BERLIN MESA

ALSO BY MICHAEL FROST BECKNER

HITLER'S LOKI
Berlin Mesa

SPY GAME
The Aiken Trilogy
Muir's Gambit
Bishop's Endgame
Aiken in Check

A NATION DIVIDED
Volume I: Episodes 101–104
Volume II: Episodes 105–108
Volume III: Episodes 109–112

Berlin Mesa

Michael Frost Beckner

Los Angeles
2022

Copyright © 2022 by Michael Frost Beckner

All rights reserved.

Published in the United States by Montrose Station Press LLC, Los Angeles.

LIBRARY OF CONGRESS CONTROL NUMBER:
2022902356

ISBN 9798985729221 (hardcover)
ISBN 9798985729238 (paperback)
ISBN 9798985729245 (ebook)

Printed in the United States of America
FIRST EDITION

Cover design by Andrew Frost Beckner
Book design by Michael Grossman

For my father

BERLIN MESA

PROLOGUE

BENEATH A FADED BLUE UMBRELLA at an unassuming café on Zurich's Limmat Quay, Nicholai Chernikov, an officer of the *Narodny Komissariat Vnutrennikh Del*, the Soviet People's Commissariat of Internal Affairs, sipped Mumm champagne and watched the summer afternoon fade into evening shadows. People lingering on the Bellvueplatz or strolling along the river wore faces reposed in the somnambulant belief they were insulated from the war by their country's neutrality. The fools. Switzerland was in it as deep as everyone, only here the war was fought in a kind of darkness where combatants rarely came face to face. Victories were marked not in territory gained or casualties inflicted, but in gathered intelligence and stolen secrets. While the clandestine war was minuscule in the scope of its action, the success or failure of a single intelligence operation was oftentimes the turning point of a nation's future.

The NKVD officer floated his pride on champagne bubbles, convinced the roll of microfilm concealed in the heel of his left shoe would prove to be that sort of success. The kind of success, once back home, a smart man could use as cornerstone to a towering career.

"Waiter. Another champagne, *bitte*?" Nicholai's *Schwyzerdütsch* was perfect, creating the illusion of a Zurich native.

The waiter acknowledged the request with a slight dip of his chin.

Now was the time to celebrate success. Nicholai would find little opportunity once he arrived in Moscow and there would be no champagne. He let his gaze travel to a brunette woman, animated in expression and gesture by her youth, seated in a wicker chair at the red-awninged establishment across from his own café. She slipped the Russian spy a pleasant smile.

Nicholai imagined her naked. Submitting beneath him. But he matched her expression—*Pleasant, oh, so pleasant, aren't we all—?* and she returned to her conversation with her older male companion, nondescript in his gray suit and dark fedora.

A cool breeze lifted from the river and sighed through the café, washing the young Russian with a wave of affection for this naïve city. He'd followed his Moscow instructors' strict orders to refrain from emotional attachments while on assignment, but they had been referring to women specifically, people in general, but not to places, he was sure. Nicholai would miss Zurich. He would miss the intrigue and excitement of this hub of international espionage. He would miss the food and the wine, the dark coffeehouses and bright markets. Most of all, he would miss the city's superior prostitutes.

The second glass of champagne arrived as Nicholai remembered evenings spent in the whorehouses off the Langstrasse. One house he'd grown particularly fond of in the last two months boasted an international array of exemplary women. Six days ago, he'd received a note from the proprietress indicating the arrival of a new girl. An Aryan blonde. One of Hitler's own. To whom—for a price—Nicholai could do anything he wanted. Yes, a night at 38 Langstrasse would be a just reward for a job well done. Like the champagne, it was something he would never find once home.

DOM PÉRIGNON WAS THE CHAMPAGNE OF CHOICE at 38 Langstrasse. Distinguishable only by the shape of their hats in the darkness of the main salon, seven men—the seventh, Nicholai Chernikov—were held entranced by the performance of two naked women on the establishment's small stage. Illuminated in the circle of a red spotlight, their bodies glistened, slick with oil, beaded with sweat. Nicholai grinned as one wilted to her knees. Her pale arms stretched behind her, fingers quivering and clutching at the fur-covered floor, while the other, a black African, enveloped her from beneath, arms snaking from behind, collapsing the first woman with a huff of pleasure as she slid her way over her right shoulder licking and kissing a path to her stomach and beyond.

"The new girl is ready, sir."

Nicholai tore his attention from the sex show to the proprietress at his side. She ran a red lacquered nail from his shoulder down his arm.

He followed the aging prostitute upstairs to a mezzanine leading to the bedrooms. They paused, watching the stage where the two performers climaxed with simultaneous moans, and the spotlight faded from red to indigo and darkened to black. Nicholai's cheeks flushed with the warmth of arousal. The proprietress ushered him into a dimly lit bedroom and left Nicholai alone.

He stepped to the lace-curtained window and made sure both the fire escape and the alley beyond were empty before he sat at the foot of the large four-poster eiderdown bed as he had a dozen times before. He undressed. He had once had the African woman but found her much more exciting in her performance this evening; this time she'd not been pretending enjoyment.

There were two mirrors in the room, one on the ceiling above the bed, the other on the wall opposite him. After neatly folding his clothes and placing them atop his revolver and shoes on the floor, Nicholai Chernikov admired his reflection and the healthy glow Zurich had bestowed upon him.

At the soft sound of the opening door, he turned to see a girl—for she couldn't possibly be yet eighteen—walk into the bedroom and shyly sit in the impression he'd made in the comforter a moment before. She wore a Prussian blue corset and garter belt trimmed in gold. Her hair was blonde and thick atop her head, and as she seductively rolled her stockings, between her legs it was flaxen there as well.

Nicholai was erect by the time he stepped beside her. He turned her pale and luminous face to his, noting something sad and familiar in it. He had the vaguest inkling he'd seen her before, but she was new, so, of course not.

She wears the look of all prostitutes.

He sat, pulling her with him and kissing her mouth.

The blonde slipped from the bed to the floor. She kneeled between Nicholai's legs and he leaned back and shut his eyes. His lungs filled and relaxed, filled and relaxed. The bed moved and Nicholai registered this as the girl's hand disappeared between the feather mattress and the box spring. Nicholai gasped at the gathering power of impending orgasm. The girl slackened in her caresses and he opened his eyes. Was she purposely holding him back?

Her rhythm continued. His stimulation increased. His eyes widened, watching her bobbing head. Nicholai noticed her scalp, the dark roots of her hair. The girl looked familiar to him because he had seen her before.

Today.

The young brunette in a wicker chair at the red-awninged café on the Limmat Quay.

Nicholai's perfectly ordered and secret world shattered into a thousand fragments across his mind. He fastened his hands on the top of the girl's head, but held back the impulse to crush her skull. He had to know who she was, whom she worked for, how much of the NKVD's mission in Switzerland was compromised.

"Wait." He slowly raised her.

As her right hand caressed his shoulder, her left hand withdrew, empty, from between the mattress and box spring.

She met his eyes and smiled. "Is something wrong, sir?"

Nicholai shook his head. He loosened the front laces of her corset, freeing her breasts. He lowered his face to their firm silkiness.

His tongue found her right nipple. As it hardened between his lips, he didn't notice how the girl's left hand strained back for the crack between the two parts of the bed. He didn't need to. He positioned his incisors over the nipple, savagely clamped his jaws, and bit it off.

The coppery taste of blood squirted into his mouth, and Chernikov hurled the screaming girl across the floor. He grabbed his revolver from his pile of clothes and aimed it at her, shouting, "Who do you work for?"

Blood streaming down her chest, the girl crawled toward the bed. "I don't know . . . I don't know what you are talking about."

As she dragged the quilt from the bed to cover her bleeding nakedness, Nicholai squeezed the trigger and shattered her left calf.

"Tell me, bitch, or die."

The girl collapsed against the side of the bed. She choked out between her painful sobs, "*Sicherheitsdienst*. We wanted to compromise you. To turn you." She pointed at the mirror on the wall behind him. "They're in there. Two men—with cameras."

Nicholai whirled to the mirror in mute shock. The girl's hand disappeared beneath the mattress again. It reappeared a second later with a silenced Mauser HSc pistol. *Phuump! Phuump!* She fired twice into the back of his head. For a fleeting second, Nicholai watched the first bullet lift the top of his skull from his cranium, before the second splattered most of his brain across the mirror and he was dead.

THE WOUNDED YOUNG WOMAN—twenty-four and better trained for her work then Nicholai had been—spun around at an urgent knocking at the door.

"What's happening in there? Open up! Open up this instant!"

The blonde slid her back along the bedpost, rising, gripping the Mauser in weakening hands. She fired twice more through the door, and there was a cry of alarm followed by the sound of fleeing feet.

The girl lurched to the dead Soviet officer's pile of clothes, collected the garments and the shoes and, trailing blood, stole to the window.

Her SD compatriots were not behind the mirror, but outside, waiting out of sight. She threw open the window and called to them. Preceded by the growl of a powerful engine, they pulled their car into a position directly below the fire escape. The girl tossed the clothes and the heavy-soled shoes into the night. She clutched the window frame and mustered her strength. If only she had found her pistol earlier. She struggled to lift her broken leg over the sill.

Below, the man of dark fedora and nondescript suit threw Nicholai Chernikov's belongings into the vehicle. He looked to the girl as she collapsed onto the rusted fire escape and, in excruciating pain, pulled onto the creaking ladder. She was halfway to the alley when she lost consciousness and fell. The SD man caught her, staggered, and almost collapsed. He hustled her into the back seat of the car and instructed the driver to head for the border.

Sixteen black-and-white photographic prints developed from Nicholai Chernikov's microfilm lay across a desk at 32 Berkaerstrasse in the heart of Berlin. They depicted thirty notebook pages from a German Communist, an escaped enemy of the Reich, working for an American war project whose secrets he was passing to the Soviet NKVD. After more than two and a half years of planning and awaiting the right moment, SS-Brigadeführer Walter Schellenberg—head of the *Sicherheitsdienst Reichssicherheitshauptamt VI*, the Reich Security Service's foreign intelligence department— had intelligence in his possession worthy of activating his and Heydrich's most daring SD operation to date.

He lifted his telephone's receiver.

"*Ja, Brigadeführer?*" came his aide's immediate response.

"Connect me with Reichsführer Himmler. I will hold the line."

"*Zu befehl, Brigadeführer.*" As you command.

Although the Third Reich had already independently discovered the content of the photographs, the fact that Schellenberg had obtained the microfilm was conclusive proof of an NKVD operation his agents in Moscow had been hearing rumors of for over a year. Last month, SD operatives in England "leaked" to the Soviets their infiltration of the NKVD's London mission, causing the Soviets to go to careless extremes in rerouting the microfilm from America through Zurich on its way to Moscow.

More importantly, the America-based traitor to the Fatherland had included with the microfilm a handwritten message informing his Soviet spymasters he would have three full notebooks for them by Christmas. In the hands of the Third Reich, these notebooks would represent nothing less than the key to swift and decisive victory for Germany.

"And what good news do you bring me this morning, Walter?" Reichsführer Himmler said when the call was connected.

"I have found a mission for one of our *Loki*."

"And which one would that be?"

"*Unternehmen Steppenfeuer,* Reichsführer." Operation Prairie Fire.

"New Mexico. I see. Our assumptions there have been confirmed?"

"They have."

"Unternehmen Steppenfeuer," Himmler's voice warmed to the news as he repeated the Loki's operational designation and dreamt of that agent's future. "From one tiny spark in the desert to an unquenchable, all-consuming mass event. From which," Himmler mused, "our New Order will be born on the firebringer's success."

PART ONE

"A knife is sharpened on stone, steel is tempered
by fire, but men must be sharpened by men."

— Louis L'Amour

1

H. Howard Hendricks read out loud from a handwritten page. "'Members of the New Mexico Board of Parole: I stand here today humbly representing my daughter, Virginia Hendricks, victim of *heinous rape* by the remorseless and unrepentant inmate Tyler Keyes: the rotten coward here seated before you.'"

Unpossessed of a shred of humility, Hendricks's claim to "humbleness" was a hollow word inserted into his speech to allow him to fill it with his plentiful hate. His abundant rage.

"'As you look to grant this human scum a reprieve—'"

A tap of an interruptive gavel provoked a flash of anger in Hendricks's faded-blue, age-watery eyes.

"Mr. Hendricks, to be clear: a 'reprieve' is a suspension of punishment." In his voice, Rudolph Schneider carried the accent of his emigrant youth. "We are discussing a parole, which is the continuation of punishment outside of prison." Schneider glanced right-left to the three other attending members of the state board. With nothing to add, he said, "Please continue," and returned his pocket-sized "travel" gavel onto Tyler Keyes's file—case and prison records, other hearing evidence—and gestured Hendricks speak.

"I'm not ignorant, Schneider—" Hendricks made the name sound a whole lot like he'd say *Kraut*—"I chose the word I see being applied in these circumstances. This is your first time, *Schneider*, leading one of these despicable attempts to subvert justice in my daughter's case, but I assure you: retired Judge Holden—who should be chairing this hearing—understood that difference you speak of and made sure—as I'm sure you will today—that Tyler Keyes's incarceration doesn't change one single, damn bit."

"Continue with your statement, Mr. Hendricks," said Schneider. He turned a sympathetic eye to the female board member on his right, "And please mind your language: we have a lady present."

"I beg pardon, ma'am," said Hendricks.

He snapped the crisp onionskin page of stationery, adjusted his half-frame reading glasses and resumed. "'*This human scum* broke into my home in the dead of night, made his way into the bedroom of my only child, and stole her most precious possessions—her innocence and virtue—in the most contemptible, vile way known to humanity. These are the facts of his brutal crime to which, with the evidence and God's truth so clearly against him at the time of his apprehension, Tyler Keyes chose not to defend himself in court and *volunteered* to the eight-year sentence he now must finish serving.'"

Hendricks paused to fix each parole board member in the eye. One after the other—bang, bang, bang, lady-included-bang like shooting cans off a fence... Or livestock thieves when the blasting of a buck Indian or a wetback bandido was still extra-judicially legal in the State of New Mexico and anything but frowned upon.

"'Eight years. Not six years. Not the six years and the hundred-and sixteen-days today's calendar indicate. Not five days from now. *Eight years*. His choice, his sentence. Within the span of my lifetime, within this county, the deserv-ed sentence would have been an eternity in hell delivered by me within my right. Eight years—'" and here he pointed at the woman appearing to hide under the felt brim of her green cloche hat—"and you, ma'am,

I know agree with me—'is a light sentence for what he did to that girl, but it is the sentence that predator and defiler was given and the sentence I will be'—excuse me in advance—'*damned* to see him serve.' Thank you."

Hendricks was of a stature that made the largest of horses look small beside him, and it took him a second or two longer than most to return to a seated posture. Mrs. Margey, the woman on today's board, who never hid from anyone, stopped him mid-stoop.

"Mr. Hendricks, while you're perfectly within your right to use your daughter's Victim Impact Statement to let us know, once again, your understandable dislike for the inmate in question, the true purpose of this statement—its only value, if you will, to this board—is to help us better understand her continued suffering, and the adverse effects the parole of inmate Keyes would have on your daughter."

Hendricks drilled Mrs. Margey with his eyes daring her to continue.

Which she did. "Many victims have found it helpful to voice how their lives have been impacted by the crime committed against them physically, emotionally, even spiritually. How they are unable to work, or socialize, or participate in society in any normal way."

"Even with this monster behind bars, the girl had to leave the country to even begin to feel safe!"

Mrs. Margey consulted her notes. "To England. Is that correct?"

"You know it is."

Mrs. Margey nodded. "Where she was recently wedded in quite an elaborate fashion."

"I wouldn't know. I didn't attend. There's a war on in case you've forgotten."

"I've not forgotten a single detail. From the war, which has no bearing, to those from the court record which no one, including Mr. Keyes, argues. The only person, I'd suggest has forgotten is the new Mrs. Baker-Davies."

The inmate in his prison denims seated in the wooden chair positioned before the panel, his back to Hendricks, who'd not shown a hint of life before, flinched as though gut-punched by the sound of Virginia Hendricks's married name. It didn't look good, and everyone noticed. And for that Hendricks felt glad.

But Schneider—who the hell was this sauerkraut?—had to jump in. He held up a sheaf of newspaper clippings. "I agree with Mrs. Margey, Mr. Hendricks. We have photos here of your daughter's wedding ball. It outdid the war for coverage for two days in every British paper. These are not photographs of a traumatized woman or a woman who, in England, would be made unsafe were Mr. Keyes conditionally released back into American society. Frankly, I find it unusual that while still Miss Hendricks, your daughter never provided a statement of her own about anything. Why do you think that is?"

"I couldn't answer that. Like you, and the rest of us in this room—*except* for Keyes—none of us have firsthand experience of the devastating ravagement of rape."

Silence followed a moment before Schneider spoke. "You may resume your seat, Mr. Hendricks, while I question Mr. Keyes as to his attitudes and prospects were we to grant him this parole."

There was no way in hell H. Howard Hendricks would listen to a word spoken by the dirt-scratch horse farmer. He liked to believe the next time he'd look upon Tyler Keyes's face, it would be the face of a dead horse farmer.

He tugged his mustache straight, one thumb and one knuckle for each side, as if he meant to tear his face in half. That's how angry Hendricks was. He shoved his luxurious silver beaver "Laloo" Stetson over his long-by-prerogative gun-metal hair he so wanted to make him look like Wild Bill Hickock. But since Hickok died while his hair still glowed healthy, Hendricks's locks resembled more Annie Oakley's who died gray. His nose and his eyes were also a lot like Oakley's and hers were seriously like Harpo Marx's. No one had ever remarked, but everyone saw in Howard Hendricks the clown. And Hendricks, a mean, and ugly man, strode for the door as the board chairman began to question Tyler Keyes.

The old sheep rancher and oilman—for that's what Hendricks was—stopped, one hand on the door, and shook his head in disgust. He knew from the tone the dirty foreigner used, that this time, Keyes was getting out.

A set-up—by whom? Hendricks didn't know and didn't waste thought guessing—that's what it was, though. He'd never heard of this German, Schneider, didn't know how he got wedged in here over Judge Holden, but it wouldn't make a difference. They had a term for what happened next in prison. Hendricks found it just as applicable on the outside. Keyes was 'dead man walking.' Whoever was helping him could suck a dick, or better, the barrel of Hendricks's dirtiest shotgun.

Convicted rapist Tyler Keyes, released on parole five days later, had told the Parole Board that although he had no living family, he had his farm to return to, alfalfa he would plant, and, having made a living out of horseflesh—breaking and training man's truest best friend since childhood when it had become apparent to everyone who knew Tyler Keyes that he understood horses in a way horses understood back—he'd go back to offering those services to ranchers and farmers and pleasure riders in the county, as he'd done his whole life. He had a string of horses, cared for these past six years by a family friend, and a steeldust filly among those, born while Tyler was incarcerated, now ready to be bred.

They gave him his parole and a whole bunch of rules he knew he'd break if he stuck around and followed the plan he'd spelled out for them. Instead of going on to Vaughn—the town nearest his old family homestead—he got off the bus in Albuquerque. Tyler Keyes went into the nearest Army recruitment office and enlisted. Told to return after noon the following day, Tyler did as much, eager to get on with his life and on out of New Mexico; getting back Virginia, fixing what he knew they'd had even if she'd forgotten—the idea of that: the only thing he'd held onto throughout his incarceration—well, he'd rolled the dice, but she'd left the table and now his stake was shot.

The recruiting sergeant slid his paperwork across the countertop, his finger like a dagger he'd have liked to drive through Tyler. He indicated the reason for Keyes's rejection.

"'Morally Unfit,' buster. So either you are a perv, a molester, a rapist, or a faggot: whatever the case, the Army—hell, the United States—doesn't want your sick ass anywhere near its Armed Services, and I do not want to see your mug inside this station a mean-second longer, or me and the boys are going to break it."

"The boys," were some enlisted fellows who had clustered around Tyler like so many bullies in a High School parking lot. The only thing going to be broken would be them, and Tyler was the man for a try, but these boys were needed elsewhere. Tyler figured he'd let the German's do the breaking if that were to be their fate. Deep down, beyond his ego, he hoped it wasn't.

And maybe he was—morally unfit, that is—if not before he'd gone in, certainly by the time he'd gotten out. That's what prison does to a man. Murder, the only actual crime he had committed, and that did it to a man real well. Unwanted by his community, by society, by an entire world war, at twenty-four years old, name ruined, spirit crushed, hope—that thing with wings—he'd find dead on its back, feet curled, hollowed out by ants on the floor of his barn.

He sent a pair of letters from the post office. One to Elijah Jefferson who'd been caring for his string. The other to Phil Dexter who'd been paying his property taxes and keeping his farm in trust so Hendricks couldn't get hold of it and ruin the Keyes family completely, which is all the bastard had ever wanted to do. Then he made his way home.

TYLER OPENED THE SINGLE-ROOM FARMHOUSE to let the air chase out the must. He went outside to the barn. Went inside to see what five years of weather had done to his tools, his tack, and his equipment. He didn't find a dead bird named "Hope." What he did find was Hendricks's foreman, Cecil O'Hara, accompanied by four of his roughest hands. They hauled him into the yard where Tyler caught a glimpse of De Baca County Sheriff Thedford's car idling down a'ways along the easement road that ran between the Keyes farm and the Hendricks sheep range. The five men did everything they could to get Tyler to fight back, but Tyler, knowing one fist from him would violate his parole and get him put back in the slam, let them beat him unconscious. He didn't really have anything better to do.

2

FRIDAY, SEPTEMBER 3, 1943

PERHAPS A THUNDERCLAP before the storm woke him, but now, standing in the doorway of Compound 3 officer's mess, watching heavy raindrops fire like tracers through the roving beams of the guard tower searchlights, Standartenführer Jürgen von Hofmann of the SD, had heard no thunder since. It was possible that the reason his eyes had opened at precisely 4:19 that morning, a full minute before the present downpour, was he'd expected it. Strange, he'd never seen the pattern before today, but lying in his barracks bunk, listening to the rain's hard hammer, he'd concluded certain storms were portentous to him. His body attuned to their arrival. Were he Reichsführer Himmler, he'd believe some strange Teutonic god loomed over him, directing his course with overwrought Wagnerian symbolism. The SS colonel sipped flavorless ersatz American coffee and allowed a faint smile to twist the corners of his mouth. His steel-gray eyes remained perfectly cold. Fixed on the rain.

"There's bread fresh out of the oven, Standartenführer. We could split a loaf before roll call. It'd be nice to have it hot for a change."

Von Hofmann turned and glanced at the twenty-six-year-old *Afrikakorps* captain stepping from behind the service counter. Von Hofmann didn't answer. The captain approached, juggling between his hands a steaming loaf of the sweet-smelling white *Kuchen* the Americans passed off as bread.

Although it couldn't be more than six degrees Celsius, the captain, Hauptmann Fritz Zundorf, eschewed the pseudo-civilian blue jeans and denim shirts provided by their captors. He wore, as always, the sun-bleached khaki shorts he'd been wearing upon his capture. Zundorf preferred to wear them for as much of the year as he could tolerate, and, to his credit, Hauptmann Zundorf could tolerate a lot. His only concessions to the early-morning chill were the trademark Afrikakorps forage cap atop his head, the coarse wool scarf made from a Red Cross blanket, its tattered ends disappearing beneath the collar of his long-sleeved desert battle tunic, and the thick woolen socks rising from his combat boots like the Tyrolean mountaineer he had once been.

All this appeared in contrast to von Hofmann's black wool SS uniform, visible beneath his unadorned, black leather military overcoat. As the searchlights swept past, the tunic's highly polished silver buttons caught the light and shot it glistening back among the raindrops. Von Hofmann looked ready for parade. Six months into his incarceration, the only imperfection to his uniform was the missing SD cuff title, ripped from his sleeve and buried in the Tunisian sand in those last dangerous seconds before capture.

It had been the right thing to do. Whereas a disguise was out of the question—his SS uniform and rank his only tool to impress absolute authority over the other prisoners—he should never have worn the cuff title into combat. When captured, his papers identified him as a protocol officer from Berlin on an inspection tour of field hospitals. If a smart British interrogator had discovered he was Sicherheitsdienst, right now he would still be under the lights in some moldy London basement, a florid-faced MI5 bastard trying to pull from him the darkest secrets of the Reich.

Instead, he was safely in position. America. Camp Santa Rosa, New Mexico.

Zundorf tore off a hunk of bread.

"*Ja?*" he offered.

Von Hofmann declined with a slight shake of his head. His mind was elsewhere. Another rainstorm.

Zundorf bit into the piece and, chewing, made his way back to the service counter for some marmalade.

Yes, von Hofmann was sure. Violent storms marked important events of his life. When he was a child, his mother told him snow had fallen for three hours in Stettin the morning of his birth. July of that year had been uncomfortable and humid, making the joint-swollen exhaustion of her final month of pregnancy unbearable. Afterward, for the rest of August while she recovered, the weather was as hot, close, and as miserable. Yet, from two until five on the morning of August second, 1900, as she lay on the hospital bed, legs spread, her entire being focused on pushing a blood-smeared, wrinkled baby into the world, snow had drifted like angels' breath across the foggy hospital windows and Stettin had found itself somewhere in the middle of December.

Von Hofmann narrowed his eyes at the pelting rain outside. In 1936, a dry alpine lightning storm had marked his wedding—men laughing, the women nervous, as he and Agna dashed from the church beneath the upraised swords of his honor guard standing at lightning-rod attention as her veil tugged the comb from her flame red hair and she laughed with joy and radiant abandon. And again, the night at Wewelsburg two years back: a heavy rain without angle, hard drops hammering straight into the earth.

If it were that kind of storm, there would soon be much to accomplish, with a margin for error at absolute zero.

3

THE FIRST PHOTOGRAPHS from the capture of Smolensk had been published in the Berlin papers and magazines, black-and-white and typical to that period of the war: a dirt road, three Panzer III tanks receding into the background, their cannons front, left, right. Village huts all smoke, flame, rubble along their flanks. Infantry surrounded by Ukrainians, showered with their flowers. A proud SS tank commander, radio headset around his neck, stared into the lens, his eyes and smile brilliant white against a smoke-blackened face.

The news of this German victory blew through Berlin like a wind behind a kite that was the collective spirit of the city. The only topic of conversation. People on the street, meeting at offices, beer halls, and parks praised the Wehrmacht for another victory, hailed the Führer for his masterful strategy, and laughed at the Communists, all while silently praying for the safe delivery of sons and lovers, brothers and husbands fighting in the east.

Von Hofmann, a major at the time, acknowledged the vast success of the first month of *Unternehmen Barbarossa.* The captured bridges and fallen cities. The hopeless encirclement of Bialystok. The double envelopment of Minsk. The hundreds of thousands of Russian prisoners. But von Hofmann couldn't be jubilant. The Third Reich's four panzer groups were overextended at close to seven hundred kilometers inside Russia. The intelligence report he'd seen two days prior showed the Red

Army, instead of weakening, adding divisions. Russia would fall, but not before the red bear took a long and quenching draft of German blood.

Von Hofmann finished his coffee and folded his copy of *Signal* magazine. His recent duties had kept him out of Russia, out of the action, but as he rose from the overstuffed hotel-room chair and buttoned his tunic, he had a vague sense that things were about to change for him.

Jürgen von Hofmann admired himself in the freestanding mirror beside the hand-carved door panels of the hotel-room dresser. His sun-bronzed complexion, a shade darker than his thick, light hair, stood out magnificently against the depthless black of his major's dress uniform. His six-foot-one frame was a steelwork of muscle, an outward testament to a body, mind, and soul dedicated to the Fatherland. He was satisfied that in forty years he'd become something beyond a mere mortal man. *Die Blitze und der Wahnsin.* The lightning and the frenzy. The Nietzschean Übermensch.

Long before he'd ever heard of Adolf Hitler or his National Socialist Party, von Hofmann's worldview was forged on the anvil of the modern age. Born into the greatest period of social, economic, and military upheaval the European continent had ever known, von Hofmann grew up trying to emulate a class pathetically scrambling after the crumbling pieces of an old world they blindly taught him held greatness, even as the ugly new century tore it down around their heads.

"This is the twentieth century." "No one can stand in the way of Progress." "Germany must adapt or die!"

These catchphrases and so many others von Hofmann heard throughout his youth were words he would watch take Germany and the rest of Europe into a second Dark Age, governed by the lowest common denominators of poverty, depression, immorality, and false equality.

Adapt or die? It's what you did when shipwrecked on an island, or lost in the woods. How is a society lost or shipwrecked? By denying the compass of the past and cutting the anchor on the traditions of history. Uncontrolled progress had turned every great culture into dust. That was fact. Von Hofmann wasn't about to let it happen to Germany. He vowed, when the time was right, he and others like him would seize the reins on progress. They would take control of this runaway twentieth century and put it back on track. They would drive it toward the greatest goals of their ancestors.

The fulfillment of this vow was a long time coming. Von Hofmann survived a world war. He watched Germany degraded by feeble politicians. Hypnotized by the false intellectuals. Confused by the apologists, and overrun by artists and Communists, Jews and free-thinkers. His gray eyes became cunning. They suggested danger, suggested, as his father had been fond of saying, the eyes of a wolf the old man once watched maul two peasants while on a hunting party in East Prussia. It was pure, cold danger without malice. The wolf had chosen the moment not simply to survive, but to assert its dominance over the landscape and everything that moved upon it. Like the wolf, this was von Hofmann's moment.

Von Hofmann exited the hotel onto Wilhelmstrasse. Soldiers and civilians sprinkled both sides of the swastika-festooned street. The day was overcast and muggy, hinting at a coming rain. A black Mercedes pulled to the curb. The driver, an expectant SS-*Hauptsturmführer*, moved onto the sidewalk.

Clicking his heels, the officer thrust out his arm. *"Heil Hitler!"*

"Heil Hitler."

Von Hofmann let the captain open the rear door for him. He slid into the back seat. The captain took his place behind the wheel and smoothly engaged the steering-column gearshift. He eased the Mercedes into traffic and von Hofmann caught his eyes flicking to the rearview mirror to study him. Sensory perceptions, razor sharp from years of training, von Hofmann had the infallibility of radar in picking out the slightest anomalies in any environment, to register their blips upon his consciousness as warnings even before he understood the precise nature of the threat he faced.

His eyes drifted to the right-side mirror, where he discovered three machine pistol-toting Waffen-SS in a Volkswagen Kübelwagen fall into position behind them.

The captain spoke. "For your protection, Sturmbannführer."

"I had no idea how dangerous Berlin had become for me."

The captain offered nothing back and concentrated on the traffic.

As they drove toward the heart of the city, von Hofmann puzzled at his situation. Two nights previously, he had received an urgent "top secret" message summoning him to a face-to-face meeting with SS-Brigadeführer Walter Schellenberg. Although they had never met privately before, there was nothing strange about this. Von Hofmann assumed details of his next assignment required an in-person meeting. Yet, since when did a captain and three Waffen-SS escort a major to meet with his commanding officer? Von Hofmann reassured himself all would be made clear once he arrived at RSHA Headquarters at Prinz-Albrecht-Strasse.

The Mercedes shot past Prinz-Albrecht-Strasse.

"Hauptsturmführer, our turn," von Hofmann said as the Air Ministry and the Führer's private office swept by in a blur.

"I beg the Sturmbannführer's pardon. The general has moved his offices. Didn't you know?"

They passed the Reich Chancellery and the Propaganda Ministry.

Von Hofmann said nothing.

They turned left through the Brandenburg Gate, continuing in silence through the park and out of the Tiergarten district into Charlottenburg.

Von Hofmann racked his brain to make sense of his situation. He had done nothing to warrant arrest or imprisonment. He rejected the possibility of execution. After all, his most recent work monitoring security among the foreign recruits at the SS training camp at Sennheim, Alsace-Lorraine, had been the picture of obedience and loyalty for the entire five months he'd served there.

Maybe he should have made a few examples.

Nonsense. The situation at Sennheim had been uneventful precisely because von Hofmann had carried out his duties perfectly, exuding enough power and instilling enough fear in the young men to wither the hardiest seeds of dissension. He'd turned those conquered youths away from the soils of their fallen cultures. He'd made them face the future as proud, unwavering, unquestioning soldiers of the greater Reich.

They wended their way along the tree-lined Reichenhaller Strasse, turned north onto Berkaer Strasse, and pulled to the curb. The trio of Waffen-SS stopped a respectful distance behind.

Von Hofmann stepped from the Mercedes as the driver said, "Number thirty-two, Sturmbannführer."

Von Hofmann faced the building. An example of late art déco architecture, it was a curvilinear four-story building made of alternating bands of brick and concrete. Von Hofmann recognized this address, but was unable to place it until he entered through the narrow, unadorned wooden door. 32 Berkaerstrasse had been an old folks' home for Jews. It lifted his mood to see the building put to better use.

A GENERAL'S AIDE led von Hofmann into Schellenberg's office, where he sat at his desk, an overhead light bathing him in a golden aura. Von Hofmann saluted. Schellenberg didn't look up from the file he was reading, giving von Hofmann a moment to study his superior. Walter Schellenberg's boyish look was deceiving. His rise through the SS hierarchy had been meteoric, culminating in his little-disguised ousting of his SD boss, Heinz Jost. Most found Schellenberg charming and elegant; von Hofmann knew him to be ruthless and dangerous.

The brigadeführer met Hofmann's gaze. "No doubt you believe your talents were wasted at Sennheim?" The tone of Schellenberg's voice was detached, clinical, like a doctor.

"Brigadeführer?"

Schellenberg stared at him, waiting for von Hofmann to continue speaking. When he did not, half of Schellenberg's mouth twitched into a sly smile. "They were wasted, I suppose."

He flipped back through the file to von Hofmann's SS service records.

"All the way back to your first personnel report, I find only good things about you. Surely, Sturmbannführer, you're not perfect?"

"I am what my record states."

The other half of Schellenberg's mouth completed his smile. "I had forgotten you'd come to us hand-picked by Obergruppenführer Heydrich." Reinhard Heydrich was the chief of *Sicherheitspolizei*—the security police—and the SD, Schellenberg's superior, yet the general intoned the fact as if asking a question.

"August of '33 . . . I escaped to South America following the Beer Hall Putsch—I had led an armed uprising that day for the Führer in Regensburg. Eight years spent in Buenos Aires, 1923 to '31 . . . The next two years I resided in New York City. The Obergruppenführer found me there."

"Ten years is a long time to be away from your Fatherland and your party."

"It was good to have a reason to come back, and a cause to come back to."

"You have performed admirably ever since," said Schellenberg.

He rose and indicated the door. "Come, there is someone awaiting us. He wants to talk with you."

"Regarding?"

"*Ein Fall von höchster Sicherheit.*" A matter of the highest security.

THE MERCEDES AND SOLDIERS had been Schellenberg's personal escort. In this same manner, von Hofmann accompanied the general to an airfield from where they flew to Westphalia.

Another Mercedes and another contingent of Waffen-SS drove them through the rain-wet night, until traversing a series of short, steep switchbacks, they approached a huge and menacing structure perched on the edge of a cliff. They passed through the fortified gates, and von Hofmann swallowed his excitement at the sight of Wewelsburg Castle.

They pulled to a stop in a cobbled courtyard lit by flickering gas-fed braziers on the walls. Two iron torches burned beside the massive doors. Von Hofmann and Schellenberg exited the car. A platoon of SS Honor Guards snapped to attention, twenty-five pairs of hobnailed boots throwing sparks across the stones. Von Hofmann paused long enough to take it all in. Before him towered Reichsführer Himmler's architectural paean to the tales of the Teutonic Knights and the Arthurian legends that fevered his imagination. Wewelsburg was a seventeenth-century fortress, renovated at an astounding cost of more than six million reichsmarks. Especially impressive when von Hofmann remembered the concentration camp labor that did the work came free.

Obergruppenführer Heydrich met them at the door, taking von Hofmann's hand like an old friend's. "At last we meet again," he said.

Heydrich's handshake was like a cluster of bones, his fingers inordinately long and thin. A tall man with a voice both high-pitched and reedy, baby blue eyes small and darting, his lean figure perversely distorted by wide, feminine hips. Heydrich reminded von Hofmann of a spider. Each time he saw him, it surprised von Hofmann by how this strange configuration of weak attributes in a man could produce such a tangible and overwhelmingly sinister effect. Heydrich led them across the threshold.

Brief pleasantries exchanged, the chief of the SD silently maneuvered von Hofmann and Brigadeführer Schellenberg into a vertical maze of dark corridors and ornate chambers connected by wide, dramatic flag-draped stairways. Von Hofmann concealed his awe at what was nothing short of a cathedral dedicated to the religion of the SS. Bas-relief swastikas adorned wall niches, stone eagles perched above portals, and filling every room was the plunder of nations. Himmler's presence, like heady incense, exuded from it all.

They entered an immense library lit by candelabra von Hofmann presumed had been brought in for this occasion since the dark electric lighting overhead was clearly a functioning part of the castle's restoration. Heydrich indicated von Hofmann should sit on one side of a wide table while he and Schellenberg selected seats across from him.

Von Hofmann's eyes traveled along ranks of bookcases that disappeared into darkness. "Impressive."

"Reichsführer Himmler's library contains over twelve thousand volumes dedicated to the study of Aryan Science curated by the scientists of our *Ahnenerbe* think tank," Heydrich said, and abruptly changed the subject. "I have followed your career closely, Sturmbannführer von Hofmann."

"Thank you, Obergruppenführer, I am honored by your attention."

Von Hofmann could hear Heydrich's breathing like a reptile hiss.

The chief of the SD folded his hands and proceeded with business. "Your military record shows you were captured in the Great War. I believe you told me the story a number of years ago. Please refresh my memory."

Heydrich's mind was sharper than any von Hofmann had ever encountered. There was only one reason Heydrich would ask to hear the story a second time. Somewhere in the shadows of this room, Reichsführer Himmler watched and listened, judging him for some important purpose von Hofmann could not guess. He walked a rope over an abyss, and while he did not know where it stretched, he was eager to make it to its end.

He focused his mind.

Although it grieved him to remember the war itself, von Hofmann was proud of his service to his country. He would tell his story briefly and without embellishment. "As an infantry lieutenant, I was wounded at the Second Battle of Marne and taken prisoner by the Americans."

Schellenberg took out a cigarette. Von Hofmann paused while he lit it.

"Removed to an enemy hospital in the rear, I waited for my chance. Overpowering a night orderly, I escaped. On my way toward our lines, I crossed paths with an American courier. I beat him to death with a brick."

Von Hofmann noticed a wrinkle crease Schellenberg's brow.

"All I needed was his motorbike, but I ended up with plans detailing an American offensive to take place in the Argonne Forest. I presented these to my commanding officer, who in turn took them to Generalleutnant Baron von Haldbeck."

Von Hofmann paused, not liking what the memories did to him. The fire they ignited in his blood, always started in the back of his head, before moving to the surface of his face. He spoke rapidly, hoping to beat it. "The next day, my captain informed me I was a fool. Used as a pawn by forces of Allied counter-espionage. The battle plans were fake."

Sweat gathered beneath the inner band of von Hofmann's hat. His throat constricted. He coughed once to clear it. Heydrich indicated a pitcher of water and a glass. Von Hofmann poured from it and drank. "Thank you." He returned the empty glass to the table. "Of course the Allies carried out their offensive as the plans described."

The water hadn't helped. Perspiration rolled down his temple past his ear.

"If the generals had listened to you, you believe we might have won the war?" prompted Heydrich.

"No, Obergruppenführer. The weak, stupid, and lazy who comprised our government had already guaranteed ultimate defeat. But I will believe, until the day I die, the one hundred thousand casualties we suffered those thirty-odd days were tens of thousands of casualties I'd offered the means to prevent."

Von Hofmann's memories of the German defeat humiliated him. Like Schellenberg, like Heydrich, like Himmler, the Führer and so many others, the disgraceful treaty of Versailles and the

"November Criminals" who signed it left von Hofmann with feelings of violent rage and total impotence.

Both Heydrich and Schellenberg studied him as he wiped a sweat droplet from the side of his nose. Von Hofmann performed the action slowly, deliberately. He refused to let them discern any greater sign of his emotional discomfort.

"I have discovered your immediate commanding officer of that period, Hauptmann Vogel, was shot and killed in a Berlin cabaret in 1919. The murder has never been solved."

Von Hofmann narrowed his eyes. His nostrils flared.

Heydrich continued, the pitch of his voice getting higher. "And General von Haldbeck and four members of his family died in a fire at their country estate in Bavaria two weeks later. In fact, over the next two years, every officer who served on the general's staff above the rank of major—eight men and their families—met untimely ends."

How long had they known? Von Hofmann locked eyes with Heydrich. He had nothing to hide. On the contrary, he was proud of his actions. "They were failures. All of them."

"You murdered all of them because they had 'failed' you?" Schellenberg took the tone policemen use to goad suspects. He ashed out his cigarette.

"Murdered? No. They had failed the Fatherland. My conscience is clear."

Heydrich took water. His glance darted to Schellenberg and back to von Hofmann. "You served your Fatherland in the Putsch of '23. A warrant was issued for your arrest, yet you managed to avoid capture and escape the country . . . A year after I brought you back from the United States, you served your Fatherland once more in the purge of the homosexual leadership and the treasonous members of the *Sturmabteilung*."

Again, Heydrich let the statement hang like a question. Von Hofmann's mind raced. To this point, the interview had focused on his ability to escape dangerous situations—wartime capture, criminal detection, political arrest. Here was a question that could only be about one thing. His capacity for killing. It made no sense. If they simply wanted him to kill or assassinate someone, why go to all this trouble?

What had Schellenberg said? *Ein Fall von höchster Sicherheit.* A matter of the highest security?

"Yes, Obergruppenführer Heydrich. I was infiltrated into an SA group on the first of June, 1934. From the list of names I submitted to you, eighteen out of eighteen were shot for treason."

"Ten of them—"

"Pistol shots to the back of the head. By me. As prescribed. Oh, there was an eleventh that night."

Both Heydrich's and Schellenberg's faces drew blanks. Von Hofmann smiled. Here was something they didn't know. "A few hours after dawn on the second of July, I shot a man in the face. A gypsy street rascal. He'd made a remark about the Führer I didn't like. I taught him a lesson."

Von Hofmann glowed to see Schellenberg's grin, Heydrich's dancing eyes, and it all came clear. This wasn't so much about his abilities—everything they had so far discussed was a matter of record—this was about his initiative, and only initiative would get him across the tightrope. They were waiting for him to impress them.

He shifted his gaze past Heydrich and Schellenberg, focusing on the place where the bookcases converged into shadows. Von Hofmann stood and, extending his arm in the Nazi salute, boldly remarked, "Reichsführer Himmler, I could also detail my activities in Poland."

Schellenberg pursed his lips. Heydrich remained unperturbed, and from the shadows came a faint chuckle, followed by a confident, "In English?"

"If it pleases you, Reichsführer," von Hofmann responded in perfect American English.

"At ease, Sturmbannführer," said Himmler. He emerged from the darkness. "And, please, do go on."

Von Hofmann recounted his work on August 30, 1939. In the company of fifteen SS officers disguised in Polish uniforms, he staged attacks along the German border. They shot up and seized radio stations. They burned customs sheds. And, after the attacks, von Hofmann delivered the "canned goods."

The "canned goods" were an idea he had demonstrated to Gestapo Gruppenführer Heinrich Müller before the first mock-skirmish. By administering lethal injections to concentration camp prisoners, their bodies could be clothed in uniforms and brought to the "battlefields," where, shot full of bullets, they were strewn across the sites. "After all, we had to have a few German casualties. And, like 'canned goods,' they were cheap, proved easily transportable, and stayed fresh to the minute of use. Highly effective."

By the time von Hofmann finished, Himmler had crossed to the table and taken a seat. Von Hofmann was pleased to hear him share a laugh with the others, rolling his eyes and tilting back his head.

The Reichsführer was the strangest of them all. An awkward, unhealthy-looking, nearsighted man, he appeared more the fussy chicken farmer he'd once been than the brilliant architect of the SS and the chief designer of the Reich's racial purity standards. Looks be damned: von Hofmann loved and admired, no, worshipped him almost as much as he worshipped the Führer.

Himmler looked at Heydrich and Schellenberg. "You have done an excellent job. This officer is perfect."

He addressed von Hofmann. "Obergruppenführer Heydrich has a proposition you'll find intriguing, Sturmbannführer."

Von Hofmann fixed his attention on Heydrich and went completely still to hide any indication of the adrenaline rushing from his gut to ice the fire in his brain.

"The Führer has always known we would eventually have to fight the Americans. He'd hoped to have both England and Russia firmly in his grasp before proceeding. Unfortunately, recent reports from Brigadeführer Schellenberg's agents in position inside the United States confirm that President Roosevelt is actively seeking an excuse to enter the war. It could come at any time."

Heydrich met von Hofmann's eyes. He held open his bony hands. "Our situation is this: Britain has begun bombing us, while our early estimates of Russian fighting capabilities were grossly undercounted. We are in for a protracted struggle on the Eastern Front, meaning we are currently incapable of opening a front against the Americans in the west.

"The Führer's concern is, as the war progresses, we will have no way to check the Americans' military and industrial output. Over time, as their war machine grows, their armies swell, and their morale is raised by the peace within their borders, the Reich will burn beneath their falling bombs. We will rely more, and more, on conscript soldiers, and the morale of our people will be sorely tried. The Führer believes our only salvation from the Americans is to find a way to bring the war directly to their homeland."

Von Hofmann considered the situation. How could these men—the Führer—be afraid of the Americans? The United

States Army ranked nineteenth in the world. Portugal had a larger army. The latest intelligence von Hofmann had seen regarding the Americans concerned their maneuvers in Louisiana the previous summer. The US Army consisted of just over two hundred and sixty thousand men. By contrast, Poland fielded fifty-two divisions and close to three million men against the Wehrmacht. Germany conquered Poland in less than a month. While, granted, the US Army might have grown in a year, they didn't stand a chance against the mighty Third Reich.

Or did they?

Heydrich wasn't a man to make outrageous statements.

Von Hofmann looked back on his two years in America. He tried to envision that vast land more clearly. There were plenty of men to turn into soldiers—true—and the United States did have a tremendous manufacturing capability, bolstered by near unlimited raw materials. But, he remembered, the major industrial centers were near the coasts—most on the Atlantic, some in the Gulf, the remainder on the Pacific.

Perhaps they were testing him.

From behind thick lenses, Himmler probed von Hofmann's face. Schellenberg scowled. He lit another cigarette. They waited for von Hofmann to speak.

"Our U-boats can handle their east coast and the Gulf of Mexico. Given time, our Imperial Japanese allies will invade their mainland from the Pacific Ocean in the west, and commence the bombing of their industrial complex. America might be put quickly in check, I imagine."

"The Gulf we can certainly watch, but you've forgotten the size of their eastern seaboard." Himmler spoke as if von Hofmann were a student. "For every ship we sink, a dozen slip past. As for the west? We would be fools to put the future of the Reich into the hands of the mongrel Asians, Sturmbannführer. The American question is for us in this room to answer. Preferably, right now."

Von Hofmann burned with embarrassment. The Reichsführer sat back in his chair, smiled with a sneering contentment at having made his point, and returned his attention to Heydrich.

"You should recall," said Heydrich, "our *Unterseeboots* are not equipped for the amphibious landing of troops, so an invasion of any effective size is not a possibility. We have also ruled out the use of our Luftwaffe and our agents already in place in America. The former, because we have no aircraft with the range for bombing or paratroops missions. The latter because, as you know, foreign spies are never one hundred percent reliable. Even if they were, they are unfit for the type of combat we envision."

"What type of combat is that, Obergruppenführer?"

"Trust us. We have found a way to bring the war to the American homeland," said Heydrich. "As with the last war, there will be victories the Allies will win, and there will be German soldiers taken prisoner."

Heydrich turned to Schellenberg. The brigadeführer took up the briefing in his area of expertise: stolen information. "The English have discussed with the Americans the burden of German POWs. Britain is small and already we have verified that their camp facilities are near capacity. They have asked America to take ninety percent of German prisoners of war once America enters the conflict. This number is divided over branches of service and theaters of operation. For example, as it would pertain to you, all SS troops captured in the Mediterranean and African theaters will go to America. My agents in Washington confirm these discussions and report that America is willing to go along with this protocol. Camps are already being located across the United States."

"'As it would pertain to me?' I'm not sure I follow."

Himmler leaned toward von Hofmann. His eyes sparkled with excitement. "The operation we are planning concerns you being among these prisoners, Sturmbannführer."

Von Hofmann barely followed their reasoning, and what he did follow he didn't like.

Heydrich spoke. "We call it *Unternehmen Steppenfeuer*. Operation Prairie Fire. For the next six months, you will undergo rigorous training in the arts of escape and evasion. Guerrilla warfare and hand-to-hand combat. Sabotage and assassination. Training complete, you will be captured by the Americans, who will transfer you to the United States. Once inside an American prisoner of war camp, you will assemble a squad of loyal soldiers from among your fellow prisoners and await orders. Do you have any questions?"

Von Hofmann's heart hammered. Allow himself captured? His mind spun. "I will be doing this alone?"

Heydrich glanced at Himmler. The Reichsführer gave a shrug.

"There will be at least nine others," said Himmler. "I call you my ten Loki." He leaned forward and grinned at von Hofmann. "You know Loki. From Wagner's *Nibelungen Ring*. The giant who forced his way into the company of the gods. Cunning, witty, skillful. He is the calumniator of the gods and the contriver of all fraud and mischief."

Himmler was silent a moment, and then added more formally, "Of course, for security purposes, you will never meet the others while training, nor, once captured, will your missions ever overlap."

"And when I receive my orders, what will my mission be?"

Schellenberg smiled his school-chum smile and raised his eyebrows as though amused. "That, Sturmbannführer, can't possibly be known. After all, the war with America has yet to be declared."

Von Hofmann scowled.

"Don't worry, you will not be forgotten." Schellenberg tapped the end of yet another cigarette on the tabletop before jabbing it between his lips and lighting it. "Really, you must see yourself as one of the Führer's most powerful and potentially deadly weapons. His only way to strike a direct blow to the enemy's heart. How that blow will be most effective must be well calculated and perfectly timed. It is, truly, something we cannot possibly register right now. Timing is the essence of Operation Steppenfeuer."

Von Hofmann directed his attention back to Himmler, who was saying, "Now you see why your training will be so diverse and your capture so very necessary. You must be ready for anything, with a contingent of German soldiers prepared to follow your command. When the time comes, you and your men will wage war against the enemy on a scale that could be as large as the liberation of all your fellow prisoners in camp after camp—the formation of an army group inside America—or repeated hit-and-run commando operations to destroy individual industrial and military centers and wreak havoc across their countryside.

"Whatever the individual task you are asked to perform, know, if it succeeds, it will be a deathblow to our enemies. What do you say, my friend?"

The idea was extreme, but it had come from the very top, where success was demanded, failure unconsidered. Those selected to achieve that success were those deemed most able to face long odds and meet them victoriously. The longer the odds, the greater the glory.

It was daring. It was desperate.

Von Hofmann went to Nietzsche: *Du hast ihm die Gelegenheit gegeben, Charakter von Größe zu zeigen, und er hat ihn nicht ergriffen.*

Er wird dir das niemals vergeben. You gave him an opportunity of showing greatness of character and he did not seize it. He will never forgive you for that.

Von Hofmann weighed his words. *"Meine Ehre heißt Treue."* My honor is called loyalty. The SS oath.

Himmler offered von Hofmann his hand. "Then I congratulate you on the occasion of your promotion, Standartenführer von Hofmann."

AFTER A STRANGE MEAL that Himmler described as the traditional feast of a Teutonic Knight the eve before battle, von Hofmann took a long steam in the castle's subterranean baths while Jewish tailors from a local camp, tailored his uniform to fit his new rank. By mid-morning the following day, he and Schellenberg arrived back in Berlin. The brigadeführer rewarded von Hofmann with three days' leave before he was to report at The Hague to commence his training.

Salutes exchanged, Von Hofmann declined the military escort home, preferring to walk. He took the Wilhelmstrasse through historic Dorotheenstadt to Unter den Linden Boulevard until he stood beneath the Brandenburg Gate. How different the magnificent edifices and heroic monuments of Hitler's grand city appeared this time as he passed. They were part of von Hofmann, he a part of them, and the bond intoxicated him. Their power increased his strength.

Von Hofmann boarded a bus for the rest of his journey. He glowed with pride at the awe and fear his uniform and new rank of Standartenführer reflected in the faces of all who beheld it. Upon reaching the Zehlendorf district, he left the bus and resumed walking toward the Schlachtensee neighborhood, where he and Agna made their city home, overlooking the lake.

He passed a toyshop. A child's hopper ball caught his eye. Patterned on its sphere was a map of the globe; the Third Reich, appropriately oversized, was the dominant focal point, facing outward below the two-hand grip, while the Soviet Union was the ball's base upon which its rider would bounce. It amused von Hofmann. He purchased it for his four-year-old son, Martin.

That evening, von Hofmann made love to Agna. The first time, he did it slowly and tenderly, much as in the early days of their marriage, when he'd been most excited hunting out her pleasure. Later, in full darkness, von Hofmann took her violently and triumphantly for pleasures all his own. Now, as she slept, sated and exhausted, his mind went back to Wewelsburg. About one thing he had no doubt: *If I'd refused, I'd have not have left the castle alive.*

4

FRIDAY, SEPTEMBER 3, 1943

"Look at him standing there, Hastings. Reveille ain't yet blown, and he's out of his barracks, hanging around in doorways like he owns the fucking camp. Stinkin' goddamn Nazi bastard son-of-a-Berlin-whore," said Lieutenant Colonel Lucien G. Marls, commandant of Camp Santa Rosa, to his intelligence officer, Major Lyle Hastings as they marched—or, in the case of Marls's 280-odd pounds, waddled—along the gravel walkway through the pouring rain to the Compound 3 officers' mess.

Hastings held the umbrella over the two of them, but it did little to protect his fat commanding officer, who cursed and sputtered about rain, and New Mexico, and the "fucking goddamn Army." An act, of course. As much as Marls hated Standartenführer Jürgen von Hofmann, for all intents and purposes, the "goddamn Nazi bastard son-of-a-Berlin-whore" kept him his job. Hastings, called up to service from the United States Army Reserve, was happy to be serving his country in a job that kept him close to home—Albuquerque, the wife, their two cats, Bread and Butter. But Marls? He was Regular Army all the way and would've been cashiered three years ago had Uncle Sam not needed everyone to fight the war.

Even the rottenest apples.

Reveille blew. The two Americans stepped up to von Hofmann and Zundorf in the doorway to the mess. Salutes exchanged all around.

"What brings you out so early in this is awful weather, Colonel? Have I forgotten an American holiday? Or perhaps you have finally won the war," von Hofmann said.

Marls frowned, but von Hofmann didn't give him a chance to get angry, because, laughing good-naturedly, he pulled a typed letter from his overcoat pocket. He handed it to the fat camp commandant.

"As you requested, these are the German officers I have convinced to join the work program. I earnestly hope they will set an example for the other camps. Maybe help with your promotion?"

Marls gave the sheet a cursory look. Fifteen names, six of them captains. Although encouraged, German officers were not required to participate in off-camp agricultural labor programs.

Marls's face took the countenance of a grinning pig. "Fine work, von Hofmann. Just sorry I don't see your name on the list." Marls passed the sheet to Hastings. "Major, check these boys out, make sure they're all clear from an intelligence standpoint."

"Yes, sir."

They all stood there, smiling like the best of enemies.

Across the 350-acre camp, 2,879 German prisoners of war from the Wehrmacht, *Kriegsmarine*, and Waffen-SS, 626 of them officers, having finished making their bunks, assembled in the dirt quadrangles of four separate compounds for roll call. Von Hofmann loved this time of day, the sound of the men coming together, the *Feldwebels* and other noncoms shouting orders. It reminded him of home.

What does the pig want? von Hofmann phrasing it aloud, "So how may I help you, commandant?"

"Got a call last night. About a thousand new prisoners comin' in—last of Arnim's boys from North Africa, and the first from Sicily since we chased your asses out, I hear tell."

Von Hofmann's face remained impassive at the announcement of the fall of Sicily.

Marls snorted. "They'll have been on a train for three days, and'll be mighty restless. I'd like to count on your help organizing 'em. You know. Like last time. Cut the officers from the enlisted men and sort the problem boys from both?"

"Herr Commandant, so many men? But of course, I will do what I can." Von Hofmann saluted a second time. "Now if you two will excuse us." He didn't wait for Marls's leave. "Come Hauptmann, the men get wet waiting for roll call."

Von Hofmann led Zundorf into the rain.

Behind him, with a muttered, "Arrogant bastard," Marls pulled a plug of chewing tobacco from his hip pocket. He bit off a chaw and spat out his breakfast.

5

In darkness, Tyler Keyes left the emptiness of the family homestead farm on the back of his sixteen-hand bay quarter horse, trailing the steel-dust mare on a short rope, into the wind and cool an hour before the sun burst across the land with silent thunder from the east. He left, followed by the whickers and nervous snorts from the rest of his string—nervous because they had no idea why he was taking the mare—and met the morning's burning gold upon his face: he, the bay, and the steeldust mare the only significant features on an endless expanse of New Mexican prairie. Out here, where his were the only human eyes to see this land, he wrapped himself in the calm comfort that he was alone in the world, and this world would not, could not change. It existed before him, through him. It existed beyond him, his hard and damaged past, his unrequited, unreconcilable future.

Tyler Keyes listened to his horse, its lungs a bellows between his legs, he also listened to the mare behind. A horse that today would either make or break the only ambition left in him.

The morning wind shifted. It took with it the smell of horse and leather, giving Tyler a breath of sage. He considered the money in his pocket. He'd not mentioned price when he'd written to Phil Dexter in August. Tyler hadn't remembered to ask if the studding fee had changed since he'd gone away. Not that he could do a thing about it. What he carried in his pocket was every dollar he possessed.

Ahead, the rails of the Santa Fe branch line winked silver. As Tyler approached the tracks, and Vaughn materialized in a scattering of indistinct buildings beyond, a gleaming freight came screaming from the west out of Albuquerque, causing him to rein back hard on his bay, causing the steeldust to jump and kick backways in the unusual way she had. Tyler watched the train clatter past. Some passenger, but mostly open freight cars—it made no difference—as the cargo in both was German prisoners of war packed tight and looking, in the snapshot glimpses his eyes could catch, as if this was no worse and probably a lot better than where they'd been and how they'd gotten there. They were the enemy, or at least its representatives, though they and all of that weren't his concern and never would be. *Morally unfit.* And that put them a battlefield spot above Tyler Keyes in this war.

The flatcars jounced and groaned and rattled past. He clicked his tongue and left the prairie, crossing into Vaughn.

6

THE ARRIVAL OF THE NEW PRISONERS was a cold and muddy mess. Inside a prisoner gymnasium, von Hofmann assisted a group of American Military Police whose task it was to check incoming prisoners' belongings against the inventory provided from the ports of embarkation. They recorded thefts or losses, as well as indicated anything the prisoner picked up along the way, which wasn't subject to confiscation as unacceptable for prisoner possession. A dull process, but the room was dry. More importantly, a certain combination of possessions was a prearranged signal from Berlin.

Seven hundred and eighty-six prisoners into the day, von Hofmann watched a sickly looking *SS-Schütze*, a private, step to the table clutching a red leather-bound American Standard Bible. A pair of Ray-Ban Aviator sunglasses protruded from his tunic pocket. The sunglasses were confiscated, to the chagrin of the German private and the consternation of the rest of the MPs baffled over why they hadn't seen them first, but as the MP tried to take the Bible, the young prisoner fought for it until von Hofmann intervened.

"Sergeant! Release the boy's book."

The MP did as von Hofmann ordered. He had a sober appreciation for how the German stood with Marls. "Just doing my job, Colonel. It's not on the list. I have to check it, sir."

"Sergeant, it's a Bible, not a bomb. You've stolen his glasses, isn't that enough?"

The sergeant didn't answer. He glanced at his fellow MPs for support, but they were busy with other prisoners. They had no beef with von Hofmann. He could make their life difficult if he wanted, but he often made it easier.

The Bible and the glasses were a prearranged signal from Berlin. Von Hofmann addressed the private in German. *"Wie ist der werte Name?"*

"I speak English. My name is Helmut Veit."

"You have been to America before?"

"I have been to Milwaukee. Twice. Their weather is nice, but I prefer my beer German." He smiled as though he'd made a joke.

Von Hofmann had turned the recognition phrases in his head a thousand times since Himmler gave them to him back in Berlin on the day before he'd left for North Africa. Had Veit said "Once" it would mean he'd been compromised and von Hofmann would be forced to wait for a second courier. "Twice" meant the operation secure and to proceed directly with the orders the young private carried.

"C'mon, Colonel, you look at the book if you want, but one of us has to."

Von Hofmann held out his hand, "Herr Veit, your Bible."

"Zu befehl, Standartenführer." He passed von Hofmann the red leather book.

Von Hofmann flipped through the pages and probed the binding with the index finger of his right hand. There was nothing out of the ordinary about the Bible, yet somewhere within its pages, his orders were concealed.

He returned the book, saying, "You will find much in this book to help your days here. If you ever need to talk, I am always accessible."

"Thank you, Standartenführer."

As the private moved off, the MP caught von Hofmann's eye.

"I take it the Bible's okay, Colonel?"

"No, Sergeant. Inside that book is Hitler's plan to overthrow your country."

The MP noted the Bible on his sheet, chuckling at the ridiculous notion. Von Hofmann joined in the fun, patting him on the back, but his mind was already far from the room, racing ahead to the time he would hold that Bible again, the moment when two years of waiting would end and he would finally know his objective in America.

7

Phil Dexter's stallion stood seventeen hands of Kentucky thoroughbred muscle, blood, and bone. At the sight of the steeldust mare, it reared, whinnying, forelegs boxing air.

"Nice to see you, Tyler." Phil Dexter's greeting accompanied his handshake. "Didn't know if'n I would."

"You got my letter?"

Phil Dexter had. He stepped past to examine the mare. Liked what he saw. "You're fixing to make yourself a lot of horse—this here filly."

Tyler said nothing. Phil Dexter called to his wranglers in Spanish and they came over. They led the steeldust into the corral to be covered by the stallion. Tyler Keyes and Phil Dexter watched the mating horses for a minute before Phil Dexter looked Tyler Keyes dead in the eye and said, "Howard Hendricks tried to convince me not to go through with this. Told me I'd be doing you a favor."

"You don't say."

"Seeing as t'how he delivered the same note to you by special messenger—" he looked pointedly at the yellow bruises, flaking scabs of O'Hara's visit to Tyler's face—"and you're here in spite, or to spite, it…" He rubbed his stubbled chin. "You're man enough to know your business. Wasn't gonna bring it up, but my Mrs. Dexter was awful close with your mama. Even after all these years, after you paying your debt to society, she still sees trouble 'tween you, him and that girl a'his."

"Forget about it. I have."

"We want you to be careful there, Tyler—Virginia being back like she is with a husband 'parently still overseas—s'all."

Overseas? Tyler hid his surprise. "I've always taken right care of myself, sir."

"You have. 'Nuf said."

The steeldust stood wide-stanced, head bowed, flanks aquiver. Tyler handed Phil Dexter the envelope of cash. The horse rancher accepted it without discussion of price, nor did he open it to count the bills before tucking it inside his vest.

"Speaking of Mrs. Dexter, she'll want to see you at supper, and you'll want to tell her you got that face as a going away present from the yard boys at the Pen Road Inn."

"I think that's a good idea, sir."

"As for your gal," he nodded at the steeldust. "We'll cover her twice more over the next four days. Andy threw his saddle in with the Navy—if you can believe that, kid never much a swimmer—so you can take his room in the main house."

Tyler nodded his thanks, and Phil Dexter smiled, and he gave a variation of what he'd said off the bat—"Yup, we're gonna fix you up with a lot of good horse—" but threw in to close: "And how 'bout, fuck Howard Hendricks for the sour piss-for-blood he is?"

8

"IT IS TRUE ABOUT SICILY, Standartenführer. The Italians are out of the war. Any day now, the Allies will land on the continent. The Führer has plans to crush them before they reach Rome, I promise you that," Helmut Veit said with the hard-edged conviction of angry youth.

They stood at the far north fence of the camp recreation field. Von Hofmann considered the frail private beside him who, cheeks flushed pink with fervor, saw the Reich's inevitable triumph as stark and bright as the thick white clouds that punctuated the expansive blue of the New Mexico sky like the explosions from one hundred cannon fired in victorious salute.

A whistle blew behind them. Two teams of enlisted prisoners joined in a soccer match.

Veit was eighteen years old. He was representative of an entire generation weaned on the Führer and the glories of the Third Reich. Loyal and obedient, they were the new order, born to die for Germany.

"What of the Russian campaign?"

"A stalemate for now, and we move toward another long winter," Veit said. He looked von Hofmann in the eye. "Do not think the war goes badly, Standartenführer. As we speak, the Luftwaffe completes final tests of rocket- and jet-powered aircraft that will soon make them invincible." He gripped the fence, watching the shadows of the high clouds sail over the rocky desert. "Researchers for our V-weapons projects inform the Führer that within a year they will give him more and better bombs that at a push of a button—"

"You, let go of the fence!" an MP yelled from the guard tower thirty feet away as he swiveled his .50 caliber Browning machine gun in their direction.

Veit sneered, but von Hofmann said, "In two seconds, he will use it."

Veit's tight lips quivered, still learning the difference between a boy's pout and a man's fury. He removed his hand from the fence.

"You were saying about the V-weapons, Veit, 'at the push of a button . . .'"

"At the simple push of a button, not only will our supersonic rockets be able to cross the channel to targets in England, but they will cross the Atlantic. We will rain devastation upon New York and Washington, and anywhere else on the eastern seaboard we choose. This is why I come to you with orders from Reichsführer Himmler. It is time to bring Operation Steppenfeuer to full operational status, Standartenführer."

"I will take the Bible, if you please."

On the road beyond the perimeter fence, two MPs patrolled past in a jeep. Veit followed them with his eyes. When he spoke, his tone had lost all life. He sounded like a recorded message from Berlin.

"I have been instructed to tell you to activate your primary team. A tunnel will be dug and an escape prepared for the twentieth of December of this year."

"And the Bible? My instructions?" Von Hofmann extended his open hand.

"Not until you report to me that the tunnel is complete."

"I report to you?" Von Hofmann's hand struck, clamping around Veit's throat. "You will give me that Bible now."

Veit choked and he struggled in von Hofmann's grip. His hand went to his tunic, withdrew the Bible, and fumbled it into the Standartenführer's other hand. Von Hofmann drilled him relentlessly with his gaze before releasing him with a shove.

"That wasn't too difficult, was it?"

"Standartenführer, please. If the tunnel were discovered, and you were found out? Those orders are evidence the Führer does not want found in your possession. Reichsführer Himmler told me to convey this to you as a direct order."

"Your failure, not mine." He considered the book. "Now, how do I find my orders exactly?"

Veit paled. He drew to rigid attention, clenched his jaw and spoke through pursed lips, bracing for a blow. "Standartenführer, I am not to receive word until the tunnel is complete."

"How?"

"I don't know."

"Liar." Von Hofmann backhanded him across the jaw.

"Standartenführer, it is the truth. I do not know!"

Von Hofmann struck him a second time, splitting Veit's lip and knocking him to the ground.

"I swear on the Führer's name! I am not to find out until the tunnel is complete!"

Von Hofmann towered over the young soldier. He'd invoked the Führer's name. For someone like Veit, it was a sacred oath.

"Get up."

Veit staggered to his feet. "You have your duty, Standartenführer, as I have mine. *Es is ein Fall—*"

"*Von höchster Sicherheit.* I am well aware, Herr Veit. If I find you are lying, your death will be extremely unpleasant."

"Thank you, Standartenführer. You have my honor and obedience. I will not fail you."

He retreated a single step, brought his heels together with a smack, and gave a respectful, "Heil Hitler" before melting through the crowd of enlisted prisoners racing by, yelling as they chased their football.

Von Hofmann opened and closed his fist, focusing on the strength of his grip, the blood pumping in and out of his fingertips. He'd come too close to killing the private. He would be more careful in the future.

9

FIFTY MILES AND A WHOLE 'NOTHER WORLD away from von Hofmann and the war prisoners of Camp Santa Rosa, Tyler spent a moment stroking the steeldust's nose, talking to her, helping her calm after her third and last covering by Phil Dexter's stallion. His bay saddled, saddlebags filled—Mrs. Dexter having forced on him some new thermals she'd bought for her son and unnecessary for winter aboard a ship on the Pacific, those, a couple pair of blue jeans along with a bag of coffee, bag of corn meal for the one side, bacon and a few pounds of beans, "if only to remind you to eat," for the other—Tyler offered his thanks and Mrs. Dexter clucked and clutched him and said:

"Now you make me a promise you'll stay away from the past. Even if she comes looking to rub your face in it—running off and marrying that Chip-Cheerio. Girl turned out just as untrustworthy as her father and you're better off now. I'll just say so."

Tyler stretched his lips in the approximation of a smile.

"You go right on, Mrs. Dexter. Lot of work ahead of me, smoothing over five years of weather on the property. That and getting my alfalfa in, ma'am."

Mrs. Dexter had known Tyler Keyes since she'd midwifed his delivery, and she wasn't having any of this non-answer. "Then I'll go right on and tell you: Mrs. Olsen called from her husband's drugstore-diner—" she shielded her mouth with the back of her hand to scoff, "*her* diner counter, by-the-by—and if she didn't put up to me a warning. Virginia has shown up four of these last five days you've been here." She swung her head side-to-side, now playing innocent to go with her: "Gal just lingers over her burger or a piece a'pie, but she's lying in wait for you. Whether she's in on it or not, Hendricks and his Sheriff Thedford are using her games as bait."

At this news, Tyler wanted to get moving. He gripped his reins in the space between his ring and middle finger and his bay perked up as if the key been turned in its ignition.

"Whatever there's left to say about Virginia, she'd never be party to something like that."

"She didn't lift a finger—"

"All right, Mrs. Dexter…" He used a soothing tone, saw her agitation, and through that her maternal love for him. "Lookit: I've no desire to go back in the poke. I'll stay clear of High Street which can't get you to Mr. *or Mrs.* Olsen's establishment if you don't go down their street."

"It would save me gobs of worry."

"I know it would, ma'am." And, darn it, if she didn't have to start rolling tears, and Tyler had to climb out of his saddle. He comforted her in his strong arms and, never one to lie to a woman, he felt a bit of the heel.

A TIP OF HIS HAT AND TEN MINUTES LATER found Tyler at the top of High Street. One minute after that, he parked his bay in the street in a space meant for the perpendicular parking of a car. He looked down on a little blue Triumph convertible beside him. He didn't need to guess who owned it. Although the front glass of Olsen's Drug and Diner was streaked with dirt, the auto's owner was sitting at the counter and, having turned her stool away from her burger, was matching his look of "so this is where our life's brought us," with her look of…what-he-did-not-know. Every detail of Virginia Hendricks—or Virginia whatever-that-surname she'd hitched up to—seared Tyler's vision. Her copper-colored hair, a magnet to the sunshine; her sapphire eyes, tossing the dancing sparks of her inner fire; her brushstroke mouth ready to give the smile that had once been his alone; her nose upturned in permanent challenge the curved slope to its tiny summit dusted with a fairy's breath of cinnamon freckles. Tyler didn't fool himself thinking she was the kind of beauty you'd ever see on the silver screen; Tyler saw her beauty as the kind that stood out against the unbounded prairie beneath the western sky and lit golden by the sun.

Just one look, he'd promised himself, but now that he'd taken it, he wanted to take more. Take her. He watched himself ride inside, right through the doors. Ignoring Mrs. Olsen's yelping, scoop Virginia up, swinging her onto the saddle behind him.

He knew exactly how that would feel—the fit of her hand, her lasso ring waist, sack of feathers weight, her settling in behind him, her lips to his ear urging him as she once had: *"Rake your horse and we'll ride out of this hell forever."*

"Time, Gingersnap. We have plenty enough of it to give waiting a little more. When your father comes after us, we gotta have the law behind us."

But the law hadn't mattered—not in De Baca County, not when her father owned it—and here Tyler's rational mind blew out the phantom smoke of fantasy and ordered his heels to give a "move along" scritch.

Tyler's bootheels didn't move. Virginia was standing now. Raising her hand to her face. Not knowing any better, the sun found her wedding ring and sparked its sparkler. She must have noticed then, because she closed her fist and dropped her hand. Tyler just shook his head—regret and disappointment—that became a goodbye nod. Because that's all he'd come to do. It was all that lay left between them.

In that "damn you, Tyler Keyes," way she had, Virginia shoved off the dirty glass, heading for the doors, headed for a scene, but by the time the bells jingled and she was on the sidewalk, Tyler was already down the road. He didn't turn at the words she chased him with:

"Then go to hell for all I care! You damn coward!"

He'd already been halfway there, because he'd not pulled her into the saddle behind him, the one time it would have made the difference in everything, and he wouldn't be like he was today: sitting tall but sitting alone. Half-wondering, half-accepting her last words against his character a judgement he'd been trying to hide from six years and more than one hundred days on the way to this moment.

Hurting like one thousand hells, Tyler sealed his heart as securely as the barred gate on his former cell. He gave a tap of the hat to the sheriff's deputy in the Guadalupe County car who, doing the bidding of Sheriff Thedford, looked dissatisfied to discover he hadn't caught the pair of them in any matter that could be construed as together.

10

ON VON HOFMANN'S WRIST, the second hand of his Hanart Luftwaffe chronograph—to his mind, the most accurate of all military wristwatches—swept past the twelve. "Sixteen thirty. We will begin without Leutnant Wolters. Leutnant Gauss, the door."

The dimple-cheeked Afrikakorps lieutenant with a head of hair as black as the Ruhr coal the men of his family had mined for generations, stepped to the door of von Hofmann's barracks. Gauss kicked a wooden wedge into the crack at the floor before pressing a thumbtack into a knothole.

Von Hofmann addressed the assembled members of his primary team. "The dirt we excavate weighs roughly one ton per cubic meter. The tunnel I've plotted will be five and a half meters below ground and seventy-seven meters in length, which necessitates our disposing of—at the least—eighty-point-five tons of earth.

"Hauptmann Zundorf requested each of you to develop a formula for disposal. I will start with you, Obersturmführer Mesmer."

Mesmer, a strong, wire-framed SS tanker and a wizard with anything mechanical, answered in the crisp, clipped sentences of an officer used to dealing with rigid commanders. "Seven meters beyond the southern fence. A cement culvert runs alongside the perimeter patrol road. The guards say it is for flood control. The Amis offer a copy of their American Farmers' Almanac in the library. I have studied the historical weather patterns of this region. It confirms the next four months will average thirty-eight centimeters of rain."

Mesmer paused, shifting his steady glance from von Hofmann to Zundorf, including both his senior officers, in his conclusion. "All gutters and drainage systems for the four prisoner compounds flow into the culvert. Dirt can be stored in flour sacks from the mess hall. Hidden in the rafters of our barracks until it rains. At such a time, it will be the simple matter of pouring the dirt into the gutters. This would be safest to carry out at night."

Zundorf glanced at von Hofmann. When the Standartenführer didn't speak, he said, "And if it doesn't rain?"

"Each barracks' rafters can support at least two tons. Bagged. The guards have never checked rafters. Of course, hiding that much dirt would involve the confidence of many more prisoners . . . But it will rain, Herr Hauptmann Zundorf. Almanacs don't lie."

Again, Zundorf gave von Hofmann a questioning glance. This time, the Standartenführer met it with a slight nod.

"It will rain," von Hofmann stated as fact. "As for engaging the confidence of more prisoners, I already have in place a secondary team of thirty-seven enlisted men. They are excellent soldiers, all of them party members, dedicated to me and to the Führer. They will faithfully dispose of the dirt any way I prescribe."

"That answers any questions about my idea," the one called the Tiger interjected without waiting for acknowledgment.

With any other officer, von Hofmann would never tolerate this violation of the chain of command. But the Tiger was not Afrikakorps standard issue. Before the war, he'd been something of a celebrity—his nickname, along with his bashed-in nose won in the boxing ring. While still in the Hitler Youth, the Tiger won a gold medal as a middleweight boxer in the Berlin Olympics. "For the Führer and the Third Reich," he'd told the reporters. He went on to compete professionally before taking a commission in the Wehrmacht, where his boxing career continued. Middleweight champion of the *Panzerarmee Afrika*, the only time he came face to face with an Allied soldier was when he and some 125,000 other Germans and 115,000 Italians were surrendered by Arnim earlier that year and the North African war ended in Germany's defeat.

Von Hofmann had chosen the Tiger for his primary team for three reasons: his English was fluent; he was an ardent Nazi; and backed into a corner, he was the toughest son of a bitch von Hofmann had ever seen backed into a corner.

"At zero-seven-thirty each morning, ten buses take three hundred and twenty prisoners to work programs on area farms. The enlisted men you've mentioned, Standartenführer, can smuggle the dirt out of camp in the pockets of their clothing. We could sew Mesmer's flour sacks into the lining of a greatcoat. They could put dirt in their canteens, their mess kits, anything they carry. All they'd have to do is dump it out in whatever bean field they're working in. I bet we could get rid of almost all our dirt—"

A commotion outside interrupted him.

"Gauss, see who it is," von Hofmann ordered.

Still minding the door, Gauss pinched the thumbtack, pulled free the knothole. He peered into the compound.

The work buses had returned. The enlisted men and few officers who went with them were arriving late from their work details and were complaining about it. Gauss caught sight of Leutnant Wolters. His right arm draped around the shoulder of a short, middle-aged, barrel-chested sergeant, Wolters clenched his face in pain as he limped toward von Hofmann's barracks.

"Here comes Wolters and some Feldwebel, sir," said Gauss. "He's limping. He looks hurt."

"Wolters or the Feldwebel?" von Hofmann said, suspicious.

"Herr Wolters."

"Let them in."

Gauss pried the wedge free and opened the door as Wolters and the sergeant mounted the barracks steps.

When they entered the room, the Feldwebel released Wolters. The larva-pale, bald lieutenant hobbled to the nearest cot and sat. A small, hardcover book with a garish cover fell out of his desert trousers.

"Mission accomplished, Standartenführer," he grinned, collecting his Karl May western novel.

In civilian life, Wolters had been a teacher, so von Hofmann understood where his constant need for reading had developed, but he felt it also distracted young Wolters. Had Leutnant Wolters's mind been focused on their mission, rather than Wild West serials—German and superior to American westerns, though these were—this middle-aged Feldwebel would not be at the Standartenführer's door. Wolters would need corrective attention.

The sergeant who'd brought Wolters came to rigid attention. He threw a salute. "Heil Hitler!"

"Heil Hitler, Herr . . ." von Hofmann searched for his name.

"Schmidt. Gunter Schmidt, Standartenführer."

"Of course. Thank you for attending to Leutnant Wolters." He indicated the door. "Good day."

Schmidt remained at attention.

"Dismissed, Feldwebel."

"If it's all the same, I'd rather the Standartenführer let me remain."

Zundorf shot to his feet, but von Hofmann stayed him with a wave of his hand. Von Hofmann faced Wolters, who was in the process of removing the heads of two pickaxes from where he'd tied them around his left thigh. Concentrating on the tools, Wolters spoke. "He caught me stealing these."

"You will look at me when you address me, Leutnant."

Wolters's eyes flashed to von Hofmann.

"*Zu befehl*, Standartenführer. He caught me stealing these from the farmer's supply shed. He wanted to use them to kill the driver and our guard and steal the bus to escape. He would have turned me in if I didn't tell him what I needed them for."

Jürgen von Hofmann glared at Wolters.

The Feldwebel said, "In the past four months, I have come to the Standartenführer with four escape plans. The Standartenführer has refused me, but now I can see why. I beg the Standartenführer, let me join his escape."

Von Hofmann scrutinized the sergeant.

Schmidt clenched a fist and thumped his chest. "I'm built for digging tunnels. I've dug them before. I am a mole. I could out-dig any man in this room."

Von Hofmann fancied him more a tough, old Spanish fighting bull than a mole. He remembered Feldwebel Schmidt. Half a dozen years older than von Hofmann, the sergeant was also a veteran of the Great War who used that era's irritating third-person form of address between noncoms and officers. Schmidt had come to him before with escape ideas. Brazen, outlandish ideas. One had involved inciting a general riot, seizing a guard tower, and taking over its machine gun. Another had been stealing a bus and crashing it through the gates. The other two he couldn't recall precisely, but one had centered on some kind of bonfire. It was possible the last had been a tunnel.

Von Hofmann didn't want Schmidt. No question, something needed to be done about this obtrusive sergeant. Von Hofmann's inclination was to kill him. He dismissed the idea. The body and explanation would create problems with Marls. Too much to risk this far into the operation. Von Hofmann needed the fat American blithely complacent. For the time being, it would be safer for von Hofmann to include Schmidt; kept on a short leash, he could be controlled.

"Welcome aboard, Feldwebel Schmidt."

He noticed Zundorf's disapproval. He would explain to him later, after he'd dealt with Wolters. "Once we finish our discussion on dirt disposal, Leutnant Wolters, you and I will have a private discussion on security and your continued involvement in this operation."

Wolters stiffened. His blood rushed to the surface of his ghoulish skin. Von Hofmann was pleased to note the rest of the team avert their eyes, as if the mere sight of Wolters might contaminate them with his shame.

"*Zu befehl*, Standartenführer." Wolters's voice trembled.

The remainder of the meeting went quickly. Never once did von Hofmann's eyes leave Wolters, trapping him in their gaze with the cold detachment of a scientist watching an insect kick on a pin.

Zundorf waited until the others were out of sight before he went back to the barracks' door. Wolters had made a stupid mistake. If a guard instead of Schmidt had seen the pickaxes, they would all be "cooling off" right now in one of Colonel Marls's hotboxes, or worse, von Hofmann would be on his way to the maximum-security camp at Alva, where the hardcore Nazis were imprisoned. Whatever his mission, he would never get the chance to accomplish it from there.

Wolters needed censure and discipline. Absolutely. But Zundorf cringed, sickened by the sound of heavy blows coming from beyond the wooden door. This was not his way, not the way of the Afrikakorps. It was the way of Berlin, the Gestapo, the SD, and Zundorf had no stomach for it.

Surely von Hofmann was killing him. Zundorf had known Wolters since he'd transferred into his company in Tripoli. He'd saved Zundorf's life at Tobruk. His love of German western author Karl May and his encyclopedic knowledge of his books, and characters and their adventures, had, surprisingly, been a pleasant distraction from the reality of their journey across the American West to their dull and shameful prison camp captivity. Wolters was a brother and he didn't deserve this, but Zundorf was pledged to von Hofmann. Von Hofmann commanded here, not Zundorf. He had no business, no right to question the actions of the Standartenführer. He was ashamed.

Zundorf noticed the book, its spine broken from when von Hofmann wrenched it apart and hurled it through the door. He retrieved it. *Winnetou, the Chief of the Apache.*

Walking from the barracks to the prisoner library, where he could repair the book, Zundorf told himself von Hofmann was doing the right thing. An hour later, smoking his fifth cigarette and drinking another countless cup of coffee as he waited for the glue to hold the book binding fast, Zundorf almost had himself convinced.

11

MONDAY, NOVEMBER 15, 1943

THE STEELDUST MARE MISCARRIED at 6 a.m. Dr. Vickery, the only vet Tyler knew who didn't take orders from Howard Hendricks, drove in from Valencia after that. He said, "You could be looking at a dead horse on top of the foal embryo."

"You're saying this was poison?" He stroked the steeldust's neck as she lay in distress in a bed of fresh hay on the floor of the barn.

"I wouldn't say it out loud in court."

Tyler knew what he meant and didn't blame him.

Vickery continued. "There's a dozen ways to make something like this look natural, but yours was a horse going into this all set to carry through to term, and I am not unfamiliar with your troubles."

"Nobody in these parts is."

Vickery gave Tyler a sympathetic sneer. "That's why we have a free and dishonest press."

The vet was looking for a sneer on return, but Tyler didn't have it in him. Gazed fondly at the steel dust. "She'll get better? Be able to try again?"

"Give her a couple cycles to heal. Meanwhile, I'll give her a vitamin boost and, with your permission, a dose of antibiotics."

"Like used on people? Since when?"

He nodded. "Mixed right for horses, they've been doing wonders for the last two, three years."

Tyler gave his permission wondering if somewhere along the way they'd flip it around to find a measure of horse sense they could administer to people. He'd be first in line.

Tyler Keyes worked his bay horse through a tough patch of mesquite, touched his spurs to its ribs, and proceeded over the worn edge of a mesa that dropped into the twisting length of Rattlesnake Canyon. A late decision had given him a late start. The sunlight was lifting from the deepest parts of the canyon he was headed for below, leaving it gray and a deepening blue that matched the melancholy inside him.

From that morning in front of Olsen's until this afternoon when he'd let the steeldust run free, he'd exhausted himself with work. He'd wired and reposted his fences. Baked bricks, patched and plastered his adobe walls. Replaced broken vigas and laths in his roof and ceiling. He'd gotten in the late summer alfalfa. Adequate rainfall germinated the seeds, followed by forty-eight frost-free good growing nights and days to build the carbohydrate reserves in the crop that they'd carry through winter.

He'd harness-broke a pair of draft horses for Archie Rosenberg's Land O' Milk & Honey dairy, and an Arabian to the saddle and bit for the Bernals' granddaughter. Both clients were over from Lincoln County. His local clientele, built up since he'd acquired a reputation for having the "touch" with spirited horses since the age of ten, had all been warned off business with Tyler at the time of his parole—warned off by Hendricks, whose warnings, unheeded, were always paid back as trouble. Last week, when Rosenberg came for his Percherons, he told Tyler that since Tyler's visit to Phil Dexter in Vaughn, Hendricks was making it known through his foreman O'Hara (Rosenberg used the Yiddish *nokhshleper,* 'flunky henchman'—a more apt description Tyler had yet to hear) that Hendricks planned to bleed Tyler dry—mentally, physically, financially—and, once little more than a stick-and-scrape scarecrow, kill him.

There'd been no new business since and there wouldn't be any to come. O'Hara was spreading the word not because people knew Hendricks word was good, but because they knew once the boundaries of his word were set, anyone who crossed them would suffer the same fate.

Tyler wasn't afraid of Hendricks's threats. Tyler Keyes had ridden with death for most of his life. His great-grandfather had been murdered by raiding Comanche. His great grandmother— the soft death—had fallen asleep in her chair, smiling at his two-month-old self cuddled in her lap, and never awoke. Tyler's grandparents died when he was six, his grandfather following his grandmother four months later because he couldn't bear to be without her. Then came the ones that cut closer. His mother dropping dead from a stroke the day after his sentencing. His father's heart giving up three years back and thirty years too early. All of them sad. All painful. All of them: kinds of death life could guarantee.

Grinning Earl Descheenie, his death, it seemed to Tyler, fell outside that guarantee. A Navajo con one week short of parole after ten years inside on a drunk-driving homicide. No, he wasn't guaranteed the death he got. Tyler was coming back to the yard after a week in the infirmary two months and three beat-downs into his incarceration. No bearing on the why of it, but the day happened to be Tyler's eighteenth birthday, and he happened to be smiling stupidly to himself when Descheenie's shiv came at him in an upward arc. It was the Indian's lack of commitment to the kill that allowed Tyler a single sidestep and a fateful grab.

Tyler left the old man's sharpened fence-wire shiv deep in Descheenie's chest and vanished among the felons in the yard.

He didn't look back. He couldn't look back. The old man's last whispered words echoed in his head before he took the shiv deep.

Tyler had never killed a man, never in his wildest dreams imagined that he ever would. It was all he could do to conceal the competing desires to scream, to vomit, to collapse in tears, to cackle and crow at having beaten death by trading his for another's.

No one gave him up for the killing. Not because Tyler was liked. Tyler Keyes was a piece of meat someone had upped the contract from a beatdown to a rub-out and, at that moment, he was still a dead man walking. The only friend Tyler had made since arriving inside the New Mexico State Penitentiary was his cellmate. The man he'd just killed.

Scream. Vomit. Cry. Cackle. Breathe.

Nobody fingered Tyler to the hollering guards because the kill itself was righteous. Self-defense. That wouldn't preclude someone else from going after the thousand-dollar payout on Tyler, but that would take time to set up. Meanwhile, later that night, Tyler put fire to the cell he'd shared with the Indian, following the sacred Navajo custom for the dead. It earned him twenty days' solitary in the boiler room hellhole, but it gained him the lasting respect of every Native American in the prison. Since the Indians ran the yard at the "Pen Road Inn," no one after that went for so much as a dime on the contract from Virginia Hendricks's father.

Dr. Vickery had called on Tyler this morning to check the steeldust mare. Some more vitamins, another dose of antibiotics, and Tyler and the vet watched the mare shake her head and whinny, kick her feet in that unusual way she had—half-prance, half-gambol—into the yard full of delight. She'd needed only four days rest and looking after, before she was back with the herd, tragedy put behind her, while Tyler's mood continued along the getting-worse track it had been hard-galloping these seven weeks since he'd played the fool hunting out Virginia and allowing them both to torment each other.

The vet left, happy to say the steeldust would be ready to try again come New Year's.

Tyler watched spirals of dust trail Dr. Vickery's Hudson as he drove out the right-of-way through the Hendricks range that surrounded Keyes's farm. Tyler's recent backbreak had bought him a year's worth of financial survival. A few weeks remained before he'd have to batten down for winter. Tyler was tired of Hendricks, of the death that man hurled like lightning bolts with superhuman impunity. He loved Virginia, but he didn't know her anymore. By the time the vet's coupé was out of sight, Tyler had decided he needed to leave the farm as well.

Not that he was afraid of Hendricks and his threats, but he had voluntarily taken an eight-year sentence to protect Virginia until she became adult and able to make her own decisions free in a couple years' time from her father's legal grip. He'd do the time between, until she could get before a judge and spell out the truth, and they could seize the future they'd wanted since their first sticky-lipped, cotton-candy kiss at the state fair when they were nine.

At seventeen, never once in trouble with the law before, Tyler was slammed into a ten-by-eight cell in the state penitentiary. A damned and frightened kid with a price on his head in the yard, and she'd never wrote him once. Not once. Instead, Virginia left New Mexico, found someone else, married him, and upped his sentence from eight years inside to life wherever he ended up.

He'd left this afternoon because since that day in Vaughn, he couldn't get Virginia Hendricks out of his head, and its pain was apt to destroy him. It was time to release her, to take a hard look at his life—the rest of it and how he'd arrive there—and there was only one place on earth where he could do that: the fishing camp passed down to Tyler by his father, who'd been shown it by his own father when just a boy.

South of their place, just below the Chaves county line, hidden halfway up Rattlesnake Canyon where the Headwater, Blue Hole, and Rattlesnake Springs all come together in a rocky bowl, lay a deep, clear and cool little lake. A lake shaded by old cotton-woods, its surface broken by the occasional jump of a cutthroat trout while the big black bass hid at the bottom, waiting for a fight. Tyler's grandfather had built a campsite, a cabin, and a corral, and, Tyler suspected, stocked the pool some forty years back. Black bass are not native to New Mexico.

Tyler Keyes had no idea how long he'd be gone. He'd just grabbed the jeans and thermals Mrs. Dexter had gifted him, a buck-skin shirt a pair of Mescalaro teenagers had brought—a trade for a bitless bridle with sidepull reins Tyler had promised their father he'd give them when he got out; he put his string of horses to pasture, his eyes lingering hopefully on the steeldust; he mounted his bay and left.

Tyler guided the horse through an uneven corridor of jagged boulders, wending his way through juniper and the clutches of brittle, twisting piñon that dotted the sand-colored east wall of the canyon. In less than an hour, he would be at the cabin. A breeze blew south down the ravine at his strong back as he rode the bay into the shallow bed of Rattlesnake Springs. The dying sun still had a last gasp in it and drew out the pinks and reds from the gorge's upper walls while the canyon rim glowed violet against the faded-blue-jean sky. Somewhere a quail called and was answered, and Tyler's mood softened with the familiarity of this landscape.

The evening star rose, and by the time it glimmered high above, Tyler was looking at it as a reflection in the fishing hole. He'd corralled and fed his horse, rubbing it down with a handful of grass. He'd opened the cabin and thrown his gear on one of the bunks. Now, seated on a rock beside the water, he let his heart fall to pieces. Life without Virginia. She hadn't fought. She'd become someone else.

The night grew colder as the darkness deepened. Tyler listened to the rustle of bat wings as they reeled above the water, hunting insects. He mourned Virginia and for all he'd lost. And an idea wormed its way from the darkest corner of his mind. He'd ridden with death for most of his life. How the last three—his mother, father, Descheenie, though all forced by Hendricks—had been caused by him. How he ached half-dead already. How he'd never have a life without Virginia and how a life without Virginia wouldn't be life at all. Why wait? Wasn't this why he'd come here alone?

It would be easy to end it. The idea worked its way like water across a stone, searching for a crack.

Was this the answer? To die. To take a plunge into the big pool and drown?

Without love, without family or friends, a reputation ruined, and your name soon erased from the land, what was there for him, anyway? Tyler stared at the water's surface. He tried to peel back the reflections and get to the cold depths, the silence, and the peace promising itself below. Would it be difficult to drown yourself? Not if you went deep enough to start.

Find a large rock on the bottom. Wedge a foot under, good and tight. Wait and run out of breath. He could do that. He was sure of it. Might as well get it over with.

The air was still. The water flat. All feelings buried and waiting for him to join them. Tyler rose to his feet.

His heart ripped open one more time. "God dammit."

Every Keyes who'd come before deserved a better end. Water doesn't break rock. Suicide would betray their honor, betray his line.

Descheenie caught his eye one second before he attacked.

Everything Tyler's people ever worked for, everything they'd loved, feared, and fought against.

He grabbed for Descheenie's shiv and Descheenie forced its handle into Tyler's hand.

All their tears, and all their dreams for a better future, Tyler had no right to take and drown and turn to miserable failure.

Descheenie's fingers closed Tyler's fist around the blanket-wrapped handle. Their eyes remained locked. "Got the cancer, kid. Not the way a warrior goes."

The Navajo pulled Tyler into his chest. Shiv first. "Be the brave I done never were."

Tyler's first night in lock-up, the Navajo had told the young horseman about the fire ritual. He knew what it would earn Tyler. With that shiv, that life sacrifice, that ritual fire, Descheenie had saved Tyler Keyes for his future.

Tyler howled his pain into the empty night. He threw himself into the water and sank to the bottom. When he could no longer hold his breath, Tyler accepted the water's cleansing renewal and pushed to the surface, bursting forth to fill his lungs with precious air. Tyler's duty would be life.

12

SUNDAY, NOVEMBER 28, 1943

FIVE AND A HALF METERS beneath Camp Santa Rosa, von Hofmann's tunnel angled southwest from under the hollow wooden altar inside the prisoners' chapel. One and a half meters wide by another meter high, it cut through a hard caliche cap into a tough composition of red sandstone, siltstone, and Triassic rock Marls, Hastings, and the Army Corps of Engineers who'd located the camp believed impassable, but in fact was perfect for tunneling, in that it needed little support or bracing.

This amused von Hofmann as alone, shirtless and crawling on his elbows, he pushed a sputtering candle made from a tin can filled with a coil of bacon-fat-impregnated rope in front of him and inspected the shaft. Cold and dry, a chalky gray dust hovered in the thin air.

As usual, Nietzsche was right. "*Was mich nicht zerstört, macht mich stärker.*" What does not destroy me makes me stronger. The beating of Wolters had been a good thing. Although all visible reminders of the event were gone, its mental presence remained like thick scar tissue between the Standartenführer and his subordinates. Already it had borne a significant effect on the team's performance. Von Hofmann was proud of what he had accomplished. In two months, they'd dug fifty-eight meters. The tunnel ran laterally from the chapel, beneath the ends of two prisoners' barracks in Compound 2, continued under the prisoners' laundry, and stretched the length of the utility area. Von Hofmann calculated they were five meters shy of the outer fence. Fourteen meters beyond stood the cluster of four piñon pines von Hofmann envisioned for the location of their escape hatch.

The only fault von Hofmann found with his tunnel was its length. The training he'd undergone at the RSHA mock POW camp sixteen kilometers from the spy school in The Hague stressed the rule of thumb pertaining to tunnel construction: "*In jedem Gramm von ausgegrabener, existiert eine Tonne von potentieller Katastrophe.*" In every gram of excavated dirt, there exists a ton of potential disaster.

Von Hofmann had turned over the question of location a hundred times in his mind. The selection of the chapel had been a choice forced by necessity. Of all the buildings in the prisoners' domain, the chapel and the showers were the only structures with floors and foundations touching the earth. The corrugated tin barracks, the prisoners' PX, hospital, and work sheds all perched on concrete pylons one meter above the ground, affording a view of anything moving beneath them, not to mention exposing the mouth of any tunnel to the inclement weather of the encroaching winter and the grim possibility of flooding. Von Hofmann shuddered.

To drown in one's own escape tunnel? Pathetic.

When von Hofmann was ten, his mother slipped while preparing her bath. An hour passed before anyone checked on her. When the housekeeper did, she screamed at the sight of her mistress sprawled naked, half in, half out of the tub. The face was blue and puckered in the water, hair floating around it like a golden corona of light. Von Hofmann's mother was dead, and from the moment they brought her to the parlor and his father removed her rings, von Hofmann considered drowning the most repulsive and humiliating way to die. Drowning was the only thing that frightened him.

As for digging from the showers, his compound's showers were closer to the perimeter fences by over fifteen meters, but the MP guards monitored their usage. While his men going to dig in the chapel at night played a longer, deadly game of tag with the watchtower searchlights, the complete inattention the Americans paid the little church at all other times offset the danger. Prisoners' religion was sacred in Camp Santa Rosa. Marls and his MPs didn't give a damn about it.

Von Hofmann was reconciled to the chapel. Were his instructors with him, they would be hard-pressed to find a better location for a tunnel in Camp Santa Rosa.

The sound of digging increased as von Hofmann neared the tunnel's end. Gauss turned and greeted him while Mesmer loosened the earth with a pickax. Von Hofmann gave the pair a few words of encouragement. He passed them the canteen of water he'd brought, some hard bread and dried fruit stolen from the kitchen, and relaxed while they gorged themselves until the food was gone and the canteen empty. After thanking the Standartenführer, there was nothing more to say, and the two junior officers went back to work.

Von Hofmann tied the ends of two sacks of dirt together and draped them across his neck. He wedged around and headed out of the tunnel.

The disposal of the dirt was flawless. The Tiger's plans for the work parties to dump it on the farms had been an inspiration. Did Veit have any idea how they were doing it? Probably not. Veit was merely a *Jungvolk* errand boy. At least once a week, von Hofmann noticed him sitting outside his Compound 1 barracks, eating a candy bar and reading a book, eyes bulging ridiculously behind thick reading glasses.

For two weeks, von Hofmann had spent every night attempting to discover his orders in Veit's Bible. He'd carefully taken apart the binding. He'd examined the spine and the covers. Nothing concealed within either. He'd read the book three times from cover to cover, hoping to find something meaningful inserted into the text by its Nazi publisher, but the words inside the book contained no message at all. Humiliating as it would be, he'd have to wait for Veit. Those were Reichsführer Himmler's orders. Von Hofmann allowed his dedication to Himmler to guide his emotions and allow him patience.

Once he received his orders, von Hofmann would need a significant way for Veit to serve the mission and his Fatherland. A permanent way. As much as von Hofmann despised the arrogant, insubordinate private, he did not believe in wasting men. He had seen enough of that in the first war. No, Veit would serve his purpose—become the centerpiece of the escape—and as it came to him, Von Hofmann judged his plan for Veit so ingenious Reichsführer Himmler would applaud him for its innovation.

But the applause would come later. After his successful completion of his mission. His proud return to Berlin. Letting his imagination run, von Hofmann accidentally jammed his shoulder into the tunnel wall. With a heavy thud, the tunnel collapsed on von Hofmann's back and buried him alive.

Wolters breathlessly caught Zundorf behind the officers' mess. "The Standartenführer's buried, Herr Hauptmann."

"*Scheisse.* Marls is looking all over for him. How did this happen?"

"I don't know. Schmidt and the Tiger are digging him out."

They made strides from Compound 3 into the prisoners' common area.

"What about Mesmer and Gauss?"

"They were digging at the time. Schmidt sent me to get you—"

"You take orders from a Feldwebel?"

"What? No, Herr Hauptmann. There wasn't room for me to help dig. I wanted to get you."

"Not what you said, Herr Leutnant," Zundorf added. "Watch that Schmidt. He is not like us. He has already gotten you into trouble once."

Wolters nodded. They continued in silence.

The Tiger let Zundorf and Wolters into the chapel. Von Hofmann slouched on a pew, his arms and legs spread wide. Schmidt was talking to him, von Hofmann silently agreeing with whatever the sergeant said.

"You're all right, Standartenführer?" Zundorf pushed his way between von Hofmann and the sergeant.

"What does it look like?"

"And Mesmer and Gauss, they are okay, too?"

"They're bagging the dirt and setting a brace," said Schmidt.

Zundorf cast a sidelong glance at the sergeant. "What caused the cave-in?"

"The section you and Wolters dug last night collapsed."

"What are you suggesting, Feldwebel?"

"Nothing, Herr Hauptmann. As I was telling the Standartenführer, there was no possible way you or Wolters could have known the dirt in that section was any different from the rest of the tunnel and needed special bracing. Otherwise, you would have been more careful, spent more time and set a proper brace."

Zundorf's body clenched like a fist, but von Hofmann interjected. "An accident, plain and simple. I'm just glad Schmidt was here to pull me out."

Von Hofmann rose. He'd predicted the rivalry between the sergeant and his captain from their first exchange. Von Hofmann used it to his advantage, playing the pair off each other in order to get the best of what these two men had to offer. Inside, he smiled. It seemed to be working.

13

IN VON HOFMANN'S EYES, Colonel Marls's office was an affront to the profession of arms. Coffee mugs and dirty glasses. A plate covered with the crumbs of Marls's lunch. All of them paper-weights to the scattered files and documents covering every surface, like painters' drop cloths, collecting the dust blowing in from the open window. Two half-filled spittoons stood on either side of the wide desk. Three bottles of different whiskeys were displayed on a credenza, above which hung the moth-eaten head of an unfortunate mountain lion. Von Hofmann was certain the lion would have killed Marls had they ever faced each other. Probably still could. In the midst of it, filling an oversized chair behind the desk, sat Marls, hands folded before him, his fat fingers a mound of pulsing slugs.

Colonel Marls held von Hofmann in a half-closed, heavy-lidded stare. Von Hofmann didn't wait for an invitation to sit. He took a straight-backed chair and pulled it close to the edge of the desk. He raised a questioning eyebrow at the camp commandant, inviting him to speak.

"Where the hell you been, von Hofmann?"

"I beg your pardon?"

"You heard me. We had an appointment."

"Of course we did. Fifteen hundred hours, which it will be in . . ." His eyes caught the second hand of Marls's wall clock as it swung for the twelve. ". . . thirty seconds."

"Dammit, von Hofmann: fourteen hundred—two o'clock—not three!"

Von Hofmann gave a skeptical smile. "Fourteen hundred? My apologies."

"Don't play games with me, Colonel."

Von Hofmann raised his hands, palms facing Marls, in mock surrender. Marls snorted and picked up a copy of the *Phoenix Sun*. He flung it at his prisoner. Von Hofmann caught the newspaper and turned it over. He glanced at the headline.

Two Nazi Prisoners Escape Humboldt Camp. Von Hofmann perused the article, caught Marls's eye. "Perhaps they took a sight-seeing trip to the Grand Canyon?"

"Try Mexico City, smart-ass." Marls pulled his immense girth from his chair and leveled a finger. "This I won't have, Colonel. Not in my camp. Not on my watch. Do you hear me?"

"Colonel, I won't be baited into guessing why you have chosen to lecture me for the foolhardy venture of two misguided soldiers I've never heard of from a camp I have never seen."

"Look here, von—"

"I may be a prisoner, but I am also an officer and a gentleman. I am ascribed certain considerations by the Geneva Convention. I find your tone and implication outrageous."

Marls frowned. The Nazi's voice had dropped to a disquieting pitch. Marls picked at a sore on the nape of his neck, and then cleaning his fingernail with his thumbnail, hesitated before asking, "You get many requests for escapes from the enlisted men? The officers?"

Von Hofmann gave a short, congenial laugh. "Nine."

"Thatta no?"

"That's a yes: one, two, three, four, five, six, seven, eight, *nine*. I have had nine requests by men desiring to escape Camp Santa Rosa and return to their Fatherland."

Marls's mouth gaped. Von Hofmann noticed bits of tobacco in his teeth.

"Nine requests, huh? That's sure a damned awful lot." He clicked his tongue, trying to recover the initiative he'd never had.

"Well, you've slipped this much, von Hofmann. You oughta just tell me when they plan to break. And don't bullshit me because I know an escape is in the works."

Von Hofmann looked properly aghast. "I don't believe this, Colonel Marls. It is as if we are not speaking the same language. Obviously, I rejected these requests! And I will continue to reject all escape requests that come my way. Frankly, you are not the judge of human nature I thought. Do you assume I would tell you of any requests if there was an escape in the works? What kind of Judas do you take me for? I am under no obligation by said Geneva Convention or otherwise to share with you this kind of information. I do so only out of my belief that by working together we can do our share to make this a shorter war."

Von Hofmann rose. He flung the newspaper into Marls's chest. "Be glad our agendas are the same on this point, Colonel. Now, if you will excuse me, this meeting is over."

He left the building. As he passed beneath Marls's open window, von Hofmann heard the distinctive sound of glass against glass, liquor trickling from a bottle.

14

FOUR UPROOTED PLANTS lay in the dirt before Tyler's boots at the foot of his front porch stairs. Onion-like root bulbs eaten on two of them, the other two: masticated stems and flower stalks. Dr. Vickery had come by in the afternoon to confirm cause of death and help Tyler execute the proper paperwork. The crematorial pyre for the steeldust mare had burned all night in the front yard but hadn't attracted any visitors. It smoked and smoldered now, in the hour of dawn, a pit of charred wood and wood ash, horse bones and teeth, and Tyler waited. His octagonal barrel Winchester '94 lay across his lap.

Cecil O'Hara drove through Tyler's gate in his maroon Ford pickup. A city-hauler with a four-cylinder tractor engine, Tyler couldn't see the point of for ranch work but, then again, O'Hara didn't do the kind ranch work associated with trucks or dirty hands.

He was alone and as he came to Tyler his nickel-plated .45 automatic glint in first light high on his hip. He stopped a conversational shooting-distance from Tyler who didn't rise, nor move the rifle across his legs, although, in his mind's eye, gun smoke already curled: O'Hara twitching out his last couple heartbeats in the dirt.

"Saw the glow of your fire over the ridgeline from the Triple H."

"Neighborly you, coming over to see if I had an emergency."

O'Hara indicated the plants at Tyler's feet with a thrust of his chin. "How many horses you lose to them death camas?"

"Just the one you wanted me to lose. Could've poisoned her outright all at once—taking the mare when you aborted the foal. To that, you could have taken the whole string although not so many were as trusting as that steeldust to be handfed poison. Guess it's just that right amount of cruelty Hendricks likes to set himself apart with… A nokshleper just takes orders."

O'Hara smacked his lips like a horned toad catching a gnat. "Can't say I'm an American Bund member like your pal Schneider to know how to translate no Kraut talk. But I am here to talk."

"Don't know Schneider, though I'm thankful he's more honorable than the former judge Holden. Don't imagine he's Nazi, but the word's Yiddish—that'd be Jewish—so the American Bund Nazi thing don't fly your eagle."

"You calling me Jewboy?" O'Hara's palm moved to the butt of his pistol.

"I'm calling you a motherfucking-horse-killer-son-of-a-bitch whose dirt I'll piss on right after I plant you in the grave I kick your maggot-bait corpse into. That'll be your first drop on your way down to the fires of hell."

O'Hara's eye twitched as his fingers tremored like spider legs, but Tyler didn't move his gun. He laughed.

"You and I both know you'll only ever get me in ambush. You walked up front here because Hendricks doesn't want me dead yet. Knows you won't shoot 'cause you're a leash-dog. Knows I won't shoot because I'll kill you and that'll get me lit up like a Christmas tree in the chair back in the smoking room of the place I got no intention of going back to."

To prove his point, Tyler laid his Winchester aside. He stood. He walked up to O'Hara and gave him a poke in the chest to accentuate these words: "I'm gonna kill all a'you at once and I'm gonna get away with it."

O'Hara was a tough guy. O'Hara had killed men. Had with his gun, and not always in the back in ambush. But this morning he lifted his hand from his pistol and pushed it inside his jacket to fish out an envelope. He ground down his fury with his nicotine-stained teeth before he could get out, "This is a bank draft drawn on the account of H. Howard Hendricks, from the First National Bank of Santa Fe, in the amount of five thousand dollars."

"Looks like ass paper to me," Tyler cracked.

"Stop fucking with me—because I'm this close to breaking orders!" Spittle flew in Tyler's face.

Tyler dialed his tone down a notch. "It's fifty percent more than what-all land and property I got. Plus, maybe, double the two horses."

"You're only worth lead to me, but that's not how Mr. Hendricks sees it. He's willing to be generous to get you gone. It expires Friday the twenty-fourth of this month. He'll expect you to cash it before end of business that day and haul on outta here before that point in time."

"Christmas is a time of miracles, but I wouldn't hold my breath for that one, pal-I-mean-nokshleper."

O'Hara flipped him off. Back inside his truck, he stomped on his gas pedal. He puttered out of Tyler's yard.

15

MONDAY, DECEMBER 20, 1943

A T HALF PAST NINE, Lieutenant Colonel Lucien G. Marls dropped the dog-eared copy of Raymond Chandler's *The Lady in the Lake* onto the floor beside his bed. He shut off the light. He relaxed in the dark, listening to a mean winter wind pummel his buttoned-down camp. He still liked *The Big Sleep* best, with its story of cheap pornography and that little slut Carmen Sternwood, who enjoyed posing for dirty pictures. *The Big Sleep:* where he'd gotten the idea to photograph General Asher's daughter, Janet, in the first place. He'd managed to save a few of the best photos of her for private time. He still enjoyed them more than any woman on any night.

Janet Asher. An interesting piece from his past, a squalid but damn-hot episode that would have destroyed the career of a lesser soldier. But not Marls. No, sir. The way he looked at it, he'd been able to use it to dump an eyesore of a wife and get a general to understand a court-martial wouldn't be enough to protect his daughter's reputation, but that a promotion and Camp Santa Rosa would produce—to use a pun and badly—"no *negative* repercussions."

By lying to himself that self-corruption and the corruption of others throughout his life had made Marls into the smartest man he'd ever known was the paramount height of his inexorable stupidity.

As sleep crept upon him, Marls warmed with visions of how he'd made Camp Santa Rosa a model POW camp with a reputation that stretched all the way to Washington. It had been easy. Germans were a race used to strict discipline and order. Early on, Marls learned the best way to handle them (whether the government allowed it or not) was to turn them over to the strictest disciplinarians he could find. Their own officers. It had now reached the point that, outside of camp security and military bureaucracy, the camp was run by that smug bastard von Hofmann. Sure, he talked tough, played the all-knowing Aryan superman before Marls, and sure, he strutted and thundered like a tyrant before his men, but 99 percent of the time, his attitudes belied his actions and von Hofmann ended up kissing Marls's fat ass before doing precisely what the commandant ordered. Yep, Marls had von Hofmann's number: vain, stupid, and pliable. A protocol officer who farts like the rest of us, for Chrissakes.

Terminally deluded, Marls believed he was one inspection away from having his transfer accepted, packing his kit, and heading the hell out of this miserable desert to the fame and valor he'd be sure to steal overseas.

AS MARLS SLEPT the sleep of a self-righteous fool, the sharpened end of a thin iron rod pierced the surface of the desert floor emerging behind a copse of four piñon pines fourteen meters beyond the camp's outer fence. Two meters below, standing near the top of a rickety wooden ladder, the Tiger withdrew the rod. Sand showered his flattened nose. He grinned at the panzer-pilot three and a half meters further below in a chamber widened out at the end of the tunnel.

"We've made it."

"Have we?" Mesmer asked, not ready to believe escape and freedom were so close.

"Take a look at your wick."

Mesmer glanced at the bacon-grease candle in his hand. Wind blowing in from the hole flickered the flame.

"Next stop, Christmas in Mexico," the Tiger said.

He disengaged a pick from where he'd jammed it into the tunnel wall. He told Mesmer to hurry back for von Hofmann and the others while he widened the hole.

Mesmer left, taking the candle with him, and for a time, the Tiger was in darkness. The Tiger closed his eyes against the dribble of soil and sand and drove the pick into the earth above him, expanding the escape hole until he'd cleared enough of a gap to fit his head and shoulders through.

The Tiger wiped his eyes, pinched dirt from his nostrils. He let his gaze wander south and contemplated the night from the other side of the barbed wire. The wind cried across the desert, rippling the surrounding dunes in a wash of sand the color of molten lead. It rolled down a ragged slope scattered with massive rocks that would be boulders to giants. The Tiger turned. Warm breath measured out in vaporous trails. He peered through the arthritic, vibrating branches of the four piñons back to the camp. Fourteen meters away, the barbed wire of the outer and inner perimeter fences glowed dully in the brightness of a waning moon. The wind drove dust devils through it, murky and ghostlike, obscuring the camp in an aura of unreality, until both wire and sand sparkled in the light of the guard tower searchlights rhythmically scanning the dark shadows of Camp Santa Rosa for trouble.

"Stupid Amis," the Tiger muttered and ducked beneath the lip of the tunnel and out of the cold wind. He lifted his face, squinting against trickles of sand. He looked to the stars and remembered Mexico.

After winning Olympic gold, the Fatherland sponsored his professional career, and he found himself boxing around the globe. On the train from Mexico City, he'd had his first woman. A dusky señorita with odd egg-shaped nipples. He'd rolled off her sweat-glistening, brown body and gazed through the open window at the Milky Way. The rush of the clattering train had given him the brief sensation of falling upward into the stars. With a throaty laugh, the Mexican whore coaxed him back to strength and he'd entered her again.

The Tiger waited for von Hofmann and the others, excited by the prospect of seeing Mexico a second time. He'd make sure there'd be time for a woman before they headed home.

He looked proudly at the Afrikakorps cuff title on his sleeve and smiled.

Mexico.

INSIDE THE PRISONERS' CHAPEL, von Hofmann folded Agna's letter; all he had with him of his wife. He'd been made to beg for it by his British captors, groveling, building on the illusion he was a Berlin protocol officer, weak and frightened. Later, after processing in America, when he received his next correspondence from Berlin, his rage almost caused him to destroy this letter and, in the end, he'd kept this one and tore the later, final letter, to pieces. This letter was the one that willed him to fight.

Jürgen, my beloved,

Our little Martin cannot decide which he prefers more to play with: the ball painted as the world, or the glider airplane you made from the balsa kit before you left. You would be proud of him; he knows the airplane is delicate and he takes great care not to damage its tissue-paper wings. Martin cannot decide, so chooses to play with both. He circles the airplane around the bouncy globe and says, "My airplane is bringing Papa home."

I understand things are difficult, but I am much happier you are a prisoner rather than dead.

I am writing to ask for your permission to travel. I do not want to remain in Berlin with Martin any longer. This has nothing to do with the bombing and rationing, as the British aim poorly and our status allows certain comfort.

It becomes a question of the home in Kitzbühel. The home given from my parents to you at our marriage. You must agree that Martin, at four years of age, should be more afraid of nanny goats than all the marching and constant military

[Here the rest of the paragraph was censored].

I know you find the chalet drafty, and moldy, and out of the 'limelight,' but I have no light whatever-so-much without you by my side with me on your arm. Please let us go home. We cannot take [two sentences censored] *and in this, I am not questioning your authority or working against your ambitions. Our son deserves a boy's childhood, and that childhood can be his in Kitzbühel.*

We love you. We love the Führer, and the Reich. We simply want to be home in Austria while you are standing brave and noble, forced away from the two people who love you most.

Von Hofmann relieved Gauss at his lookout spot at the door. He peered through a spyhole into the windswept night and watched the searchlights pan the prisoner compounds, glad to see the slight figure of Schütze Veit zigzagging through wind and shadow.

None of the others were aware of the private, and except for Zundorf, had the slightest inclination of Operation Steppenfeuer.

For their money, they were betting on a run for the border. A mad dash to freedom. The sudden inclusion of Veit into their midst would trip their suspicions and cause no small amount of tension. As it should be. The last thing von Hofmann wanted was his team punch-drunk with the excitement of escape, celebrating that they'd made it and were somehow free from duty. The moment they ascended beyond the fence, von Hofmann wanted them sober, alert, dangerous. He needed hard, obedient soldiers, and his plan for Veit would accomplish this.

Von Hofmann tested the prick of sharpened metal inside the pocket of his black leather overcoat. He refused to see his plan as anything more than a necessary command decision.

"Standartenführer, we've made it!"

Von Hofmann heard Mesmer's enthusiastic whisper behind him at the same time Helmut Veit dashed from the corner of the PX and up the chapel steps. Von Hofmann wrenched open the door and jerked the private inside.

"So it is finished, Standartenführer?"

"Of course. Now, the key to the Bible."

Veit hesitated. He shifted his gaze to the men of von Hofmann's team. Their expressions ran the gambit from the surprised curiosity of Mesmer's face protruding above the rim of the hole to Schmidt's hostile disdain as he glared at the private from his position at his back-wall lookout post.

Envy played across Veit's features. He thrust a hand inside his tunic. To von Hofmann's surprise, all he pulled out were his reading glasses. "Turn to Daniel, chapter two, verse twenty-seven."

Von Hofmann located book, chapter, and verse: *Daniel answered in the presence of the king, and said, "The secret which the king has demanded, the wise men, the astrologers, the magicians, and the soothsayers cannot declare to the king."*

"What is this shit?"

"The glasses, Standartenführer." Veit bent them so that one lens positioned behind the other. "The period is a microdot. Look."

Von Hofmann took the glasses and held them over the open book. The two lenses had not been ground for reading and one on top of the other became, in essence, a microscope. The period became a document.

"Good luck, Standartenführer." Veit saluted. "Heil Hitler."

He was opening the door, but von Hofmann instructed him to wait.

The top portion of the micro-photographed document was revealed as a map, while below were two series of numbers—von Hofmann's encoded orders. The orders were brief, and not at all what von Hofmann expected. Von Hofmann fought to control the tremor of frustration running through him. He abruptly pocketed the Bible and the glasses as the rest of his team watched with growing concern.

"Is something wrong, Standartenführer?" said Zundorf.

"All is well." His voice was tight, strained.

"If that is all, Standartenführer . . .?" Veit murmured.

"You've been ordered to accompany us."

Veit knit his brow. "You are quite sure?"

Violence flared in von Hofmann's steely eyes. He would have acted immediately had not the bullish Schmidt started over. "Look, who is this? What's this all about? The tunnel's ready. Let's get out of—"

Zundorf intercepted him, grabbing his collar. "This is none of your concern, Feldwebel. Get back to your position until further ordered."

Zundorf twisted his grip on Schmidt, shoving him back toward the back wall with more brutality than necessary. The sergeant's face flushed red. Fists clenching, he prepared to throw himself on Zundorf when von Hofmann moved between them.

"Enough!" Von Hofmann's eyes bore into Schmidt, warning that a challenge to Zundorf was a challenge to him.

Schmidt straightened up. He backed off.

Calm returned to von Hofmann's voice. "Feldwebel Schmidt, take point. Lead the others to the end of the tunnel." He turned to Zundorf. "Herr Hauptmann, you'll follow behind Gauss and Mesmer. Veit and I will be right behind you."

"*Zu befehl*, Standartenführer," Zundorf said and moved to the altar.

Following Schmidt, the men descended one after another until von Hofmann and Veit were alone in the chapel.

"I do not care to have my authority questioned, Herr Schütze."

"I apologize, sir. Your order came as a shock. I cannot imagine Berlin would want me to join you."

"You had no idea of my orders?"

Veit stiffened, taking offense. "Of course not, Standartenführer. The Bible passage only came last week—'My honor is my—'"

Von Hofmann waved him silent. "Yes, yes, 'your loyalty,'" von Hofmann completed the SS oath for him. "I understand."

He led Veit to the tunnel entrance. "Although my orders were not specific regarding my mission, Herr Reichsführer Himmler made it clear what I am to do with you."

"The Reichsführer mentioned me specifically?"

Von Hofmann forced pride into his face. "From here we travel to meet a civilian agent at a prearranged rendezvous. Afterward, you are to go with him and he will arrange your escape back to Germany. It seems while we are, shall I say, expendable after our mission is complete, you are not." Von Hofmann gestured into the tunnel. "I'll be right behind you."

Veit entered the dark closeness of the tunnel.

Von Hofmann pulled the wooden altar over the mouth of the tunnel. What he'd told Veit had been partially true. His orders had been vague with regard to his mission. The first string of numbers had been a basic numeric substitution code that instructed von Hofmann to keep the Bible for later use as a code key. The second string of numbers was the date and time for a rendezvous, compass bearings, and a two-digit number corresponding to a preset sign and countersign von Hofmann had memorized in training. All to bring him face to face with an American spy recruited by the SD years before the war. It made von Hofmann's temples throb with humiliation.

Whatever the individual task you are asked to perform, know, if it succeeds, it will be no less than a deathblow to our enemies.

The idea of Himmler entrusting a mission of this magnitude to some treasonous American stooge was dangerous. Von Hofmann couldn't imagine a more unreliable cog in the Nazi espionage machine. Von Hofmann puzzled Himmler's rationale as he crawled toward his unknown future. By the time he joined the rest of his team, tentatively awaiting orders at the end of the tunnel, von Hofmann understood. The magnitude of his assignment dictated the roundabout arrangements. To smuggle the exact details of his assignment into the prison camp would have been too much for Berlin to risk. Just as Veit had been ordered to retain the secret of the Bible to protect von Hofmann were the tunnel discovered, the specifics of his mission—be it sabotage, assassination, or any of the other activities he'd trained in— Berlin would only deliver at a time and place that offered the assurance von Hofmann was capable of carrying them out. And the use of an American? Its necessity seemed twofold. First, as an American, the man would have to-the-minute intelligence of von Hofmann's area of operations—something Berlin could never provide. Second, if the American spy were to be compromised, the most the United States would get from him would be his radio and, if this spy was stupid, von Hofmann's encoded orders for the target—worthless without the Bible in von Hofmann's pocket. These lengths of security were not for von Hofmann, but for the mission. Operation Steppenfeuer would not be exposed until its success was guaranteed. Von Hofmann's ego swelled for that prospect and its attendant glory would be his and his alone.

"All clear?" he said to the Tiger.

"*Jawohl*, Standartenführer. It is a beautiful night for an escape."

"Then, men, you will follow me."

Von Hofmann scanned their faces. Determination burned in their eyes. "Once out of the tunnel, immediately head south into the boulders. I'll wait for you there."

Von Hofmann moved to the front of the group. He climbed the ladder and entered the night. He squatted in the swirling sand beside the escape hole and shielded his eyes. He studied the camp for any change in the pattern of searchlights, the appearance of any additional guards, vehicles, foot patrols, dogs . . . All was well. Von Hofmann pivoted south toward freedom and made a low dash into the enveloping arms of the windstorm.

16

THE MEN GATHERED around von Hofmann in the shelter of two sandstone domes as the Standartenführer located true north with the miniature compass he'd made from the broken edge of a magnetized razor blade. He calculated their escape route accordingly. No one spoke, but the wind whining over the boulders was an eloquent expression of the team's anxious desire to get away from Camp Santa Rosa as fast as possible.

Standing apart from the officers, no one experienced this anxiety more than Schütze Helmut Veit. The events of the last half hour had taken him by surprise. Try as he might to beat it back, a monstrous foreboding threatened to overwhelm him and cause him to run howling into the desert storm. Foolish, of course. Veit had just become an escaped prisoner of war. His heightened emotional state was natural to his newfound status. He cast a furtive glance at the others. He convinced himself he saw in their faces the same emotions they saw in his.

Good Nazis. Every one of them dedicated to the Führer.

And von Hofmann? Veit's feelings for that stalwart genius left him discomfited. Von Hofmann was Aryan perfection. With effort, the private subdued the primal warnings oozing from the mud of his subconscious and shuffled forward like a lamb following the flock as von Hofmann led them into the flying face of the storm.

FOR OVER AN HOUR, they proceeded south at a brutal pace, each man's visibility reduced to the back of the man in front of him. Von Hofmann picked his way through a labyrinth of cholla and rock and soap-tree yucca, keeping a plumb line south until the path ran out and von Hofmann teetered on the dark, knife-cut edge of a mesa. Grit assaulted him like ocean waves sweeping from the valley below. A lesser man would have been compelled to turn back, finding the cliff impassable, but von Hofmann had prepared for this in training and in recruiting Zundorf. He instructed Zundorf over the rim of stone. The young alpinist nimbly charted a path down the rock face marking handholds and footholds with flour from a sack on his belt. Von Hofmann followed, waiting at the bottom as Zundorf made five more trips guiding the other men, struggling against wind and darkness, down the mesa's jagged face with a tireless agility that would make a mountain goat blush.

Thirty minutes later, they stood in the stony shelter of a natural amphitheater. Ringed by large smooth rocks, its floor was pitted and grooved. Wheatgrass grew from these cracks, while rainwater stood collected into clear pools in the holes and hollows.

"We rest. Five minutes. It would be wise to quench our thirst and fill canteens before moving on."

The men eagerly went to the water. Von Hofmann watched them as he dusted off his uniform. He focused on the necessity of what he was about to do, not considering the young man's right to his own life or its meaning beyond his use in taking it. A line from Nietzsche sprang to mind. *"I love all those who are as heavy drops, falling one by one out of the dark cloud that hangs over men . . ."*

The men drank.

Von Hofmann edged toward Veit.

The private had found his own natural basin of drinking water and, crouching before it, scooped a palm-full of cool liquid into his mouth. He gargled, swished it around. Close behind him, von Hofmann slapped the dust from his trousers.

Moved closer.

"*. . . They herald the advent of lightning, and, as heralds, they must perish.*"

Veit spit across the ground. He drew more water, drinking this time, tilting back his head to relish its sweet taste in his dusty throat.

There was a rustling of cloth, a faint scratch of metal. In the split second it took Veit to realize it, the Standartenführer whipped a barbed-wire garrote around Veit's throat. Veit grabbed for it, lunging forward, splashing into the drinking water, clouding its surface as his boots stirred sand. He was no match for von Hofmann, whose only movement against the private's struggle was an abrupt twisting of his wrists.

The razor-sharp wire tightened, dotting Veit's throat with red as the barbs punctured flesh. Von Hofmann sawed for his jugular.

"*Behold, I am a herald of the lightning and a heavy drop from the cloud, but this lighting is called overman.*"

Veit's body jerked in strangulation, and Von Hofmann swung him around to face the others so they could watch him die.

"Private Veit won't be coming with us."

Von Hofmann noted the collected horror on the faces of his men, who formed a semicircle before him in the pale cast of moonlight. With a final twist, he severed Veit's jugular. Blood squirted, darkening the pool around his and Veit's boots. With a final quiver, Veit slumped in the Standartenführer's arms.

Holding the corpse before his men, von Hofmann spoke. "At the camp, this 'trusted' countryman volunteered to the enemy detailed information on our units in the field and our industries back home. Hiding among the one hundred and twenty thousand German prisoners spread throughout this country, perhaps he believed he was beyond the Führer's grip . . ." Von Hofmann paused, loosening the tension in the wire. His reward was a spray of blood. "He was mistaken."

Von Hofmann hurled the body into the dirt at his team's feet. Gauss recoiled as Veit's arm flopped across the toe of his left boot. The others remained motionless in shocked revulsion, which is what von Hofmann wanted.

"From here we move south as quickly as possible." Von Hofmann assumed the formal tone of battlefield command. "The next five hours before dawn and with it the discovery of our escape will decide our fate. Have no illusions about the skill and sheer manpower the military police and the Federal Bureau of Investigation will draw upon once the manhunt commences. If we do not succeed in putting as much distance as possible between ourselves and our pursuers this night, we will not succeed at all."

Von Hofmann let his words sink in. Schmidt used the opportunity to step forward and extend a pair of binoculars he'd carried inside his tunic.

"I stole these this morning. The Standartenführer will find them useful?"

Von Hofmann accepted the high-powered field glasses. "Very good, Schmidt."

"Anything to help the Standartenführer's escape."

"If we were escaping," von Hofmann said, finding the perfect segue into the words he'd prepared for this moment. "Like you, the Americans will have every reason to assume we are heading for the Mexican border. But know this: I have chosen you for something far greater. We are once again combatants in this war, ground forces of the Third Reich, on a mission to inflict nothing less than a mortal blow against our American enemies."

Von Hofmann watched the effect of his words on the men. As he spoke, they instinctively gathered themselves into rigid attention. The violence of his treatment of Veit, coupled with the grand inspiration of his words, had triggered the proper reflex. These men were soldiers once again.

Sober. Alert. Dangerous.

Von Hofmann gave a final glance at the corpse at his feet. "As for our traitorous friend? In death he will aid our enemies yet again"—he fished a small piece of notebook paper from his breast pocket—"and in so doing redeem his life to our cause."

He crouched and wedged the paper into the hollow space behind the rectangular clasp of Veit's belt buckle. Von Hofmann quickly went through his pockets, making sure they were empty. Aside from a handkerchief, he found nothing. He left the pockets untucked. Von Hofmann stood. He cared nothing for the dead boy soldier but that he had done what had been required. He could never have included Veit with the team as his orders *had* recommended. An outsider, weak and without combat experience, Veit would have put their lives in constant jeopardy. On the other hand, he knew too much about the operation for von Hofmann to risk leaving him behind. From the beginning, Veit's death had been inevitable and all von Hofmann could do now was take comfort in the assurance that in a war in which there are few good ways to die, he had given Veit the chance to serve his fellow soldiers, Himmler, and the Führer with the honor the boy so craved. It was more than most could ask for and receive. Von Hofmann wiped his hands before leading his men along the columnar base of the mesa.

Long after the Standartenführer and his men had disappeared into an arroyo, dawn came like a trickle of blood on the edge of the world. A cold wind crept into the amphitheater. It found the ends of the barbed-wire garrote embedded in SS-Schütze Helmut Veit's throat and rhythmically tapped them against the ground like the tick of death's watch.

Operation Steppenfeuer had commenced.

17

TUESDAY, DECEMBER 21, 1943

SPECIAL AGENT IN CHARGE TOM CARTWRIGHT of the Federal Bureau of Investigation, Santa Fe, lit his sixth Lucky Strike of the morning. He stood at his second-story office window inside the new wing of the Federal Building on Lincoln Avenue, staring between the slats of the venetian blinds at the tan volcanic stone towers of Santa Fe's St. Francis Cathedral without seeing them at all. His mind had wandered back to a woman he'd met on the train between Washington, DC and New York City back in '18. She, a legal secretary, headed to Manhattan to find a job. He headed up from Bureau training, looking for a way to spend the long weekend before graduation. Neither of them had been to New York before. Their expectations were high. Perhaps, had they ventured it alone, the weight of the city's massive indifference might have crushed them, yet by joining forces, they managed to find for themselves four days of adventure and magic that transformed their nights into a state of bliss. Cartwright had long ago earmarked the weekend as one of the most memorable of his life. After graduation, he'd naïvely contemplated tracking her down through the job she'd taken, sweep her off her feet and marry her, but that was twenty-five years ago, and today, Cartwright was damned if he could remember the girl's face let alone recall her name.

If he'd forgotten that—the essence of a memory he'd once treasured—he wondered how many events of lesser importance from his life had left his mind entirely. Memories were a man's frame of reference; he drew from them; they defined who he was. So if you lost them, who were you?

At 4:23 that morning, Cartwright had been awake and drinking coffee when he'd turned forty-seven. It was 8:15 now, and in less than four hours, he might as well have continued aging all the way to sixty. What the hell? Maybe memories were like the dead. Sometimes they twitched, but they never came back to life. Better to bury them and move on.

Special Agent Burley walked into Cartwright's office with a flimsy yellow sheet from the teletype. Cartwright turned away from his view of the church. He was a big man, muscular and well-proportioned, with the rough comportment and hard-edged countenance of man poured from iron instead of flesh and bone and blood like the rest of the population. He was tough and dangerous, grown more so over the years as the good hands dealt him became fewer and farther apart. Cartwright acknowledged his subordinate with an inquisitive lift of his eyebrows. His career was not unlike the girl in New York. In the eyes of the Bureau, his quarter century of hard, honest service amounted to little more than a nameless, faceless weekend. Nothing wrong with that, but nothing to hang your hat on.

"Tell me we got ourselves the second coming of Billy the Kid," he said.

Special Agent Burley gave a grunt, less a laugh, in recognition of Cartwright's joke. "Nothing that solid. But it could pan out."

He handed the sheet to Cartwright. "It's from the War Department by way of Mr. Hoover's office. Been a prisoner escape out at Santa Rosa."

Cartwright didn't bother to look. With more than a hundred and twenty thousand Axis prisoners spread out in camps across the nation, escapes and escape attempts had, in the last year, become little more than a nuisance. As recently as November, the escape of two German POWs from Humboldt Camp, Arizona, turned out to be as serious as the prisoners walking through the front gates when a guard wasn't looking and hitching a ride into town because they wanted steak dinners. Before agents dispatched from Phoenix were able to apprehend them, the two boys had eaten their steaks, washed dishes to pay for them, snuck into an Edward G. Robinson movie about North Atlantic convoys, then homesick, walked back to camp and pounded on the gates until let back inside.

Cartwright flipped the sheet onto his desk. "Probably some horny Kraut kid chasing a dirt-scratcher's daughter and missed the bus back from his work program."

"Don't think so. Says there's a tunnel. And it's not a single runner. Six officers and two enlisted men are missing."

Cartwright's disappointment ebbed. Eight men and a tunnel could have promise. Some, anyhow. Cartwright ashed his cigarette. He studied the telex. Aside from what Burley had told him, there was no other information.

"Who do you want to put on this, sir?" Burley asked.

For the first time that morning, Cartwright grinned. "Hell, Burley, it's my birthday today. Wouldn't seem right if I didn't handle it personally."

Cartwright found his jacket, hat, and his overcoat. He half suspected the military police would have their prisoners back before he got to the camp, but once a POW escaped, he fell under Bureau jurisdiction. That meant if it happened in New Mexico, Cartwright carried ultimate responsibility.

"Pass this on to Arizona, Texas, Oklahoma, and Colorado to be safe." Cartwright returned the flimsy. "And have Special Agent Torres put in a request to the War Department for all prisoner records and intelligence they have on each one of these eight characters."

"Sure, chief. Anything else?"

"Yeah. Get your things. You're coming along. We're going to see what the hell goes on in that camp."

Cartwright followed Burley out of his office, only to pull up short. He turned, stepped back inside, and opened his desk. He snatched his Colt Detective Special .38 revolver and two extra packs of Lucky Strikes. After all, there was a slim chance this escape could amount to something real, and Cartwright always went prepared.

THEY TOOK ROUTE 285 south from Santa Fe. Cartwright drove, his left hand steady at twelve o'clock on the wheel while his right, holding his cigarette, moved restlessly between three, his mouth, and six o'clock with a hypnotic regularity Burley had grown accustomed to in the three years he'd spent in the passenger seat. The pair rarely spoke when driving. This morning was no different.

The wind from the night before had picked up again. The highway undulated through a course of brown and gray hills dotted with juniper and piñon, sheep and cattle poking out between them. Cartwright noticed small patches of dark-bellied clouds gathering along the snow-speckled reaches of the Sangre de Cristo, Sandia, and the Jemez Mountains surrounding the country like scouts charting a raid.

Cartwright finished off one cigarette and used its butt to burn his way into the next. He exhaled the fresh smoke through his nose. At this rate, he'd smoke three packs easy today. No matter, Cartwright liked to smoke. He'd picked up the habit as a kid in the Army—13th Cavalry—but in those days, he'd rolled his own. If someone handed him the makings, would he still remember how? Nah. Just another particular of his life forgotten, like the woman from the train. What the hell? It didn't matter whether he could roll his own anymore or not. Lucky Strikes were better than the shit they took with them after Pancho Villa.

Of late, Tom Cartwright missed the Army. Well, that wasn't exactly true. None of the five thousand troopers who'd followed "Black Jack" Pershing into the hell of Mexico in March '16 ever missed it, but recently he'd taken to imagining where he'd be if he'd stayed in. Armor Branch, most likely. Along with the rest of the horse soldiers, he'd have traded in his saddle for a tank. If Cartwright had survived th First World War and come out with his spirit intact, he'd be guiding the boys fighting their way up Italy's tough old gut right now, maybe having already found his moment of truth again, a truth so elusive to him in law enforcement.

He'd had it once. The kind of glory a man can only have when taking life's supreme test, choosing to face death alone over something no more tangible than a belief in right over wrong. He'd ridden into Mexico, ready with the rest of them to make the bandit Pancho Villa pay for violating the sovereignty of the United States of America in his murderous raids into New Mexico. But after forty days of savage heat, nights of bitter cold, his company had missed the only two engagements of the Punitive Expedition. Guerrero and the town of Parral. Tom Cartwright was fed up with General Pershing, Pancho Villa, the state of Chihuahua, and every goddamn greaser in it. A point he made clear to his sergeant, who, like sergeants throughout the ages, responded by giving him the shit detail.

The daughters of a widowed American schoolteacher had been abducted after a raid. Girls, ten and twelve years old, thrown across the saddles of two Villistas to be shared with a third somewhere off in the desert. They'd assigned Tom Cartwright an Apache guide named Galgo.

His sergeant had said, "Give it two days. If you don't find them by then, you'll rejoin the company here." He indicated a place on his map.

Cartwright, nineteen at the time, had been young, but not too young to know what was going to happen to those girls would happen a lot sooner than two days—sand filling their eyes and mouths as they silently screamed their torture from beneath a shallow grave. To Cartwright's reckoning, the detail would be a soul-sucking waste of time.

Every step of the way through the cold and dark, without food or the prospect of bedding down, Cartwright complained and cursed the Apache, who seemed to lead him aimlessly through the desert.

"Your days with the Thirteenth Cavalry are over, old-timer."

Cartwright watched Galgo swaying on his pony, focused only on himself. The girls didn't become a reality to Cartwright until on the morning of the second day. They found the remains of the Villistas' camp. Galgo let him go in alone.

Broken bottles.

Marijuana cigarette roaches.

Some cut ropes, ends tied to a tree.

Strands of blonde hair caught in bark. A collar torn from a nightgown. An impression on the dirt, left to tell of a body writhing on its back.

Blood-thickened sand.

Cartwright wept by the pissed-out fire and the Apache wordlessly watched. The Apache said, "If we are to find the two golden-hairs, we must ride as one, read sign together."

"Yeah, well, sorry. I don't know what you're talking, you crazy old bat."

The Apache closed a wizened hand tightly over Cartwright's fist. "You cannot look with your mouth. If you close it, your eyes will open wider, and I will teach you how to see."

And he had, changing the course of Tom Cartwright's life, transforming him from wet-nosed soldier, to tracker, stalker, and ultimately a symbol of law and justice that belonged to something greater than himself.

18

Halfway from Santa Fe to Santa Rosa, Cartwright angled his black government Packard into a dirt lot off Route 285. The filling station, adobe brick store, and café that comprised Clines Corners and marked the junction with Route 66 welcomed them with all the enthusiasm of a cluster of rotting teeth in a dead mule's grin. Cartwright opened the door and climbed out as the heavy dust from their arrival swirled into the dirty wind.

"You're driving from here, Burley. Get some gas."

Cartwright headed away from the car. A teenager in a stained straw cowboy hat ambled out of the filling station, gaping at Cartwright on his way to the pumps. The FBI agent stalked toward the other two buildings. A tumbleweed bounded between the store and the café, caroming off the porch to attach itself to the cuff of Cartwright's trousers like an angry dog as he edged around the dead, gray wood of the hitching post. Cartwright shook his leg, sending the tumbleweed across the dirt lot, where it joined five more of its kind bouncing across the highway in a pack. Off in the southern distance, a long, thin cloud trailed like a pennant from the summit of the Cerro Pedernal. Over seven thousand feet above sea level, the flint peak was an outstanding landmark in an otherwise flat expanse of country. Prospectors frequently camped at its base, and its crown was riddled with pits and excavations where, for as long as Cartwright could remember, they'd hunted for a buried cache of Apache gold. They wouldn't be there digging today. Not the smart ones, anyway. The end of the cloud clinging to the peak meant only one thing: a drenching rain and the pounding of lightning.

A storm was coming, Cartwright thought, that was for sure, but it was taking its time getting here, which meant when it hit, it would hit hard. Out here, the land teamed up with this kind of weather to play at killing men. Cartwright shook his head, not envying those foreign prisoners getting caught unprepared in that mess.

He entered the store and looked around. A withered woman, her tan arms and face covered with a fine hair like a tarantula's, looked up from behind a chipped glass counter that displayed Pueblo turquoise, set in silver, lying upon wads of cotton used for stuffing quilts, all of it—including the woman, as far as Cartwright could tell—coated gray with dust.

"Interest you in something, mister?"

"Telephone, if you don't mind." Cartwright placed a nickel on the counter as an incentive.

The woman smiled, showing the most perfect set of teeth Cartwright had ever seen. She gestured to the phone mounted on the wall beside a Coca-Cola icebox. "Goes in and out when the wind gets like this. Can't promise you nothing."

Cartwright wondered whether her teeth were real. "Happy to take my chances."

He walked to the phone, and the nickel disappeared as if it had never existed. He lifted the receiver, turned the crank, and was rewarded with a connection. He asked, and the operator put him in touch with Camp Santa Rosa.

His conversation with Major Hastings pretty much proved Cartwright's theory that the Army put its most useless officers in charge of its prisoners of war.

No, they'd not caught any of the prisoners. No, they didn't have a trail. No, they hadn't contacted the railroad. (The Southern Pacific ran a straight shot south out of Santa Rosa down to

El Paso and Mexico beyond). The Army assumed the FBI would handle all that. Cartwright gave an exasperated snort and asked the intelligence officer what the Army had handled.

"I've assembled everything we have on the eight escaped prisoners. It's waiting for you here at my office. Now, regarding the railroads, I could certainly—"

"The Bureau will handle it, Major Hastings."

"Okay. Just fine," Hastings said, tension straining his voice. "Is there anything else I can do for you right now? Answer any questions?"

Cartwright lit a cigarette. He inhaled before he answered. "Tell me, Major, the escaped officers. Any stand out to you as ringleader?"

"Absolutely. Standartenführer Jürgen von Hofmann. Senior prisoner here at camp. Uh, was."

At camp? Was he playing Boy Scouts? "'Standartenführer,' what the hell's one of those?" Cartwright squinted through a coil of rising smoke.

"It's colonel. In the SS."

Cartwright didn't respond. His earlier sensation of being sixty squeezed from his body by a strange mixture of disbelief, dread, and a hopeful clarity of purpose. He slowly said, "Could that be possible, Major? The Bureau is under the impression all SS prisoners are held in the maximum-security facility at Alva over in Oklahoma. The Army playing games behind Mr. Hoover's back?"

"Um, no games. No, sir. Our camp population is six percent SS, most others have nine or ten. You're right, of course, Alva is over ninety-five percent SS, but just 'cause they're the worst trouble-makers. That's actually what Alva's camp's for: high-risk prisoners, the violent, die-hard Nazis, men prone to violence, escape . . ."

"And this von Hofmann?"

"He wasn't a combat soldier. War Department considered him low risk."

Cartwright cut in with a blistering laugh. "Sounds like y'all are a bunch of idiots out there. Can't wait to make your acquaintance, Major."

Cartwright hung up.

He had the operator connect him to his office. Special Agent Torres, whom Burley had put on the desk for this assignment, took the call. Cartwright's orders were brief and to the point.

"Get in touch with Southern Pacific. I want a sweep of every train and rail yard between Santa Rosa and El Paso. Contact the El Paso office. Put 'em on special alert. These prisoners might already be in town looking for a way into Juárez. And—most important here, Torres—get everything we have, what the War Department has, and even what Colonel Donovan's Office of Strategic Service has on an SS-Standartenführer Jürgen von Hofmann. You got that? SS-Standartenführer Jürgen von Hofmann." Cartwright took a long drag from his cigarette. "I want it in two hours when I call back from Santa Rosa."

"Yes, sir."

Cartwright sizzled out his cigarette on the side of an ice cube in the soda cooler. He turned, caught the eye of the woman behind the counter. From the way her mouth hung like a broken barn door, Cartwright understood she'd listened to every word and that her perfect teeth were the real McCoy. He crossed to her and withdrew his black leather ID case. He snapped it open three inches from her nose.

"Repeat anything you've heard—even guess you've heard—and you'll be committing a federal offense. Do that and I'll come back here and bury you myself."

He spoke in a tone calibrated to frighten. A rich, smooth voice that, like motor oil in a racing engine, glided effortlessly over and around words of heat and violence. Tom Cartwright had discovered the voice in a cantina in a fly speck of a town in the Sierra Madres called Namiquipa. It was always effective.

Burley was waiting for him behind the wheel, engine running, as Cartwright slid into the Packard beside him. He read the worry line dropped between his superior's eyebrows.

"Problems?"

Cartwright gave him a sidelong glance and then jerked his chin at the road as an order to drive. Burley put the Packard into gear and eased onto Route 66, heading east.

"Problems, you bet. But only in the finest sense of the word," Cartwright said. He slipped a fresh smoke from a crumpled pack and into his mouth. "This escape might shape into something interesting, Burley. Might be some work in it for us after all."

Cartwright struck his lighter. Lit up. Burley gave him a curious frown. Cartwright filled him in on his conversation with Major Hastings, then he gazed across the prairie stretching south until it met the sky. They made better time now than they had on the first leg of the trip. The wind was at their back and the highway descended over two thousand feet in the fifty-seven miles that lay between Clines Corners and Santa Rosa. They shot past some old corrals. Cartwright caught a fleeting glimpse of a tawny mustang running the fence, tail and mane flying off the horse like sparks dancing in the wind.

The beast could smell the coming storm. It ran because it was scared.

19

"WHAT DID YOU FIND on this von Hofmann?"

"Three things, sir." Torres's voice crackled over the telephone wires as Cartwright sat behind Marls's desk using the commandant's telephone. He was alone in the messy office.

"First two are interesting because they contradict each other. The War Department is sending overnight copies of their interrogations with Standartenführer von Hofmann, but I had them read me in."

"Summarize."

"Standartenführer Jürgen von Hofmann. Captured by British forces in North Africa on March seventh, 1941. His interrogation corroborates his papers in that he was a protocol officer on a field hospital inspection tour. He was put in Camp Santa Rosa because he was considered a low-risk prisoner."

"Yeah, yeah, Torres, I know all that. That doesn't contradict anything."

Cartwright spoke more sharply than he intended, but he'd already given a cursory look through the eight prisoner files Major Hastings had prepared. Eight model prisoners, nothing particularly outstanding about any of them. He was impatient to look at the tunnel and meet the camp commandant Colonel Marls of whom his negative opinion continued to grow.

"The contradiction comes from Washington, sir. I spoke to the OSS as you asked. They were extremely uncooperative, which wasn't unexpected."

Cartwright made an encouraging sound. He was familiar with the closed-door policy of the Bureau's wartime intelligence counterpart, the Office of Strategic Services. The power struggle between J. Edgar Hoover and William 'Wild Bill' Donovan was legendary. A question of jurisdiction. Hoover had the western hemisphere and domestic intelligence, including Central and South America, while Donovan had the eastern hemisphere.

Colonel Donovan, a recipient of the Congressional Medal of Honor in the First World War, concerned himself primarily with the war in Europe where, according to rumor, his clandestine operations were brilliant. But occasionally, Donovan's work spilled across the Atlantic. Six months after Pearl Harbor, OSS agents broke into the Spanish embassy in Washington to crack a safe and photograph badly needed German cipher books. Hoover, getting wind of the operation and seeing a chance to embarrass his rival, had FBI Agents raid the embassy and sabotage the mission.

Afterward, Donovan said, "The Abwehr gets better treatment from the FBI than we do."

The Abwehr was the German military intelligence service, and Cartwright, although deft enough never to voice anything resembling a negative comment against Hoover or the Bureau, couldn't deny that Donovan was right.

"I was pretty persistent, though," Special Agent Torres continued. "Finally got someone to admit they'd heard of him. They're sending us a German newspaper photograph from von Hofmann's hometown showing him being awarded an Iron Cross back in thirty-nine. He wasn't a protocol officer then, sir. They told me his uniform is Sicherheitsdienst."

"What's that, Gestapo?"

"No, sir. To hear them say it, it's the SS Security Service. They control all Nazi Party intelligence. Their primary function is keeping tabs on all threats to the political body of the Nazi party from within and without. Von Hofmann is no mere protocol officer, sir."

"Well, frost my balls and call it a cupcake."

Cartwright loosened his necktie and his eyes moved to the door. It was ajar. Through the crack, he could see Burley questioning Major Hastings in the hallway as they waited for him to finish.

"You still there, sir?" Torres said, thrown by the silence.

"Yeah. What else you got?"

"Something from our own files. In 1932 and '33, von Hofmann lived in New York City. He was under our surveillance. Was peripherally involved with the American Nazi Party. Never broke the law, so we never picked him up. We'll have all that by morning too."

Cartwright sank back in Marls's chair. He couldn't believe what he was hearing. A colonel in the SS Security Service? Von Hofmann's capture had been a magnificent stroke of luck for the War Department, the information he must possess of staggering importance, yet the Army had somehow let him slip through their fingers. And now he was making a break for freedom.

It was then that Cartwright understood he was on the brink of the greatest case of his career, and in it, he'd rediscover his moment of truth or be damned in trying.

Cartwright commended Torres for his work and instructed him to prepare the official transfer of jurisdiction papers to present to the War Department. "We'll use their manpower, we'll have to, but they've screwed this up plenty already and I want them to know in no uncertain terms who's running this show."

"Yes, sir."

"And get back in touch with the OSS. That picture must've accompanied an article of some kind. Leastways a caption. I want it, and I want whatever else their file contains."

"That was all they said they had."

"That's bullshit, Torres. If they try to give you that same song and dance, you have permission to dangle me as a carrot. Tell them I will personally do Mr. Donovan any favor he asks if they go the distance with me on this. Got it?"

There was a long pause at the other end. "Sir, if the Seat of Government finds you just said that, you're going to end up worse than Purvis."

Worse than Purvis. Torres was right. The FBI divided itself into two parts: "The Seat of Government," Hoover's Washington bureaucracy filled with the deskbound promotion hunters, fawning and fatuous to their dictator Hoover, and "The Field," filled with men like Cartwright whose only ambition was to be on the front line fighting crime. Melvin Purvis, special agent in charge of Chicago, had been a "Field" man in 1933 when he solved the Hamm and Factor kidnappings. He tracked, caught and gunned down John Dillinger in '34. He did the same for Pretty Boy Floyd a few months after that. But Purvis made a mistake. By taking credit for his successes rather than rendering them as tribute to J. Edgar Hoover, he offended the director's tremendous ego.

Hoover took immediate action to belittle the hero. He sent Purvis on long, pointless inspection tours of the Bureau's most remote offices—Santa Fe being one of them. Disparaging and false stories appeared in newspapers attributing Purvis with outlandish and embarrassing activities. Every field agent in the Bureau, including Tom Cartwright, understood these stories to be fabrications planted by Hoover. No one said a word, and Melvin Purvis resigned.

Purvis, Cartwright had heard rumors, now worked for Donovan and the OSS.

Cartwright shrugged the weight of Torres's warning from his shoulders. He'd take his chances with Hoover. He needed what Donovan had.

"If I were you, Special Agent Torres, I'd try to make sure the Seat of Government doesn't find out."

"Yes, sir. Will that be all?"

Cartwright glanced at Burley and Major Hastings. They were silent. Waiting. Nothing else to say between them. Time to move on. Cartwright finished with Torres and joined the two men outside the office.

"Seemed like you had a lot to talk about in there. Something happen?" said Hastings. Nervous. Polite.

"Bet your sweet ass, Major," but Cartwright didn't bother to elaborate. Leading the way outside, he said, "I'll see that tunnel, then find me Colonel Marls."

THE MOOD ACROSS THE CAMP was ebullient. Prisoners everywhere, enlisted men mixing with officers, noncoms not even attempting any control. It was as if the day had been declared a holiday, which was probably what the officers had done. Cartwright carried no animosity toward these Germans clothed in denim work outfits, black "PW"s stenciled on their back. They boisterously jostled his party as a group of billy-club-wielding MPs escorted the FBI men and Major Hastings across the gravel pathways of the commons to the prisoners' chapel. Another force of MPs stood as a cordon before the chapel door. They took swings at the crowd of prisoners, who heckled and jeered them. The prisoners were quick enough to keep out of reach of their sticks.

Cartwright, Burley, and Major Hastings slipped past the soldiers and disappeared inside. Hastings showed them the tunnel entrance. Both FBI men saw it for what it was.

"This isn't sandbox play here," Cartwright said.

Burley clarified for Hastings. "The men who dug this are experts."

"Major, any of those files suggest one or more of the prisoners have engineering experience?"

"No, sir, though they could have applied skills from their civilian occupations."

Where the hell else would they have gotten the experience? Cartwright mocked to himself. He said, "How'd you find the tunnel, Major? They leave it open or what?"

"It was pretty carefully disguised by the altar." Hastings tilted the wooden construction to emphasize his point.

"They were discovered missing at roll call, just after reveille at five. A patrol of the perimeter discovered the exit hole while we were still searching the camp. We simply followed the tunnel back into here."

"And what time was the tunnel's exit discovered?"

Hastings paused. He spoke softly. "Between nine thirty and ten."

"Between? That, nine forty-five?"

"Uh, yes, I believe so."

Cartwright flashed Burley with a disbelieving glance. Burley rolled his eyes while taking notes. Hastings caught the nonverbal exchange as intended.

"Lights out are at . . .?"

"Ten p.m. but, there's no evening roll call."

"Delightful. Why?"

"It isn't mandatory because of the camp's remote location. Colonel Marls abolished it two weeks ago at . . ." Hastings's eyes darted between Cartwright and Burley like a rabbit facing coyotes.

"I didn't get that?" said Burley.

"Go on?" added Cartwright.

"The Colonel abolished evening roll call at von Hofmann's guarantee there'd be no escape attempts."

From outside, the raucous sounds of the prisoners bled through the door.

Hastings defended himself. "I was strongly against it."

"I'll bet," Cartwright said. "So you say the prisoners were discovered missing at five?"

Hastings was clearly too afraid to say any more. Cartwright appreciated that.

"The Bureau was informed at—what time would you say that was, Burley?"

"Eight fifteen, chief."

"Eight fifteen. Means Mr. Hoover's office got it from the War Department at about eight, and the War Department, I understand, sends this kind of thing immediately." Cartwright's eyes connected with Hastings's. "Tell me right now what went on from five till eight."

Hastings paled. "Colonel Marls said we should catch von Hofmann ourselves. Keep the trouble to a minimum. He was still out there looking when I decided to report the escape."

"I see."

To browbeat Hastings any further would be counterproductive. Cartwright lit a cigarette. He offered one to the major. Hastings no-thank-you'd it away.

"You know, Burley, the more I hear about this Marls, the more anxious I am to meet him."

"You're telling me? I'm interested in seeing the color of his uniform."

"Colonel Marls is a decent officer with a tough job."

"We all got tough jobs, Major. But instead of doing his, your decent colonel has gone and made mine a whole lot tougher."

MAJOR HASTINGS TOOK THE LEAD in his jeep while Cartwright and Burley followed in their Packard, leaving the camp for the grove of piñons and the escape hole, which was surrounded by six more MPs. Burley parked the car beside an army truck. As the FBI agents headed across the hard packed sand for the tunnel, two Army Corps of Engineers officers emerged from the hole. One set and sighted through a surveyor's level while the other worked out some calculations in a green notebook.

"To look at 'em, you'd guess they haven't figured out the thing's a tunnel yet," Cartwright said over the wind.

Burley didn't comment, and Cartwright turned to identify what had captured his subordinate's attention. Escorted by three additional shotgun-toting MPs, Lieutenant Colonel Lucien G. Marls waddled from a pile of boulders to join them.

One look at the slovenly commandant and Cartwright was sickly amused why only eight prisoners made the break.

Marls spit tobacco juice into the open hole just missing the engineers. He extended his hand to Cartwright. "Colonel Marls. Been out hunting a trail, but this damn wind ain't making things easy for any of us."

Stoney silence.

"And you are?" Marls said.

Cartwright ignored Marls's offered hand, opting instead to light another cigarette. He stared at the glowing tip of the Lucky Strike as he exhaled. When the FBI agent spoke, it was slowly, enunciating each syllable with relish. "SS-Standartenführer Jürgen von Hofmann. Sicherheitsdienst—SS Security Service—the guys even the Gestapo's afraid of."

Marls's grin dissolved to a look of befuddlement.

"He's the one that got away," Cartwright said. "Remember? Big mistake letting a prize catch slip through your fingers, Colonel."

"*Sicher-sick*-whatever-the-hell-you're-saying, I have no idea what you're talking about, Agent . . ."

"Special Agent in Charge Cartwright. Oh, and I believe you. I can imagine you don't know much about anything. Why von Hofmann was here, under less-than-minimum security instead of with the rest of Hitler's hard core at Alva, is something I assure you will come out in the wash."

Marls's jaw had been working furiously as Cartwright spoke. He spit another stream of tobacco juice into the hole. "The Army can take care of itself."

"I'm looking at how the Army takes care of itself. Not reporting the escape for three hours sounds like a cover-up. Ever hear the phrase 'aiding and abetting a fugitive'?"

Marls licked his lips and smirked. "F-B-I. Always the tough guys, always Hoover's boys versus the world, that it?"

"Watch out for Colonel Five-Squares-a-Day, Burley. Catches on quick."

Marls's face flushed crimson and his cheeks inflated with air, giving him the appearance of an angry tomato. "Look here," he spluttered, "This is my fucking command and I don't have to take orders from you or—"

"I'm precisely who you will be taking orders from now on." Cartwright jabbed Marls's chest with his index finger. "Once von Hofmann and his men poked their head through that hole, they became fugitives of the Federal Government under jurisdiction of the Justice Department, which means the FBI, Colonel Marls, which means me, which means your authority stops at that fence. Step beyond it with some notion of playing posse behind my back and you'll be breaking federal law. You know what that'll mean, fatboy?" Cartwright lowered his tone. "After you're court-martialed, I get to throw you in the pen."

Having chewed his tobacco to a froth, Marls needed to spit before he gagged. He gave it his best shot. His best would never be good enough. A long glob of tobacco juice dribbled down his chins and across his uniform blouse.

"Oh. One more thing . . ."

Marls sneered at Cartwright with undisguised hatred.

Cartwright flicked the butt of his cigarette into the dirt. "Fill in the fucking hole."

20

THE AGENTS GOT BACK INTO the Packard and out of the wind. "You carved that moron a new asshole. Wise to alienate the Army?" Burley said.

"I only alienated that son of a bitch. Had to. He's not as stupid as he seems." Cartwright responded.

"What are you talking about? One look at his sty of an office tells me all I need to know about the sad sack."

"Absolutely, Burley. So my guess is a slob like that'd only make and hold lieutenant colonel if he's as shrewd as the pig he resembles."

Burley frowned. He would buy it, although he came from the city and had never considered "pig" and "shrewd" as two words you'd pen together. Cartwright was a farmer's son. Burley got the point.

"See, Marls has fucked up bad—real bad. He knows the only way he'll keep that oak leaf from blowing off his shoulder is by somehow making me look worse than him and single-handedly saving the day," Cartwright said. "Better trying to tie him up and muzzle him here than have to constantly deal with him in the field. If I'm any judge of character, this isn't the last we're going to see of Colonel Marls."

He lit a fresh cigarette and fell silent. He let his vision sweep out across the mesa. He closed his lighter, smothering the flame, and dropped it in his pocket.

"So, does that mean we're using the army or not?"

"We're using them. Can't help it. We'll need their manpower for roadblocks, ground searches, aerial recon." Cartwright flicked ash. "My guess would be if our fugitives don't split up, they'll head straight for El Paso, try to filter from there into Juárez."

Beyond the edge of the mesa, large black birds rode the thermals, spiraling in and out of towering sandstone spires.

"Have Major Hastings put together a comprehensive plan he can get going within the hour. I want you to get back in touch with HQ. Get everyone in our office into the field. Also, see if Denver can spare us a half dozen or so agents. Then touch base with Texas and Arizona. I want them fully apprised. And start greasing the machine to get me some of their men. If this goes as planned, we'll either catch 'em on the run, or sweep them into our nets within three days."

Burley made some notes in his book. Cartwright opened the door and stepped from the automobile.

"Where are you going?"

Cartwright indicated the black birds soaring in the distance. "That many buzzards—we got ourselves a corpse."

Burley furrowed his brow.

"Von Hofmann and his fellow escapees wouldn't have wasted time killing their own food so close to the camp, unless what they'd killed wasn't food..."

"I'll call in a team of crime-scene technicians, sir."

Cartwright winked. "Attaboy." He moved back to the cluster of soldiers.

Clenched fists positioned on his ample hips, Colonel Marls let Cartwright take Major Hastings's jeep and watched him go. He didn't imagine the FBI agent was going to find anything down that mesa. No way that pansy martinet von Hofmann would risk climbing it. The face was impassable to all but an expert mountain climber, and it dropped into a maze of dead-end draws. Escapees wouldn't waste their time with that shit.

Special Agent Burley called to Hastings, offering him a ride back to the camp in the Packard, informing him that he needed his help in organizing military checkpoints.

Marls smiled, listening to the conversation. Agent Cartwright hadn't scared him one flipping bit. Already the power was coming back to the him.

"Say, Major," Marls said, stopping Hastings before he joined Burley.

"Colonel?"

Marls spit. He lowered his voice. "Lyle, you fucked the cat by calling this in and getting these feather merchants involved, but that's all said and done and I'm gonna forgive you." He put a meaty hand on his intelligence officer's shoulder. "You do know this is our ticket outta here . . .?" Marls continued. "No more prison camps. No more pinto beans. Work with me on this—just the two of us, now—we nail that rat bastard von Hofmann, and I'll make sure you come out of this as big a hero as me. You hear what I'm saying?"

Hastings flinched as Marls slipped his arm across his back like a pal, or a boa constrictor, and guided him forward.

Although it came as a shock to Colonel Marls, Cartwright's discovery of the dead German prisoner was a matter of little surprise to the FBI man. What puzzled Special Agent in Charge Cartwright was the cause of death. Von Hofmann had garroted one of his own men. Cartwright stared at the body. He couldn't make sense of it. Although coyotes had gotten to the corpse sometime in the night, chewing off most of its face, half its fingers, tearing apart its uniform, and dragging it into the rocks, Cartwright didn't dare touch what remained until the crime-scene technicians arrived. All he could do was wrinkle his brow in consternation at the lethal barbed-wire garrote wind-ticking from the corpse's neck.

Five hours later, the body was identified as SS-Schütze Helmut Veit. Major Hastings, having been good enough to take Cartwright's fifth unanswered phone call to Colonel Marls, informed him that, ". . . No, Veit wasn't a snitch. I'd say he had only minimal contact with us since he'd been brought into the camp."

The dead man had provided one clue. While searching Veit's clothing, a crime-laboratory technician found a scrap of paper with Spanish phrases on it hidden in the clasp of the belt buckle. Von Hofmann had missed it in his own cursory search of the body, and it now corroborated Cartwright's suspicion von Hofmann was indeed running for Mexico.

By this time, Cartwright had established his field headquarters in the El Royale Hotel in Santa Rosa proper and had confirmed the deployment of military checkpoints. He'd heard back from the Southern Pacific Railway, relieved when their chief of railroad detectives told him a sweep every train, rail yard, and station from Santa Rosa to the El Paso border crossing, had come up empty. The railway was now secure. The press had been gagged—taken care of with the usual assortment of promises and threats. And although Cartwright was disappointed the fugitives had been running for approximately twenty-four hours and no trail had yet been located by man or dog, he was confident that the net he'd set was wide and deep. Soon, the harsh winter country would tip the scales against von Hofmann. He and the other escapees would show themselves as desperation for food and shelter made them bold and careless.

The radiator heater popped and clanged in the corner by the bed. Cartwright moved out into the hall where he watched a pair of agents carefully wrestle the last of three teletypes up the old, dark stairs. Cartwright dug out the final cigarette from his last pack of Lucky Strikes. He fired it from the butt of the smoke he'd just finished. He leaned over the stair rail and hollered to the front desk.

"Calling Señor Rodriguez!" He caught a glimpse of dark eyes shining from Rodriguez's leathery face. "Would you do me the favor of sending your boy to fetch some Lucky Strikes?"

"No Lucky Strikes, jefe."

"Sorry to hear that, but whatever they got a fresh carton of, please-and-thanks."

He checked his Hamilton wristwatch: nine forty. No later than ten p.m., the machines would be tapped into the phone-company wires and photos of each of the Germans distributed to every city and town, one-horse main street, and Indian reservation by midnight.

Rodriguez's gleam-groomed nephew returned a couple minutes later with a carton of Old Golds and a grin. All the boy could find and better than nothing. Cartwright thanked the smile with an old Standing Liberty quarter that had found its way into his pocket.

Cartwright started up the factory chimney of his mouth. He was secure in the knowledge that it's impossible for man, animal, objects, even weather to move through any environment without leaving sign. And all sign could be cut. He smoked, speculating on the sign von Hofmann and his men were leaving him this cold and bitter night. No matter how careful they'd been at concealing their passage since the murder of Veit, they were marking the landscape and the landscape was remembering.

"But why the hell go and murder the kid?" Cartwright said to no one in particular. A most important question, it hung in cigarette smoke and stared back at him unsmiling like a ghost.

21

Naked and weary with fatigue, von Hofmann and his team forded the Pecos River at Windmill Canyon, where it ran wide and relatively shallow north of Fort Sumner.

Hauptmann Zundorf stumbled in the bone-chilling current. He cursed for not paying attention and paused mid-river, teeth chattering as he caught his breath. He had to clear his mind. It swirled with images of the night before and that strange, sorry boy soldier, Veit.

The gush of blood. The horrified look of betrayal flashes obscenely to acceptance as if dying is his duty.

Zundorf didn't know if any of the rest of the team realized von Hofmann had lied about Veit's treason. Veit had come to the church with von Hofmann's orders. Had he been treasonous, as von Hofmann wanted them to believe, he would have also brought Marls and his MPs. So why did the Standartenführer murder him so viciously?

Wolters leaned in. He huffed in Zundorf's ear, "I don't even have a name. I'm known as *Bloody Fox.*"

Zundorf met the ghoulish grin splayed across his face. "Is now really the time for this?"

"'Are you surprised?'" continued the young man. "'I have to say that my parents, my family, and their companions were murdered in the Llano Estacado.'"

Zundorf, wet and cold, and ticked off, gave Wolters a dirty look. "You *Kampfmüde?*" Battle fatigued.

Wolters grinned. "I know this land."

"You don't." Wolters looked crushed. Zundorf sighed. "You're quoting your books."

"*Der Geist des Llano Estakado.* Karl May's masterpiece. He lived this and I *know* it. Don't you see? I can help the Standartenführer find his way," Wolters said.

Zundorf gave him a hard look. "Ghost stories: bad idea."

"Bloody Fox *is* the ghost!" His own ghostly eyes gleamed. "Did you know the tactics—our Führer's tactics—in North Africa were based on Karl May's teaching about the Apache? The Führer said so."

"Leutnant Wolters, you need to be quiet!"

Wolters urged, "The water runs out soon after this river. We must make our trek based on windmill wells." He grinned, loopy and ghoulish. "A farmhouse. A single family home. That's how we survive."

Zundorf shoved him forward. Wolters splashed. Zundorf stood, unsure; a little defeated; worried.

"What are you stopped for, Zundorf? Keep moving," came von Hofmann's harsh whisper.

Zundorf waded forward.

The wind whipped the water off the surface in a stinging, icy spray. Each man was soaked to the skin, uniforms and footgear off to keep them dry, their bodies shivered with violent spasm. Von Hofmann estimated the temperature close to freezing, with the wind taking it somewhere below. It was hard going, and von Hofmann had been pushing his team without rest. It could not be helped. They had lost precious time that afternoon navigating over and around seemingly endless volcanic mesas, a warped landscape that had them covering three, maybe four kilometers of march while only making a single kilometer of forward progress.

At seventeen hundred, before the last weak light of day faded behind the long stretches of gray-washed clouds that covered the land, they'd seen a cone of dust rising in the distance. Von Hofmann climbed a hill and through his field glasses witnessed a convoy of three military trucks racing south along a dirt road. They were attempting to get ahead of von Hofmann and the prisoners. Trying to cut them off. So now, although their supply of food was short and it was imperative they find weapons, transport, and some kind of clothing to disguise their uniforms, von Hofmann chose to avoid the town of Fort Sumner knowing the FBI, US Army, or some other brand of law enforcement lay in wait.

They made the western shore. the team huddled, shivering among the cottonwoods and willows, tugging on clothing, dry socks and boots they'd carried across the river. Ready again, von Hofmann refused to let them rest. No one complained. They silently filed onto the vast grama grassland of the Llano Estacado. In the moonlit cold, it reminded the SS colonel of the Polish steppes.

Unternehmen Steppenfeuer. Operation Prairie Fire. The name made sense. This was land he could burn across uncontrolled. It made him glad. Von Hofmann had heard Wolters's conversation with Zundorf. And he was certain that ahead waited a farmhouse or ranch where he would take what he needed.

22

WEDNESDAY, DECEMBER 22, 1943

GRAY MOONLIGHT stabbed beneath the farmhouse door and through the old triangular gun ports in the ironwood shutters to vaguely illuminate a dusty, four-room adobe farmhouse. It appeared as if it were lost in a time when life, liberty, and the pursuit of happiness were purchased at the price of sweat, bullets, and blood. Large only by the standards of the last century, the main room contained the necessities for a hard range life and little else. A wide plank table dominated the room's center, its varnish long worn away, polished smooth to its ironwood heart by generations of anxious elbows and arms. The caress of hands folded in grace. Against the back wall of the farmhouse, a smoke-blackened iron stove told of a bountiful land and appetites to match, while the scorched iron pots and cooking utensils above the counter and the sink hung with the promise the cupboards would be full and the chairs never vacant. The only item in the room to indicate the twentieth century was the First National Bank of Santa Fe bank draft drawn from the account of H. Howard Hendricks and made out to "Mr. Tyler Keyes" for five thousand dollars that Tyler had punched through with the protruding head of a nail tapped into the wall long ago to hang a calendar from Olsen's Drug and Diner, compliments of the Coca Cola bottling company.

A large stone fireplace divided the main room in two. Embers glowed beneath the ashes spread across the iron grate. Tyler's Winchester '94 perched on deer-hoof hooks over the mantelpiece back in place after he hadn't used it on Cecil O'Hara for poisoning his steeldust dead.

On the other side of the chimney, a matching hearth opened onto the larger of two bedrooms. On the big mesquite bed, hand carved by Tyler's grandfather as a wedding gift to his bride, Tyler Keyes lay beneath the quilt reining in the last straggling minutes of sleep which, these days, ever barely came or found itself accepted.

Outside, a barrel dumped into the dirt.

Prison-sleeping with an eye always open, Tyler sat up, knitted his brow. He waited for another sound . . . Nothing. Maybe he'd imagined the first.

Screeeaaah . . . The slow swing of his barn door.

Tyler's soul sank. Was this O'Hara and Hendricks's rough-housers two days early for the trouble they'd cause him when he didn't cash out to Hendricks—? But the sounds didn't continue. He counted a full two minutes. Relaxed back into his pillow. He closed his eyes.

The distinct clomp of feet moving onto his porch.

He sat up. This wasn't men who knew the place, knew their business. Weren't cowboy boots either... Maybe he had forgotten to latch the barn last night and his bay horse had wandered out hunting weeds. Tyler had cleared the yard, but some poked through the porch planks. Shit. All he needed was the bay to crash through and break a leg. He rolled out of the bed, ready to sort out this unusual 3 a.m. alarm clock. He fished his cleanest pair of dirty blue jeans from a pile and hop-stepped his way to the front door.

Thud. Thud. A body hit the heavy timber, testing it. This was no horse.

"Hey! That you, O'Hara?"

Thud. Thud. Thud. Someone was trying to break in.

"You seen my Winchester! Speak up or it's going to do the talking!"

Tyler lurched to the hearth and snatched the weapon. Cheek against the stock, he swung the barrel round to the door only to balk in an instant of confusion: the sound of movement, the testing of the adobe walls, came from all sides of the house.

Tyler swept his gaze from each of the shuttered windows to the *thud-thud-thudding* of the front door. He worked the Winchester's action, levering a bullet into the chamber. This wasn't O'Hara, these were strangers and they'd surrounded him.

"Whoever the hell you are, you got all of three seconds to clear out before I open fire."

The door exploded inward. Tyler squeezed his trigger, and the rifle leaped in his hands. He snapped off a second shot at chest level as the farmhouse filled with a guttural cry. More than twenty sheep stampeded inside, bowling Tyler backward into the stove. As scared, stupid mad-eyed woolly bulldozers swarmed the house, a rush of humiliation replaced Tyler's adrenaline. He picked himself up, swearing. Kneed, shoved, kicked his way through the mass of living sweaters onto his porch to gaze across his farm. Over three hundred sheep milled about, eating and bleating, trampling and destroying what had yesterday been a salvageable fifty acres of a tired hundred-acre spread.

The cold air turned Tyler's breath to thick, white vapor that stood out against the pre-dawn moonlight. Tyler ignored the chill as he looked up at moonbeams piercing through a patchwork of rain clouds that checkered the sky. He looked to the eastern border of his property. He could just make out a place along his fence where the new posts and barbed wire had been ripped down to drive the herd onto his land. Tyler burned with humiliation.

"Stupid, stupid. Damn-fuck-fool!"

Why'd he think Hendricks wouldn't have forced the deal? Long as Tyler could remember, Virginia's father had worked at running the Keyes off their property and incorporating it into his range, which encircled the Keyes's hundred acres with thousands. Hendricks fought twenty years to get his hands on it. When he couldn't wrest them from Tyler's father, he made life brutal for the man. Challenged his water rights and dragged him through court. Pressured buyers away from his crops. Bribed the seed sellers to sell him second-rate seed. But Tyler's father was tenacious. He fought Hendricks tooth and claw, like a panther, fighting right into an early grave.

Tyler watched the devastation of his farm. A chill that was more than an effect of the weather ran through him. He gripped his right shoulder with his left hand as though to hold his frame from bursting. Farming had never been his passion, but Tyler owed it to his family, his forebears, their memory, and maybe to himself. Those weeks at the fishing camp, he'd come to grips with the fact it was this land, these hundred acres watered with their blood, that shaped his meaning of life. This land was the only connection Tyler had with that. He'd learned to walk, to laugh, to cry here, and in every step he took, his every smile or frown, this land grinned and wept and spoke through him. If he lost it, he would be losing the last part of that made him a Keyes. More than wanting, Tyler needed it alive to be alive.

Hendricks had never gone so far as back an offer with ready cash, which is what the harpooned bank check was, overvalued by 50 percent. The sheep were more Hendricks's style. It was the carrot and the stick. Only this time, the stick was an ax across Tyler's neck. The sheep had been in his fields all night. Tyler's alfalfa—his only chance at survival after the killing of his mare—obliterated and with it, the last of all his hope. In half a year, ten months at the most, even if he sold his every last horse, he'd never have enough money to stay on. Hendricks had said he would kill him and this was the end of that hangman's rope.

Tyler's fingers dug into his bare shoulder. The muscles in his face, his back, his body, clenched with a will he refused to let be broken.

He pushed his way out of the barn through a sea of wool, leading his big bay into the yard. Its neck twitched with nervous anticipation as Tyler double-checked its tack, then pulled on his gloves. He wore black boots and the dirty, faded blue jeans, the Apache buckskin and a hip-length, fleece-lined range coat. He was dressed for work. He paused to adjust the brim of his sweat-stained Stetson. Tyler gripped the saddle horn, got his foot into the stirrup, and, with a creak of leather, swung into the saddle.

With a click of his tongue, Tyler urged his horse forward. He needed to condense the flock before guiding it toward the open fence. It was hard, tiring work, but Tyler Keyes was one hell of a cowboy, and, as he spent the morning expertly gathering, moving and cutting the herd back out onto Hendricks's range, he appeared the sum total of the American West, sitting tall in his saddle.

Minutes past eight, five hours after he'd awakened, Tyler drove the last of the bleating livestock from his property. He jumped from his horse and set to work on the downed section of fence he'd located on his eastern border—the last of what turned out to be three breaks in his property. On two of them, they'd cut the barbed wire and pulled it back, but on this section they'd taken their time. They'd unstapled the wire from five of the posts, dug out the stakes, and laid them across the loose wire to pin it in a wide corridor for the sheep. Tyler righted the piñon posts. He rehitched the wire—a glove- and hand-shredding process made all the more difficult by the surge of a huge flock itching to get back inside. Maintaining a threatening "Ha! Ya! Ha!" he worked his way to the finish.

Tyler led his horse from the fence and mounted, firming his Winchester in its saddle boot. He dug spurs into his horse's ribs and raced to the fence. He jumped it, scattering sheep before him, and headed into the endless plains, riding into the face of a hard December wind.

23

Tyler rode to Hendricks's ranch. He tried to plan for his encounter with the old man, but found the closer he got, the more his mind turned to Virginia. He hated to admit it, but she'd consumed him these last weeks since O'Hara had delivered the bank draft and passed on Hendricks's ultimatum—take the money or be destroyed. In whatever way Tyler had occupied himself since, memories of Virginia cropped up to puncture his every thought. He had the nagging suspicion this sudden play for his land was about her return. But she was married, so why the violence? Hendricks understood him well enough to know Tyler wouldn't get in the way of that. What the hell? He'd completely avoided her these last three months; what explained the mix of obscene generosity with outright hostility?

Three months, 110 days, and he didn't do the math to convert 2,640 hours into minutes. That would lead to seconds and each of these he'd measured as hours.

She *was* married, Never to be his again. When Tyler tried to get to the heart of it, the fire of his ego evaporated logic and left him angry.

All the time in the State Penitentiary, the only news he'd ever gotten about Virginia was when O'Hara visited to show him the British newspapers' announcement of Virginia's wedding.

Pointless to keep on about her. Tyler scratched his cheek. He focused on the beat of his horse's hooves. He watched the clouds. He listened to the rhythmic creak of saddle leather. He tried to whistle a festive "Hark the Herald Angels." Real jolly.

His mind remained fixed on Virginia.

Tyler's bay trotted at a calmer pace as he guided it along the dirt road to Virginia's father's ranch. He reined short before the massive black and gold-highlighted iron gates that, rising from a gravel crossroads, stood fenceless on the plain, proclaiming to the empty landscape this was indeed the entrance to the "Triple 'H'" Hendricks Ranch.

The idea of passing beneath the ridiculous gate like a vassal entering the dominion of his lord disgusted Tyler Keyes. He rode into the drainage ditch alongside the flood-prone road and navigated around the gates.

Ten minutes later, as Tyler and his bay followed the road down a steep grade that dropped from a shelf of limestone buttes into the ranch proper, he had no idea a pair of wolf-gray eyes followed his passage.

STANDARTENFÜHRER JÜRGEN VON HOFMANN watched the cowboy head toward the ranch, confident he was unseen as he laid at the rocky edge of one of the buttes, his men hidden in the limestone formations behind him, resting out of sight.

They'd arrived shortly after two that morning, having hiked along the line of buttes for most of the night. Upon discovering the dark, remote, and sprawling ranch a kilometer beyond the protective shelves of stone, von Hofmann decided it was here he'd take what he required to proceed with his mission. His rendezvous with the American spy was twenty-eight hours and approximately one hundred and sixty kilometers away. Time was running short.

At first, he'd planned to infiltrate the ranch and steal what he needed before dawn. But before he'd had a chance to organize the men, seven heavily armed horsemen rode out of the night, heading straight for the ranch. The riders' sudden appearance, the instant suspicion it brought that they were riding for von Hofmann and his men, had driven him to cover. When the riders passed his hiding place, von Hofmann noticed most of them swayed drunkenly in their saddles. Three thirty in the morning, conspicuously armed, drunk—had they been on some kind of raid?

Von Hofmann caught a glimpse of their leader, a man adorning long silver hair, ramrod-backed with the carriage of a baron. Eyes that blazed with malice. He was sober, and as he'd ridden by, the man's sharp criticisms of his cowboys carried back to von Hofmann on the wind, and the Standartenführer warmed with aggressive excitement, the kind known only to a soldier hidden in ambush.

He and his men were back in the war.

Dawn followed in stillness, and von Hofmann ordered his men to sleep. They had been on the run for more than thirty hours, crossing this rough windswept, multileveled prairie without rest. The men were grizzled and filthy but thankfully, their physical raggedness had yet to overtake their spirit. Although tempers had flared one time or another, there had been no fighting among the team.

Twice since the escape, Army patrol planes had forced von Hofmann and his men to hide. By fluke of luck, the first time they'd been at a windmill for water and able to hide among the cattle. The second time, they were leaving an arroyo when Wolters heard the sound of another low-flying plane. For thirty-five minutes, they'd hidden among the juniper and sage until the reconnaissance aircraft moved its box search, flying on to another grid. Von Hofmann was convinced they had gone unobserved.

As with the case of their pursuit, their luck extended to include the weather and water. The skies, overcast and threatening a storm since their escape, kept the temperature cold enough to be conducive to hard travel, and they never had any trouble finding streams, wells, or windmills to provide a constant supply of fresh drinking water. Food was another matter entirely. The supply they'd brought from the camp had dwindled to a few hard rolls and some dried-out chicken they finished before bedding down. Now they had nothing. Von Hofmann had seen hunger make soldiers fight like ferocious animals, but it dulled the rest of their senses, making them careless. Von Hofmann couldn't afford careless men. After dark, they would make their move.

Von Hofmann raised his high-powered field glasses to his eyes. He'd studied the ranch off and on for most of the morning. This time, he chose to study the new cowboy. He tracked him past stockyards, corrals, shearing pens—then, where the road branched out—between workshops, tack rooms, and bunkhouses. The place bustled as a dozen Mexican and Anglo-American ranch hands, too young or too old for the war, tended to the business of sheep.

From the way the ranch hands stopped to watch the cowboy, it was obvious he wasn't expected. Von Hofmann wondered whether this newcomer brought word of their escape. He regretted not having stopped him when he'd passed, but there was nothing to do about it now.

Von Hofmann switched his view from the cowboy and focused on a pair of two-ton canvas covered trucks that had appeared since the last time he'd reconnoitered the ranch. A few sheep herded from the truck beds went into a corral. The vehicles crossed the compound and pulled into a garage.

He noted the garage location, then let his magnified vision travel back to three stories of Victorian splendor. The mansion sat against a backdrop of low, stark hills, peppered with sleek gray pumpjacks sucking black, liquid cash from the ground. Once again, he watched the cowboy who rode up to the porch.

Words exchanged. A figure disappeared into the house. Von Hofmann imagined himself living inside one of Wolters fanciful books. Was this young rider quick on the draw?

He chuckled to himself only to lose all humor as the deep growl of approaching aircraft brought him back to this century. His century. His war.

24

Virginia was not at Oxford. Not in the London Blitz. Not on the Atlantic Ocean. She wasn't in a courtroom watching Tyler plead no contest to her rape. Her sleep-fogged brain located body and soul as she awakened to the growl of approaching aircraft. Her bedding, headboard, and canopy, all pink satin bunched and buttoned, resembled nothing so much as a coffin fit for a dead girl.

Her childhood bedroom.

The Triple H Hendricks Ranch.

Three "H"s for three kinds of past, present, and future hell.

Virginia rose from her bed. The drone of aircraft engines increased in volume from the west. Before looking out the window, she'd already identified them as four-engine long-range bombers. She parted the curtains and confirmed two V formations of B-17 Flying Fortresses. Ten aircraft each. The delivery run from California—destination: England—for raids into Germany.

B-17s. Cousin to the British Arvo Lancaster. The aircraft her husband Paul had lain on his stomach inside the clear Perspex nose. Nine missions, Germany and back, his eyes buried in the bomb sight. Over target, once the bombing run commenced, he took control of the aircraft until he released the payload and snapped the bombing photograph, then the pilot retook control and turned for home. The tenth time, Paul and the six other men of his crew never completed that turn.

A German flak widow at twenty-three.

After the empty coffin funeral, Virginia stood in the church sacristy with her former in-laws to determine her name, her settlement, her riddance.

"It's the logical thing," Paul's father had opened fire, followed by salvo-by-battery: Paul's mother, his father, then mother and father again and again. "A clean breast of it." "You're still young. Another life, another family to look forward to." "Your own father—a very wise man: complete agreement." "The privilege to be allowed civilian passage back to your own shore's safety is not to be turned down." "We're only saying what we know Paul would say." "What our son would want, dear."

More than once, Paul's words to his wife had included that he didn't particularly care for his parents.

"I'll go." And Virginia patted her belly. "At least I'll have his child to comfort me," she said, and left them suitably horrified.

That night, she'd boarded the *SS America*, a civilian ocean liner called into service by the US Navy, chased by Paul's imploring parents she stay and raise their grandchild in the bosom of his—or hers, you never can tell—heritage and the people who loved Virginia most. Virginia heard their words as much the same as the shrieking of the gulls that swirled over dock and overhead. Lying back upon her cabin berth she entertained her private amusement, smiling for the first time, it would seem, in weeks. No child was forthcoming. Unbeknownst to Paul, she'd taken the appropriate precautions for the nineteen months of their short marriage. Virginia would write his parents with the truth but wanted them to stew a little for their treatment of her. She'd get to it with the new year.

She looked at the wedding ring on the vanity. The table had been her mother's when she'd been alive, before father—wanting a son to carry his name—forced himself and a second child upon her and, true to the doctor's warning after Virginia was born, killed both her mother and the baby boy with its birth.

H. Howard Hendricks was familiar with rape long before Tyler Keyes came into his crosshairs.

Virginia pushed the wedding ring over her knuckle. Did she love Paul? Then? Now? Ever at all? With Paul, it had been platonic for three years. A friendship sparked by his fascination with American "hillbilly" music.

Paul had just returned his original fiancée to her rooms at Somerville College, Oxford, when he'd heard Roy Acuff's 'Wabash Cannonball' playing too loud through Virginia's open window. Paul crooned along badly enough from the lawn below to cause Virginia to thrust out her head and, as miserable and friendless as when she'd arrived in England three weeks earlier, curse him away. This revealed her New Mexican twang.

"Jesus wept. A genu-ine cowgirl."

At sixteen, Virginia had developed the habit of never letting the opportunity for a snappy retort go wasted. "You're a genu-ine horse's ass. Shoo-fly."

Paul didn't. Instead, he made like a fool, turning circles, craning his neck to view that equine posterior she'd indicated, until the recording ended; he laughed, asked Virginia if she had any of the Dixie Clodhoppers as good as the Acuff.

Wishing she weren't amused, and securing his promise he'd leave her alone after she played it, Virginia played the record. By the time it ended, their friendship had begun.

Paul was a third-year undergraduate in biology at Queens' College, as awkward as he was smart. Ranked the top biology undergraduate in the entire university, the boundaries of his awkwardness were . . . boundless. Paul had known this for as long as he could remember. He'd developed a thousand little ways to embrace every curbside trip and altar-rail stumble, each non sequitur and way-off-the-mark laugh, each ankle-biting dog he tried to pet, dance-floor collision, and stranger's wailing toddler he'd frightened with a wink or hello. Shortly after *The Wizard of Oz* came to London, Paul picked up the nickname "Scarecrow." The nickname fit. By the time he made it through officer training, flight school, and onto his crew, few of his RAF mates could identify him by his given name. But everyone knew Scarecrow.

His university fiancée, the hard-toothed, biting-mad Meredith who declared love to Paul in snappish declarations of her plans to spend his family fortune, but showed it with irrepressible passion that bordered on the mystical. Meredith became Virginia's second friend. This after Virginia suggested as scandalously sarcastically as possible, if money's all Meredith wanted, Virginia's father's fortune was larger and she was just as available as Paul. "I only suggest it," she teased, "because your course of study seems preoccupied by feminist poetry of a certain scandalous point of view."

"The difference between the study of and the writing of is the difference between identifying experience and experimenting in it."

"I'm not sure that doesn't mean the same thing."

"I'm sure it doesn't either. Stick around, Gin. And have a toddy to honor the sweetest syllable of your de-lish name."

One friend became two, became five, six, ten at any one time with Paul and Meredith's rotating circle of Oxford characters— all of them three or four years older than Virginia—all of whom welcomed the ironic New Mexican cowgirl into their wit-fueled, boozy-intellectual, communist and fascist-wary, Chamberlain- and Churchill-weary, island-neurotic clique.

In the little over six years Virginia spent abroad, they were the length and breadth of Virginia's experience of England. The rest of the soppy, sooty-citied, too green countrysided country she despised.

Virginia had arrived in England three weeks after her sixteenth birthday. A birthday commemorated by her father's exertion of cash influence to secure her "visiting student (ineligible for degree)" status at Somerville while, locally, the old man put out the contract to kill Tyler Keyes in prison for having raped his daughter.

Tyler Keyes served six years of an eight-year sentence. And, while he'd never responded to a single letter she'd written to him, Virginia was certain Tyler continued to love her as deeply as she'd always and carelessly loved him. To protect him from further harm from her father, she had, upon learning of his pending parole, agreed to Paul's marriage proposal one night in London during the Blitz and quickly wrote her father. She and Paul eloped two days after his break-up with Meredith who'd quietly moved into the home of her poetry professor and his adventuresome wife. The ball—oh, God, the gall of the ball—came one week later, ending short hours before Paul made his enlistment into the RAF.

Virginia twitched her finger feeling the weight of the ring. The Baker-Davies family millstone. They'd had six days together before Paul reported for training, which would be the longest consecutive period they'd ever spend as man and wife. He'd wanted to pilot a Lancaster, but bomb aimer was the role assigned. This was not due to technical or physical disqualification as a pilot, he'd told Virginia, but rather for the mental qualification of zero moral hesitation in releasing twenty-eight thousand pounds of high-explosive bombs at the push of the button onto sleeping German cities. Military targets and otherwise.

Virginia asked him once about the civilians caught below. He'd said, "They don't care about ours and I don't think about theirs."

A reoccurring nightmare Virginia would have found her trapped each night, a kind of invisible, indestructible visitor, in a cellar belonging to a beautiful German woman with hair, red like her own. Each night, unable to warn the woman or her children,

Paul's bombs plunged through their cellar ceiling, engulfing them in flesh-and-bone-melting fire Virginia would watch until she jarred awake in breath-caught terror.

She dressed. Virginia had loved Paul in every way he'd wanted, and she was secure that he'd known this and had been happy with her. But now that he was dead, now that she was home, now that Tyler was free and nearby and he had seen her, now that her father and his men had ridden out and ridden back in the middle of the night: Tyler Keyes would come. So she'd wear the ring and use it alongside the large, black silk Civil War mourning rosette of her grandmother's.

She stabbed its oversized hatpin, a wicked-looking skewer made for heavy Victorian fabrics, through her dress. A black flower of death symbolically knifing her heart. A talismanic weapon she'd use to compel Tyler safely away (if he'd truly become the beaten man, the coward, she'd seen him act in Vaughn), or drive him toward a more calculated course of action.

That's what it would boil down to in the end ever since that day in September when she'd returned from Vaughn and her father wrenched her from her car having been called by the local deputy.

"That's the last time you'll be seeing Tyler Keyes whose life gets shorter and shorter with your pushing."

"Are you threatening murder?"

"Anyone can threaten murder. The question you should be asking is if I'm a man capable of getting away with it."

25

The perception Hendricks had of his study was round and distorted, as he viewed it through the double barrels of the nineteenth-century Italian 12-gauge shotgun he had bought last month at auction in St. Louis. The silver and gold inlaid engraving that depicted two pheasants on the wing against a background of the Italian Alps was exquisite. This shotgun was one of a kind and had cost Hendricks more than he'd paid for the sports car he'd recently purchased for his ungrateful daughter. The premier gun collector in the Southwest, this was a work of art and worth every cent.

The insides of the barrels were immaculate. They faintly glowed as he turned the weapon toward the lights illuminating the rest of his collection. An exotic assortment of firearms. Everything from three fourteenth-century 21-bore Japanese matchlock temple guns—silver damascened with clouds and rising herons, their black lacquered stocks displaying seven large gilt monsters of the Tokugawara family—to the beat-up Peacemaker Pat Garrett fired into Billy the Kid not twenty-five miles away at Pete Maxwell's house in Fort Sumner.

But his collection would not have been complete had it not also contained a variety of modern weapons, which, although not having individual distinguished pasts, would have gripped the imagination of any gun aficionado for what they represented. He'd built an entire display case for his collection of "100s." Fifteen important American firearms with the serial number 0100. His favorite among these: a never-before-fired Thompson M1928A1 submachine gun.

The door opened. "Why'd you do it?"

"Do what, girl?"

"I talked to some of the hands," Virginia said, walking into the room. "You and O'Hara and the little night ride you took to tear up Tyler's place. Some say, last month, you killed his breeding mare."

Hendricks picked up a polishing cloth and set to wiping the gun of fingerprints. He looked from the barrels to his daughter.

"Made for Jim Fisk. Ever heard of him?"

"Answer me, Father."

"A scandalous railroader. Missed his chance to use this piece when he got shot by the boyfriend of his mistress. Stupid bastard died before he could find a shell."

Virginia watched her father walk the weapon to the space he'd prepared inside the "historical" case.

"I've done as you've asked. I've not seen him. Contacted him. You said you'd buy his place."

"Boy needed some encouragement."

Before Virginia could respond, Hendricks's balding, skulking foreman, Cecil O'Hara, entered past her.

"Excuse me, Mr. Hendricks, but Tyler Keyes is outside."

Hendricks looked from O'Hara to Virginia. He grinned. "Encouragement." He asked O'Hara, "Is he armed?"

"Rifle in his saddle boot."

Virginia went to the window and moved the curtain. Tyler Keyes sat on his horse at the veranda rail. She dropped her hand, allowing the curtain to close.

"If I'd stayed in London, this wouldn't be happening."

"Don't be so sure about that. Anyway, your place is home now. With family."

"With you."

"Who could possibly love you more than your father?"

He rose from his deep leather chair. He'd never be caught like Fisk. In matters of violence, Hendricks always saw it coming and struck first, fast, hard. He'd shoot a man in the back to protect what was his or gain what was not. Hendricks locked his collection and, ignoring Virginia, followed O'Hara from the room.

HENDRICKS STEPPED ONTO THE VERANDA that circled his entire mansion and was itself twice as wide as Tyler Keyes's house. Tyler, astride his horse, faced him from the rail. Hendricks's house servant, Señora Gúzman, met him with a glass of iced bitters. He sipped. He savored.

"Well, well, Tyler Keyes. I'm told you wanted to see me?" O'Hara chuckled.

Tyler considered the rancher. He said nothing. The silence was uncomfortable.

"Well?" said Hendricks.

Tyler pushed his hat back on his head. Took on a puzzled expression. "I've no idea what you've been doing in private to those sheep of yours, Hendricks, but they arrived at my place this morning pretty shook up."

Tyler spoke loud enough for the ranch hands in the corral behind him to hear. They snickered. Hendricks's face turned to stone. He set down his drink and took three steps to the veranda railing. "Men have died for lesser remarks."

"I hear they've also died from what they've caught from your sheep." Tyler locked eyes with the rancher. "Don't cut my fences again."

"Cut fences, Mr. Keyes? News to me. I'd say what, with the thunder last night, the sheep spooked. You're the bad-luck victim of a stampede."

"There wasn't any thunder last night."

"No? Well, knowing how once sheep get started on something sweet like alfalfa," he shook his head with mock sympathy, "holdin' a five-grand draft of mine made out in your name must seem mighty generous, considering what the bank will give you when you go belly at New Year's."

"You got it all figured out."

"Gifted that way."

Tyler's eyes searched the face of the house, hoping to catch sight of its other occupant. "Tell you what," he said. "Virginia comes outside right now and tells me she wants me gone, I'll go tonight."

"Don't push this the wrong direction, Keyes."

Tyler did. "Virginia!"

"Keyes, your parole's still in effect and it includes a restraining order from seeing that girl."

"VIRGINIA!"

O'Hara's hand dropped to the butt of the .45 holstered on his belt.

Hendricks raised his voice. "I'll have you back in prison so damn fast. Then I'll seize your cow-dip mudhole for nothing, that's what you want."

But as he spoke, the front doors opened, and Virginia stepped outside.

Tyler didn't hear his voice say, "Virginia," his eyes jacklit by the black mourning rosette over her heart.

Virginia considered him without speaking.

"You're not needed here, girl. Get back in the house."

Virginia crossed the veranda to the steps, her eyes never leaving Tyler as she walked up to him. Tyler looked from the mourning ribbons to her face. Her husband was dead.

"I didn't know. I'm sorry."

"Germans killed my husband. Nothing of yours to be sorry about."

The coldness in her voice wounded him. He jerked his chin at her father. "He's offered me five thousand dollars for my family place."

"That's a lot of money."

"Do you want me gone?"

Her face was set hard. She didn't say yes, but neither did she say no.

"C'mon. Just climb on my horse. Let's just get out of here." He held out his hand to her.

O'Hara gave Hendricks a look. Hendricks gave a subtle shake of his head.

Virginia said, "You're embarrassing yourself. I just came out to say goodbye . . . It is a lot of money." She weighted the last three words. Then she turned for the house.

"Don't."

She stopped, her back to Tyler. For an instant, it appeared she'd turn and say something else, but she moved into the house and shut the door.

"Got your answer, Keyes." Hendricks said, "I'll expect word from my bank before close of business. Oh, and tell you what—You go ahead and throw in that rifle. Your court terms don't allow it to leave your property and I promise I'll give it a place of honor in my collection."

"Closest you'll get to this rifle is a mark in its stock because if you come onto my property again, I'll kill you."

He wheeled his horse and shot off.

26

Tuesday, February 12, 1924

*V*IRGINIA REFUSED TO CRY. *Five years old and hearing her mother's wrenching pain screamed through the door of her bedroom upstairs. Hearing Señora Gúzman and the doctor yelling, "Push! Push! Push! Breath—deep breaths—Push!" her tiny body hummed with an unnamable fear as she sat on the straight-backed chair beside the grandfather clock. Daddy, at the second floor railing above her, gripped it in white, bony fists, smiling and telling her it sounded bad, but was really all right.*

Virginia drew comfort from the strength of his voice.

Silence came suddenly. Her father whirled from the railing. Virginia wanted to follow, but he ordered her not to move from the chair. She licked her lips and craned her neck. She strained to hear.

A baby cried.

The baby was outside of Mommy's tummy now and Virginia ached to know its name and what it looked like.

Faint voices.

She tried to discern who spoke. Mommy, the doctor, Daddy. Her heart beat faster. Everything was good.

"Virginia," Daddy said, coming back into view at the railing, "you have a brother."

Virginia's eyes went wide. Her very own brother. Daddy's smile melted her as it always did. He put a cigar in his mouth. He lit it with a match.

"Hurry, sweetheart, Mommy wants to see you."

The room was dark, but Mommy's face was a glowing white light. When she saw Virginia, her sweat-dewed features brightened even more.

"Sweet pea." Her voice soft and Southern. "You see your baby brother?"

Virginia froze. "Mom-my?"

The bed sheets piled at the foot of the bed were bloody, and worse was the struggling, howling creature Mommy clutched to her bare bosom. A wave of dizziness crashed over Virginia. She staggered, colliding with the doctor's knees.

"It's all right, Virginia," her mother said. "I'm fine now, see?" She smiled, tender and pretty, as proof.

Virginia looked from Mommy to the baby-creature, to Señora Gúzman preparing a basin of water by the shade-drawn window.

"The bath is ready, ma'am. Shall I wrap Howard Junior when I am finished?"

"Give him my yellow shawl."

Virginia ran from the bedroom in terror.

Señora Gúzman was a señora without a señor. Daddy said she'd lost her husband and her baby before coming to work for them. Virginia didn't know if she would ever find them again, or if Señora Gúzman was even looking. She moved into the house the day after Little Howie came. Daddy said it was because Mommy had no milk and Señora Gúzman did.

Mommy's blood was sick from pushing Little Howie out of her, and Virginia wasn't allowed to see her. Virginia missed Mommy. Missed her voice. She missed how she'd sing her a song every night after prayers. Now Daddy turned out her light and they didn't say prayers. The only singing Virginia heard anymore was Señora Gúzman. She would sing in her own language to little Howie as she nursed him, the baby wrapped in Mommy's favorite shawl.

For two weeks after the baby arrived, Virginia never strayed far from Mommy's room. She'd listen all day to the clock and pretend it was Mommy's heartbeat. The doctor came each day, and each day he seemed much grayer, until finally, he came out and told Daddy, "She'll speak to you, and then with Virginia."

Daddy went in and Virginia waited in the hallway, listening to the grandfather clock's lonely tick.

The door opened. "Go on in, Virginia. Mommy's waiting for you."

Virginia crept into the dark room. Strange, sharp smells she didn't recognize frightened her.

"Virginia?"

"Yes, Mommy." Virginia climbed onto the fat chair at the side of her bed. "When are you going to get better? I miss prayer-time."

Virginia twisted onto her knees so she could lean across the bed on her elbows. Her mother hooked Virginia's hair behind her warm and tiny ear. "I'm not, sweet pea. I'm going to heaven."

Their eyes met. They stared at each other for a long time that, when Virginia remembered it, was never long enough. Virginia looked away.

"You don't have to go, Mommy."

"It's what our Lord wants, I'spect ."

A tiny hole opened inside of Virginia. It crumbled and widened like the riverbank when Daddy took her the time it rained so much and they watched the water rising, eating away the earth. Virginia laid her head on Mommy's chest, her eyes fixed on the end of the bed. "You should stay, Mommy."

"I know you want me to." And she stroked Virginia's hair. Her hand was like a feather. Virginia heard the thump of her mother's heart. It sounded far away.

"Will you do something for me, sweet pea?"

"Uh-huh."

Already the beat was slowing.

"Love your father and your baby brother. And care for them as if you were both of us . . . Promise me?"

Virginia turned her head to use her other ear to hear her mother's heart, and again their eyes met, and Virginia gave her promise.

Mommy smiled. A tear rolled from her lower eyelid. She took her hand from Virginia's head.

"Don't go, Mommy. Please?" Virginia said, terror welling up from the hole inside her.

The heartbeat was almost gone.

Mommy lifted a finger. She caught her tear in the cup of a fingernail. More difficult than dying itself, she forced her finger to touch the teardrop to Virginia's lips. Virginia's tongue licked the teardrop salty into her mouth.

"Now you'll never be without me."

The river surged, and the ground beneath Virginia's feet disappeared. Daddy caught her in the air and pulled her back. This time Daddy wasn't there to catch her and Virginia knew what it was to fall. Her mother was dead.

Little Howie died two days later.

27

THURSDAY, DECEMBER 23, 1943

IT WAS AFTER MIDNIGHT when H. Howard Hendricks poured his nightly snifter of Napoleon brandy. That look on Tyler Keyes's face when his daughter told him to drop dead. Ha! Crushed. Destroyed. Humiliated. Only one outcome would prevail. Keyes would take the five thousand dollars, or he would play it true to form. Go off half-cocked and do something rash that would bury him. Either way, those hundred acres would belong to Hendricks.

Hendricks relished the irony. If the father had been smart, understood what the Keyes people had been sitting on for four generations, Tyler would be wealthier than Hendricks.

Back in '31, Hendricks invited two promising young chemists, A. K. Teplitz and J. K. Rogers, to the Triple H. When no one else was interested, he'd allowed the pair to conduct field research on their controversial theories of surface geochemical testing for petroleum excavation. They'd located the twenty-five wells scattered across his range that sucked an endless stream of money into his bank, but their most significant discovery that trip, conducted in the dead of night, had been within the boundaries of the Keyes's farm. Testing there concluded the largest oil deposits in the region belonged to Keyes.

He'd offered money, fair market value. He'd tried to side drill any number of times. He'd employed a dozen tactics to ruin and run them off. The Keyes held on. When he'd put the boy in prison, he'd hoped he'd have it then, but that old badger Phil Dexter had taken on a conservatorship, kept the taxes current, and Tyler Keyes still owned the farm when he was paroled.

Not for long now.

By New Year's at the latest, the land would belong to Hendricks, and Tyler Keyes would be gone. In time, Hendricks would find his daughter a suitable—no, better word, a "governable" husband for the girl to produce him an heir. Her spirit was weak. Always had been. In time, she'd come around. Or not. Fate had dealt him a terrible hand, taking his son and leaving the daughter. But he'd played tough and he'd played the odds and knew he wouldn't crap out again. Hendricks wouldn't lose sleep over the girl. She'd end up fine.

Thunder crashed. Hendricks stood and polished off his drink. He glanced at the window, but there was no lightning and the glow of his lamp prevented him from seeing beyond the glass. He left the room, not seeing the German face peering back at him.

From his vantage point on the veranda, Feldwebel Gunter Schmidt watched Hendricks leave the study. Thunder rolled across the prairie. Sent forward to reconnoiter the house, Schmidt had kept to shadows in his approach. He circled the mansion in a wide, careful sweep before moving onto the veranda and risking a look inside. He watched the old man drink his brandy. Von Hofmann had instructed Schmidt to keep his eyes open for weapons, but this?

Schmidt hadn't counted them, but there must have been over fifty firearms in the study, a third of them contemporary. Useful. And more than enough to equip their squad.

Like a boy outside a toyshop coveting the entire Christmas display, Schmidt found it difficult to tear away from the window. When the old man stood and looked out, Schmidt had been rooted to his spot. The old man hadn't seen him and now, having closed and locked the cabinets, was gone.

Things were coming together. Important things. For the first time since the escape, Schmidt was struck with the powerful sense this mission that the Standartenführer had presented them with, this idea that they were not going to Mexico but taking arms inside their enemy's homeland and fighting as ground forces, was something they could achieve.

Schmidt was anxious to get back into the fight. He hated the Americans. He hated them for capturing him, for involving themselves in a European conflict that was none of their business. America. With its bogus democracy, its hollow belief that all men are created equal. As if the peasantry was equal to the gentry, the Arab equal to the Pole, Pole equal to Aryan. The mule equal to the thoroughbred?

Schmidt hated that America couldn't see Germany fought to topple a fractious collection of self-serving, weak nation-states modeled on the mistakes of the first forty years of the century, to create a strong, unified Europe under a single flag: an order of the future. Hadn't America gone after and achieved the same kind of unification during their Civil War? Hadn't they taken this land from the natives because they needed space for their people to grow? *Lebensraum* was the same. The need of the German people for living space in Russia. As the thunder boomed again much closer, Schmidt relished the idea of bringing these hypocritical people the taste of war.

He had been in the German Army for twenty-seven years. With the Standartenführer, he had finally come under the command of an officer whose passion and sincerity for his cause, whose standard set for himself and for his men, and whose willingness to fight was equal to Schmidt's own.

Hauptmann Zundorf might officially be von Hofmann's second-in-command, but Zundorf's mountain climbing utility had ended. He didn't possess the courage or conviction to succeed in the military aspects of this undertaking. Schmidt did. Now, more than ever, Schmidt was determined to supplant the conceited fucking Bavarian in von Hofmann's esteem.

28

Through a dirt-smeared pane of glass in the bunkhouse wall, Wolters counted ranch hands gathered around a table. Their tanned, sun-lined faces bathed in the pleasant glow of a kerosene lantern. They grinned and laughed and passed a bottle of tequila, shooting the breeze as Wolters had always imagined. Would he have to kill these men who, with hats hanging from their chairs, gun belts wrapped around their waists, resembled the heroes of Karl May come to life? The cowboys had been the good guys.

He ducked beneath the sill and whispered to his captain, "Six cowboys. Stupid drunk."

Zundorf patted Wolters's shoulder. He took a hatchet from his belt and handed it to him. "Last resort," he said, before scurrying across the dirt lane to the second bunkhouse where Gauss waited.

"Could you get a count?" Zundorf asked Gauss, noticing that, unlike Wolters's window, the bunkhouse window above Gauss was dark.

"There are seven bunks. All occupied." He added, "One is . . ." he pantomimed the act of masturbation.

Zundorf gave Gauss a ball-peen hammer. Gauss turned it over in his hand. He gave his captain a quizzical look.

"It was all I could find. But remember, von Hofmann's orders are for us to avoid violence if possible. We are not here to take lives. We will get our trucks, food, and better weapons without anyone waking."

Gauss nodded nervously.

Zundorf said, "I'll report to von Hofmann. Be back in a couple minutes." He took off in a crouching run toward the work sheds and garages that lay between the bunkhouses and the mansion.

THE RAIN ARRIVED all of a sudden and steady. Gauss peered through the slanting drops toward Wolters. He waved the hammer like a toy and Wolters grinned feeling sick; his books had taught him what inevitably came next.

ZUNDORF REACHED THE GARAGE at the same time Mesmer and the Tiger forced the lock and stepped aside. Von Hofmann rolled open the wide wooden door, revealing the pair of two-ton canvas covered trucks he'd seen earlier. The word *Ford* stood out in black against the chrome of both their grills.

"Mesmer, get these vehicles ready to go. Tiger, do whatever he tells you."

"*Zu befehl*," they responded in unison.

Mesmer and the Tiger moved between the trucks. Von Hofmann crooked a finger at Zundorf, beckoning him out of the rain.

"I find it remarkable you aren't cold in those shorts, Herr Hauptmann."

"My legs don't notice."

Thunder exploded on top of them and tumbled around the sky with haphazard fury that made conversation impossible for a full five seconds.

"Rain is a good sign for me, Herr Hauptmann. Tell me what you found."

"In the west barracks are six men, awake and drinking. In the east barracks, seven occupants are all in bed."

"You understand, our success relies on the avoidance of violence."

Zundorf did.

"However, if one of them stirs and there's a chance he'll raise the alarm . . . It will be best to leave no witnesses."

Zundorf gripped the handle of the bailing hook protruding from his waistband and gave a single affirmative nod.

Schmidt ducked inside. He spoke without waiting for von Hofmann's permission. "I would report to the Standartenführer that the house is dark. Everyone has gone to bed."

"Any sign of weapons?"

There was a flash of lightning accentuating the excitement on Schmidt's face. "The old man is a gun collector. Trust in the Standartenführer's genius to have led us to such an incredible stockpile."

Von Hofmann wore the compliment like an olive wreath. Zundorf, who should have been equally as glad of Schmidt's discovery, seethed with jealousy. He turned to watch Mesmer. The tank officer lay across the front seat of the first truck, head buried beneath the dashboard. The Tiger stood by, holding some clippers, a screwdriver, and a wrench they'd dug from a toolbox.

"Excellent, Herr Feldwebel. Take me to them," said von Hofmann.

Schmidt stepped back. The Standartenführer faced Zundorf. "When Mesmer has these trucks running, rejoin Gauss and Wolters. I count on you to make sure this goes smoothly."

Von Hofmann and Feldwebel Schmidt moved off into the rain. Zundorf turned back into the garage. Four dirty canvas dusters hung on a row of pegs with a moth-eaten hat and the odd piece of tack. Zundorf grabbed the coats and tossed them into the back of one of the trucks before heading into the rain for the bunkhouses.

He was certain von Hofmann saw through the sergeant's wheedling. Zundorf was an officer; he held a special position in the Standartenführer's trust, not Schmidt. Still, Zundorf couldn't deny the nagging suspicion that at times it was as if von Hofmann was buying into Schmidt's sycophancy, almost as if to pit the sergeant against him.

He rejoined Wolters and Gauss, slipping under the cover of the west bunkhouse eaves. He leaned against the side of the steps to the bunkhouse door. What did it matter, anyway? Let Schmidt play his games. Zundorf was a combat officer. He knew the battlefield, how to lead men, and make them fight. He'd proven this to von Hofmann in Africa.

He freed the bailing hook from his belt and weighed it in his hand. He watched the square of light from the bunkhouse window reflected in the wet dirt beneath his boots beginning to puddle. Watched and waited. He had never killed civilians before. He hoped he wouldn't tonight.

Wrapped in his fleece-lined range coat, Tyler sat on his porch, grimly watching lightning lance the eastern sky near the Hendricks ranch as the storm headed his way. The blade of Tyler's pocketknife flashed in his hand, showering the empty supper plate at his feet with cream-colored curls of wood as he transformed a pine burl into a raven.

Tyler worked the small blade in and around a tiny knot, transforming it into an eye, while his mind cast back to that afternoon. Virginia. In mourning for a man she'd given up all their promises to marry.

Germans killed my husband. Nothing of yours to be sorry about.

Purposely cold. Purposely fenced off.

He whacked the raven's eye from the head, the head from the pine burl, now carving nothing.

A Virginia he didn't know.

You're embarrassing yourself. I just came out to say goodbye . . . It is a lot of money.

He hurled the piece of wood into the rain. It did not make sense. None of it. Especially her last bit about the money. Virginia relished in sarcasm. Those words of hers had that kind of bite. But Virginia hated money. It had poisoned her father with greed. Greed, she blamed for the death of her mother and infant brother. She called money the great American prison. Her prison they'd planned to escape the day she turned eighteen. Tyler had considered her marriage a life sentence she'd condemned him with, but the life sentence she'd always believed her cruel punishment was her father's fortune.

Virginia, today, on that porch, the words she'd spoken, the deadness to him he'd seen in her eyes, was a Virginia Tyler didn't know because it wasn't the real Virginia.

It is a lot of money.

No. Sarcastic as Virginia could be, she would never cut with that knife. Tyler pushed to his feet. He understood. She'd chosen those words because only he would understand her true passion behind them.

Like Grinning Earl Descheenie sneaking the shiv into his hand at the yard gate, who'd attempted to kill Tyler in order to secure Tyler's safety after he was gone. Virginia's sarcasm had been for her father. Far from sending Tyler away, Virginia was calling him back.

Tyler went inside. When he came out, he held Hendricks's bank draft. He shoved it in a pocket. He adjusted his Stetson, grabbed his rifle, and, striding to the barn, met the rain head-on as it arrived.

VON HOFMANN DID NOT WANT to risk the noise of breaking the study window. He and Schmidt circled the veranda until they found an unlatched window. Von Hofmann motioned the bull-like sergeant through and then followed him into the dining room.

From the dining room, they crossed into a parlor and passed into the entry hall. Lightning crackled. It filled the entry hall with color as it flashed through the stained-glass panels that framed the front door. To von Hofmann's left, wide stairs led to a landing where a grandfather clock ticked-tocked at the point the stairway made a right angle, ascending over a dark corridor to the second floor above. Von Hofmann faced the study doors across the entry hall and directly ahead.

Schmidt pushed open the double doors and von Hofmann stepped inside. His boots sunk into the thick rug, a sensation long denied. Carpets filled the house in Kitzbühel. He pushed memories of his wife's family home from his mind. He would never return there.

Schmidt closed the doors and crossed to Hendricks's desk. Von Hofmann watched Schmidt open the desk, produce a key with a flourish—von Hofmann loathed dramatics—and unlock the gun cabinets one by one. Von Hofmann opened the main cabinet to stare at the most magnificent collection of firearms he had ever seen.

VIRGINIA SAT AT HER DESK in the dark of her bedroom, listening to the cadence of falling rain. She set down her pen and folded the piece of stationery along its center. She pinched the crease between her index finger and thumb and pulled the letter through.

Letter? Note, really. She didn't have a letter's worth of words to leave her father. All she had to tell him was she was going and would be pleased never to see him again.

Virginia clutched the folded sheet of paper, turned and faced the mirror. It was too dark for her to see more than her silhouette, but the Virginia she was looking for didn't need light for reflection. She'd stood in front of this mirror innumerable times, and now she visualized herself as she had been. The black dress she'd hated that Señora Gúzman had forced her into for her mother's and her baby brother's funeral. Señora Gúzman had worn Mommy's yellow shawl. She saw a little girl in denim covered with dirt, bits of alfalfa tangled in her hair after the hay fight with Tyler Keyes at the state fair where they'd stolen their first kiss. Her earliest memory: her mother looking something like Virginia looked now, but more beautiful, holding her in her arms before the mirror and saying, "That's you, sweet pea. That's my Virginia."

So many good and bad memories lived beneath the surface of her looking glass. Virginia remembered standing in front of it in the silver luminescence of June moonlight after she and Tyler made love for the first time. She remembered the ache between her legs, muscular and of the body, yet also divine and of the spirit and unlike anything she had ever known possible. Alone in her room, she'd touched herself, needing to make sure what had happened had happened, and her hand came away with the proof that Tyler had been there and joined with her and she'd believed it would be forever.

And afterward: "Put me up in your saddle tonight. Rake your horse and we'll ride out of this hell together."

Virginia had been sixteen for only one hour on the night when Tyler came through her window and awoken her as he'd slid into her bed. They had gone into Fort Sumner to celebrate her birthday the night before. To see "Garbo laugh" in *Ninotchka* at the Bijou theater. Virginia had met Tyler as usual in the back row as *The March of Time* unspooled. They'd laughed as they always did when Tyler read the credits, emphasizing every syllable of narrator Cornelius Westbrook van Voorhis's name. They'd held hands through the segment on the Archduke Otto of Austria, petted throughout the Texas Centennial Exhibition, and kissing, missed entirely the final segment entitled *Crime School,* a fictional case history of a poor boy who becomes a criminal and is sent to prison.

That one might have been worth watching, but if Garbo laughed in *Ninotchka,* Virginia and Tyler missed that, too. One minute Melvyn Douglas was meeting Garbo at the Eiffel Tower and Virginia was threading fingers through Tyler's hair pulling his face to hers, and the next Garbo and Douglas were gone, the theater empty, and she was ready for all of him and the future between them the act would seal.

They'd parked out by the Atchison, Topeka, and Santa Fe Railroad tracks and Virginia had begged for it then, but Tyler, laughing gently, told her she wouldn't be legal until after midnight. Her hand in his lap let Virginia know that waiting was as difficult for Tyler as for her, but he drove her to her father's gates, parked and tiptoed her home in the moonlight.

All through the night, she lay beneath the covers, wishing Tyler could be there with her.

Before dawn, he was.

Virginia wrapped her arms around him, held him close, and as she did, she warmed to his skin and understood he was nude. Tyler's hands slid the thin satin straps of Virginia's nightgown from her shoulders, and as he pulled it down the length of her body, his mouth met each new inch of exposed flesh with luxurious kisses. Their bodies spoke. Virginia's uncomfortable but urgent, Tyler's slow, careful, gentle. The pain gave way to pleasure and Virginia's body came alive. Each of Tyler's thrusts became deeper and more confident. His need to be inside her matched her desire to consume him, and for an instant there was oneness, then both their bodies shuddered and they plummeted headlong into a pool of sensation.

Afterward, they'd emerged sweat-slick and breathless and laid on the bed watching the sky through the window, the stars like a million diamonds spilling from the black velvet bag of the horizon and they recited the litany of their love and their future.

Tyler left on his horse without her, and Virginia awoke with the dawn and stood before the mirror and found the proof of what they'd done.

Thunder and lightning exploded in tandem. When she'd lost her virginity, there had been no blood when there should have, but that balanced with the times there had been blood when there should not. In the mirror, she could still see the swelling and the dried blood from later that morning after Señora Gúzman announced to her father she'd seen Tyler Keyes leave Virginia's bedroom. To back up her meaning, she produced the stained sheet from Virginia's bed. Virginia claimed it her right. She was sixteen. The rights to her sex were hers alone.

Note in hand, seeing memories in her mirror, Virginia remembered exactly what she'd told her father across the breakfast table.

"If you don't like today's birthday, then you'd better not come to my eighteenth."

"Shut your mouth, girl."

"Because that day's the day I leave this prison for good. I'm marrying Tyler Keyes—"

The back of Hendricks's hand struck Virginia's face.

"You want to talk about prison? Good. Because that's where Keyes is headed, soon as I get Sheriff Thedford out here."

"*Daddy*, didn't you hear what I said? I turned sixteen at midnight."

"Señora, what time did you see Tyler Keyes leave my daughter's bedroom?"

"Ten thirty p.m., Mr. Hendricks. God's truth."

"Liar!" Virginia shouted.

Hendricks smacked her again.

"That dirt-scratcher raped you." He went for the telephone.

"The only rape that ever took place in this house was the one that killed my mother and my brother."

Virginia saw his third blow coming. She fastened a furious smile on her face and faced into it.

VIRGINIA TURNED AWAY from the mirror. She slipped her arms through the sleeves of her double-breasted wool wrap coat, straightened it and the dress she wore beneath, before tying the belt around her waist. She put the note into her coat pocket and tied a scarf over her thick, copper-colored hair.

She picked up the small suitcase of clothing she'd packed. Nothing else she owned she particularly cared to see again. Virginia planned to start her life with Tyler without any encumbrances from the past.

No, there was one.

Virginia went to her vanity. She retrieved her wedding ring and her mourning rosette. Was it for Paul? Her mother? Newborn Howie Jr.? Or some forlorn hope Gettysberg uncle? She didn't know if Tyler would understand, because she didn't understand. But Tyler was the only person who could save her from her guilt.

She left her room for the last time in her life, and Virginia didn't consider what would happen if Tyler hadn't understood the message behind her cruelty that afternoon. She loved him and believed, even as his hurt made him try not to, that he loved her. She would stick to him like angry bees, or one of his beautiful, faithful horses. She would change his mind, force him to reckon with the past, and see the futility of defending that farm of his fighting her father. She'd convince Tyler their happiness waited for them, right now, in some other place . . . any place, but New Mexico.

Virginia was halfway down the stairs when she heard a sound behind the study doors.

Ned Gault, his kid brother Frank, and Norris O'Conner were the last three ranch hands left at the table when the mescal bottle gave up its last shot. Thunder shook the bunkhouse. Ned stood and announced he was turning in. When neither of the others responded, he zeroed in on Frank. "It's late. Hit the sack, kid. We got a load a'work tomorrow."

Frank stared out the window at the water pouring from the roof. "Shore is a goose-drownder."

Norris rose from the chair beside him. "No shit, Frank. Gonna wash the piss off right my boots if I can't hold my pecker straight."

Norris groped for his fly and stumbled to the door, not bothering to find his hat. He entered the storm. Preoccupied with his fly-buttons, he didn't see the German soldier wedged alongside the six front steps, gripping a bailing hook.

Norris O'Conner walked blindly past Zundorf and stepped between the bunkhouses. Norris got down to business. He sighed. Was giving a shake when lightning ignited the sky, etching Wolters as clear as day as he squatted in the dirt less than a yard from where he'd pissed.

Norris gasped.

Wolters lurched to his feet. Rain ran off his Afrikakorps forage cap and down his grotesquely pale face. He raised the hatchet to strike but didn't, and the man staggered backward, inadvertently adding his own momentum to the swing of Zundorf's bailing hook.

The Afrikacorps captain drove it into the soft, thin bone of Norris's temple. The sharpened tip dug into the ranch hand's brain, killing him. Zundorf let the body fall in a shudder of disgust as Ned Gault stepped into the doorway to see what was taking Norris.

What he saw overwhelmed his tequila-muddied mind with such disbelief he never stood a chance. Zundorf snatched the fallen cowboy's gun. Norris had never been, nor would ever be, quick on the draw. The .44 boomed in Zundorf's hands.

VIRGINIA STOOD AT THE STUDY DOORS. Someone was moving about inside. Could it be her father? She grasped the right-door latch and turned the handle, then paused, remembering she'd heard him go to bed some time before. Whispered, indistinct voices came from behind the door and Virginia recalled her father's words.

Anyone can threaten murder. The question you should be asking is if I'm a man capable of getting away with it.

Tyler wouldn't have accepted her father's money. She'd bet her life on that. Were her father and O'Hara planning another night ride to his place to finish him?

Virginia feared to release the latch. She put her ear to the door. Outside, the gunfire began in earnest.

AWAKENED BY GUNSHOTS, Hendricks peered out his third-story window. From this vantage point, he could see the flash of gunfire around the bunkhouses. Hendricks had seen Ned Gault buy the bottle of mescal homebrew from José, the groom's son.

"Wild kids, want to drink Mexie hooch and shoot up the night?" he said.

Hendricks stepped to his dresser. From the space behind it, he pulled a Remington pump-action 12-gauge.

"Shooting them is going to help?" Señora Gúzman said from the bed. "Come back to me, *querido.*"

"Just gonna put a little three-quarter baby pellet in someone's ass, is all." His hands shook with equal parts excitement and age as he shoved the shells into the breach. "Keep warm."

Schmidt piled the last load of ammunition atop the stack of weapons he and von Hofmann had selected, which lay across a drapery torn from its rod. The Thompson gun was separate from the group, loaded and ready, von Hofmann having rewarded it to the Feldwebel.

"It appears someone stirred," said von Hofmann.

29

Von Hofmann selected a WWI-era Luger. The outbreak of violence annoyed him, but what to expect from this American cowboy gun culture? He chambered a round. He instructed Schmidt to pick up the weapons.

Schmidt raised a hand in warning. He directed the Standartenführer's attention to the doors. The left latch pointed at the floor in a cocked position. They watched it slowly release.

Von Hofmann looked from Schmidt to the Tommy gun.

Virginia retreated into the entry hall, confused by the gunfire outside and the foreign language she'd heard within. The study doors exploded from their frame in a hurricane of wood and lead. Virginia dropped to the floor.

Badly shaken, but otherwise unhurt, she focused on two soldiers stalking from the study. Smoke curled from the barrel of the short one's Tommy gun. As if in a waking nightmare, Virginia recognized their German uniforms.

"Young ladies should be in bed," von Hofmann said in perfect English.

Schmidt aimed his submachine gun at her, ready to finish her off at the same instant O'Hara lunged from the corridor beneath the stairs, his .45 automatic covering the Nazis.

"Stop where you fucking are," said O'Hara.

Von Hofmann fired his Luger. The bullet punched through O'Hara's chest, hurling him into the wall. His blood smeared across the white wainscoting as he twisted and sank to the floor. Virginia screamed.

"Stay down, girl," Hendricks cried from halfway down the stairs.

He fired the shotgun. The spread of birdshot peppered the wall above the Nazis. Von Hofmann grabbed Virginia by the hair, ramming the barrel of his pistol into her throat, pulling her close enough to smell her sandalwood soap.

"Fire again, old man, she dies."

Virginia's eyes focused on her father, frozen behind the shotgun's barrel, finger quivering at the trigger.

No one moved or spoke. The grandfather clock ticked a metronome of perversity.

Von Hofmann's eyes remained fastened on the rancher. "Schmidt, take the weapons and get to the trucks."

Schmidt disappeared into the study. He reappeared with the bundle of weapons and ammo slung over his back. Schmidt kept his Tommy gun aimed at Hendricks as he stepped around von Hofmann and Virginia to exit through the front door.

Lightning flashed. Hendricks glimpsed the silver death's head insignia on von Hofmann's battered hat.

"Who the hell are you?"

"An officer of the Third Reich. Welcome to my war."

Hendricks let his gaze travel from von Hofmann to Virginia to O'Hara, whose blood puddled between his legs and across the floor. Fright clutched at his old heart, weakening his resolve.

"Look, whatever this is, it doesn't have to involve the girl."

"She's your daughter, no?" Von Hofmann watched the old rancher's nerves weaken him further. "You love her . . . don't you?"

Hendricks's face quivered. In that instant, the guiding light of his life snuffed out and lost its meaning: money, land, sheep, and oil, and power—controlling people, building an empire from nothing—a wisp of smoke. All that remained—the true light, the light of heaven—was the child he had made and loved as strongly as any father ever loved a daughter. The child he had turned his back on, hated, and beaten. In this split second, he didn't know why. He spoke her name. A kind of one-word apology trying to recapture and pass to her the emotions he'd had the first time he'd put voice to it.

Their eyes connected. The only emotions left: sorrow and regret.

Von Hofmann saw this and used it. "There's no way you'd ever pull that trigger." Moving the Luger, he fired.

His first bullet blasted through Hendricks's shoulder, knocking him backward across the stairs. Virginia cried out. Two more fast shots from von Hofmann chased Hendricks crawling around the corner and out of sight.

Virginia tried to fight free from the SS-Standartenführer's grip, but von Hofmann wrestled her around and hauled her through the front door into the violence of the storm.

"You don't have to do this. Let me go. I can't do anything to you."

Too bad for her, death would ensure that. But as von Hofmann increased pressure on the trigger, lightning flashed. Virginia's face, upturned, twisting back, illuminated in electricity. Oval and unblemished. Rose paint-stroke lips. High, rounded cheeks. Eyes of turquoise green framed by thick red hair that was flame against the night, and those pleading eyes pulling him into their pools to drown with her.

His heart froze. He hated drowning, knew it lurked with his death, but he hated losing her more. His finger slackened. He couldn't destroy her.

Not again.

Cold rain pummeled Tyler as he arrived at Hendricks's gates. Thunder bellowed and jagged lightning leaped to the sky, casting the massive iron letters in white-hot brilliance. Tyler stood in his stirrups and skewered the bank draft on a spear-tipped fence post. The crack of a distant rifle grabbed his attention. Not many good reasons for that this time of night. Storms tended to bring out the worst in people. He rode hard through the gates. The gunfire increased.

HENDRICKS LEANED AGAINST THE WALL of the second-story hallway gripping his shoulder that throbbed numbness to searing pain in time with his hammering pulse. His hand soaked with blood and he pulled it away from the wound. He looked around, panicked and confused. Oil paintings and photographs depicting his ancestors, his life, and his family adorned both walls. The old man sucked deep breaths, desperate to fight off enclosing shock. He couldn't recognize any of these faces pulsing at him from each side. His sixty-seven-year-old brain had snapped and he didn't understand his situation. Nothing meant what it should.

Soldiers? The war? They couldn't be, but who were they?

Why did they have his baby girl?

He'd ask his wife. She'd have the answer. She always had the answer. He tried to single out her portrait face, but her colors mixed and swirled and burned before his eyes.

Hendricks needed something to anchor on. He found it in the 12-gauge hanging from his hand. Stop them. Kill them.

He pushed from the wall. He tottered to the window at the hallway's end. He smashed the glass with the gun butt. He tumbled onto the veranda roof. The drenching rain invigorated him.

SCHMIDT RELOADED the Tommy gun on the front steps as von Hofmann dragged Virginia across the veranda and took cover beside him. The Standartenführer looked down the road that led from the veranda straight off the property. Zundorf, Gauss, and

Wolters had taken position behind a short wall of fertilizer drums. With guns recovered from the bunkhouse cowboys, they traded fire with a group of Mexican workers moving through two large corrals on the left, but a moment later, the Germans were pinned down and out of bullets.

"Where are my trucks?" von Hofmann said.

As if in answer, the two trucks roared from the garage, Mesmer behind the wheel of one, the Tiger at the wheel of the other.

The trucks careened through the mud and rain. Zundorf barked, "Use the trucks and fall back."

Wolters and Gauss followed his example, scrambling from the drums to the cover of the trucks. The Mexicans' guns hurled lead after them as the Nazis moved with the trucks toward the veranda.

The trucks maneuvered into position on the lane in front of the mansion, fifty feet from the veranda steps. Three Mexicans with rifles dashed forward across the last corral. Schmidt pulled back the bolt on his Tommy gun and rushed to meet them.

"March." Von Hofmann pushed Virginia off the veranda ahead of him.

ONE HUNDRED YARDS AWAY, Tyler reined his horse alongside a row of stables. The horses inside the stalls were jittery. Their nervousness affected Tyler's bay, making it stamp its hooves. Tyler slipped from the saddle and roped him to a stall door. Tyler didn't care what had motivated this fight or who was fighting. All that mattered was Virginia's safety.

He drew his Winchester from its scabbard and went forward on foot. His nerves hummed in anticipation of violence. It made Tyler hyperaware of his life and his surroundings and the colors of things, adrenaline making them bold in the rainy darkness as he approached the stable's corner.

Two corrals spread between his position and the mansion. Tyler could see the flash of gunfire. He was filled with the crazy urge to race out shooting. He fought it back. Leaned out a little farther to get a better view of the house. Some type of machine gun barked, cutting apart three Mexicans inside the far corral.

Time to move.

Tyler threw himself over the first corral fence. He sprinted fifty yards through rain and carnage toward the last Mexican huddled, eyes closed, behind a water trough. The man's rifle, butt-down in the sludge, rising between his legs so that the barrel touched his lips. The Mexican's lips moved in prayer. Bullets whiffed past Tyler's ears as he belly-flopped to the mud beside the man whose dark eyes popped open. Heavy raindrops hitting the overflowing water trough splashed the Mexican's face with a constant spray.

They shared a frightened look. "Who the hell are these guys?" said Tyler.

The Mexican hadn't listened, didn't understand, or plain didn't care. He screamed as he rose and fired at the trucks. Three bullets hit him in the space of two seconds. His legs buckled, and he fell over backward, dead before he hit the ground. Lead continued to chase the dead man, and Tyler hugged the wet, sheep-shitty earth, gritting his teeth at the sound of bullets whining overhead.

Tyler waited until a break in the gunfire. He levered his Winchester and pushed to one knee to return fire. In the instant that it took his eye to find a target, he came unstrung by the realization he was aiming at Virginia.

"Shit."

Tyler's rifle shook in his grip. He watched von Hofmann throw Virginia into the rear of the second truck.

LIGHTNING FLASHED. Schmidt saw Tyler. His Tommy gun spit lead, driving Tyler back behind the trough.

Von Hofmann lunged to the cab of the second truck. "Tiger, in the back with the girl! Schmidt, the front with me! The rest of you, let's move!"

Zundorf flashed jealous eyes at Schmidt, who continued to fire at the trough as, responding to the Standartenführer's orders, Gauss and Wolters piled into the rear of the first truck. Mesmer put it in gear and hit the gas. Schmidt gave up on Tyler and, hoisting the bundle of weapons and ammunition into the cargo bed, ducked to the cab and climbed behind the wheel of the second truck.

HENDRICKS, SLIP-SLIDING ACROSS WET SHINGLES, had to act fast. His vision was fading from blood loss, but he could see enough to pick out von Hofmann as the Nazi levered into the passenger side of the second truck.

BOOM. Hendricks fired, riddling its side with birdshot. As the second truck moved after the first, von Hofmann gripped the door with one arm, swinging his Luger around, following the path of his eyes as they picked out Hendricks who, having slipped to a sitting position with the recoil, frantically tugged his shotgun's pump.

Von Hofmann squeezed the trigger three times, each shot tearing into the old rancher's torso.

Virginia wailed.

Hendricks flopped onto his back. Caught by gravity, he slipped to the edge of the veranda before plummeting from the roof to plop raggedy and lifeless into the mud.

TYLER ROLLED FROM BEHIND THE TROUGH. He spun under the corral fence onto the road and found his feet as the first truck bore down on him. The distance between Tyler and the truck was less than ten yards as he let his Winchester blaze. His lead shattered the windshield. A bullet found Mesmer on a ricochet, plinking into his abdomen. The truck went out of control, passing Tyler within inches.

Inside the covered truck bed, Zundorf and Wolters hit the deck, Tyler's bullets whizzing around them like a swarm of hornets.

Gauss fought his way around Mesmer, bloody and groaning. He grabbed the wheel and regained control of the vehicle. Tyler spun to face the second truck.

Von Hofmann extended his arm out the window. He drew a bead on Tyler, but as he pulled the trigger, Schmidt accelerated. Von Hofmann missed his shot.

Tyler's Winchester slipped from his grip as he rolled back to his feet. The second truck whooshed past, its tires spraying mud. With no time to retrieve his weapon, Tyler ran after the truck, his mind set on saving Virginia.

"Tyler!"

The truck splashed into a deep rut. Schmidt ground the gears as he downshifted. He floored the gas pedal, the wheels spinning wet and muddy for a couple seconds, and then the truck lurched forward. Those three seconds were all Tyler needed. He leaped for the truck's rear gate. Inside, the Tiger wrestled Virginia to hold her back.

"Help! Tyler!"

Tyler seized a handful of the Tiger's sleeve and pulled him off balance.

"Jump, Virginia! Now!"

Virginia lunged for freedom, but the Nazi viciously elbowed her with his free arm, toppling her deeper into the truck. Tyler cocked a fist, but the Tiger struck first. He pounded Tyler's jaw with jackhammer force. Cloth tore. Tyler flew from the back of the truck. He hit the rain-running earth with only a fragment of the Tiger's cuff in his hand.

Virginia fought her way to the gate. Her eyes met Tyler's. She cried out for him. The Tiger grabbed her again and yanked her back.

Tyler pushed out of the mud as, engines roaring, the two trucks ran parallel up the road. The truck carrying Virginia accelerated into the lead, and the madness of the storm swallowed them both.

Panic set in. The fragment of the Tiger's uniform fell from Tyler's fingers. He sloshed back for his rifle—losing his footing, falling twice before finding it—and chambering a round, he brought it to his shoulder. Nothing he could do. The trucks and Virginia were gone.

Tyler fired into the rain. Shot after shot after shot until he was empty and howling with impotent rage to the uncaring tempest.

Slowly, he took in the ranch around him. A scatter of bodies lay out by the bunkhouses. A half dozen more in the corrals. He was the only survivor. He and Virginia. But who were these killers? Why had they taken her—and where?

Only one reason violent men steal a woman.

He'd learned enough in prison to know men's basest desires, and how long they would make them last before a ruined body was killed and tossed. If Tyler would see Virginia again, he had to take pursuit, and now.

30

TYLER SPLASHED BACK through the mud to his Stetson. He snatched it, fit it on his head, and turned toward his horse. Lightning flashed, revealing Hendricks's body. He looked at the corpse. What the hell had happened here? But Hendricks couldn't reveal the answer, and Tyler didn't have time to let it matter.

He started toward the corral. A flicker of movement from behind the house caught Tyler's attention, and Tyler swept his rifle around as he pivoted, only to discover a group of Mexican women converging from the peasant shacks out back. He could guess their emotions as they stalked toward him. He lowered his gun.

He called to Señora Gúzman. "They've taken Virginia. I'm going after her."

She didn't respond. No one did. They kept stalking forward.

The sound of something spoken in Spanish rose from them, one voice building on another, each taking up an indistinct chant. They were calling him something. Tyler shifted his eyes from the women back to Hendricks's body. And Tyler understood.

"Wait a minute. This isn't what it looks like."

"*Asesino!*" Señora Gúzman led them in shouting. Murderer!

Tyler glimpsed knives, and tools, and stones clutched in their hands.

"*Asesino! Asesino!*"

"Look," he said, sidestepping in the direction of his bay, "this has nothing to do with earlier. I just got here."

The women, loved ones dead around them, didn't listen. They would avenge themselves on Tyler Keyes. A rock flew from their midst. It struck Tyler in the chest. Others glanced off arms and shoulders. The women rushed forward. Tyler ran. He vaulted the corral fence. The screaming women chased him with a hail of lethal projectiles. The handle of a spinning knife hit him with little force, but the rocks and chunks of brick that pounded his back and shoulders hurt like hell.

Señora Gúzman found Hendricks's shotgun. She aimed and fired.

Birdshot spattered his range coat, nicked his neck and jaw. He grabbed his horse, freed the reins, and whipped into the saddle as a bottle shattered against the stable wall. A shard of flying glass embedded into the back of his hand. He flicked it away, his heels jabbed his spurs, and the horse took off at a run.

Señora Gúzman watched Tyler flee. Tyler hadn't shot Hendricks, but she didn't care. The man she loved was dead. She could not let Tyler escape. He'd ruined her life and now she would ruin his. He must die. While the other women let their anger turn to grief and went to the bodies of their husbands and sons, she gripped the shotgun in one hand, pulled her skirt past her knees with the other, and ran for the road. She drew on hate to give her strength and as she ran, her yellow silk shawl flew from her shoulders. The hammering rain beat it into the ground.

Tyler hurtled headlong into the rain. He passed beneath Hendricks's gates and lightning leaped across the sky to show the emptiness of the flooded crossroads ahead. Tyler wheeled the bay in a spray of water, unsure of which way to continue. Maintaining the same direction on the main access road out of the ranch would lead southeast about forty miles to Roswell. If they'd driven north, they'd hit Vaughn in three miles. If they'd left the road and cut across the prairie west, in five miles lay the town of Corona, a small trading center on the edge of the Cibola National Forest.

Without knowing the men or motive behind this violent set of events, Tyler had no way of knowing which way they'd run. He wrenched his horse around in widening circles, hunting for tracks, but the gravel roads flowed with rivers of rainwater. Tire tracks were nonexistent.

Then he saw it. Rainbow swirls of oil. His bullets fired at the escaping trucks had been effective. He'd damaged one of the vehicles, and its oil leak continued north. Tyler urged his bay forward, but the horse faltered. The sound of a kiss was the command to run, but all it earned was the animal to hobble forward and stop.

The bay had thrown a shoe. Tyler swung from his saddle. His horse, naturally built "downhill"—high in the croup and low at the withers—made the bay a long strider. It tended to overreach its hind foot when nervous or overexcited causing the rear shoe to collide with the front heel. At the first sounds of gunfire, Tyler had heard the metal-on-metal ring of his horse's shoes. Add human fear, death, and Tyler's urgency for pursuit to the bay's emotional mindscape, pile on that the violent weather, and Tyler was lucky the bay had thrown only one.

Until Tyler replaced it, he wouldn't be able to ride. Unable to ride, he'd never catch up. Tyler crouched in the rain-running gravel and lifted the bay's left foreleg. The shoe was gone. That was good. Ridden on, half-mounted shoes drive nails into a horse's sole, laming it out of commission for days until they heal. That hadn't happened. Upside. The downside was, hard riding in the rain had softened its hooves. Once the shoe was gone, the over-reaching hind foot had kicked off a chunk of hoof to go along with the iron. That meant the right front shoe needed pulling and that hoof short-clipped to even out the two front legs, or as his father used to joke, he'd only ride around in circles.

Tyler tore a swath of lining from his coat. Tore it into strips. He packed the sole and wrapped the hoof, pastern, and fetlock. He stroked his bay's nose and apologized, pulled the reins over its head, and led the bay forward on foot.

Señora Gúzman reached the gates, mud-splattered and winded. The crossroads had flooded as they did in the strongest storms every few years, and the river of water raged over her ankles, pulling hard. She grabbed the gates to keep upright.

She had never wanted to believe what her mother had told her when, at fourteen, she'd given birth to a beautiful baby boy outside of wedlock. *"Dios y la Sagrada Madre te a abandonado."* God and the Sacred Mother have abandoned you. Señora Gúzman's mother took the infant outside their Juárez shack. Leaving her daughter alone and crying, begging God for forgiveness, she drowned it in a puddle.

"Señor Gúzman" was a brand name on an empty coffee can. She didn't know which man or teenager she'd been selling her sex to had impregnated her. She took the coffee man's name and left Mexico, refusing to believe her mother's words could follow her into New Mexico. She worked as a wet nurse—the only skill she had—and for a time, life had been perfect.

But it had been without God.

Dios y la Sagrada Madre te a abandonado.

The force of the floodwater grew strong. It was dangerous to remain at the gates. Señora Gúzman would find her shawl, cover the face of the man she loved, and do what she should have done from the beginning. She would turn her back on God and ask the devil to help get her revenge.

PART TWO

"The true man wants two things: danger
and play. For that reason he wants woman,
as the most dangerous plaything."

— Friedrich Nietzsche

31

THE SMELL OF SHEEP and their urine, reminders of the truck's last occupants, assailed Virginia's nostrils. She huddled in the farthest corner against the back of the driver's compartment. The thrum of wind and rain added to Virginia's misery as she recalled the foul way the German seated by the gate had handled her into the truck. The pressures of his grip, the rubbing of his fingers, the private places they touched: all suggested more than a soldier's brutality. He exuded sexual violence the way garbage exudes stench. She caught his eyes shamelessly caressing the curve of her breasts. Virginia pulled the edges of her wrap coat together, her knees to her chin, covering her body. She fought for calm.

"*Ich werde sie noch sehen, da bin ich mir sicher.*"

"What?"

He smirked. "You would like to know?"

Virginia clenched her jaw.

"I said, 'I will see them yet, I am sure.'" He wiggled his eyebrows.

Virginia's stomach knotted with disgust. She had to control her emotions. Only then could she take the offensive, give as much as she got and maybe, if she could find out what this was all about, find a way around this vile man and affect her escape. It wouldn't be easy. Virginia had never known fear as she did now. Horrific images of the last hour clawed their way forward. Nazis gunning down O'Hara in the house. The ranch hands in the yard. Her perception of the world obliterated in a deluge of gunfire and blood.

Her father. The mighty H. Howard Hendricks. Virginia had despised him for so long, and yet, as she'd watched him torn down by bullets, his final act on this earth was the sacrifice of his life in a futile attempt to save hers. She couldn't put a name to her strange sorrow and angry loss. She could only hear his voice. *Virginia.* He called her by name for the first time in years. It was the last thing she would ever hear him say. Death should not have come for him this way. It shouldn't have come for any of them.

Virginia prayed for strength. She prayed for guidance and clarity. She prayed for justice and in her prayer, she prayed for Tyler, but between her and the comfort of God loomed the face of the Nazi officer who had taken her. Virginia couldn't shake the hold of his dead, gray stare. She was one more dead thing in his sight. Then the lightning flashed and her eyes had brought life back into his and he'd spared her.

Since childhood, Virginia had noticed how men looked at her. All men. It was primal and had everything to do with her female sex. In her teens, she'd learned to distinguish the intent in strangers' eyes, between the male admiration of most and the animal lust typified by men like the beast guarding her in the truck. She found neither in how the Nazi officer had looked at her. His murderous eyes had transformed into heartbreak. She'd seen that look once before in Tyler's face in court the morning of his sentencing. It was the heartbreak of love.

So powerfully did this notion strike Virginia that the downy hair on the nape of her neck tingled and stood on end. Her pulse quickened and an instinctive warning surged from her subconscious with tidal-wave force. It drowned all ideas and memories. The concept of time, past, present, and future engulfed by visions of blood. Her blood pouring from her body while she lived. That officer: his cold eyes changed to fire, burning with heartsick hunger—a screaming, sick, tragic savagery.

The wave washed over her and withdrew. It left Virginia strangely centered, adrenaline-full of the determination to fight.

"You disgust me. You're not soldiers, you're murderers and thieves."

"Is there a better way for escaped prisoners of war to behave in the land of their enemy?"

"I'll tell you one thing: whatever happens to me, you'll never get out of this land alive."

"Do not worry so about us. We will manage. But maybe you would like to guess what will happen to you, *Fraulein*? That game might be fun to play."

"Games are for children. If you want to play, play with yourself, pig."

The Tiger scowled. He rubbed his thumbs over the joints of his scarred fingers.

"What? You want to hit me again, tough guy?"

"If you don't keep your mouth shut, I'll do more than that."

Virginia didn't doubt he meant it, but she had to keep pushing.

"As if you'd be brave enough to do anything without his orders." She cocked her head at the cab where his commanding officer sat.

The Tiger curled his lip.

"You're nothing without him. You don't know why he took me or where we're going."

The Tiger chuffed, turned and looked at the rain, the following truck.

I'VE BECOME A MURDERER. Hauptmann Fritz Zundorf loaded ammo into the firearms inside the back of the second truck. *A cold-blooded murderer of civilians.*

He'd killed at least four innocent men tonight and that, his heart told him, was murder. Not that his ego didn't protest self-defense. This is war. Given the chance, they would have done the same to him. What of it, anyway? It's not like killing men was a new experience. Zundorf couldn't count the number of enemies that had fallen to his guns. He didn't lose sleep over it. As an officer in the Deutsche Wehrmacht, it was his job to destroy the enemy in combat.

But the enemy had always been in uniform. That enemy understood the stakes.

A hook through a man's brain. Bullets fired into the bodies of drunken cowboys. Murder, not warfare. These men tonight weren't soldiers. They died at home. Some in their beds. None on the battlefield.

Zundorf refused this. He was doing his duty. Hadn't he, the day he'd enlisted, sworn an oath to follow the orders of his superiors and fight to win the war for Germany and the Third Reich? Wasn't following von Hofmann the fulfillment of his oath? Of course it was. Zundorf understood the importance of the Standartenführer's mission. Von Hofmann was leading them back into the war. While this operation was different from anything Zundorf had ever encountered, no military authority in Germany would judge his actions incorrect. How many times had he called those military authorities hypocrites?

I've become a murderer.

No. Civilian casualties are part of war. They die en masse by each side on every front from the air, from artillery, from street fighting every day. It is an imperfect world. It's why there are wars in the first place. Civilian death, a sad, bloody facet of that imperfection. He didn't ask that cowboy to come piss outside, but when he did, what choice was Zundorf left? He couldn't take him or any of them prisoner. Couldn't let them go. Anything but what he'd done would have jeopardized the mission. *A hook through a man's brain, bullets fired into the bodies of sleeping boys. Murder, not warfare.*

Zundorf focused his attention on Wolters. The lieutenant wore a sullen expression as he listened to the thunder and watched the wind-whipped downpour. "Is everything all right, Herr Leutnant?"

"There was a girl I was acquainted with at university in Heidelberg. We studied together for our teaching degrees. She was a friend of my sister. That's how I was able to meet her. But she was nice to me. I used to pretend if there hadn't been a war, we would have married. It was stupid. Immature. I know I'm ugly," he said and met Zundorf's curious gaze with the look of a man shoveling dirt over the grave of his emotions. "I am only reminded of her because she had a face like this girl the Standartenführer took from the farm. Brown eyes, you understand, but it was much the same . . ." Searching for the word, he circled an open hand around his pale face until he found it. "Fullness."

In the two years Zundorf had known Wolters, close as they'd come in battle, he had never heard the lieutenant offer a single, personal detail of his past. Zundorf burned with a sudden shot of nerves. Consumed by his own doubts and guilt over the killings, he hadn't yet considered the implications presented by von Hofmann's kidnapping of the girl.

Duty, honor, a casualty of war?

Zundorf buried the questions and gave a meaningless nod that served only to tell Wolters he'd heard him.

"I hope he just kills her, Herr Hauptmann. I hope he doesn't do something horrible and make us watch."

"Stop it. The Standartenführer isn't like that. He's a family man. You've seen how he pores over his wife's letters."

"*Letter*, Herr Hauptmann. There is only the one. She stopped writing him," said Wolters.

"Shut up and load."

Zundorf tossed a box of cartridges into Wolters's lap. A guilty stare passed between them. Wolters selected a pistol. He thumbed bullets into its magazine.

Schmidt, like the others, was also curious about the girl, and in a way, his opinion encompassed the only two possibilities for her under their specific circumstances. "If one could ask the Standartenführer a question?"

Von Hofmann shifted his glance from the sweep of the windshield wipers to the sergeant beside him. His raised brow invited Schmidt to continue.

"The girl—is the Standartenführer going to give her to us to 'keep up morale,' or was she simply cover for our escape? Deadweight. I could take care of that if the Standartenführer would like."

Schmidt posed the question openly, his eyes never leaving the road ahead. Nothing more lurked behind the query than his desire for clarification and guidance.

"My plans for the woman are none of your business, Herr Feldwebel. It would be wise for you not to bring her up again," von Hofmann growled.

Schmidt frowned. They were descending the back of a butte and he shifted unnecessarily, the nasty grind of the gears substituting for the snide retort he would have made to any other officer. He'd served under too many men who had used the same imperious tone to cover a weakness of spirit. But von Hofmann wasn't weak. Standartenführer von Hofmann was Harz granite. Like him. Together, the two of them were going to make this thing work. Like inside the house: Schmidt on the submachine gun, von Hofmann with the pistol. Glorious.

It wouldn't hurt to remind von Hofmann. Remind him one more time who stood most faithful beside him, making the mission happen. Schmidt glanced at the Standartenführer. He appeared to have retreated into troublesome thoughts, so Schmidt did not speak.

VON HOFMANN PUZZLED over the question of the woman. Why hadn't he shot her back at the house? Because, like something out of Nietzsche, the omen had pointed her to him. Had he pulled the trigger, he would have destroyed her face without ever seeing it. But lightning flashed. Intervened. She'd looked into his eyes, and there she was a decade ago and returned to life.

Von Hofmann couldn't deny his wife's presence growing in his mind since before coming upon the ranch.

This woman isn't Agna. She never would be—could never be—her . . .

. . . be Agna.

His single-word response to her last letter. One stupid word written without thought. *"No."* And Agna never wrote him again. She kept her marriage vows. She didn't stop loving and obeying him. She'd remained in Berlin with Martin, and remained there still, eternally waiting for word from him before she could move on.

This woman wasn't Agna. So why had the lightning lied?

32

THE STORM SLACKENED to light rain at three twenty in the morning when Tyler hit the highway where Route 285 intersected with 60. The north-south 285, coming in from the east on its way to Santa Fe. Route 60 stretched east-west and perpendicular to the muddy road Tyler walked his bay since Hendricks's. Rain-soaked and miserable, Tyler stopped. On dirt, there had been the benefit of deep tire ruts in the mud. Here was pavement in three directions. He examined the blacktop. Distance stretching over lengthening time, combined with steady rain . . . the oil trail was gone.

Lightning flashed deep within the angry cloud-curtain in the distance ahead as the electrical heart of the storm paused atop Gallinas Peak in the Cibola forest on its race across the state. North, east, or west? A one-in-three guess. Tyler swept the compass points with his gaze. The wrong guess doomed Virginia. His bay nuzzled his shoulder. He stroked its muzzle, drawing on the patience in its eyes to maintain his own.

The bay shuffled its feet and bumped him.

"I'm getting there. Hold on."

Tyler's horse didn't need soothing. The bay was the alpha of Tyler's herd. Well-trained, it abdicated the alpha role to Tyler, but only to a point. The instinct remained and remained clear. Between some horses and men, this led to aggressive behavior. It stemmed from the simple factor that men were men and horses were horses. Tyler's unique affinity with horses removed that factor. His human nature blended with horseflesh. It allowed for give and take. It allowed for mentally connected teamwork.

The bay flared its nostrils. It raised its head, curled its upper lip and flehmened, pushing scent particles through the structure in its nose. Horses flehmen when they search for a scent that interests them. While horses aren't as good at *specific* scent recognition as, say, a dog, their long heads give them a large nasal cavity, making them extraordinarily capable at identifying predators, other horses, humans, and objects. No one would dare tell Tyler dogs were smarter than horses. Horses were smarter due to a herd animal's higher-attuned, sensitive social and emotional intelligence. This gave them conscious command of more facial expressions to communicate with humans than dogs. Even more, he'd heard somewhere, than chimpanzees. When a horse rolls its eyes and mocks a person, or looks down its nose in disdain, it means it.

Tyler loosened his hold on the reins to give the bay its head. His horse walked west with surety and purpose. They merged onto Route 60 and continued walking.

The thunder came with a hollow boom that tumbled across the land. It echoed the sound of the earlier gunfire, and more than anything, reminded Tyler he was no closer to an explanation for the events he'd witnessed since the first muzzle flash. Why had these men taken Virginia? What had they been doing there in the first place? Robbery? A kidnapping plot? Tyler Keyes wasn't Howard Hendricks's only enemy. Could this have been some kind of brutal revenge? Tyler didn't think so. None of these obvious crimes justified the havoc those men wrecked upon that ranch.

Tyler couldn't recall ever hearing of anything so violent happening in New Mexico since the time of the Apache and Comanche raids of the 1870s, like the one that had claimed the life of his great-grandfather two generations before he was born. And that wasn't crime. That was nations at war. Native tribes versus colonizing settlers. It didn't explain what had driven these men tonight to commit their savage acts.

Or did it.

War.

Tyler leaped for the truck's rear gate. Inside, a figure wrestled Virginia to hold her back.

"Help! Tyler!"

Tyler seized a handful of the man's sleeve—a uniform sleeve—*and pulled him off balance.*

"Jump, Virginia! Now!"

Virginia lunged for freedom, but the man—a soldier—*elbowed her with his free arm, toppling her deeper into the truck. His fist pounded Tyler's jaw. Cloth tore and Tyler hit the rain-running earth with a fragment of the man's cuff.*

He'd seen a ribbon on the cuff. On it, a word . . .

Afrikakorps.

The men who'd taken Virginia were enemy soldiers. Nazis.

A sickening fear overcame Tyler. He recalled hearing about the PW camp at Santa Rosa. How farmers in Guadalupe, San Miguel, here in De Baca County, could get cheap German field help to replace their own workers fighting the war. It was an easy guess this group of men were escaped prisoners of war, and more than a guess, Tyler understood by their murderous actions they would never allow Virginia to survive. If the Army or the FBI caught them, they would fight it out, using Virginia as their shield. And men like this, if they ever made freedom having stolen her for the only purpose desperate men steal a woman—they would kill her out of hand.

33

*I*N C*ARTWRIGHT*'S DREAM, *Galgo cut sign, teaching him. He spoke to him about the wind, and how to read its message of time on hoofprints in the sand. About the hoofprints, and how they told more about the men who rode horses than anything ever printed in words. He showed Cartwright how a trampled patch of grass told a story about the older golden-haired girl twisting from her captor's saddle. How a wild sage became her hiding place where her frightened fingers snapped off the ends of stems. A frightened child wanting to run, but knowing she could not leave her sister to the bandits who searched the dark and cursed. The old Apache spoke these words not to the young trooper Cartwright who'd been there and had seen it, but to the Cartwright of the FBI as he and Galgo sat in his Packard waiting for von Hofmann and the other escaped prisoners to get off the Greyhound bus in El Paso near the Mexico border crossing.*

The buses came and went. In each of them, Cartwright saw the Nazis visible through the windows as they pulled into the terminal, but each time a bus emptied all its passengers, the Nazis were never among them. They disappeared only to turn up, visible again, through the windows of the next bus.

The buses came and went.

Cartwright was unconcerned. He continued his conversation with Galgo. He told the Apache that the older girl surrendered before dawn and rejoined her abductors. He read this in the sign. Sign that gave no indication of a struggle or a chase, just a faint trail of footsteps back to the bandits' horses. Galgo approved. He asked Cartwright if he wanted to go on. As is the way of dreams, with his yes, Cartwright was again young.

THE SUN DROOPED in the colorless Mexican sky, and the afternoon heat hammered its last hour across the anvil of their backs. Cartwright and Galgo worked their way through the red volcanic rubble toward the crest and the culmination of their journey together.

"They're right up ahead, aren't they?" Cartwright said.

Galgo handed him his caliber .30 model 1903 Springfield rifle. Cartwright's hand shook as he took his weapon. Could he kill a man?

"Maybe we should try to bargain for the girls."

"That is not a choice these men consider. Peace for them is all of us dead. You, me, and the two golden-hairs."

Cartwright watched him pull the beaded leather sheath off his own rifle. One braid of black human hair and another of brown hung from the harness buckle. Galgo stared at the weapon as a supplicant might stare at the cross. When he spoke again, it seemed to Cartwright he also spoke to his gun.

"The Apache knows no pity. Our name means 'the enemy.' We have already won our fight with them."

Galgo smiled a smile Cartwright would never forget. It froze time, and for the rest of his life when Cartwright thought of a smile—read, or heard the word—in his mind, he'd picture Galgo's face the moment before he let loose death upon the mountain.

The firefight was brief. An exchange of eight shots so confusing and fast Cartwright never once pulled his trigger, and saw nothing until a horse with an empty saddle, stirrups flapping, ran perpendicular to his sights.

"Did you get 'em?"

"One. You saw his horse."

Two of the bandits had gotten away, but they'd left something behind. A little girl's body twisted between two stones at the bottom of a gully. Much of the white cotton nightgown bunched around her waist was damp with blood.

"Oh, shit," Cartwright said. "God damn! Shit!"

She was the younger of the two. The ten-year-old.

Galgo retrieved her. The child was alive.

Cartwright attempted to give her water. He watched it dribble across her chin and down her delicate neck. A pretty face beneath the dirt.

Cartwright stroked her forehead. He prayed on the mountaintop. Prayed to God to save this girl, to save her sister. And in this prayer he begged for their lives. He swore he would trade his own for the two who'd done this. Cartwright might not have been the law, but he begged God to make him justice.

"You will find the Mexicans," said Galgo.

"What about you?" said Cartwright.

"The little one must not be moved. I must stay. I will make her well."

"It'll be dark soon. Without you, how am I going to follow their trail?"

"You will follow it and you will kill them. When you do, cut out their eyes. They do not deserve to find their way to the afterlife."

Galgo stepped past Cartwright and sat beside the girl. He sang a strange and low tuneless song.

Cartwright pursed his lips and looked at the sky. A fingernail of sun glowed briefly in the center of a blood-red stain of light lying across the eastern horizon. It winked and was gone, leaving Cartwright alone in the sudden desert night.

Special Agent Burley rapped once on Special Agent in Charge Cartwright's hotel-room door. "You awake, sir?"

Cartwright's eyes snapped open. "Am now."

He threw off the shabby covers. Swung his feet onto the floor. He ran his tongue over the front of his teeth as he strapped on his wristwatch. 4:58 in the morning.

"All right, Burley. Good or bad?"

"About as bad as you could imagine, sir."

"You'd be surprised how far my imagination can stretch."

Cartwright crossed the room. He picked up a pack of Old Golds off the floor by the dresser.

"Well, sir, that's about as bad as I'm told it is."

Cartwright already knew the pack was empty, but he stuck a finger inside and searched it, anyway. Still empty. He crumpled it and tossed it in the wastebasket.

"Okay, so von Hofmann's brought the end of the world and we're riding him down into hell. Sketch me a map while I get dressed."

"There was a mass murder last night at a ranch about twenty miles south of Fort Sumner. About twenty men are dead, if the local sheriff's to be believed."

"Got any reason not to believe him?" Cartwright tucked in his shirt.

"Well, it's all kind of patchy. He's going on the report from an eyewitness. He called us before he headed out to the scene."

"Any suspects other than our fugitives?"

"Our fugitives weren't mentioned. Only suspect seen was a neighbor. Name of Keyes. Tyler Keyes. He'd been by there midday yesterday, threatening the rancher's life. Witness also puts him armed and at the scene the time of the murders. She tried to detain him, but he took off on horseback."

"Twenty dead? Sounds excessive for one man. Sheriff must agree our Nazis were involved."

"I asked him. He won't. Stubborn on the point. He says this Keyes fellow is good for it. He only called us because that was the drill assigned." Burley paused. "But, sir, his witness also reported a dozen firearms and ammunition stolen as well as two trucks. Even if Keyes were involved, what did he do, drive one truck while his horse drove the other?"

Cartwright grinned, tightening his tie. "And the sheriff said . . .?"

"I didn't mention it and he hadn't figured that out yet."

"I'll bet," said Cartwright.

He slipped his .38 into his shoulder holster. Sheriffs in a town the size of Fort Sumner were politicians, not detectives. Politicians always came to crime scenes with axes to grind.

"Two days I've been hoping von Hofmann would slip and leave me a sign, but twenty people?" He grabbed his trench coat. "Sweet Jesus."

"You agree von Hofmann's behind these murders?"

Cartwright joined Burley outside his room.

"Burley, twenty people killed in one night—if that number is reasonably correct—goes way beyond the realm of any 'mass murder' I've ever heard. Sounds like a battle to me." He shook his head and heaved a sigh, which ended in a hack. "So much for a quiet escape 'Down Mexico Way,' huh?"

They headed for the stairs.

Burley hummed the *ay yay-yay's* from the Gene Autry song. Then he said, "Maybe all the ground patrols and air searches spooked von Hofmann and he got reckless. Decided he better be prepared to fight his way across the border like a soldier."

"Maybe."

In the lobby, Cartwright found Special Agent Torres and put him on Tyler Keyes. "Get his entire recorded history. Means I want to know if he's been in trouble with the law before. I want to know if he's a Republican, a Democrat, National Socialist, or Communist. I want to know the kind of grades he got in school, if he went to college—why he's not serving Uncle Sam and still playing cowboy 'round here—I want to know everything down to the last tooth he got filled."

"And you want it in an hour."

Cartwright chuckled. "I'm a generous man. Take two."

Before leaving the hotel, Cartwright told Special Agent Burley to send the crime-scene technicians from Santa Fe out to the scene before the sheriff made a mess of it. He stopped in the lobby restroom long enough to wash his face and run a comb through his hair. Upon emerging, he bummed a handful of cigarettes from one of his agents coming across the dirt parking lot with a bag of donuts and some coffee from the diner across the street.

Cartwright had already lit up by the time the rear wheels of the Packard hit the road.

They headed down the graded red dirt stretch of Route 84, south toward Fort Sumner. It was still dark, but the rain had stopped, and the morning air blew through Cartwright's window with a freshness that reinforced his belief that nowhere else in America was the air as pure and fragrant as the air of New Mexico. This was never more apparent than after a storm. The crisp aroma of burning piñon preceded the appearance of an adobe hut on the left side of the road. Smoke curled from its outdoor cooking *horno*. An old Hispanic woman feeding pigs inside a muddy pen stopped and watched the Packard pass.

She and her hut were the last signs of human life on the road between Santa Rosa and Fort Sumner. Cartwright sped into shadow-bound cane cactus and juniper-studded plains, he smoked and let his mind focus on the status of his operation.

The fugitives had been on the run for more than fifty-five hours, but Cartwright was less worried now than he'd been at the beginning of the manhunt. His agents in the field, working with local law enforcement, had investigated and then secured every town between Santa Rosa and the Mexican border. Following Cartwright's request Tuesday afternoon, twenty-three agents from the neighboring states were ceded to his control and inside his borders. By eight o'clock yesterday morning, he had sealed the eastern, western and northern boundaries of New Mexico tighter than a coffin.

The Army was out in force. Along with their roadblocks now staked across all US and interstate highways, the military provided dawn-till-dusk air reconnaissance from Clovis Army Airfield. Additionally, an infantry company deployed out of Fort Bliss, Texas, conducted ground sweeps of the desolate areas along New Mexico's southern border, while thirty recruits and their officers in from Fort Sill, Oklahoma, patrolled the Llano Estacado south from Santa Rosa, each one of them itching to get his first crack at the enemy on a home-turf advantage. If all this didn't ensure the job done, the army also provided Cartwright access to a contingent of ten military police personnel from Fort Bliss, who were prepared to step into El Paso in support of the six FBI agents Cartwright had positioned there in case things got too heavy when von Hofmann made his break for Juárez.

Cartwright crushed the butt of his cigarette into the ashtray while inhaling from the next. Until Burley had awoke him at two minutes to five that morning, he'd been certain the hunt for von Hofmann would end in El Paso. He'd telexed that to Washington, and Hoover's office had agreed. They'd advised that he relocate to El Paso after lunch today if nothing else turned up in the vicinity of Santa Rosa.

Something else had turned up. A massacre. The body count estimated at twenty dead.

As Cartwright steered the Packard across a narrow wooden bridge spanning the engorged and raging Alamogordo Creek, he reevaluated what Burley had said about von Hofmann on their way downstairs.

Maybe all the ground patrols and air searches spooked von Hofmann and he got reckless. Decided he'd better be prepared to fight his way across the border like a soldier.

The idea didn't ring true. Sure, a fugitive with military experience would view his escape in military terms, and therefore have a necessity to arm, but Cartwright couldn't accept a soldier of von Hofmann's rank and specialized SS training would neglect the military tenet that stealth outweighs all other factor when moving successfully behind enemy lines.

So what was von Hofmann's real motivation in attacking the ranch and leaving behind a pile of dead like a billboard? *Here I am, come get me . . . ?*

Cartwright tried to imagine von Hofmann's state of mind at the time of the attack. He had studied enough criminology to know a psychological transformation had taken place in von Hofmann and his men somewhere after the twenty-fourth hour of escape. During the first twenty-four hours of any manhunt, the fugitive is on the run, and his actions, defensive in nature, are under the control of his id. The instinctual impulse and demand for immediate satisfaction of primitive needs consumes him. Survival. The fear of pursuit and capture. The desire to put as much distance between himself and his pursuers as quickly as possible dictates his every decision.

Human beings measure their lives in terms of days. With the twenty-fifth hour, an exhilaration of having eluded pursuit takes root in the fugitive's mind. It allows the fugitive's ego to reassert control over his psyche. The fugitive takes stock. He looks back over the mistakes and successes of his first day's run. He begins to plot his ultimate escape. The longer the fugitive is free, the more rational his plans can become.

Von Hofmann hit the ranch last night past the forty-eight-hour mark of his escape. Von Hofmann would not have acted recklessly because he was spooked. He would have been calm and calculating. He would have acted as he did because getting those trucks and those weapons was more important than any need for stealth and secrecy.

Why? What kind of plan would von Hofmann be following that had him compromise his position? Have him give his pursuers a fresh lead in exchange for a handful of weapons and a couple trucks? Why these specific, deliberate choices?

And what about this Tyler Keyes? Could an American be involved in a Nazi prison-camp break?

34

DAWN CREPT UP on Tyler's back in bleak whispers of gray. There had been no more rain since he had started on foot. He entered the town of Vaughn through outlying farms and houses. Elijah Jefferson, a longtime friend of his father, was retired now from the horse trade, most of that business having gone over to Phil Dexter. He ran the Vaughn service station for some out-of-town owners. He had given Tyler his first job with horses at age nine and sold the bay to Tyler as a colt two years before Tyler went into the penitentiary. Tyler saw the Gulf Gasoline sign rising over the far end of the next block and headed toward it.

Tyler made his way onto Eighth Street. A yellow Dodge truck approached in a clatter from the west. Tyler stopped in front of St. Mary's Catholic Church to let it pass. It slowed, stopped. A farmer, his stout son at the wheel, leaned out the passenger window.

"Looks like you had a rough night. Lame?"

"Threw a shoe."

"Old man Jefferson does some farrier work up ahead at the Gulf station. Opens in about an hour."

A black Packard barreled toward them. It blew a stop sign, honked and swerved. Tyler caught a glimpse of two men, over-coats and fedoras, the bigger of the two catching his gaze as they shot past.

"These jerks from Santa Fe. Need to put a light in. Put a cop on it," said the farmer.

"Yep."

The farmer gave him an up-down look. "Jefferson'll fix you right. Get dry. Stay warm and have a Merry Christmas."

A wave. They jounced off.

Tyler didn't wait. He wasn't going to involve Mr. Jefferson anyway. Outside the garage door, Tyler pulled his Winchester. He put the steel butt plate against the lock and drew it back, preparing to smash it.

"You won't be able to pay the damage if I shoot you."

Tyler turned and faced Elijah Jefferson and his black pump-action trench gun that seemed a living extension of the darker hands that held it.

"Tyler Keyes. Hell. Why'ntcha just roust me?"

"Didn't want to wake you."

"I haven't slept since I was seventy."

He studied Tyler with watery old eyes. When he spoke again, it was as if they'd already had half a conversation. "Two Hendricks trucks passed through here a little over two hours ago. One didn't sound too good. Probably won't last much longer."

His eyes challenged Tyler to deny his purpose. When Tyler didn't respond, he indicated Tyler's rifle with a thrust of his shotgun barrel.

"Hendricks finally kilt?"

"He is."

"You kill 'im?"

"Nope."

"Shame. Kill anyone?"

"Maybe."

Jefferson tightened his lips, allowing his gray scrubby mustache to tangle with the grizzle below his lips.

"You're going after 'em."

"They took Virginia."

The old man fished out his keys. "Step aside."

He unlocked the garage. "Sassy ain't in no shape to be going after nobody."

Sassy was what Jefferson called the bay colt when he'd sold it to Tyler and kept insisting ever since. Tyler honored his horse's sense of pride by never speaking its name.

"You'll need another horse." He rolled up the garage door.

"Just a pair of shoes."

"Yep. And another horse for the Hendricks's girl." His dark eyes challenged Tyler to deny him. "Pick one out while I shoe." He added as an afterthought, "They took the county road toward the Cibola. You'll find a couple boxes 30-30 in that there drawer. This type a whisky picnic you're going to break up—only your rifle needs do the talkin'."

35

Daylight returned to the earth with the rising sun. Cartwright's vision drifted through the windshield over the soap weed and buffalo grass, their stalks and drooping leaves glimmering with raindrops. He hoped to hell something at the crime scene would give him the answers he sought. There were too many questions where there shouldn't be. The suspicion there was something terribly wrong with this operation chewed Cartwright's consciousness. It had haunted him like a specter at his side from the moment he'd found Private Veit's corpse dancing with the vultures in that windswept sandstone maze. But try as he might, Cartwright couldn't formulate his suspicion into words. Like his dream of the Nazis on the bus, each time his shadowy suspicions would step into the light and take form, they jumped to another corner of his mind to grind their teeth on his brain again.

Something was wrong. Wrong with von Hofmann—he wasn't following the rules—"Like he's up to fucking-something-else."

Special Agent Burley raised an eyebrow at Cartwright through the haze of smoke. "Who? Von Hofmann?"

Cartwright flashed his subordinate a troubled look. For a split second, it didn't register he'd spoken. "Something's not sticking."

Burley waited but Cartwright chose not to elaborate. "I don't exactly follow, Chief. Something's not sticking since when?"

"Since the goddamn beginning. Since Private Veit. Why did von Hofmann start his escape with a stutter step?"

"Veit found out about the escape, wanted in, but von Hofmann didn't want him. Not wanting to kill him in camp, risk an investigation, von Hofmann waits to kill him after the escape."

"That doesn't take into account who these two men are. Von Hofmann's trying to make good an escape: he doesn't want bodies piling up from the get-go. So why kill Veit at all? What threat could a measly private pose to a colonel in the SS? For Chrissakes, are we to believe von Hofmann couldn't have just bared his teeth and growled, taken care of the kid that way? I don't believe it."

"But von Hofmann did kill him."

"That's right. He drew Private Veit into his confidence, made like he was part of the team, but all the while, von Hofmann has been handcrafting a brutal weapon and waiting for just the right time to murder the sorry sap."

"Great. Then we charge him with premeditated first-degree murder and fight with the army over who gets to buckle the electric-chair straps. How does any of this lead you to von Hofmann being up to something else?"

"The murder weapon."

Burley reacted with bewilderment, but Cartwright gave a grim smile.

"That's where this thing gets weird. Von Hofmann lures the guy out of the camp and garrotes him. Burley, how many real garrote murders you ever hear about? Not strangulation—like a rope, or a drapery cord, a stocking in a fit of passion—I'm talking about the specific Spanish execution method with designed and intentional throat-cutting."

"You hear about it from time to time out of New York, or Chicago."

"That's right. The occasional Sicilian crops up with a piano wire embedded in his throat. But would you say the garrote was the modus operandi for most mob killings?"

Burley raised his eyebrows, allowing Cartwright to answer his own question.

"No, it is not. The Mafia understands the old-fashioned intimacy involved in murdering with the garrote. It is not a weapon you use on the street or with an enemy you want plain dead. For that, it's Tommy guns, firebombs, and stilettos, and that's because the garrote is inefficient and there are too many variables. You need total surprise *and* intimacy. It takes too much time, and it creates too big a mess. That's why the Mafia tends to only use the garrote within 'the family.' They use it to send a symbolic message—not to the guy they've iced, but to everyone else.

"If von Hofmann simply wanted Veit dead, he'd have done it with a shiv or a knife. He could've hit the guy over the head—shit, you saw Veit, he was a little mouse—von Hofmann could have used his hands to snap that neck a'his. Any other method would have been easier, quicker. Whole hell of lot cleaner too."

Burley nodded.

"But von Hofmann chooses the garrote," Cartwright said. "Something Veit has done or said has worked its way so far under von Hofmann's skin, giving him not only a strong motive to take his life, but the desire to take it in the most dramatic way he can imagine."

Cartwright exhaled smoke. "Now picture the murder itself a minute. They get out of the camp, run for a couple hours, leaving no trace behind, and then stop. Maybe to rest—there was water there—so probably stopping for a drink. Von Hofmann steps behind Veit, but the private's not suspicious, and before he knows it, von Hofmann has thrown the garrote around his neck and is brutally killing him in front of the men, making sure by his death, von Hofmann's own message is clear."

"Not to me, sir."

"That's because the message isn't meant for you or me, Burley. He's delivering it to his men. Think about it. Where are the others while this is taking place? Standing right there, watching. Did they know about it beforehand, know they were safe from von Hofmann? If so, the murder was an expected part of the escape they were willing to stop for, get over with, and go on. In that case, why the garrote?"

"The others had no idea von Hofmann was going to suddenly murder the private."

"Right. So now how does the murder play? Picture this: focused on escape, just a brief stop for water, suddenly von Hofmann goes nuts on this guy. You watch as your colonel rips out Veit's throat. All that blood gushing from his jugular for effect . . . He's sending you a message."

As Cartwright took a hit off his cigarette, Burley tried to develop it further. "Okay, so what kind of message would he need to send his men? He doesn't need to assert control over them. They're professional soldiers and he's their commanding officer. They'd follow his orders to the letter."

Cartwright interrupted. "Unless his orders are so extreme as to make loyal officers balk . . . Say, like Veit, each of them believes they're heading to Mexico and freedom. What would be the worst order they could possibly receive?"

"That they aren't going to Mexico and they're going to die?"

"You're being facetious, Burley, but you've hit the nail right on the head," Cartwright said, seeing the shadows of his suspicion coming into the light. "Let's go back to von Hofmann. A member of the SS Security Service, who, we're told, control all Nazi Party intelligence. Their primary function is monitoring threats to the political body of the party from within and without. Von Hofmann is a treasure trove of information, who up to now's been lucky. He's hidden this little fact from us pretty well, but once on the run, he has to assume the worst-case scenario: if we catch him, we've found out who he is."

"Sir?" Special Agent Burley gestured at an Army roadblock they fast approached.

Cartwright clicked his tongue. "I see 'em."

He eased his foot off the accelerator and onto the brake. "With him being a Standartenführer—full colonel—what he knows must be astounding. No two ways about it, von Hofmann has to make Mexico."

The Packard glided to a stop inches before an Army captain who looked to be a year or two away from retirement and a master sergeant who looked a year or two over. They stood in front of two Willys jeeps that faced each other across both lanes but were staggered so that a vehicle, once inspected, could negotiate between them. That is, once the rest of the soldiers moved from behind the jeeps' hoods. In all there were ten wet-behind-the-ears recruits, each shouldering a .30 caliber bolt-action M1903A3 rifle aimed at the Packard. Not one of them looked qualified to use it.

The captain, clutching his sidearm, stepped to Cartwright's window while the sergeant, who carried a Thompson, positioned himself a few feet from Special Agent Burley's window.

The captain rapped on the window with the barrel of his .45. "If you could please roll down your window all the way and show me some identification, sir?"

Cartwright complied. He handed over his leather ID case. With that, the captain said there was no need to identify Burley or search the trunk. Cartwright asked how long they'd been in place.

"The storm made it impossible to get out here until about four thirty this morning."

Cartwright thanked him. If von Hofmann had traveled this way, he'd have passed before these troops deployed. He made a mental note to have them leapfrogged further out. They drove on.

Less than two minutes later, Cartwright formulated his conclusion. "What if, as von Hofmann murders Veit, he tells his men their purpose is not escape, but to stay in New Mexico to fight a suicidal diversionary action while he makes his bid for freedom alone?"

"It sure would explain why he needed the weapons and the trucks and didn't mind giving his position away to get them," Burley offered.

"Sure would," Cartwright said, but as he rolled onto the access road to the Hendricks ranch, his spectral suspicions returned and he wasn't sure he had it right at all.

36

Colonel Marls beat the FBI to Hendricks's ranch with twenty minutes to spare. He'd shared the previous afternoon with a bottle of Ten High whiskey and his telephone. By seven p.m., every sheriff and police station within the state was acquainted with Lucien G. Marls, Lieutenant Colonel, USA. They understood he was the commandant of the PW camp the Nazis they'd been hearing about had escaped, and had been advised if and when von Hofmann turned up inside their jurisdiction, a telephone call to Marls was their national duty in wartime. "After all," he reminded them, "these are my boys, and I'm the one who has to bring 'em home and lock 'em back up when this whole thing's finished." This made sense to the law enforcement officers. In New Mexico, if a convict escaped from the penitentiary, you could bet your life his warden would be in on the chase every step of the way. And that's how Marls's name found its way onto Sheriff Thedford's need-to-know list—right *above* the phone number for Special Agent in Charge Cartwright of the FBI.

Colonel Marls released the top edge of the jeep's windshield as Major Hastings came to a mud-flinging stop beside the sheriff's Studebaker. He waited for his body to settle. He mopped his flushed and sweaty face with yesterday's handkerchief. He felt like canned shit. Too much fucking whiskey. Or not enough. He should have taken a little hair of the dog before he and Hastings raced out here, but he'd shaved the whole dog last night. Any minute, he expected Special Agent Cartwright's Packard to sweep down the lane toward the house, and he hadn't the time, or the inclination to face off with that smart-ass bastard again. All he wanted to do was to talk to the witness Sheriff Thedford had told him about on his call. Talk to her, get some kind of lead, then get the hell out of there before anyone else was the wiser.

"There's the sheriff, sir." Hastings nodded toward the house.

A skinny, old lawman with a face like a melting candle, a little gray Clark Gable mustache perched on his lip, was coming out of the house, arms piled with bed linens.

"Sit tight, Lyle." Marls levered his hulk from the jeep. "And keep your grapes peeled for the Feds."

Hastings bobbed his head unenthusiastically. Marls crossed through mud to the house. He stepped around a body covered with a yellow silk shawl. Marls lumbered up the mud-tracked steps to meet the sheriff on the veranda. They exchanged introductions, a handshake, and Marls went straight to his point. "You said you got an eyewitness, Sheriff? I want to talk with her while you get on about your business."

Sheriff Thedford thought about it for all of half a second, then shrugged his agreement.

"Señora Gúzman?" The sheriff addressed a cluster of Mexican women gathered together with a Hispanic priest. "If you could spare the colonel a minute?"

Señora Gúzman stood up from a wicker chair. She stepped over the shotgun at her feet, and as she approached, Sheriff Thedford explained she'd been Hendricks's house servant for almost twenty years.

"Señora Gúzman, this is Colonel Merles—"

"Marls."

"Marls from Santa Rosa prison camp. A group of German war prisoners escaped from there on Sunday night. He was curious if perhaps you or any of the other women saw anything that would indicate their involvement here?"

"Tyler Keyes did this," she said. "He came in the afternoon. He swore to kill Señor Hendricks. Last night when it was over, Tyler Keyes was standing over Señor Hendricks with a rifle. I pray to God he hangs for what he has done."

Her eyes burned with passion, as if Marls and the sheriff were implicated in Tyler's guilt. It made the Sheriff uncomfortable. Marls was too hungover to give a shit.

Sheriff Thedford thumbed an itch on the edge of his right nostril. "I'm sure we'll all see justice done," he said, "and by my book, it's a long time coming."

He gave Marls a knowing look. "Like I told you over the phone, Colonel. This case is cut and dried. There's been bad blood between Tyler Keyes and Hendricks longer than I can remember and I turned seventy last May. Keyes raped Hendricks's daughter, you know."

"Uh-huh," Marls grunted, not because he cared, but to keep the conversation fluid.

Sheriff Thedford's gaze returned to Señora Gúzman. "Ma'am, you answer the colonel's questions. Me, I left my deputies out at the bunkhouses. There's a lot of bodies out there and we didn't bring nothing to cover them with."

Sheriff Thedford took his leave and headed across the ranch with the sheets. Marls followed him with whiskey-aching eyes as he fished his plug tobacco from the breast pocket of his uniform blouse and chomped off a chaw. He worked the tobacco into the worn place at the bottom of his right cheek next to the gum. He got it lubricated just right before he spoke to Señora Gúzman.

"Lady, I feel like shit today, and I got troubles worse than a bull that wakes up from a night of screwing to find itself in the Juárez bullring. Your sheriff ain't too bright, but the FBI is, and I'm smarter than them. Among other things, I know you told the sheriff some trucks were stolen, and I know you also told him Tyler Keyes cowboyed on out of here on horseback. Now either you're a liar, or you're suffering from what my ex-wife called 'selective memory.' Whatever the case, now's the time to come clean and tell me which way those trucks went."

"You call me a liar? Go to hell, *gordo*."

Marls clutched her shoulder with a meaty hand. He circled her, placing a wall of flesh between Señora Gúzman and the other widows.

"I don't have time to play games with you, baby." He spit over the veranda railing. "Just do yourself a favor and answer my question, hmm?"

From beyond the corrals came the sound of approaching automobiles. They were black Packards. The ache in his head became more acute.

"Tyler Keyes killed Señor Hendricks. That is all I know."

"Maybe, but whether he's hooked in with my Nazis, or your Señor had hisself the unluckiest night of his life, my prisoners were involved. They took some trucks and some guns—right? They went somewhere. Where?"

Car doors opened and closed.

Marls fought the urge to look. The woman was pissing him off. She had what he wanted to know, but the way to get it—the right approach—was out of his brain's grasp.

"Hey, Colonel, what are you doing here?"

Marls turned. The speaker wasn't Special Agent in Charge Cartwright or his sidekick, Burley. Two carloads of FBI crime-scene technicians busied at their vehicle trunks, pulling out the camera equipment and oversized leather suitcases that contained the other tools of their trade. A middle-aged G-man, Special Agent Dunlap, moved to the bottom of the veranda steps. Marls had met him over the body of Private Veit. Special Agent Dunlap was the kind of straight arrow, go-to-church-Sunday bastard Marls's own father had been. Marls liked Agent Dunlap about as much as he liked Agent Cartwright.

Special Agent Dunlap crossed his arms, waiting for an answer.

Señora Gúzman retreated to her seat, the priest, and the shotgun.

"Listen, Dunlap, I take orders same as you. If you have a beef about me being here, tell it to the War Department."

"Does Special Agent in Charge Cartwright know you're here?"

"Who the hell you s'pose I'm waitin' for? Santa Claus?"

Special Agent Dunlap frowned.

"So?" Marls pushed.

"So, Merry Christmas," Special Agent Dunlap said and turned his attention to the sheriff and his two deputies entering a corral.

Colonel Marls smiled. He was free to continue with the witness. He approached her chair. Señora Gúzman was reciting a rosary.

"I want to make a deal with you, honey."

She ignored him.

"Sir," said the priest, coming to his side, "she prays. Give her this time alone."

"Get lost, Padre, or you'll wake up in a bloody heap a week from Tuesday."

The priest hesitated. Marls tensed as if ready to make good his threat. The priest backed off.

The cadence of Señora Gúzman's words never broke. Marls crouched. He closed his hand around the stock of the shotgun. He tried to lift it, but Señora Gúzman held the barrel with her foot. She fell silent. She looked him in the eye.

"You possibly don't understand, this Tyler Keyes is nobody compared to the people I'm after," Marls whispered. "I'm gonna let you in on a little secret. See, I know how the FBI works. If they catch him, they're gonna make a deal with him. Maybe let him off scot-free if he testifies against his Nazi pals . . ." Marls paused, giving her time to go over his words in her head. "Something tells me you wouldn't like that." He squeezed his eyes into devious slits and patted the gun. "Uh-uh. Just wouldn't be the same as taking this and splattering his head like a pumpkin—hell, it's what-all he deserves, ain't it?"

Señora Gúzman's answer was painted across her visage in miniature brushstrokes of tight facial muscles. Tyler Keyes must die.

"That's what I wanted to see." He smacked his lips, sucking saliva through his tobacco wad. "Tell me what you know, and promise you won't tell it to the FBI, and I swear to you on this cross"—he fingered the crucifix hanging from the rosary that dangled from her fist—"when I find Tyler Keyes, I'll present him your bill and make him pay in full." Marls tapped the cross, made it swing like a body on a gallows noose. "When I finish with him, I reckon they'll have to bury him in pieces."

"You'd do this even if it turned out he wasn't involved with the others?"

There came the sound of another automobile.

"If you tell me where those trucks went? I don't fucking care if he's Eleanor Roosevelt."

"Tyler Keyes rode north. He went after the trucks."

Marls patted her knee. He lurched to his feet. Ignoring the priest, who glowered disapprovingly, he strode to the steps. It was a third black Packard. Special Agent in Charge Cartwright was behind its wheel. Marls sucked tobacco juice, cupped it in the middle of his tongue, then jettisoned it into the mud.

37

"**S**ON OF A BITCH," said Cartwright.

He glared at Colonel Marls so hard he didn't notice Sheriff Thedford, who leaped from the middle of the drive like some kind of lunatic rodeo clown, waving a scrap of fabric at a big, black Detroit-built bull.

"Shit!" Cartwright swerved to miss the old man.

He pulled over and parked. "Burley, find out what Colonel Marls is doing here and detain him while I deal with the sheriff."

"If he tries to leave, can I arrest him?"

Cartwright made a snap decision. Marls must have come here for something, which meant if he left, he'd gotten it. "Actually, Burley, let him leave. Then follow him."

"Are you sure?"

Cartwright pointed at himself. *You questioning me?* Special Agent Burley gave a fake smile before focusing his attention on Colonel Marls. Cartwright stepped around the car and moved to the sheriff's side.

"I almost ran you over, Sheriff. It was explained to you, you weren't to move about the crime scene."

"You the Special Agent Burley I spoke with?"

"I'm Special Agent in Charge Cartwright." He pointed to the scrap of muddy fabric dangling from Sheriff Thedford's hand. "Find something, Sheriff?"

Sheriff Thedford blinked. He twitched his hand. "Hell, yes I did. Proves your Nazis were here after all."

He handed Cartwright the torn-off end of a khaki sleeve. Cartwright examined the fabric. A white-bordered brown ribbon dangled, wet and muddy. Stitched across it in white, block-letters was the word *Afrikakorps*. Cartwright clicked his tongue at the inevitable.

"It'd make sense, though." Sheriff Thedford took back the scrap of cloth and buried it in his pocket. "Señora Gúzman claims Keyes rode out of here on a horse, but if he didn't, who drove the second truck?"

"My word, that's sharp thinking. How many dead do we have, Sheriff?"

"Uh, thirteen."

"Not twenty?"

Sheriff Thedford shrugged. Cartwright walked in the direction of the mansion. Sheriff Thedford moved alongside him.

"The family among the dead?"

"Hendricks is, but there's no sign of the daughter, Virginia. Señora Gúzman says she wasn't here last night. I went upstairs. Her bed wasn't slept in. Lucky thing too—don't want to imagine what Keyes would have done to her."

"You've had trouble with Keyes before?"

"Trouble? Six-seven years back, he raped Howard Hendricks's only child when she was just a kid."

"How young?"

"Fifteen at the time of the rape."

"Why do you qualify it 'at the time of'?"

Sheriff Thedford scrunched his face, preferring not to answer.

"Wipe the rat face and answer me, Sheriff."

"She turned sixteen the next day."

"Age of consent, this state."

"And a gentleman waits for it."

"How old was this Keyes back then?"

"Almost eighteen. That's an adult around here."

"*Almost* sounds like seventeen. Not an adult anywhere." Cartwright said, "What did he get?"

"Eight years, state penitentiary. Paroled at six."

Cartwright didn't comment again, and the sheriff interpreted his silence as agreement.

They passed a pair of Dunlap's men photographing .45 caliber shell casings before bagging them. One of the men gave a low whistle and looked at Cartwright.

"Someone's gotten their hands on an automatic rifle, sir. A Thompson, or maybe an M3."

Cartwright nodded, and Sheriff Thedford waggled his head in disgust. "It figures Tyler Keyes would turn out a Nazi collaborator. Just makes me sick. Why, if he was here right now, I'd shoot the son of a bitch."

Cartwright raised an eyebrow. "It's nice to know the law's in such fair and capable hands in Fort Sumner."

"Agent Cartwright, that piece of fabric I found proves Tyler Keyes is a Nazi. Along with that, last night he came out here and murdered my best friend. I am entitled to my opinion without being mocked by you, sir. Do you have a problem with that?"

A crime-scene technician sketching the location stepped out of their path as they came to the corpse of H. Howard Hendricks. Sheriff Thedford was angry and waiting for an answer. Cartwright turned his attention to the body. A puddle filled an impact depression surrounding it. His eyes traveled to the roof, retracing the path of the fall, then over to the broken window.

"This, no doubt, is Mr. Hendricks."

Sheriff Thedford still waited on Cartwright's response.

"Sir, I believe this belongs to one of the Mexican women," an agent said, handing Cartwright Señora Gúzman's shawl.

Cartwright passed it off to Thedford. "Sheriff, you have no legal jurisdiction in this case. It's not your fault and I don't hold it against you, but I want to make it clear where we're starting from."

Cartwright noted Sheriff Thedford's expression didn't change. He'd have to push a little harder. "The problems—plural—I have with you, Sheriff, are that everything you've said and done reflects a total and complete lack of experience and understanding of detective work and the law. I'm sure when Special Agent Burley spoke with you, he told you to wait for us in your car. That was important for my crime-scene technicians, but you chose not to, and your presence moving about the crime-scene makes their job more difficult. This"—he snatched the piece of uniform from Sheriff Thedford's pocket—"is evidence. Not a souvenir. You should have left it where you found it."

Sheriff Thedford's face colored.

"Finally, since you obviously have a personal stake in the fate of Tyler Keyes going far beyond this case, you are unreliable as a source of information. Your opinion—especially when it comes in the form of a threat to commit a Class A felony against a witness and probable suspect in a federal crime—is nothing I want to hear. This case is too important, and every minute of my time you waste, you Christmas wrap for those Nazis I'm charged with capturing."

"If you aren't the most arro—"

"Hold it! That's opinion, and I told you I don't want it." He lowered his voice to its soft, dark, menacing tone. "If this is too difficult for you to handle, Sheriff, and you still have the urge to shoot somebody? Go shoot yourself."

Cartwright screwed a cigarette between his lips, waiting to light it to see if the sheriff wanted to go another round. Sheriff Thedford remained silent. Cartwright returned to a more professional tone of voice. "Thank you for your time, Sheriff. You may go over to your car and relax, or whatever you want to do, until I send you and your deputies home."

Sheriff Thedford bristled. He handed Cartwright the shawl. "This belongs to Señora Gúzman," he said and went away.

Cartwright stepped onto the veranda. Flashbulbs popped inside the house. The strobe of white light through the open door and through the stained-glass windows took the aspect of a surreal echo of the previous night's storm. Cartwright faced the grieving women.

"Which of you is Señora Gúzman?"

Señora Gúzman stood at the farthest end of the veranda, leaning against a wooden post that supported the roof. Her back was to the federal agent. She didn't turn or respond.

The priest walked over to Cartwright.

"Please, sir, she is communing with God," he said. "I cannot allow you men to continue to badger her."

"Really?" He blew smoke through his mouth and nose like some kind of devil. "Well, I can appreciate that," Cartwright said, his left hand disappearing into his trench-coat pocket, "but I have it on His authority that right now, Señora Gúzman needs to be communing with me. *Comprende?*" He snapped open his leather credential case.

The ID always had the same effect on honest citizens. It rendered the priest speechless.

"Señora Gúzman," Cartwright said.

She gave him a reluctant glance.

"I'm Special Agent in Charge Cartwright of the Federal Bureau of Investigation. I'm sorry to interrupt, but you and I need to speak. Right now."

Señora Gúzman considered Cartwright before addressing the priest in rapid-fire Spanish. It was too fast for Cartwright to translate.

"What'd she say?"

"She said that she and the other women have loved ones lying dead out there. She will not talk and neither will any of them until they can attend to the bodies and I can administer the proper prayers."

Señora Gúzman faced the post again, seemingly going back to her prayers.

Cartwright ashed his cigarette. He stared at the tip. He kept his attention focused there as he dropped his voice a few decibels and said, "Señora Gúzman speak much English?"

"Uh, yes, sir."

"I guess she lost her husband or a relative last night?"

"The Señora has been a widow for many years."

Cartwright registered a small look of surprise. What the hell was this woman up to? "You said you couldn't allow 'us men' to continue to badger her. Who are you including with me?"

"The colonel," the priest said. "If you would like, I will try to convince her to speak with you, but she's probably just irritated from her conversation with that rude man."

His voice trailed off as Special Agent Dunlap moved to Cartwright's elbow. "Have a second?" said Dunlap.

"Yeah." Turning back to the priest, he said, "Father, do that—go talk to her. Oh, Father? Ask if she's ever visited the women's correctional facility outside of Gallup."

"Isn't it outside of Albuquerque?"

"The nice one is . . ." He gave the priest the shawl. "I don't want to have to lock her up for withholding evidence. Tell her, would you? And while you're at it, you can inform the rest of these poor women that autopsies have to be performed on every body out there, so they can forget this waiting for prayers. My men will take their statements in five minutes."

The priest blanched. He joined Señora Gúzman and they conversed.

Cartwright took the last draw from his smoke before crushing it under the toe of his shoe. He saw Marls's jeep heading away. Burley engaged the Packard's engine. Patting his pockets for another cigarette, Cartwright faced Special Agent Dunlap.

"Here," Dunlap offered him a Lucky Strike.

"Thanks. No Lucky Strikes in Santa Rosa, if you can believe it."

"Keep the pack."

Cartwright pocketed the pack. He handed Special Agent Dunlap the scrap of fabric and explained about the sheriff. Dunlap didn't comment, and Cartwright asked for the broad strokes of what he and his technicians had discovered.

Special Agent Dunlap consulted his notepad. "Thirteen bodies killed almost thirteen ways in three separate fights. Out at the bunkhouses, those corrals, and the front of the house"—he pointed—"and inside the house. There's shell casing for a nine millimeter, forty-five caliber, thirty-eight, and thirty-thirty. In both the forty-fives and thirty-eights, there's a mix of Smith and Wessons, Colts, Remingtons, and Winchesters. It's going to take some time piecing together who did what to whom. If I may say so, sir, I've never seen anything this big or this violent."

Cartwright took a deep breath of smoke. No one had. Even Capone's Valentine's Day massacre back in '29 had only been seven dead. He picked a tiny grain of tobacco from his tongue.

"What about trucks? The trail's what's most important. Soon as you can, I need to know if they split up."

"That's turning out to be a problem, sir."

"Why?"

"It's not the tires. We've taken excellent casts from outside the garage—where the trucks were stolen—? But the road out of here . . ."

"What about it? Burley and I saw McGregor and two others already going over it when we pulled in."

"True, sir, but they haven't found anything on any of the three roads."

"I don't believe it. With all the rain? Mud ought to give us plenty."

"The roads are gravel. Although the gravel only goes a hundred yards in each direction, the continuing rain after our quarry drove out, worked in their favor. Turned the roads into rivers. There's no sign of anything."

"God damn it."

"Of course, the men will keep spreading out, hunting for tracks in every direction. Something will turn up. Always does. Just hasn't yet."

Luck was going against Cartwright on this one. It was only seven in the morning and he was already worn out by the day. He tried to suck the edge away with nicotine. "All right, just keep at it, Dunlap. I'm going inside."

Special Agent Dunlap moved off.

Inside the house, Cartwright ignored the four agents in the entry hall—tape measures, cameras, bags, and tweezers, finger-printing powders divided between them—and his eyes fastened on O'Hara, the bullet hole in the center of his chest, the pool of blood from his blasted-out back. He located a smear of blood and a single bullet hole in the wall halfway up the stairs. He let his eyes travel to his right, past a spray of birdshot high on the wall, to the thousands of scattered fragments of timber from the blown-out study doors. "Gun collection from that room?" Cartwright asked the entry hall in general.

"Yes, sir," said an agent, filling out an evidence tag for O'Hara's .45.

Cartwright let an image of events construct itself in his mind. He cut sign.

Von Hofmann blows his way out of the study with the automatic rifle. Why? Someone outside the door.

No bloodstains outside the door.

That individual retreated before the gun went off.

Was it O'Hara? Maybe.

Cartwright went back to von Hofmann.

He exits the study, moves into the entry hall. Cartwright looked at O'Hara. *Killed by a single bullet, not an automatic rifle.*

Two guns, two Nazis . . .

All right, so there's two of them. But if they'd used the automatic rifle first, why not continue using it?

"Has that gun been fired?" Cartwright said to the agent holding O'Hara's pistol.

"No, sir, not recently."

If he'd been the man by the door, he'd have gotten off at least one shot. No, he must have surprised them, come out of the doorway he'd died next to while their attention was on whomever else had been outside the door . . .

Cartwright looked back at the smear of blood halfway up the stairs. He looked at the birdshot tear high across the wall by the study doors.

Hendricks, no doubt. He retreats, ultimately onto the roof where he fell to his death . . .

Okay. Rebuild the scene. Von Hofmann chases Hendricks from the study, sees him on the stairs, fires. O'Hara surprises them from the doorway beneath the stairs and the second Nazi shoots him.

But again, no machine-gun bullets. The bloodstain on the wall framed another single bullet hole.

The action had stopped. The machine gun hadn't fired because . . . There is a third individual in the entry hall.

Cartwright created another scenario.

The third individual is at the study door. Hears von Hofmann. Dodges. Automatic weapon opens fire.

No body, no blood—third individual not wounded.

Maybe he heard the bolt of the automatic rifle, dove from the study doors. Regardless, he's on the floor and von Hofmann's man lowers the automatic rifle—a soldier would have the heavy gun, von Hofmann a pistol—to check him. O'Hara pops out. Von Hofmann kills him with a single shot at the same time as Hendricks appears on the stairs, fires, but in haste, his shot is high . . .

So why doesn't von Hofmann's sidekick rake a trail of bullets from the third man at his feet to Hendricks on the stair?

He can't bring his weapon to bear because it's covering the third man, whom von Hofmann is hesitant for some reason to kill.

So why doesn't Hendricks fire again? Take them all out with the spread of shot.

Hendricks hesitates for fear of killing the third man.

Who's the third man?

Tyler Keyes?

Cartwright didn't know much about Keyes, but he was certain from the sheriff's blabber, Hendricks would be all too happy to shoot Keyes dead.

Cartwright squatted where he imagined the third man might have been. He looked around, gauging the angles . . .

A standoff over the third man, but then, von Hofmann does fire. He moves his weapon and Hendricks doesn't defend himself.

The third party was a loved one. Hendricks couldn't shoot.

Cartwright saw it. Tangled amid the splinters on the floor, it caught the morning light like a filament of gold. It wasn't gold. It was a single strand of long red hair. A woman's hair.

An icy wave swept through him. Without a doubt, the daughter, Virginia, had been at home and von Hofmann now had her. One strand of hair and this case was no longer a middle-aged G-man's romantic wish to recapture a lost truth and prove he's made of the same stuff as the man he'd been before.

This was Mexico. All over again. His life had come full circle to hit him below the belt with the force of a runaway train.

Cartwright stood and announced von Hofmann had a hostage.

38

Nestor Cooney, the short, bespectacled bookkeeper for the Hardz Ice Company of Mountainair, New Mexico, kept his office in the far corner of the plant's third-floor storage room, preferring its wooden-shelved dimness and the company of dust motes and mice to the company of Beatrice and Lucille, Mr. Augustus Hardz's secretaries.

Nestor Cooney was a forty-one-year-old study in contradictions, but that didn't make him stupid. He didn't show it, but he knew that the girls made fun of him. The past two Christmas seasons, for instance, had proved humorous at his expense for the two secretaries. He didn't let on, but he knew why. It was last November. Nestor Cooney had returned from delivering bills to the local customers (he didn't trust the US Postal Service farther than he could spit), and, as he mounted the stairs, had heard Lucille's conspiratorial whisper, "It *is* Nestor, as I live and breathe, it is." He crept to the third floor, avoiding the step, which squeaked, and emerged in their little secretarial pen to surprise Beatrice and Lucille giggling over the latest *Life* magazine.

Beatrice shoved the magazine into her desk, Lucille scurried back to her typewriter, and, smart as paint, Nestor Cooney played dumb.

"Good afternoon, girls," he trilled and disappeared into his storage room.

Nestor Cooney waited until work ended. He waited until Mr. Hardz was locking the door before he "remembered" he'd forgotten his car keys.

"How silly of me."

He ran upstairs. He rifled Beatrice's desk. Found the magazine. He riffled that. Nothing jumped out at him. His training told him that to take more time for a thorough examination would provoke Mr. Hardz's suspicion.

Nestor Cooney bought his own copy of *Life* at Woolworth's on his way to the home he shared with his violet-haired older sister, Myra. He barely spoke two words to her over their dinner of ground beef, bean, and chile baked casserole. At midnight, drinking his fifth mug of hot cocoa, Nestor Cooney found the goddamn Coca-Cola Christmas advertisement and understood what provoked those idiots' laughter. He went to bed angry, but as he fell asleep, took satisfaction.

A lesser spy would have missed the magazine and advertisement.

That was last year. This year, what with war cutbacks and all, the Coca-Cola Bottling Company had obviously chosen to cut costs and run the same Christmas ad as the year before. The Jews running Coca-Cola would get another handful of anonymous letters this Christmas too—that is, if the postal inspectors opening people's mail for the government did not get to them first.

Nestor Cooney finished triple-checking the tape on the November receipts. He could hear the girls' little laughter filtering through his door. He knew what went on out there. Mail call.

Nestor Cooney went to the door. A crack in the wood beneath the lock plate that he'd pecked out with a penknife made a perfect peephole. He put his eye to it. As suspected, Lucille and Beatrice were huddled over a magazine, mocking him.

The Coca-Cola advertisement in question depicted a fleshy-faced, rosy-cheeked Santa Claus drinking a Coca-Cola soft drink while making his list and checking it twice. An elf dressed in Christmas green with jingle-bell shoes and beaklike nose waited at the fat man's knee. An elf with the pinched pixie face of Nestor Cooney.

"Nestor Cooney's a runaway elf from the North Pole—That's why Looney-Goony works in an ice plant," Lucille hooted.

Laugh all you want. You two, you're so clever. Nestor Cooney is a "goony"?

Nestor had heard that one, too. He wanted to spit in Lucille's face, slap her around a little like Bogart, tell her she wasn't the first to coin it, either. *"Nestor Cooney is a goony, Nestor Cooney is a goony!"* He'd heard it echo across every schoolyard he'd ever been tormented on. And Nestor Cooney had been tormented on a lot, so there.

Nestor Cooney always kept his head.

He had to. Like Santa Claus, Nestor Cooney had a list of his own. He kept it in a little black leather book tucked in the pocket of his coat, right over his heart. It was a list of radio frequencies and transmission codes. He might be Nestor Cooney the loony elf to his pathetic co-workers at the Hardz Ice Company, but to the Abwehr and, more recently, the Sicherheitsdienst RSHA VI who controlled spying in the Anglo-American sphere of influence, he was Black Bird.

How far he'd come since his student days abroad, studying radio engineering at the University in Munich and flying sailplanes as a member of the *Universität-Segelflugzeug-Schläger*, the University Sailplane Club, between 1920 and 1923.

Germany in the early twenties. Heady days indeed. Never having had a political notion in his life, Nestor Cooney chose the turbulent climate of Bavaria as the perfect hatching ground. Having been unpopular for his entire youth, he simply joined the most popular movement. He could recall as if it were yesterday, standing shoulder to shoulder with over two thousand excited

Germans in Munich's smoky, beer-pungent Hofbräuhaus on February 24, 1920. He had never seen or heard Adolf Hitler speak. The bright red posters announcing the *Deutsche Arbeiterpartei* or DAP's (German Workers' Party) first mass meeting that Nestor Cooney saw plastered around the old town where he rented a room didn't mention Hitler's name. Georg Eisvogel, a fellow sailplane enthusiast, had heard it rumored this orator, Hitler, would make an appearance. Nestor Cooney decided it might prove interesting to attend.

Nestor Cooney's first impression of Adolf Hitler was only a voice. Too short to see over the shoulders of the men in front of him, Nestor Cooney stared through the blue haze of tobacco smoke at the ceiling and listened. From its opening volley of vehement declarations against the Versailles Treaty and the November Criminals who signed it, Hitler's guttural voice swelled with passion. He read the Twenty-Five-Point Program of party doctrine decrying Marxism and capitalism. He spoke out against the Jews. He pitted himself against the government. "No," he cried, "we forgive nothing; we demand revenge! To achieve freedom takes pride, will, defiance, hate, and again, hate!"

Hitler's thundering waves of words crashed over Nestor Cooney, dizzying him in their whirlpool of power. Nestor Cooney shut his eyes and the soaring, eagle-shrieking voice that crashed against the walls of his skull became his own. Nestor Cooney wanted what Hitler wanted. He wanted to be part of the passion. He wanted to belong to something that sounded more magnificent than anything he'd ever known.

"What is beginning today will be greater than the World War! It will be fought out on German soil for the entire world! There are only two possibilities: We will be the sacrificial lamb, or the victors!" Hitler roared to his finish.

Nestor Cooney's eyes slid open. The crowd in front of him shifted. He saw Adolf Hitler throw his arms wide, point the index finger of his right hand to the ground and cry hoarsely: "Deutschland! Deutschland! Deutschland!"

There was an eternity of silence, as if Hitler's words summed up the meaning of existence and, in so doing, had eliminated the need for time to continue. A shock of sweat-soaked hair hung black over Hitler's forehead. His close-cropped mustache glistened in the light. Nestor Cooney saw the future in the now Führer's pale blue eyes and, along with everyone else in the giant hall, he embraced the rhetoric of Hitler. It imbued him with seductive, overpowering sensations of masculine strength. He'd never experienced anything like it before, but hate, he discovered, had been growing inside him all his life.

It was not entirely Nestor's fault. He'd had a bad start and a pathetic, solitary youth. The day he had been born, his father went for a newspaper and kept right on going. A year after that, his mother did her own disappearing act and Nestor Cooney found himself a bewildered toddler in the care of his eighteen-year-old sister, Myra.

Myra was studying to be a nurse. She could barely make ends meet on what little money she made taking in the neighbors' washing and mending, but she was loath to put her tiny brother into an orphanage. During the day, she watched him as best she could while she worked—he only burned his hand on the iron once. At night, she went to school. For the next three years, Myra fed Nestor his dinner, put him in his crib, closed the door to the empty bedroom, and attended night school. Nestor would chase her from the house with squawks and squalls of frightened tears, but Myra didn't do a thing about it. She was doing the best she could.

For Nestor's part, by the time he was eighteen months, he learned that crying didn't bring Myra back. By the time he was two, he could climb out of his crib without falling on his face and wait for Myra to come home in the middle of his floor. If he was still awake, she'd spank him. By two-and-half, he was able to grasp the glass knob of the bedroom door, only to discover it locked. And so, by age three, when night would fall, Nestor finally learned to put his little heart into a locked room of its own. When, one morning after Myra unlocked his bedroom door and released him and he forgot to take back his heart, his personality was complete. Nestor Cooney would spend his life an emotionless, quiet, and lonely, maladjusted human being.

Myra finished night school and landed a job caring for the third wealthiest widow in Albuquerque. At the old woman's death, her children's grief turned to shock on discovering that mother had changed her will, providing for Myra Cooney to receive half of the estate. Myra Cooney converted the bequest to cash and with her brother in tow, relocated to Mountainair, "The Pinto Bean Capital of the World," forty-six miles southeast. Later, she used a portion of the money to educate Nestor and send him abroad.

Nestor Cooney looked at the superior, precision-made wristwatch he'd brought back from Germany. Twelve thirty in the afternoon. By now, Myra would have left the house for her one o'clock hair appointment at Mañuela's Beauty Parlor, as she did every Thursday for the past five years. That gave Nestor Cooney two hours to get home, transmit his radio message, receive his final orders, then put his delivery together and go. The black shoes, gray fedora, and size forty-six long suit were already in the trunk of his car. He'd stop at the bank and withdraw the five hundred dollars transferred into his account from the Banco Nacional de Mexico. He would go to the grocery store for provisions. He would use a ration stamp for gas, and while the Hudson was filling, he'd call the airfield and check on his aircraft to make sure it would be ready for tomorrow. After accomplishing all that, he'd head for the rendezvous.

Nestor Cooney shut off his desk lamp, pushed his chair back beneath his desk, and left his storage-room office. Beatrice and Lucille eyed him suspiciously. He waited until one of them spoke.

"What's wrong?" Lucille said.

"I'm a tad puny, I'm afraid."

"There's a flu going around, you know," said Beatrice.

Nestor Cooney gave her the vague look of a sick elf. Beatrice averted her gaze and held her breath. Nestor remained where he was. Lucille suggested he go home.

"I suppose perhaps I might. Tell Mr. Hardz for me, would you?"

Lucille said she would.

Nestor Cooney left, followed by Beatrice's explosion of laughter.

39

Colonel Marls mulled over this "Tyler Keyes" as he and Hastings sped east along Route 60. He didn't give two hoots about the Mexican bitch and her vendettas. He'd have promised to blow Douglas MacArthur if it got him what he wanted. Von Hofmann was the important thing. That arrogant Nazi bastard wasn't using outside help. This meant Tyler Keyes was after von Hofmann to stop him. Hero shit. Something Marls couldn't have if he was to steal the glory. It didn't leave many alternatives.

Truth is, Marls had only one. The same damn thing he'd promised the señora.

Could I do it? Kill him?

Do I have any other choice? Alive, Tyler Keyes ain't nothing but a fucking nuisance. But dead? Hell, dead, he's anyone I say he is—the inside man, a spy . . . Make it look even better for me . . .

Marls smiled. No one was looking where he'd be looking. Everyone else was hung up on Mexico, but von Hofmann was traveling north. All Marls had to do was locate the Standartenführer, get ahead of him, and set a trap. He'd accomplish it easy enough. A flex of military muscle and he'd be on his way. Have von Hofmann by sunset. If that fucking cowboy decided to show, well, Marls would make sure there'd be enough fireworks to take care of him too.

After reporting Virginia Hendricks's kidnapping to Torres in Santa Rosa, Cartwright turned from the phone and directly bumped into one of his techs. It was the sketch artist. He offered Cartwright a rendering of Tyler Keyes. Cartwright studied it. He'd seen the face before. That morning. The last town he passed through. The cowboy chewing the fat with the two farmers in their truck. As he reconstructed the image from his memory, two details he'd noticed now took on a new significance: the rifle in the saddle boot and the young man's storm-drowned appearance. He'd been traveling long, hard hours through the rain. "Dunlap! Toss me your car keys!"

He caught them from the air and headed for the door.

Cartwright drove Dunlap's car back into Vaughn faster than he'd raced through it earlier.

He slowed, passing the church where he'd glimpsed Keyes. His eyes swept from one side of the street to the other. This time, it was he who obstructed traffic. Vehicles honked and drove around him. There was a horse corral behind the Gulf Oil station at the end of town. He tapped the brakes long enough to catch a look at each horse, but didn't see the large bay that had been at the end of Keyes's lead rope.

An old man came out of the garage and rolled down the door. He carried a World War I-era sawed-off trench gun with the relaxed grip of someone familiar with using it. He narrowed his eyes at Cartwright in the Packard, didn't like what he saw, entered his station office and flipped his *Open* sign to *Closed*.

In Cartwright's book, that earned the old fellow a knock on the window and an FBI credential up his snout. But before he parked, Cartwright looked in the opposite direction, into the plains. Tiny in the distance, he could make out a figure on horseback with a black-and-white paint mustang, trailing behind. They headed in the direction of the Cibola National Forest.

Cartwright hit the gas and cranked the wheel away from the Gulf station. The Packard launched off the roadway, in and out of a drainage culvert, and engine screaming, tires throwing mud and grass, bounced off fast in pursuit.

TYLER WAS RUNNING the horses hard, following the trucks' tire tracks and trying to make up lost time when he heard the Packard flathead straight-eight build in volume, howling down on him from behind. He caught his second glimpse of Cartwright as the FBI agent barreled past on his left then slew the vehicle crossways across his path. He didn't need to see the gun to know Cartwright was law enforcement, but the FBI agent had it out and aimed at Tyler across his hood in less than five seconds.

"Tyler Keyes, stop or I will shoot you!"

Tyler released the slipknot from the second horse's rope that ponied the one animal behind the other. He raked his spurs and kissed the air twice, signaling full gallop. He charged the Packard.

CARTWRIGHT THUMBED BACK HIS .38's HAMMER, but horse and rider were on top of him before he could pull the trigger. He ducked as they vaulted the hood and pounded the earth past him. Cartwright spun around as Tyler wheeled and dead-stopped to face him, his Winchester already drawn, cocked, aimed.

"FBI! Drop it!"

"Can't do that, sir. They got my girl," shouted Tyler.

"Drop that rifle, or I kill you," said Cartwright.

Both men took the best measure of their aim.

"Before I hit the ground, you'll be falling just as hard."

Cartwright was one ounce of pressure away from trading that lead, but he tried one more time. "I don't doubt it, but one way or the other, I'll have your shooting iron on the ground."

"Not happening."

Cartwright's instinct said to shoot now, but he held back.

Tyler said, "Those mountains behind me: that's where they are. That's where I catch them on this horse. Quietly. All you'd do in that thundering rhino is warn 'em you're coming. I ain't the bad guy here."

"Surrender and prove it."

But Tyler, keeping his rifle aimed at Cartwright's heart, signaled his bay backward, dropping sideways in the saddle as the FBI agent's weapon banged. The bullet slapped saddle leather. One hand gripping the saddle horn, his right leg hitched over the saddle seat, Tyler kicked the horse around and like a circus rider clinging to its side, took off on the bay at a run. Cartwright fired a second time, then a third. He would have hit, but his heart wasn't in it. Damn his eyes, but he believed the young man. One hundred percent.

Tyler Keyes must have figured that out, because he pulled upright in the saddle before he was out of range.

Cartwright smashed his gun back into its shoulder harness. His eyes jerked between his car and the horse Tyler let free. The FBI agent removed his fedora and extending it in one direction, his other arm wide the other, he set about wrangling the mustang.

TYLER RODE FAST. He'd known that once the FBI agent had let him threaten him without shooting back, the man wouldn't shoot him at all. It made Tyler grin for the first time in a long time. The tire tracks led onto a Forest Service fire road. He could see that the one truck was again bleeding oil. He followed its path into the Cibola wilderness.

The sun broke through the remaining scatter of ragged-edged storm clouds. Its fire melted across the wet broad back of the Gallo Mesa, seeping into the deep striations of reds, oranges, and blacks etched across the ancient stone face of the mountains before him, like war paint streaking a brave's hard cheeks. The road was steeply graded, but Tyler continued to move with speed. He passed a US Forest Service sign nailed to a pine tree: *Tag Your Buck as Soon as Killed.*

It said nothing about killing men.

40

HEADED HOME behind the wheel of his faded pea-green Hudson, Nestor Cooney was pleased. His departure from the ice plant had been without suspicion, and he congratulated himself for waiting until one of the secretaries recommended he go home. He was on the verge of greatness, something that would help shape the future of the Third Reich. Perhaps the Führer, right at that moment, was reading a file on his agent in America, Black Bird, gazing at his photograph, counting on Nestor Cooney to bring off this operation. Nestor Cooney twisted sweaty palms over the steering wheel.

The nervous excitement bubbling through Nestor Cooney's veins was almost as good as the sensation of flight. Nestor Cooney smiled, faintly recalling all the flying he'd done since September in his Twin Beech. He'd purchased the airplane from an American oilman in Tampico, Mexico, and in accordance with his orders, made diligent practice at landings and take-offs on deserted fields and stretches of highway in Rio Arriba county. The plane waited for him, hidden inside the private hanger he'd rented in Albuquerque, waited for him and tomorrow night's historic flight.

Nestor Cooney turned the Hudson west on W. Main Street, past the Shaffer Hotel and Dining Room with its four large and prominent swastikas etched into its façade. They were Indian in origin, but Nazi enough for Nestor, who drew inspiration from them every time he passed.

In 1933, on a tour of South America with his sister, Nestor Cooney entered the German Embassy in Argentina and offered his services to the Reich. After a careful investigation of his background, they accepted him into the Abwehr. He underwent training at a desolate ranch fifty miles outside of Juárez, Mexico. Two Abwehr agents taught him how to encrypt messages for radio transmission, and they taught him how to decipher the same. They gave him a Minox camera and instructed him in its use and concealment. They taught him how to spot and identify planes, ships, and military vehicles. They taught him the rudiments of surveillance and evasion. On Nestor Cooney's departure back to the United States, he received the leather-bound codebook he now carried in his breast pocket over his heart. They also gave him a keychain that, with the push of a button, would drop a cyanide tablet into the palm of his hand were he to find it necessary to still that heart to protect the Reich.

A 10-watt *Agentenfunk "Afu"* short-wave radio arrived at his house two days later.

IN THE LARGE HOUSE on Ripley Street, where Myra slept in ignorance, every Sunday morning at four, Nestor Cooney went into the basement, where he hid his radio. He would select the appropriate code, tune in on the appropriate channel, and transmit his call sign to his Nazi masters. They would respond. Then they would give him orders that generally amounted to Nestor sitting tight until the following Sunday. Once in 1937, they had chosen him to gather information on dams in the western United States. Nestor Cooney took his two weeks of vacation from the Hardz Ice Company and journeyed to all major dams in California, Nevada, Arizona, Utah, Colorado, and his own state of New Mexico. He took photographs. He talked to workers. If there was printed material for tourists, he procured such as he could. At Lahontan Dam in northwestern Nevada, he had stolen an employee schedule and timesheet carelessly left in reach across the counter. After successful completion of the mission, he drove through the night to El Paso, crossed the border at dawn, and left the bundle of material in a canvas knapsack in the second stall of the shit-versus-ammonia-fragrant men's room of the Juárez train station.

To what important purpose the Third Reich used the intelligence for—seven years and zero busted dam later—Nestor Cooney did not know.

The next duty the Abwehr asked of Nestor Cooney was for information on the warships built outside of Houston. Every other month from June of '39 through to February 1942, Nestor Cooney spent his weekend prowling the bars around the military shipyards, making friends, buying drinks, loosening tongues. Some of the friendships necessitated a level of closeness he'd not experienced before. He was not homosexual, but in the name of duty, he didn't shy away. Twice in '41, Nestor Cooney reported the launches of ships bound for North Atlantic convoys. The ships were torpedoed before they left the Gulf. It was good work, and he was proud of what he helped the German Navy accomplish.

Nestor Cooney never read about any survivors.

Then there was nothing. America was in the thick of things, but the Abwehr seemed to have lost interest in their New Mexican spy. Each Sunday, Nestor Cooney dutifully made his 4:00 a.m. Afu transmissions, and each Sunday, his position confirmed, they ordered him to wait another week.

Seventy-five weeks passed.

The war raged on.

Nestor Cooney perched farther and farther out on a branch of despair. This wasn't fair. He'd once marched with Hitler. Not ten yards behind his hero. Nestor Cooney was important to the cause, surely someone remembered.

The Sicherheitsdienst remembered Nestor Cooney and took over his control from the Abwehr on Sunday, September 5, 1943. From there, things moved faster than he could say, "Swastika over the White House." The SD wired Nestor Cooney the money to purchase the Twin Beech transport plane in Tampico. They sent him the forged government Avgas ration cards that allowed him to keep it fueled. Each Sunday thereafter, they provided Nestor Cooney one more piece of information, gave him one more task, all leading to his rendezvous today and his flight tomorrow. Christmas Eve.

Nestor Cooney pulled into his driveway at 12:51 p.m. The shades were drawn. No lights burned inside. Myra's hair was a bird's nest. She wouldn't be home for two hours. Nestor Cooney walked to the front door, unlocked it, and stepped into the wood-paneled entry hall.

He shut the door behind him and he twisted the bolt. To his right, a large pocket-door opened onto the living room. Fifteen feet farther along the wall, a swinging door led in to the kitchen. Next to the kitchen door, at the end of the hall, the basement door stood opposite the front door. Nestor approached the basement door. He turned the knob. He took the stairs in the dark as he always did, and descended into the cold, brick-walled, concrete-floored room.

Five paces right, eight paces forward, reach up . . . He found the string. With a gentle tug, he clicked on the hanging bulb.

He stood before his workbench, illuminated in dull yellow light.

A chunk of inch-thick mortar protruded loosely between two bricks on the wall behind the workbench. Nestor Cooney slipped it free. He selected a flat-head screwdriver, inserted it into the hole and released a hidden catch. A section of fifteen false bricks nailed to a plywood board popped loose. Nestor Cooney lifted the panel and placed it on the floor. In the space behind the bricks were his radio and a manila envelope. The envelope contained a road map of New Mexico, a forged New Mexico driver's license, the current schedule for Santa Fe freight, and a ticket for the Apache Flyer that ran light freight and passengers twice daily on the Denver and Rio Grande Western narrow-gauge railway between Santa Fe, and Antonito, Colorado.

Nestor Cooney uncoiled the antenna wire from the back of the radio console and walked it over to the east wall. He clipped it to the end of a coaxial cable that entered the basement through a hole it shared with a number of water pipes. The coaxial cable ran up the side of the house to an aerial on the roof.

Returning to the workbench, Nestor Cooney pulled a stool from beneath it. He sat at his radio and withdrew his codebook from his inner breast pocket. He found the day's code. He plugged in his headset, fixed it over his skull, and attached the Morse Code key. From the workbench drawer, he took out a pad of paper and a pencil.

It was precisely one p.m.

Ready to transmit, Black Bird switched on his Afu radio.

Black Bird calling Grizzly Bear, Black Bird to Grizzly Bear, he tapped out in dots and dashes. He waited thirty seconds. No response. *Black Bird to Grizzly Bear, Black Bird to Grizzly Bear . . .*

Fifteen seconds later came a single dit response. Nestor Cooney licked his lips. He keyed the day's sign: *Edelweiss.*

Avalanche, came the countersign and Nestor Cooney poised his pencil over the pad ready to receive his instructions. They commenced. His pencil flew across the page, an endless trail of letters flowing gray from its tip. One page. Another. The letters came fast. More than they had ever given him before. It took all Nestor Cooney's powers of concentration to decode it correctly.

He flipped from the third page. Started on the fourth. Rapt with concentration, he never noticed his sister appear at the top of the basement stairs behind him.

41

MESMER DIDN'T HAVE MUCH TIME left. Because the bullet he'd taken in the mad drive from the ranch deflected into him off of a ricochet, it entered at a low velocity; the lead tumbled inside rather than blew straight through. That was bad. The slug had created a three-centimeter Grade II tear to his liver on its path to perforating his bowel. Although the initial bleeding wasn't life threatening, along with the main flow of blood from the stomach and intestines, all the body's oxygenated blood from general circulation eventually flows through the liver, making his blood loss slow but continuous. The hole to Mesmer's colon compounded the dangers. Toxic bacteria from his bowels leaked into his abdomen and, pumped through his liver, spread throughout his body. His body, confusing the necessary and helpful intestinal bacteria as a major foreign infection, released an overabundance of chemicals to fight it. This caused sepsis that was fast developing into septic shock. Mesmer burned with fever. He shook with chills. He vomited poisons, blood, and other bodily fluids from where he slouched inside the cab of the second truck.

Von Hofmann checked his wristwatch. It was seven minutes past one in the afternoon. Ever since entering the Cibola wilderness, their forward progress had been a tire-spinning, muck-flinging battle. Four times, they'd been compelled to stop and the men free one or the other truck from the mire. Along the way, Mesmer's bleeding, his pain, his vomiting and moaning had distracted Gauss enough for him to miss indications that his truck was losing its own precious fluids. The engine had finally burned out in the small volcanic pass where they now found themselves.

A post-mortem inspection revealed a bullet hole high in the oil pan. Two of the vehicle's five quarts started dribbling out as soon as they'd left the ranch, until the remaining three quarts were below the level of the puncture. Under normal driving conditions, the truck would have remained operational. Uneven terrain after the town of Vaughn had caused sloshing and additional loss, until the steep incline of the mountain fire road had drained the rest of it.

Von Hofmann cursed the roads. Unimproved, they twisted and turned like a tangled net clumsily thrown across the square-cut back of this series of steep, ponderosa-covered mesas. As far as he could tell, these roads served absolutely no purpose. They serviced nothing. Impractical for quick passage through the wilderness for anyone fleeing or fighting fire, and they were too dangerous and confused for sightseeing. Idiotic roads such as these did not exist in the Fatherland.

When Germans built roads, they built them for a purpose and they built them to last. The Führer's autobahn: more than 3,250 kilometers of four-lane, high-speed, divided highways, begun at Hitler's decree in 1933. In five short years, their completion unified the Reich.

From his position beside the rear gate of the second truck, the Standartenführer watched Mesmer slowly dying inside the cab. Behind von Hofmann, her back to his, the captive sat sullen and silent. Two rough cords von Hofmann had unthreaded from the corners of the truck's canvas top secured her. The first bound her wrists behind her back, while the second cord secured the first cord to the truck bed's gate.

Von Hofmann supposed the young woman's mind raced with the desire to escape. There would be no escape. If she struggled, the only thing she would succeed in freeing were her shoulders from their sockets.

At 1800 hours, von Hofmann was to meet his American contact at the Spanish ruins of Gran Quivira and receive his final orders. According to his map (a detail taken from the US Geological Survey topographical chart of 1938), he'd come barely half the one hundred and forty kilometers between Vaughn and his destination. If Germans had built this road, he would have arrived at Gran Quivira in less than an hour. Now he'd have to fight each minute to cover the remaining seventy kilometers in the five hours he had left.

Less than five hours: it was 13:12. He prodded a piece of stone from the mud with the toe of his boot and forced himself to remain calm. The men claimed weapons and ammo. Careful soldiers, they stripped them and checked their action.

Schmidt produced the dusters Zundorf had found in the garage. "With the Standartenführer's approval, I have found coats we can use to hide our uniforms."

Von Hofmann took and examined one of the dusters. "You have anticipated my needs once again, Feldwebel."

"I found those."

All eyes flashed to Zundorf, his face tight with jealousy. Von Hofmann scowled. Schmidt chuckled.

Virginia didn't understand German, but she'd observed every move her captors made since they'd stopped. The leader, the man the others addressed as "Standard-something," handed out the long jackets she recognized from her father's truck garage. She had followed the exchange about the dusters. There was bad blood between the older, stocky Nazi, and the blond soldier in shorts. She stored this away, hoping it might later prove useful.

VON HOFMANN CONSIDERED the antagonism growing between Schmidt and Zundorf. The Hauptmann was an excellent soldier and the men respected him. He wished Zundorf hadn't made the comment about the dusters, but Zundorf could take care of himself, and meanwhile, von Hofmann had plans for Schmidt. The Feldwebel was dangerously insane. A situation that would prove problematical to a lesser commanding officer, but von Hofmann would harness Schmidt's psychotic condition to deadly purpose. Schmidt would do things no sane man ever would, which made him von Hofmann's wildcard. A time bomb he could plant anywhere at any time.

ZUNDORF AND WOLTERS BROKE BRANCHES from pine trees. Zundorf cursed his dumb reaction to something as trivial as a pile of coats. He glanced at Schmidt. Zundorf didn't even want one of the damn things. The idea of covering his uniform made him uneasy. Von Hofmann had stood over the wreckage of Private Veit and said, "We are once again combatants in the war, ground forces of the Third Reich, on a mission to inflict nothing less than a mortal blow against our American enemies." Ground forces of the Third Reich didn't hide their uniforms. Hauptmann Fritz Zundorf wouldn't jeopardize the mission, but he planned to live or die wearing his uniform with pride.

"This should be enough. Pile them here as comfortable as you can make them. Gauss, help me carry Obersturmführer Mesmer."

"I DON'T KNOW WHAT YOU'RE UP to or why you've taken me, but I'll tell you one thing: this isn't your Fatherland and you're no Geronimo. You haven't a prayer of surviving."

Her outburst caught von Hofmann off guard, and his gray eyes registered a look of mild surprise. "You Americans. Always such a clever way to turn a phrase."

"The only thing going to be turned is the earth over your grave. You ever hear that clever American phrase 'pushing up daisies'?"

"Fraulein, please believe me, I regret as much as you the circumstances of last night—"

"The circumstances of murdering my father and the innocent men who worked for him?"

"Men with guns aren't innocent."

"Men defending their homes are the soul of innocence."

"Not in war, I'm afraid."

He studied her. Her defiance, second nature to her as it was with Agna, caused him to soften his next words. "If I'd had my way, we would have taken what we needed without anyone knowing until we were long gone. As it is, you should be glad I have chosen to let you live and help me."

"Help you? I wouldn't lift a finger."

"You seemed such a prime candidate for our SS Women's Corps."

He enjoyed how his words made the muscles tighten in her neck. "Have no fear about your fingers, Fraulein. They will stay with your hands, firmly tied behind your back. You are a hostage, a bargaining chip to throw on the table, and, if necessary, a human shield. Doesn't that please you? You have made an overnight transformation. Like Cinderella—you go from nonessential peasant to important player in the future of the Reich."

"Drop dead."

"As I said. So clever." He pivoted and went to Mesmer. His pistol dangled from his hand. He addressed the SS lieutenant. "Obersturmführer?"

Mesmer struggled upright. He shook with pain and fever. "My Standartenführer."

"Your idea of smuggling the dirt from camp with the work parties is the reason we completed the tunnel in time."

Mesmer panted. Gathered strength to speak. . . "Why didn't we go to Mexico?"

Von Hofmann ignored the question. "You understand, you cannot come farther with me?"

"We didn't go home . . ."

Von Hofmann tapped the pistol against his leg. He chose his next words carefully. "I was put into the camp to complete a mission. I chose all of you for your loyalty and expertise, and out of the three hundred officers at that prison camp, you are the very best of what makes the German man the greatest this world has ever known."

"What . . . what's your mission?"

Von Hofmann looked at the others. All eyes fastened on the two of them.

"I won't know its specifics until tonight, but my training was for something that will change the course of this war. You will always be remembered to the Third Reich as part of that."

He offered Mesmer his pistol. "Would you like to do this? Or shall I?"

Mesmer indicated von Hofmann proceed. Von Hofmann cocked the pistol.

"Do you know why I joined your plan, Standartenführer?"

Von Hofmann placed the gun against Mesmer's temple. "Tell me."

Mesmer shut his eyes. "To see my children again."

"You will."

Virginia cried out. "Stop it!"

Von Hofmann glared at her.

"Leave me here with him. When they come after you, they'll have to stop for us."

The Standartenführer hesitated. Zundorf jumped in speaking English. "Standartenführer, he still has time."

"Hauptmann Zundorf! I will not give him to the enemy."

Zundorf stiffened to attention. "No, Standartenführer. Leave him with a rifle to guard our rear. Allow him the honor of a soldier's death protecting us."

Von Hofmann relaxed his grip on the Luger.

"I will hold as long as I can," Mesmer said.

Virginia gave Zundorf a thankful look. Von Hofmann noticed.

"Schmidt," von Hofmann said. "She rides up front with us."

Schmidt grabbed Virginia. He worked at the knot, untying her from the back of the truck.

"Please. *Standard-führer*. Leave me. You said I'd be a human shield. Tie me to a tree!"

Von Hofmann tucked his gun back into his belt. He stepped face to face with Virginia. "If the authorities don't come? You'd die."

A strand of copper hair hung between Virginia's eye. Von Hofmann pushed it up behind her ear. Virginia shuddered at the gentleness of his touch.

"I'm not talking about authorities," she spat. "Tyler is coming. If he finds me here, he'll give up on you."

"Your cowboy? What do I care whether he gives up?"

"Because if he catches you, he'll kill you all."

42

THE THICKEST PATCHES OF MUD made parts of the road too dangerous to ride, forcing Cartwright to walk the black-and-white mustang as he followed the path of the trucks and the hoofprints of Tyler's bay. He'd seen the thick places where the trucks had repeatedly stuck. This land wasn't made for machines. The distance that had grown between hunted and hunter on the highways was closing in the wilderness.

A wide rain runoff cut the FBI agent's path. Cartwright crossed it, ankle deep, coaxing his horse, as it didn't prefer wading. He'd not ridden a horse since his Army days, and he almost made the mistake of letting his mind wander back to that time when, coming out on the other side, the tire tracks resumed, but the bay's prints were gone.

Cartwright's hand flew to his gun as the *clack-clack* cock of a rifle behind him froze him in his tracks.

"Not much trouble tracking us, huh?" said Tyler.

"Before you were born, Mr. Keyes, the cavalry used horses instead of tanks."

"And you chased scalpin' Injuns?" Tyler stepped in close and removed Cartwright's .38 from his hand. He stepped back. "Turn around if you'd like."

"It was Pancho Villa."

"Never caught him, didja?"

Cartwright's silence was answer enough.

"Unlike you, I won't fail." Tyler said.

Cartwright watched Tyler—rifle steady on him—retrieve his horse from the thicket where he'd hidden it.

"Mind if I ask you a question?" said Cartwright.

"Probably won't answer it. Now, go in front and get walking."

Cartwright complied. "How come you let her father and that weaselly sheriff send you up?"

"No more talking."

"No one would've convicted you of rape for what happened. Unless you confessed."

"What's your name?"

"Agent Cartwright. Talk to me now—"

"Agent Cartwright, stop talking."

Cartwright stopped walking. He faced Tyler. "You could have outdistanced me the whole way. Why'd you stop for me?"

Tyler didn't say anything. He let Cartwright figure it out. "They're up ahead."

"I must've managed to hit one last night," said Tyler. He prodded him with his rifle.

"I'm bait?" Cartwright whispered.

"We can call you a distraction if it makes you feel safer."

"The hell you say. I won't be the one who ends up missing Christmas."

"Then we got to get you through this to get you to that. Now move it."

THE BAY MUNCHED WEEDS five yards from Tyler, who watched Mesmer through the trees along the high side of the pass behind the dying Nazi. He waited, his rifle aimed and ready. Cartwright was not a man he reckoned would lose his nerve and turn back. Tyler figured he would probably like the man under different circumstances. Cartwright came into view. He was without the paint horse. The sight of a lone man in a suit and fedora caused Mesmer to blink, making sure he still engaged with reality. It gave

Cartwright an edge. He lurched to cover behind the disabled truck as Mesmer's first shot ripped harmlessly behind him.

Tyler crept down the wooded slope.

Mesmer fired once more, and again. The two bullets hammered the disabled truck.

"Throw out your gun! I can help you!" Cartwright called.

Mesmer answered with two more shots into the dirt half the distance to the vehicle. Tyler wedged the Winchester barrel into the back of Mesmer's neck.

"How's your English?"

"I surrender."

"Might've done you some good before you started carrying my lead in your gut."

Mesmer tossed the rifle.

Cartwright snatched it up. He didn't bother aiming it at anyone. He said, "Where's the woman?"

The FBI agent watched the adrenaline drain from Mesmer as chills consumed him. The dying young soldier vomited bright yellow, blood-streaked bile. His eyelids fluttered. He fought them open. "She's safe . . . He's taken an interest . . . in her."

Tyler cracked Mesmer in the chest with his rifle butt. The Nazi tanker dropped, whining like a beast.

"Cool it, Keyes."

Tyler yanked Mesmer back upright and held him there. "What do you mean, 'interest'?"

"I don't know. He feels something for her—like he knows her, or wants to know her."

Tyler wound up with his rifle again, but Cartwright stopped him, a firm hand on his arm. "Von Hofmann's keeping Virginia alive. Let that be good enough for now."

Tyler lowered the Winchester.

"C'mon," said Cartwright. "Help me get this prisoner back to civilization. Have him patched up. We'll find out what he knows, why they sidetracked in this direction instead of turning south. We'll make a real pursuit of it."

"This fella won't make it down the hill. Put him out of his misery and come with me."

"There are six of them," said Cartwright knowing even if there were twice that he couldn't stop Keyes.

Tyler headed for his horse.

"I'll arrest you when I catch up to you. If you're not dead."

Tyler disappeared among the ponderosas, but his voice echoed into the pass behind him. "I'll have saved Virginia, so either way I'll be good with the result."

Cartwright allowed himself a soft grin. He admired Tyler's bravery in turning his back on him and walking away. Keyes had been smart enough to know that as long as Mesmer lived, Cartwright's first duty was to the wounded prisoner. Anyway, he wanted Tyler to go. He wanted to go with him. He saw something of himself and Mexico in the young man. Each word he'd chosen to speak since they met, the words called after Keyes now, were strictly for the record. What would sound best for both of them in a courtroom.

If it came to that—if Keyes survived, but this thing went haywire—Hoover would see to a trial. There would be the question of Cartwright having Mesmer's rifle. Why didn't he shoot Tyler Keyes when he resisted arrest? Cartwright solved this by firing off the rest of Mesmer's cartridges.

He carried Mesmer, alive but unconscious, back to his horse. He found his .38 tucked under the back jockey of his saddle. He appreciated that.

Mesmer died across Cartwright's saddle less than an hour later.

43

Only Esmee Whitefeather did Myra Cooney's hair. Miss Cooney made it perfectly clear to the other girls that it was not personal, but Esmee had been her girl for the last eight years and she wasn't about to change now. If Esmee wasn't available, Myra would just as soon go home.

But it surprised Myra to find Nestor's car in the driveway. He never came home early from work. Myra vaguely worried there'd been some kind of terrible accident involving ice. She hurried into the house and, finding the basement door ajar, stepped to the top of the stairs.

In the room below, Myra's baby brother huddled over a radio she had never seen before. Her natural impulse was to call to him, ask what hobby he'd taken up now, but something furtive about the scene stilled her tongue.

Nestor is a spy.

The revelation seared her consciousness. One thousand suspicious and hazy aspects of her brother's life came into sharp focus. His total obsession with all things German and Nazi that abruptly ended the day he'd disappeared in Buenos Aires and toured the German Embassy. Myra knew back then you couldn't just "tour" a foreign embassy. Then there were the strange car trips. The silly miniature camera she'd found in a box behind his dresser. Road maps with circled dams found crumpled in the trash. Myra hadn't seen how these things fit together. Her naïveté embarrassed her, but now she retreated from the house in fear.

Nestor Cooney finished transcribing the cipher. He put the pencil aside and, index finger cramped from writing, pecked out the verification code confirming to his contact he'd received the complete transmission. He signed off. Nestor Cooney removed his headset and broke down the radio. He replaced it inside the cubbyhole and covered it with the false brick front. With the screwdriver, he engaged the release and wedged the piece of mortar back over it, covering its existence.

He returned his attention to the pad of paper. The first part of the encoded message was easy to decipher and exactly what Nestor Cooney had anticipated—confirmation for tonight's rendezvous and tomorrow's flight, followed by a two-sentence sign and countersign he'd exchange with the SD officer tonight. Next were instructions to hand over the remainder of the three-page cipher to that officer when bona fides were established. Nestor Cooney spent a minute trying to decipher these pages, but their code was unbreakable.

Nestor Cooney shoved the cipher into the manila envelope and, turning off the light, climbed the stairs. He stepped into the entry hall, turned, and pulled shut the basement door. The front door opened behind him. Startled, Nestor Cooney dropped the manila envelope as he locked eyes with his sister.

"Myra? You should be at the beauty parlor." His voice quavered. He couldn't help it.

"Esmee's got that flu bug going around." Myra dropped her glance. "What brings you home, Nestor?"

Nestor Cooney heard the suspicion in her voice. Myra looked at the envelope. His heart fluttered in its ribcage.

Stupid cow doesn't know a thing.

Nestor Cooney offered a thin-lipped smile. "Mr. Hardz gave me the day off. For Christmas shopping."

Their eyes met again. Nestor Cooney cringed. Myra's present was already under the tree. He didn't give presents to anyone else. Myra didn't press the point.

"What were you doing down there?"

"A fuse blew."

"Oh?"

"I replaced it—was just closing the door."

"Really. What's that?"

Myra pointed at the envelope. Sweat trickled beneath Nestor Cooney's shoulders. He had to get a grip. He was overreacting. "Accounts Mr. Hardz wants looked over before Christmas," he mumbled, and scooped it up.

She doesn't know a damn thing.

"Oh, and I won't be home for dinner." He stepped straight toward her. Myra moved aside into the living room doorway. Nestor Cooney grasped the front doorknob.

If for some reason, she does know something, she'll say it now.

He waited with his back to her.

"Nestor?"

He turned the knob, palm damp on the cold brass.

"Drive carefully."

MYRA SWALLOWED the acid taste that filled her mouth. It had taken all her willpower to refrain from seizing the envelope, tearing it open, and spilling its contents. But she couldn't do that. She couldn't tip her hand. What if it had been nothing?

No, she had to let him go. For now. It wasn't a question of whether Nestor was a spy and what he was doing was wrong. Myra Cooney was no babe in the woods when it came to wrongdoing. She'd broken lots of rules in her day—fooled an old lady into giving her half her fortune—and Myra wasn't the least bit sorry for it. Hell's bells, she'd had a child to rear who wasn't hers. A child she never wanted. In her case, she was only doing what it took to survive. The perfidy of Nestor's actions was indefensible and unforgivable. In his own vicious way, he was a willfully acting partner to Nazi murder and death. Myra took a deep breath. She was a sixty-year-old retired nurse. She was unprepared to deal with espionage. The authorities would have to be informed.

Yet, how to convince them she wasn't some kind of nutcase?

The best scenario would be for Nestor to confess. That way, the FBI could find out everything from him and perhaps crack the entire spy ring if that was possible. Could she convince him to do it? It was at least worth a try. She'd find enough evidence for the authorities and present it to Nestor. Either he could volunteer it to the FBI, or she would do it for him.

Myra walked to the easy chair by the Christmas tree in the front window. She raised the shade. Nestor was sitting in his green Hudson, watching her. Myra forced a wave before she sat and opened the newspaper to read in the window's light.

She listened for the start of the car. The sound of the Hudson pulling out and fading away down the street. Myra faced the window. She watched it turn the corner and disappear.

She let a full minute pass. Nestor Cooney did not return. Myra rose and went to the basement door.

There was a light switch at the top of the stairs. She depressed the button and descended. The workbench was empty, the wall behind it solid. Her nerves hummed as she slid open the drawer.

A pencil. A blank pad of paper. A flat-head screwdriver. Nothing else.

Myra stared at the wall. She ran her hand across the bricks, cold to the touch. Her fingers passed over a loose piece of mortar. She wedged it out with her finger. It fell onto the workbench. She twisted her finger inside the hole. She found a kind of hook-like catch. Myra tried to work it open, but couldn't.

The screwdriver.

She took it from the drawer, probed the catch, and with a satisfying *click,* opened the secret panel. She saw the radio. Her hands quivered. She tipped the heavy device to look beneath it, but found no papers or anything she could take as evidence.

She could take the little camera from behind Nestor's dresser, but would it be enough? No, the radio was the key. She studied it for some kind of answer and saw the evidence she needed. The dials and knobs were all marked with German writing. She found the metal stamp with its name—*Telefunken*—and a model number. She grabbed the pencil and the pad of paper.

From outside, came the faint sound of an automobile.

Myra beat back the fear rising in her breast. She carefully copied the information.

The automobile was approaching.

Myra finished writing. She threw pencil and pad back with the screwdriver into the drawer. She pushed it shut.

The car stopped outside. Nestor had returned.

Myra grabbed the panel of false bricks and fit it into place. She couldn't make the latch catch.

The car door opened. Closed.

Myra's pulse raced. She forced the panel into place. The piece of paper clutched in her hand, she scurried for the stairs.

"Oh, no," she said aloud and whirled back to the workbench.

She snatched the chunk of mortar and, hands shaking, poked it back where it belonged.

Myra dashed up the stairs, snapped off the lights, slamming the basement door behind her as she watched a silhouette approach her front door. Atop its head was a strange-looking hat.

Myra clutched her throat. Relief washed over her. She opened the door.

"Howdy, Miss Cooney." The postman smiled. "Parked in front of your house today, if you don't mind. We're all running late, what with Christmas cards and all."

He held out Myra's mail and she took it.

"Got anything for me?"

Myra shook her head.

"Awright, I'll be seeing you tomorrow. Merry Christmas, Miss Cooney."

"Merry Christmas," she said, her hand clutching the piece of paper inside her coat pocket.

She made her way to Nestor's bedroom to find the camera and take down the same kind of identifying information as she'd taken from the radio. She had no idea she'd put the piece of mortar into its hole backward, or that when she slammed the door, the jolt and change in pressure had been enough to cause its fall.

44

A T THE BILLY THE KID STEAKHOUSE on the corner of Main and Woodbridge in Fort Sumner, Special Agent in Charge Tom Cartwright suffocated his latest butt in a smattering of congealed egg yolk—all that was left from his ribeye steak and two eggs over easy—and stared out the window. Across the street, the old, bald owner of the Bijou Theater climbed from his ladder, pulled a pair of spectacles from his front shirt pocket and squinted at the marquee. It read: *Closed for Christmas*, which pleased the man, and he wiped his hands with his handkerchief the way pleased men do, satisfied with a job well done. Cartwright sighed out his last breath of smoke.

The belly-shot German had been no good to Cartwright dead. He'd brought the body to the service station. At the sight of the corpse, Mr. Jefferson asked if Tyler Keyes had done it. Cartwright said he had, and Jefferson remarked that he'd taken plenty "Bosche jus' like that" the last go round. Cartwright asked if Jefferson would store the corpse in the icehouse dug into the earth adjacent to the garage, and the old man said, "Yap," as long as the FBI reimbursed him for the ruined ice.

FBI would, and Cartwright asked to use the phone. He reached Dunlap. Gave him a preliminary statement for his report. Arranged to retrieve the body. Mr. Jefferson walked him to his car.

"You didn't mention my helping Keyes," Mr. Jefferson said.

"Who'd you put in with, last war?"

"Oh, I was ar'dy a lifer by then. Put in for the hassle in Cuba with the Twenty-Fifth Colored in 1898. You cavalry?" Cartwright gave him half a smirk. "You sit a horse like cavalry. Twenty-Fifth folded into the Ninety-Third. Fought a hundred-ninety-one consecutive days on the front line, 1917 to '18. Five days longer than any white troops the entire war."

"I was in and out chasing Villa, but in the army I learned fast: any information you don't volunteer, you don't have to act upon." Cartwright smashed a butt, lit another. "What do you make of Tyler Keyes?"

"Hasn't had much of a chance to prove hisself—all the business bastard-Hendricks put him through—but, back in the day, you'n I'd both a'been that much easier for it if we'd had a Tyler Keyes on a gun at our side."

After returning from Vaughn, Cartwright commandeered two offices, some telephones, and typewriters in the Fort Sumner courthouse. Not wanting to head back to Santa Rosa, or especially to El Paso, before knowing where von Hofmann's trail led, he set up shop.

With witness statements being typed in one room, Cartwright took the other and made an hour's worth of calls, taking reports from his agents in the field who'd spent the night and half the morning running down false sightings and were now compelled to pass this useless information on to him. Useless information regulations compelled he write out and forward to Washington. After that, he'd waited for word from agents and Army roadblocks he'd dispatched to the towns of Duran, Corona, Tecolote, Claunch, Mountainair, Estancia, and Encino. These towns, when connected in a line to Vaughn, encircled the Cibola like a lasso. By four o'clock, he'd heard from all of them. Nobody interviewed had seen von Hofmann, his men, or the hostage, the truck, or Tyler Keyes.

All still in the wilderness. He envisioned then, before just as quickly rejecting it, a mountain assault. A stunt like that would only get his men, Keyes, and Virginia Hendricks killed.

Here was the essential problem of being agent in charge. The make-work and the waiting. In order to keep on top of a case, you had to assign every task and delegate its responsibility to someone else. Right now, scalpels cut into corpses, autopsies performed; weapons were test-fired, slugs compared under microscopes; photographic prints were tonged from their baths; cars arriving at roadblocks were being stopped and searched; potential witnesses questioned, civilians warned. You could be the guy who pulled the strings or the guy whose string got pulled.

Nobody pulled Tyler Keyes's strings, that was for sure.

The clock on the steakhouse wall over the coffee percolator read four thirty. Cartwright slid his thick mug to the table's edge, a signal to the waitress for more coffee. Tyler Keyes had cut his strings. Like he had done in Mexico.

Not so fast. Galgo cut his string. He cut Keyes's—Naw, not true, either. Tyler Keyes cut his own. Cartwright only allowed and appreciated it. While he'd spent the years tying his own back on. Hand, foot. Another hand, the other foot. One to the top of his head to give Hoover a bob whenever he tugged.

Cartwright had not heard from either Special Agent Torres, who was developing the background on Keyes, or Special Agent Burley regarding Colonel Marls. So, Cartwright put his mind to von Hofmann. Nothing he did made any sense. His individual actions did not correspond. They didn't build a context. Psychologically, in a pursuit situation, the taking of a hostage is a subconscious demand for confrontation, but these men were soldiers and, to look at their records, superior at what they did. From a military standpoint, taking a hostage would be extraneous to their mission. Virginia Hendricks was extra baggage: a security risk, another mouth to feed, a burden to rapid deployment.

What was it the dead one, Mesmer, said? *She's safe . . . He's taken an interest . . . in her."*

Von Hofmann was defeating his purpose of a quick, stealthy, efficient dash for the border.

So why the hell did he take her?

He feels something for her—like he knows her or wants to know her.

There was, of course, the obvious reason a group of males having been without a female for a long time take a woman hostage. Tyler Keyes didn't need anyone to paint a picture of that. It was why he smashed Mesmer with his rifle and why he would have kept right on going.

Cartwright knew it firsthand. 1916. Mexico. The second little girl.

The memories burned into Cartwright's mind like the fire from a filthy shot of cantina tequila. He wished he could forget. If he'd learned anything from the old Apache, it was to separate the heart from the hunt.

Mexico wasn't going to save Virginia Hendricks. Cartwright had to move. He'd left the courthouse at three thirty-five and, following the suggestion of a pretty, young stenographer, found his lunch at the Billy the Kid Steakhouse.

The waitress, having finally gotten around to the coffee, switched on the radio. Kay Kyser and his Big Band swung out their rendition of *"Deck the Halls."* Cartwright was in the process of thumbing some flame from his lighter when Special Agent Torres entered the steakhouse with a jingle of dangling doorbells. His hands held a brown envelope embossed with the seal of the OSS.

45

S PECIAL AGENT IN CHARGE Cartwright was on his feet when Special Agent Torres stepped toward his booth.

"Glad I found you, sir," Torres said.

He handed Cartwright the OSS envelope. Cartwright read the red ink stamps: *Top Secret* and *Eyes Only*.

"Agent in Charge—Easy to find."

Cartwright tucked the envelope under his arms and reached into his trench-coat pocket. He peeled off a couple bills and dropped them beside his plate. He straightened his hat, and indicated the door. "Back to the courthouse. Got a car?" Cartwright said.

"Walked," said Torres.

"Fine."

Bells jangled. They hit the street. Tired gray cottonwoods lined the sidewalk while lost-sheep clouds aimlessly wandered the sky. Cartwright and Special Agent Torres made their way toward the four-story brick-and-limestone box of the Fort Sumner court-house. They walked abreast, Cartwright's soles tapping the rough cement in time to Special Agent Torres's words.

"June ninth of 1937, Keyes is arrested for the rape of Virginia Hendricks, a minor on the night of June eighth when the crime was committed."

"She ever testify?"

"He pled no contest at his arraignment. Went straight to sentencing."

"What was her statement to the sheriff?" Cartwright said.

Torres gave him a dubious look.

"She didn't make one?"

"Her father did," said Torres.

"Was he an eyewitness?"

"No. A powerful citizen. And Keyes took six out of an eight-year ticket at the New Mexico State Penitentiary."

Cartwright huffed, annoyed.

Torres said, "Kid didn't make friends inside. Continuous fighting from the day he arrived. Within a month, he's put in the infirmary. Coma. Fifty-fifty he lives, but he pulls through. Day he comes out, shanks a guy to death."

"Charged?"

"No witnesses. But he did it."

"One of the guys who jumped him?" said Cartwright.

"His cellmate. Way I heard it: his only friend in the joint up to that point."

"Anything else?"

They mounted the courthouse steps.

Torres said, "The slug they pulled out of the escapee, Mesmer, was a Winchester thirty-thirty from the gun you saw in his possession. The judge here is adding that killing to Tyler Keyes's warrant."

"The same warrant that has Keyes colluding with von Hofmann in the Hendricks's massacre?"

"Based on eyewitness testimony—"

"Eyewitnesses around these parts are fast proving themselves blind," said Cartwright.

Torres knit his brow, bothered by Cartwright's attitude. "Then how about we add it to the warrant that has Keyes resisting arrest, seizing the firearm of a federal agent?"

Cartwright held the door for his subordinate. "Ease up, Torres, he's trying to save his girl."

Torres didn't buy it. He said, "Meantime, I'll need to have a search warrant sworn out for his farm."

The gears were turning against Keyes. Torres wouldn't find anything at his farm and, after this conversation, his defiance, Cartwright was happy to have him out on a goose chase to cool him down. He gave Torres approval to find a judge and trudged down the hall to the office he'd commandeered.

Cartwright closed the door behind him. He ripped open the envelope from Washington. It contained an officious cover letter along with the newspaper photograph of von Hofmann receiving his Iron Cross with the article in German below, followed by a third page: the typed translation of said article, and some notes on the picture. Cartwright flipped back to the photograph. "Hometown boy makes good—look at this shit . . ."

There was a hard rap on the door. Cartwright turned. "Yeah? Come in."

One of his agents let himself inside. "Sorry to disturb you, sir, but a call came from Washington while you were out. Mr. Hoover's office."

"Mr. Hoover?"

"He wanted to speak to you personally. They left the number for his direct line." The agent extended a slip of paper.

Cartwright took it. "Thanks."

Aside from a handful of telexes from the director, or the occasional call from an assistant director of administration relaying Hoover's edicts of policy, Cartwright hadn't spoken to Hoover since the muggy Washington afternoon eight years back when Hoover promoted him to Special Agent in Charge of the Santa Fe field office. That meeting had lasted all of six minutes. Santa Fe wasn't a choice assignment, nor was it important as far as the Bureau was concerned. The only reason Cartwright got the posting was because no agent senior to him wanted the job, and there wasn't anyone that week Hoover was particularly mad enough at to banish to the boondocks. Cartwright, however, had grown up in New Mexico; it was in his file, and to Hoover, it was a perfect match.

A perfect match for Cartwright, too. He liked his limited autonomy—a condition rare in the Bureau—and the farther he was from the director and his Draconian touch, the better.

Cartwright dropped the OSS file onto the desk and he walked around to the chair. He sat and fished out a Lucky Strike from the pack Agent Dunlap had given him that morning.

As Cartwright sealed his lips around the fresh cigarette, he decided Hoover must have gotten wind of this morning's developments. The murders and kidnapping out at the Hendricks ranch. Although busy in Washington fighting his paranoid and never-ending war against the "undesirables" trying to undermine the government from within, Hoover must have realized the gravity the von Hofmann case was pulling. He'd want to be on top of it so that when Cartwright apprehended the fugitives, He would be ready to take the credit.

Cartwright recalled the full alert of June '42 when Hoover "led" the capture of eight German saboteurs landed on American shores by submarine. Cartwright, and every other Special Agent, was aware (and sworn to secrecy) that a lone coast guardsman had first seen the Germans. That the Long Island police found the stash of explosives. That the FBI agents put on the case didn't find jack shit for two days until one of the German saboteurs walked into their office to turn himself in, not because of the manhunt—no, he hadn't particularly noticed any heat from the FBI—he was just tired of being a spy. This lazy German spy led the FBI to the seven other saboteurs. Hoover did nothing more than call the newspapers…and hang the enemy agent.

That was enough. After "personally breaking the Nazi spy ring," Hoover started an anonymous letter-writing campaign urging President Roosevelt to make J. Edgar Hoover the first civilian recipient of the Congressional Medal of Honor.

Hoover never got the medal, but he sure as hell got the publicity.

Cartwright lifted the telephone receiver from its cradle. He didn't have any problem with Hoover getting the credit for this case. Let him have it. All Cartwright wanted was von Hofmann dead or captured and Virginia Hendricks safe.

He smoothed the note with the number of J. Edgar Hoover's direct line on the desk a few times before connecting with the switchboard operator. "Operator, long distance. Washington, DC, Concord, six-zero, zero-zero-zero."

"One moment, please."

Cartwright lit the cigarette between his lips. As he blew out the first smoke, his eyes drifted to the photograph of von Hofmann. Taken outdoors in a medieval courtyard. Von Hofmann stood one pace out of a rank of four decorated officers to receive his medal. Cartwright turned his attention to the man pinning the medal to von Hofmann's uniform. El numero uno: Adolf Hitler. Behind Hitler were two other characters Cartwright didn't recognize.

"Mr. Hoover's office," a female voice crackled over the line. Helen Gandy, Hoover's secretary since 1918.

"This is Special Agent in Charge Tom Cartwright, Santa Fe, returning the director's call."

"One moment, please, Special Agent Cartwright."

Cartwright skimmed the article translation.

Local hero SS-Sturmbannführer Jürgen von Hofmann . . . distinguishing himself in the Polish campaign . . . awarded the Iron Cross for bravery and the Wound Badge in black . . . presented to him by the Führer at the regimental headquarters in Danzig . . . looks forward to next posting. Other officers receiving medals that day . . .

Below the translation, a drawing was a key to identify the ceremony participants. Von Hofmann was 1., Hitler, 2., and the men behind him, 3. and 4. respectively: *3. SS-Obergruppenführer Reinhard Heydrich, head of the SD. Deceased. Ref. file: CR-42-0092.*

Cartwright couldn't guess what would be in file CR-42-0092, but he was familiar with the name Heydrich. Reinhard Heydrich, officially the Protector of Czechoslovakia. The rest of the world knew him as the "Butcher of Prague." Cartwright remembered how the Czech Resistance assassinated Heydrich by tossing a bomb beneath his car, and how, in revenge, Hitler ordered the town of Lidice wiped from the face of the earth. A photograph smuggled out by the Resistance had appeared in newspapers shortly afterward. Where once had been a town of over five hundred inhabitants, there was now a field of grain.

4. SS-Oberführer Heinz Jost, member of SD, divisional chief of RSHA VI. Replaced 1941 by Walter Schellenberg. Ref. file: WS-41-0001.

A flow chart quickly assembled in Cartwright's imagination. Hitler at the top, leader of them all. Heydrich beneath him, commanding both Jost and von Hofmann. Jost next, von Hofmann's direct superior . . . Which would mean von Hofmann is, or at least was, part of this RSHA VI now led by Walter Schellenberg.

The telephone line clicked. "Please keep holding, Agent Cartwright."

Before Cartwright could respond, the line clicked back to hold. Cartwright flicked ash into an ashtray. He'd never heard of the RSHA VI. Frustrated, he flipped back to the cover letter and quickly read its contents. It wasn't so much a letter as a release form made out in Cartwright's name, threatening him with half a dozen statutes that ended with the death penalty if he "disseminated any of the documents contained herein without due authorization." The signature at the bottom read: *Henry W. Larkin III.*

The line clicked again and someone spoke. "Hello? Who is this?" This time it was the voice of a man irritated, as though he'd been the one put on hold. It wasn't Hoover.

Cartwright was getting the runaround. He didn't like it. He balanced his cigarette on the edge of the ashtray and spoke slowly, enunciating each word. "Special Agent in Charge Tom Cartwright. Santa Fe, New Mexico. I am returning a personal call from the director."

"Oh. Yes. Agent Cartwright. Yes. I see."

"Is Mr. Hoover there?"

"He is not. This is Assistant Director Tolson." His voice was as pleasant as cold coffee laced with strychnine.

An image of Tolson appeared in Cartwright's head. Slick, dark hair, dark eyes, good-looking, effete. Since 1927, Clyde Tolson had been J. Edgar's right-hand man. They dined together, spent evenings together and, although Tolson kept a separate address, they arrived at work together in the mornings. They liked to photograph each other in shorts around swimming pools, and when they took their private vacations to Florida, they only rented one room. There wasn't an agent in the Bureau who didn't know the unspoken truth: J. Edgar Hoover and Clyde Tolson were lovers.

"Mr. Hoover isn't here right now, but he left explicit instructions for you. Are you ready?"

Cartwright lifted his cigarette, took a long drag, and blew out smoke. "Mm-hmm. I am indeed, sir."

"Good. Here it is. Mr. Hoover does not want you or any of your agents to pursue the escaped PWs any further until his representative, Associate Director Parnell, arrives this evening."

"What did you just say, sir?"

"I will repeat. Mr. Hoover does not want you or any of your men to—"

"No, excuse me. That's not what I meant."

"—pursue the escaped PWs—"

"Excuse me? With all due respect to you, Mr. Tolson, and to the director, perhaps you are not aware that we are dealing with a new set of circumstances as of this morning. This isn't just a PW chase anymore, sir. We've got thirteen new murders and a kidnapping. I wouldn't like to disagree with Mr. Hoover, but I'm not aware of any situation yet invented where pulling the plug on a murder and kidnapping investigation benefits justice for the victims."

There was a long pause at the other end of the line. Cartwright had let his frustration get the better of him. He waited for Tolson's response. Nothing. Cartwright ventured, "You still there, Mr. Tolson?"

He was, and his voice came back in measured words like successive layers of ice over a freezing lake. "Mr. Hoover is fully aware of all the circumstances, Mr. Cartwright. His orders are: neither you nor any of your agents are to pursue the escaped PWs any further until his representative, Associate Director Parnell, arrives to take over the investigation this evening."

Another pause, Tolson obviously waiting for another outburst, but Cartwright took a hard hit from his cigarette and held the smoke. If he said any more, he would shortly find himself riding the "Bureau Bicycle,"—a field agent euphemism for the director's practice of banishment. The banished agent usually quit after two or three months.

"Realize, Agent Cartwright, there are certain elements of this case you do not, and cannot understand."

"I accept that as a possibility, but if you were to enlighten me, sir—now—we wouldn't have to slow the investiga—"

"It is these elements I have mentioned that will be brought to light by Associate Director Parnell, who is scheduled to arrive in Albuquerque on Pan American Airlines flight one-eleven at nine thirty this evening. Are you clear with what I am saying, Agent Cartwright?"

"Sure I am, sir. I got a comfortable chair. Guess I'll go get a paper," he said and disconnected the call.

Von Hofmann stared at him from the photo on the desk, and in front of von Hofmann, Adolf Hitler. Hitler's mouth was open—he must have been speaking—and von Hofmann was caught grinning. *Telling jokes, how nice.* Cartwright heaved a sigh, flutes of smoke trailing from his nose. There was no way he was going to stop. No way in hell. With each tick of the clock, this case took on another complexity.

Realize, Agent Cartwright, there are certain elements of this case you do not and cannot understand . . .

Cartwright turned his attention back to the packet from the OSS. "'Henry W. Larkin the third,'" he read aloud from the cover letter.

The sound of Special Agent Torres's voice filtered in from the hall.

"Torres!" Cartwright shouted. "Front and center!"

The door opened. "Yes, sir?"

Torres approached the desk. He held the search warrant. "I was just headed out to the Keyes place."

"Yeah, great. Listen"—he jabbed the cover letter with his index finger—"Get me this fellow Larkin you've been speaking with, would you?"

Cartwright turned the telephone around so it faced Torres. Agent Torres cocked his hip and gave the edge of the desk an inquisitive look. Cartwright nodded Torres to sit. He lifted the receiver and dialed the operator.

"Operator, Washington DC, please, the National Institutes of Health Building. A Mr. Henry Larkin at extension three-two-seven-two," Torres gave from memory. "Ring back when you've made the connection." He thanked her and hung up.

Torres noticed Cartwright's disturbed expression. "Is there a problem, sir? I heard Hoover wanted to speak with you."

"Nothing I can't handle," Cartwright replied. He gestured Torres out the door.

CARTWRIGHT WATCHED HIS SILHOUETTE recede beyond the glass. Nick Torres was the FBI's first and, as far as Cartwright was aware, the FBI's only Latino special agent. When it came to recruitment, J. Edgar Hoover was a notorious racist. "The average Mexican is a psychological liar," he'd said, meaning "pathological." "They don't shoot very straight, but if they come at you with a knife, watch out." Cartwright had no idea how Torres had slipped through Hoover's screening process. At the end of training graduation, each agent filed into Hoover's office to shake his hand. After they left, Hoover would turn to Tolson and pass judgment. If a recruit was a member of a minority group, had an overtly Jewish name or look, or if he was balding or had pimples, he was on-the-spot fired. Cartwright remembered a fellow in his class who had been dismissed for possessing a moist handshake. Torres came from Castilian stock, and

Cartwright guessed Hoover had mistaken his olive skin for an American of Italian descent.

Torres was married to a beautiful girl, heiress to a newspaper fortune in Chicago, which is where he got his first posting as a special agent. That's where prejudice found him. Word got back to Hoover that Chicago didn't want a greaser on their team, especially one who was bedding down nightly with a beautiful, blonde, rich WASP of a wife. Hoover moved quickly to discredit Torres and force his resignation, but luck was on Torres's side. At the bank one Friday, while he waited in line to deposit his paycheck, two men came in and attempted to rob the place. Torres shouted, "FBI, throw down your guns and put your hands on your head!" He didn't have a gun. He didn't wave a shield. He just shouted, and the nervous robbers complied without second thought.

Hoover couldn't fire a hero, so he banished Torres to New Mexico with no chance of promotion or relocation. He tried to bore him out of the Bureau. That was a year ago, and Cartwright feared it was working. Torres was a big-city boy with a big-city wife and big-city ambitions. He was committed to the Bureau, but the Bureau was unraveling his marriage. Torres had confided in Cartwright that his wife had issued an ultimatum. She was moving back to Chicago on New Year's Day, 1944, married to a Chicago agent, or divorced from a New Mexico sad sack.

The telephone rang. Cartwright picked it up.

"Your call to Washington, sir. Hold for your connection."

Cartwright listened as a telephone rang at the other end of his line. On the third ring, he connected.

"Larkin here."

"Mr. Larkin, this is Special Agent in Charge Tom Cartwright with the Federal Bureau of Investigation in New Mexico. One of my agents has been in contact with you regarding the escape of some German prisoners of war from a camp out here and you were kind enough to give us some assistance."

"Did you sign the release?"

Cartwright glanced at the cover letter. There was an empty line at the bottom of the page awaiting his signature. "Signed and on its way back to you. The reason I'm calling is I need one more thing."

"Agent Cartwright, I'm sorry, but you've received everything our office can provide you."

"You misunderstand. me I just got a question. There's a figure pictured in the photograph, Heinz Jost?"

"Yes, there is. It says so at the bottom."

"Right. And next to his name you have typed 'RSHA VI.' Mr. Larkin, educate me: what is the RSHA VI?"

At the other end of the call, Henry W. Larkin III paused, deciding whether to cooperate. "I will tell you what, Agent Cartwright. In fifteen minutes, I will be sitting down with Colonel Donovan, who has just returned from overseas. We are going to go over some things. Agent Torres, with whom I have been speaking, mentioned something about your willingness to offer the colonel a favor?"

"Anything Colonel Donovan wants. You have my word."

"I'd say it would go pretty far if, in the spirit of interagency cooperation, you bring me up to the minute on your investigation."

Cartwright rubbed his face. For what he was about to do, it wouldn't be Hoover's Bureau Bicycle. It would be dismissal with "extreme prejudice."

There are certain elements of this case you do not and cannot understand. And J. Edgar Hoover, Clyde Tolson, and their envoy Parnell, whoever the hell he is, did? If that were true, it would have to change. Because there was one thing Cartwright understood better than any of them: a young woman had been kidnapped and from where Tom Cartwright sat, he'd rather be damned to hell than put the brakes on his operation when balanced on the fulcrum of each passing minute was the difference between life and death for an innocent young woman. Fuck Washington, fuck Hoover, and fuck himself if that's what it meant. Cartwright had been here before. He'd take a page from Tyler Keyes and cut his own strings.

"Got a minute, Larkin?" said Cartwright.

"I'm all ears, friend," said Larkin.

Cartwright talked. He told Larkin everything. As Cartwright expected, Larkin asked for his leads, questioned his theories, asked for his plan. By the time Cartwright finished, he felt like a rung out washrag.

"Thank you, Special Agent in Charge Cartwright. In answer to your question, 'RSHA' stands for '*Reichssicherheitshauptamt.*' Do you speak German?"

Condescending prick. "Y'know? I don't. Be a pal and translate, Hank?"

"It means Reich Security Administration. The Roman numeral is the branch. Branch Six handles all foreign intelligence for the Nazi Party."

Time seemed to stop in the Fort Sumner courthouse.

Foreign Intelligence? That makes von Hofmann a trained spy— the protocol officer thing a goddamn cover. Hell, von Hofmann isn't escaping to Mexico—never planned on Mexico—he's going . . .

Where?

"Mr. Cartwright?"

"Thanks." Cartwright cradled the receiver.

His brain shifted into overdrive. Von Hofmann is after something, but what? Assassination: who? Sabotage: where? There was no objective within the state of New Mexico of any significant military or national value. Or was there? Cartwright understood his security clearance didn't encompass everything. J. Edgar Hoover's, on the other hand, did. If something top secret existed in New Mexico, that would explain Hoover pulling Cartwright from the case and putting his own man on it. It would make sense the OSS would know about it, too.

Maybe Donovan did. Larkin said the colonel had been overseas, and perhaps Larkin's security clearance was only as good as Cartwright's.

All of it speculation, but as agent in charge, speculation was Cartwright's job. And this rubbed right. Standartenführer Jürgen von Hofmann was after something. Something classified. Something big.

SPECIAL AGENT BURLEY sat in the Packard on the south shoulder of Route 60. His window rolled down, he aimed a pair of 7x50 field glasses across the tracks of the Santa Fe railroad and through a barbed-wire fence that stretched east and west for some two and a half miles. Beyond the fence lay Clovis Army Airfield, which was approximately sixty miles east of Fort Sumner. This was where Colonel Marls had led him. Special Agent Burley scanned the runway. A jeep drove out onto the tarmac. Colonel Marls, Major Hastings, and the driver, who appeared to be a duty officer, climbed out of the jeep.

All right, fatso, what are you up to..?

The three men lingered for a minute or two until a Cessna AT-17 trainer taxied toward them. Some conversation between Marls and the duty officer, and then Marls hoisted himself into the plane, Major Hastings right behind. The duty officer stepped back and saluted.

The Cessna swung round and rolled out onto the runway. There was a blast of exhaust from the engines as the pilot opened his throttle. He released the brakes and the trainer shot forward, racing straight for Special Agent Burley, filling his binoculars. Agent Burley lowered the glasses as with the mechanical scream of 490 horses and a violent suck of wind, the Cessna AT-17 lifted off. It rocketed over the black Packard so close Burley instinctively ducked.

Fifteen minutes later, Special Agent Burley entered the Clovis Army Airfield duty office. He flipped open his black leather ID case three inches in front of the duty officer's nose, exactly as Cartwright had taught him.

46

C OLONEL WILLIAM "WILD BILL" DONOVAN stared at Henry W. Larkin in disbelief. Donovan hadn't slept more than forty-five minutes in the past two days, and a colossal headache was trying to push his brain through the bone wall of his forehead. He hoped when it did, it would take with it his red, stinging eyeballs, their vision fading like a flashlight left on overnight. Donovan had spent the last three days in London, trying to pull two important operatives out of Paris after their covers had been blown to the Gestapo. Twice, Gestapo agents had cornered them. Twice, they were able to break to freedom. After a harrowing and miraculous escape from the city, they'd rendezvoused with a British Lysander on a field outside of Clermont. Thirty minutes later, a German Dornier Do.217N-2 night fighter shot them from the sky over the Channel. The agents had communicated that intelligence they carried was vital to the Allied plans for a cross-Channel assault on the Continent. Whatever that intelligence was, Donovan would never know. On his way back to Washington, as he'd stood in the freezing wind blowing across the icy tarmac of the desolate Newfoundland refueling stop, harried by mosquitoes big as his thumb, his sleep-deprived mind had told him at least nothing worse could possibly happen before Christmas.

That was before he'd sat down with Larkin.

He rubbed his face with both hands. As his hands slid off his stubbled jaw, the palms came together. He held them there as if in prayer. "Do I understand you? All this is taking place in New Mexico?"

"Yes, sir. And it's my belief we could cultivate this Agent in Charge Cartwright as an informer. Consider the intelligence possibilities, sir. We've never had anyone of that rank on our . . ." Larkin's voice trailed off. Donovan had stopped listening.

Donovan flicked the switch on his intercom box. "I need the president. Direct line. Top priority. It concerns Project Y."

He reacquired Larkin in his gaze, and Larkin was stunned by the change that had overcome the colonel. Where a moment before, Donovan had looked like a corpse, he now looked like he'd taken a draught of the Devil's blood, its fire coursing through his veins to bring him back to life. Larkin, a stickler for security, had never heard of Project Y, which meant it was time he left the room. He rose from his chair and retreated to the door. "If you need me, sir . . ." he said, but Colonel Donovan was back on the intercom.

"I want my car running and the driver ready for a run to the White House."

PRESIDENT ROOSEVELT SAT BEHIND the Hoover desk—Herbert, not J. Edgar—in the Oval Office. Colonel Donovan sat in one of two chairs fanned before him. The other was empty. The door opened, and J. Edgar Hoover strode into the room.

"Good evening, Mr. President. My apologies for being late."

Roosevelt inclined his head toward the director of the FBI. "Have a seat, Edgar."

Hoover took his place beside Colonel Donovan. He ignored his rival's presence.

"Colonel Donovan and I were discussing an immediate concern for Project Y security. He reports to me a German PW escaped from Camp Santa Rosa could pose a substantial threat to our most classified activities. I'd like to hear your thoughts on the matter, Edgar."

Hoover clamped his jaw as if gathering energy behind his words before firing them off in his characteristic rapid-fire machine-gun sentences. "First of all, he shouldn't be here." Hoover jerked his chin in Donovan's direction. "I do not need to remind you, Mr. President, intelligence-security for Project Y is absolutely and completely outside the jurisdiction of the OSS. Because of security leaks within that organization—leaks I have pointed out to you, Mr. President, in my memos of February twelfth, March second, and April twenty-eighth of this year—the inclusion of Colonel Donovan in the slightest way in any intelligence on Project Y, would prove disastrous."

Donovan showed no reaction. He waited for the president.

"I am sorry, Edgar, but I've chosen to disagree with you, as have General Groves and Boris Pash, who are officially in charge of Project Y intelligence."

"Exactly my point, Mr. President. Groves and Pash are in charge. I should be intersecting with them. And them alone. May I ask why they are not here?"

"They're in Switzerland, Edgar," the president said, "meeting with Allen Dulles who works for Colonel Donovan."

"The Germans aren't sitting idly by while we build an atomic bomb," said Donovan. "Their heavy-water plant in Norway resumed full production this past summer. We believe they are using it to separate U-235 from U-238. Soon they'll have enough fissionable material to build their own bomb."

"If they do," said Hoover to Roosevelt childishly pretending Donovan hadn't spoken, "it won't be on account of any failing of the FBI."

The president's cheeks flushed. "What does it take to impress upon you that security, intelligence, and counterintelligence activities on a project as potent and dangerous as the creation of an atomic bomb go beyond your petty territorial squabbles? General Groves, Colonel Donovan, and I believe this race with the Nazis is a race we can potentially lose. If we want to win this war and save the goddamn world, we must work together!" Roosevelt slapped his palm on his desk for emphasis.

The sound of the mantel clock filled the abrupt silence in the Oval Office.

Roosevelt pinched the bridge of his nose beneath his pince-nez summoning calm. "Now, about this prison break. Tell me what you are doing."

Hoover smiled. "Mr. President, you will be happy to know, everything is under control with regard to Project Y and the security threat posed by the escaped prisoners of war who are led by one SS-Standartenführer Jürgen von Hofmann. An associate director from the Seat of Government is already on his way to New Mexico to take over the operation."

"Mr. Hoover," Donovan cut in, "may we assume your agents already on the case have been alerted to the situation?"

"That would be the height of stupidity."

Donovan shot Hoover a dirty look the kind reserved for boors, drunks, and bastards. Hoover basked in it.

He said, "All intelligence and investigative work so far on Project Y has been handled discreetly by agents I have personally sent from the Seat of Government. At this point in time, while we are still uncertain von Hofmann has any idea of the project, I see no reason to break security and divulge its existence to any of my people who are not already cleared. Anyway, our problem isn't von Hofmann."

Hoover smirked, pleased to see he had shocked both men. "Whether or not von Hofmann is on his way to Project Y, or the planet Mars is moot. The FBI will stop von Hofmann, rest assured, Mr. President. The greater problem here—my problem—is, if von Hofmann is going to Los Alamos, who is he going there to see?"

"He has an appointment, for Chrissakes?" said Donovan.

Hoover stared, unblinking, at the president. "He must. He isn't going to rush the gate and see what he can grab. He's headed to Los Alamos for a meeting with an enemy spy already inside who has collected materials for a foreign government, but—and this is the tricky part—this enemy spy is not a Nazi and has no idea von Hofmann is coming for him."

"I am not sure I follow, Edgar," said Roosevelt. "Are you suggesting the Japanese have planted an agent in Project Y?"

"Hardly, Mr. President," said Hoover. He stood. He planted the knuckles of both his hands on the edge of the president's desk in his intimidating bulldog manner. "As I warned you repeatedly when this team of 'swaydo'-liberal scientists was assembled, Mr. President— I told you there would be problems with the Communists, and here am I, proven right. Somewhere on that mountain you got yourselves a goddamn Red agent."

Donovan folded his arms across his chest, and, shaking his head, gave a thin smile. "Who is it, Edgar? Oppenheimer, perhaps? Maybe Fermi, or Bethe?"

"They're all Russkie-lovers as far as I'm concerned. And don't believe it for a minute I don't have my eye on them."

"That is the farthest thing from all our minds, I am sure," Roosevelt said. "But may I remind you, the Soviets are our allies. I would hate for comments such as the ones you've just made to leave this room."

"Let us not mince words, Mr. President. The Russians are allies only so far as crushing Germany. As for von Hofmann, his being a Nazi proves my point. If the Nazis had a direct contact with Project Y, it would mean they had infiltrated it. Once inside, they would keep their cover as secret as possible in order to continue a steady flow of stolen information. Therefore, with someone already inside Project Y, they would have no reason for SS-Standartenführer von Hofmann. However, if the spy on the inside is a Commie agent, sending our secrets to Moscow, and Hitler discovered this, well, it's safe to say, if the Nazis want a piece of the atomic pie, they'd have to send a false-flag agent in pretty damn quick to cut their slice."

"May I interject, Mr. President?" said Donovan.

"By all means."

"I don't possess the vocabulary to express my personal and professional distaste for my illustrious counterpart."

"We're not counterparts."

"Ah, there goes my vocabulary. But hang on, Hoover. In this rare instance, I agree with you. His anti-Russian obsession aside, Mr. President, what he's saying—all hinged on whether von Hofmann is moving on Project Y to false-flag himself to an inside man as a Soviet spy, which I believe is likely—rings with a dark, unpleasant truth."

"Edgar, I imagine you have a solution for stopping von Hofmann and plugging this possible security leak to the Soviets?" the president said.

"I do, Mr. President. For your ears only."

"My cue. Mr. President." Donovan took his feet. "I will leave it to the two of you."

Both Hoover and the president noticed the hint of a smile playing at the corners of Donovan's lips and eyes. A great deal of strain was evident in Roosevelt's voice as he dismissed the head of the OSS. Donovan excused himself from the president and left the Oval Office.

Hoover said, "Mind if I have something to wet my whistle, Mr. President? What I have to say is rather involved."

Roosevelt gave Hoover a cold smile. "Not at all."

GIVE A MAN ENOUGH ROPE . . . Donovan had been honest about supporting Hoover's Nazi-Soviet double-conspiracy, if that's what you'd call it. But simplicity, Donovan found, is what makes for operational success. He didn't know how, but Donovan would knock Hoover down a peg on this one.

His driver waited for him. He let him into his automobile. Donovan's mind went to the FBI agent out in Santa Fe. Instinct told him Special Agent in Charge Cartwright wouldn't react well to being sidelined. And, Larkin had said, Cartwright was willing to offer Donovan a favor.

A STEWARD ENTERED the Oval Office, pushing a teacart. "Wild Turkey for the director. Nothing for me."

The drink was poured and handed to Hoover. He took a sip, smacked his lips, and Roosevelt had a fleeting image of a toad catching flies.

"Mr. President, you have read my reports, but we have never discussed the end of the war face to face."

"No, Edgar, we've not."

"I'm talking about the Reds, Mr. President. When we're finished with Germany, we are hardly going to have time to breathe before we find ourselves at war with Russia. And the Russians, I am afraid, will have one major advantage over us the Nazis and the Japs never had."

"That being?"

"Well, I'm not saying anything new when I tell you, Mr. President. Our nation is riddled with Communist subversive elements. When it comes time to face off with the Soviet Union, we're going to find ourselves crippled to inaction by the active and dangerous Red fifth column here at home. Unchecked, the groundswell here will destroy America. If we plan to win that fight tomorrow, measures must be taken today to protect ourselves at home. That means securing an inside track."

WASHINGTON WAS ABOUT DEAL MAKING. Roosevelt watched the door to the Oval Office shut behind Hoover. Deals had gotten him to the White House and kept him there for three terms. So what was one more? Sure, what Hoover wanted put a bitter taste in his mouth, but the truth was Roosevelt didn't want Stalin to get an atomic bomb any more than Hoover did. Though he'd never consciously admit it, playing hardball with Hoover on something this important to the FBI director was out of the question. Not with what was in the director's secret files about him, his cabinet, and, most damaging and disgusting, the things about his wife. Hoover was a spoiled child, and Washington, his playroom; if he didn't get his way, he'd break all his toys.

Roosevelt lifted the telephone receiver and called his close friend and personal adviser, Harry Hopkins. "Harry, I need someone to find General Groves in Switzerland. I must speak with him as soon as possible."

47

At 17:05, the clouds threw a blanket over the sun as the stolen truck battered its way up the last of the high mesas into a state of surreal half-light. The dirt road meandered through piñon and juniper trees, tall and full, and closely packed. The only visibility afforded to Virginia was the bit of road ahead. She was wedged into the center of the front seat between Schmidt at the wheel and von Hofmann against the door. The Standartenführer's eyes blinked, fighting sleep. Virginia's hands remained bound. The road narrowed. The distance between turns shortened. Branches scratched the vehicle's sides and wove a net of brittle limbs above it. The truck rumbled over a rise and the vast openness that exploded before it dizzied Virginia with an unexpected sensation, like a bullet shot into the sky.

Overcome by the effect, she shifted her gaze to von Hofmann, involuntarily sharing the moment, hating herself for doing it, but his eyes remained shut.

His hand latched tight on her wrist. "Agna."

Virginia wrenched away. Von Hofmann's eyes flashed wide. Fearful. Trapped. Awake. She hadn't noticed before—the man wore a wedding band. Virginia's revulsion increased at what it meant. He loved? Was loved? Did he have a family? The ring gleamed, daring her with its answers.

He noticed. All he said was, "Feldwebel, stop the truck."

Schmidt complied. The plateau stretched one kilometer west, like the finger of a god high above a landscape of rolling hills speckled green beneath a silver ceiling of low-pressing clouds. It narrowed in width from two hundred yards where they sat, to fifty yards at its tip, the entire length having a downward pitch of three, almost four percent. Ahead of the truck, the road continued, a gray scar through a wide, circular field of dry sand scrub that extended to the first crumbling walls of the ruins of Gran Quivira. Two thirds of the way across the mesa, rising from a knuckle of earth like the stones of an intricate ring, stood an abandoned church. Its two empty, broken towers commanded the mesa, silent sentinels to pueblo peace, Spanish conquest, Apache violence.

Von Hofmann swept the landscape with a keen eye. Nothing moved, not even the wind. The silence that cloaked the mesa was the safe, cold silence of the grave.

"*Fahren Sie in die Ruine.*" he said. Drive into the ruin.

"*Zu befehl*, Standartenführer."

The truck rumbled over the open field and entered the eight-hundred-year-old maze of roofless, multileveled dwellings. Here and there, the road branched deeper into the pueblo. Pits and mounds of chipped stone and dirt indicated the abandoned diggings and shafts of archaeologists and treasure hunters. A weathered plank bridge carried the road over a deep trench, the bottom of which ran with a street from a second, more primitive civilization.

"The problem with America—you have no honor for your past," von Hofmann said in English. "The future you pile on top of it is temporary, then left to rot."

"You don't know the first thing about Americans."

"In Germany, cities older than the one below us still stand occupied," he said.

"Not if our bombers keep up the good work."

Her words appeared to affect the Nazi officer with greater force than she would have expected, anticipated.

"Tell me your name."

"Tell me who Agna is." When he didn't respond, she pressed. "When you grabbed my arm, you called her name. Is she your wife? You miss her?"

Von Hofmann slapped her face. The sting on her cheek warmed Virginia. She reminded the Nazi of his wife. It had saved her life and continued to keep him off balance. It wasn't as physical a weapon as a stake, but before this was over, she'd drive it through his heart.

"You've spared my life. I'm thankful for that, and I spoke out of turn. I'm sorry. My name is Virginia Hendricks."

"What I said about America wasn't entirely fair."

He spoke as if the Agna exchange had never transpired. Virginia pretended she didn't notice—calculated so that he would.

"The pure chain of the German ethnic past is unbroken since before the Teutonic Knights, while this ruined 'civilization' was built by savages. Americans deserve credit for dealing with your undesirables in the same way Germans now deal with ours. I'm speaking, of course, of the Jews."

Virginia played sheepish to his condescending superiority. She recognized in his emotional seesaw the weakness of a personality of extremes. Extremes engendered recklessness, and recklessness—dangerous in this man as it was—could create opportunity.

The shattered towers of the Spanish church disappeared from sight as the ruined pueblo walls loomed higher. The truck drove under a freestanding stone arch onto a field of gravel and short, tufted grass. A kind of plaza before the church. Beyond, the road continued off the plateau in steep switchbacks that dropped to a lone highway leading north.

Schmidt halted the truck for a second time and von Hofmann jumped from the cab. Zundorf and Gauss hopped from the back, followed by Wolters and the Tiger. Schmidt shut off the engine. They joined von Hofmann. Each man carried a handgun in his belt and a shoulder weapon they'd selected back at the pass where they'd left Mesmer. Virginia remained in her seat.

"What about her?" said the Tiger.

"Out." Von Hofmann jabbed a finger at the ground.

The Tiger pulled Virginia from the truck. He prodded her with his foot. "*Schnell. Mach schnell.*" And he knew in that moment, he would have his way with her that night.

Virginia moved forward, but, unable to use her hands, legs stiff from the tortuous journey, balance eluded her. Zundorf lunged and caught her.

Virginia's eyes met his with silent appeal. Zundorf scowled. He steadied her and pushed her back to the Tiger with what sounded to Virginia like a reprimand.

She had seen something in his eyes—behind his scowl—something that once again set him apart from the others. She couldn't pinpoint its essence, but as von Hofmann barked orders to his men and she was hustled toward the church, it came to her.

Shame.

48

S PECIAL AGENT TORRES found the Keyes farm without trouble. He parked beneath the windmill and stepped from his car. Above, the vanes creaked, rusted and forlorn. Torres looked out over desolate farmland. The sorrow it reflected crept termite-like through the cracks in his forthright veneer to feed on the contempt he kept so carefully hidden. Contempt for New Mexico and its suffocating provincialism.

Torres moved onto the porch and knocked on the door. "FBI. I have a warrant to search the premises."

He waited. No response. Torres tried the door, found it unlocked. He entered.

The place was a mess. It stunk of animals. Their shit littered the floor. A Winchester .30-30 cartridge box lay open and empty on the plank table. Torres's eyes shifted to the fireplace. A deer-hoof gun rack was empty above the mantel.

He found no outward evidence to indicate any association between Tyler Keyes and the Nazis.

Torres had not realized how badly he'd wanted to prove Tyler Keyes was a spy. Secretly, Torres had harbored hopes that in breaking this part of the case, Hoover would recognize his worth, pull him out of this Podunk hickdom and transfer him back to Chicago. Save his dying marriage. Keyes was a nobody. He had nothing to do with the Nazis. A pipe dream exploding in Torres's face.

He hated Tyler Keyes. Hated New Mexico. It wasn't fair. In eight days—New Year's Eve—he would lose the only thing that mattered to him. Torres could not allow, would not allow it.

Torres pulled out all the drawers. Pawed through cupboards, the hutch, dumped a chest. Peeked under the bed, then in a burst of fury, threw the bedding into the ashes of the fireplace and flipped the mattress to the floor. He found matches by the stove. Without thinking much about it, he lit one and threw it into the debris. Torres stalked back to his car. Emotionless, he watched the farmhouse burn, and he prayed to God in heaven for some way out of his dilemma, not knowing his salvation was closer, inbound on the Pan American flight one-eleven from Washington.

49

Concealed between two limestone boulders at the western edge of the plateau, Leutnant Wolters scanned the valley through the field glasses. He caught sight of Nestor Cooney's Hudson as it appeared on the horizon, a speck of green like one of the thousands of trees come to life and marching inexorably toward him. He scrutinized the car as it snaked through the low hills toward the plateau and, by the time the setting sun made the thick, low clouds appear like a wall of fire descending onto the mesa, he was certain the driver was alone. Halfway up the plateau, Nestor Cooney switched on his headlamps. Three minutes later, he failed to notice the flare of a match as he passed a pair of limestone boulders, but Schmidt, Tommy gun cradled in the crook of his arm, saw Wolters give the signal and he lit his own match for Zundorf who had climbed the side of the crumbling southern bell tower.

"He's here, and he's alone, Standartenführer," Zundorf called to von Hofmann waiting impatiently inside, then Zundorf struck a match across the stone and held it toward the ruined pueblo where Gauss and the Tiger guarded their rear.

Nestor Cooney entered the church and squinted in the dim light. Scattered masonry and fallen timber, the jagged pillars of broken arches, and the dark, cluttered entrances of the cave-like side chapels and sacristy gave the impression God had left the mesa in a violent hurry. "Anyone about . . .?"

The *clack-clack* of a bolt thrown and closed on a rifle was his answer. He whirled to find Zundorf perched like a gargoyle on the broken wall above him. His gaze dropped to the door where Schmidt stepped into view, the Tommy gun level with the spy's chest. Nestor Cooney's arms flew into the air like a brace of flushed quail.

"Turn around. Slowly."

Nestor Cooney did as instructed. Before him stood an SS-Standartenführer, Luger aimed and ready.

"These ruins are cold," Nestor Cooney spoke in German.

"Out here, the sun is cold. Tobacco keeps me warm," von Hofmann responded.

"I quit smoking on my birthday."

Sign, countersign.

Von Hofmann shoved the Luger behind his belt. "Hauptmann Zundorf, keep him covered. Feldwebel, go out and search his car. When you're finished, resume your patrol of the perimeter."

"I brought a sack of food. And there's a change of clothes for you in the trunk, Standartenführer," Nestor Cooney said.

"Feldwebel, you will take those items to our vehicle before returning to your patrol."

"*Zu befehl*, Standartenführer," Schmidt said, and retreated into the falling night.

Zundorf jumped to the dirt floor behind Nestor Cooney. His rifle never wavered.

Von Hofmann studied the American spy with the same critical eye he'd used to judge recruits at Sennheim. The SD recruiters had done adequately with this one. The man was a dust mote; the kind of person one never paid the slightest attention to unless it was to laugh. While he didn't look like he'd be much help in a fight, there was just the right amount of fanaticism in his eyes that said he would murder if he had to, or if captured, take the cyanide tablet von Hofmann was sure he carried close at hand.

Nestor Cooney broke the silence. "It is truly the greatest honor of my life to have been chosen to serve you, serve my Führer, and serve the Fatherland, Standartenführer."

"Are you German?"

"Not exactly, sir."

"'Not exactly?' Is that a riddle?"

"No, sir— I mean, I was born American, but I became a man in Germany. I went to school there, years ago. I was in Munich in '23 for the Beer Hall Putsch. I marched into the Odeonsplatz no less than ten yards behind the Führer. It was glorious. I remember it like yesterday, standing in front of the Bürgerbraükeller. Our surprise when the Führer drove up—"

"How nice." Von Hofmann held out an open hand. "My orders, if you please."

Nestor Cooney stopped warbling and withdrew the envelope from his pocket with a timid hand. "Of course, of course, Standartenführer. Do forgive me. As I said before, this is quite the honor. Truly." More gush as he clutched the envelope.

"Now?"

Nestor Cooney handed von Hofmann the envelope. Von Hofmann ripped open its seal. He examined the contents: a road map and a driver's license in the name of Victor Rogers; a train schedule; a train ticket; a bundle of American money . . . Von Hofmann thumbed the bills.

"Five hundred dollars, Standartenführer."

"Hmm." Von Hofmann pocketed the first five items from the envelope. He turned his attention to a sixth: the four-page handwritten cipher.

Von Hofmann withdrew the Bible from his black leather jacket. He followed the steps that converted it into a variation of an unbreakable onetime code pad. It was December, the twelfth month, so he turned to the twelfth book of the New Testament: Colossians. Adding the digits of the date together—two plus three—gave him a chapter: five. Colossians only had four chapters. All this meant was that after reaching the last chapter, von Hofmann went back to the beginning of *Colossians* and continued from there. The fifth chapter counted was chapter one. Last, he noted the day of the week. Thursday, the fifth day. Every fifth letter in chapter one, *Colossians* would be ignored.

Von Hofmann had his key.

He fished a pencil from his pocket and, sitting on a block of fallen stone, wrote his translation beneath the encoded letters. The first letter of the cipher was the letter "H". "H" is the eighth letter of the alphabet. Von Hofmann counted eight characters into chapter one, skipping the "a" in "an"—the fifth letter—to arrive at "O", which he wrote beneath the "H". Next, came a "V". The twenty-second letter of the alphabet. Von Hofmann counted twenty-two letters (discounting every fifth) and found a "B". Third was an "I", ninth letter of the alphabet, according to his key: a "T" in *Colossians*.

A minute later, he had his first word: OBTAIN.

Von Hofmann had spent hundreds of hours training on this code and once familiarized with the key, worked quickly.

OBTAIN THREE NOTEBOOKS FROM NKVD SOURCE DR. KLAUS FUCHS.

Virginia hadn't understood why they stopped at the ruin until she heard the arrival of Nestor Cooney's car. A meeting was taking place with an American spy. A traitor. For the handful of minutes he'd occupy the Standartenführer and the other Nazis' attention, Virginia would make her escape.

If she could.

She lay face down on the dirt floor of what had once been the sacristy. In addition to the rope around her wrists, the Nazi called Schmidt had trussed her ankles and gagged her mouth. Virginia twisted onto her back. She curled her body, pulling her knees as tightly into her chest as she could. She rocked back and forth on her spine, straining to pull her wrists as far apart as possible in order to slip her hands beyond her hips. The rope dug into her skin, each millimeter further agonizing gain, but the space between her forearms was not wide enough. She continued to stretch. Her elbows ached. Something inside her left arm soundlessly snapped like a broken rubber band. The muscles spasmed. Quivered uncontrollably. Tears rolled down Virginia's cheeks. The pain shouted for her to give up, but she forced one last concerted effort.

With a sudden release of tension, her forearms slid over her hips. Virginia rolled onto her side, sucking air through her nose. Her wrists were now beneath her buttocks. She scraped off her shoes and waited until the most intense edge of pain dulled. She returned to her back and rocked again. With each roll, she lifted her wrists higher along the backs of her legs toward her ankles. Her heels rubbed rope. Virginia stopped rocking. Thankful her gag stifled the sound of her sharp cries, she worked her feet up and down until the curve of her heels hooked beneath the knots. Using her feet as levers, she stretched her arms. Her left shoulder popped, dislocated. She buried her face in the dirt and smothered her scream in the gag and gravelly sand. But her loose arm, lengthened once out of its socket, was all she needed. Her hands crested her feet and came up in front of her.

Virginia wiped her wet cheeks on her upper right arm. The pain in her shoulder was intense. It burned and it tingled up and down the limb, which, along with her fingers, was useless. Hands still knotted together, she raised them to her face and ripped the gag from her mouth. Virginia set her teeth to work on the knot between her wrists.

Tyler Keyes cautiously rode his bay from the tree line and onto the northern edge of the plateau. Softened by the dusk, the harsh lines of broken walls dissolved one into the other in shadowed layers that deepened from misty gray to rich dark blue until they blended indistinctly into the inky black stain of the Spanish church, its broken towers giving it the appearance of a smear across the sky. Viewed in the deceptive light of falling night, the ruins ahead of Tyler did not appear ruined at all, but alive, as they'd been so many hundreds of years before. Tyler's father had first shown him this optical illusion. They'd camped here when Tyler was a boy, which is how he'd known to leave the road before it trapped and forced him down its tunnel of trees onto the plateau at the strategic disadvantage of silhouetting on a rise without cover. His father had shown him that, too, and explained how none of it was an accident of nature, but a feat of defensive engineering accomplished by the pueblo's original occupants almost one thousand years before. Zuni Indians had planted and tended the trees, dug the mound, and cleared the field that bordered the pueblo as a killing ground for their enemies.

Tyler didn't know whether he'd find his quarry within this ancient pueblo, but if he did, his only chance lay in surprise, so he left the road early and fought his approach through the dense forest.

With a tickle of spurs, he urged his horse toward the pueblo. Foliage grown up along the side of the mesa made an intermittent partition along the edge of the field. Tyler used these clumps of cactus and sage, the occasional scrub oak and javalina bush for concealment, but this camouflage thinned dramatically the closer he got to the ruins. Twenty yards out and in the open, Tyler drew his Winchester and urged the bay faster.

GAUSS CAUGHT SIGHT OF TYLER KEYES six meters from the ruin. At the sight of the hat and the Winchester, he understood this was the cowboy who'd killed Mesmer. He was sure of this, and his response was automatic. He swung the rifle, putting the cowboy's head like a melon on the wall of his sights. He quietly opened the bolt and chambered a round.

Fifty yards away, Tyler stopped. He turned toward the road.

Gauss steadied his sight picture. He had the cowboy dead. He took three pounds of slack from the trigger and savored a shooting breath when Tyler abruptly disappeared from Gauss' sight behind a wall.

"*Scheisse.*"

Gauss glanced back in the direction of the Tiger's position halfway into the pueblo. Zundorf had given express orders to signal the Tiger at the slightest sign of trouble, but the dark of night had become complete and Gauss had no idea if the boxer was looking his way. If the cowboy hadn't noticed him, to light a match now would risk giving away his position.

Gauss vaulted over the wall. He landed in a crouch on the dirt road. He rose and, holding his rifle at ready, moved into the ruins in the direction of the cowboy's position.

TYLER FILLED HIS LUNGS with the cold night air. He'd been right. The Nazis were here. When Tyler picked out a hint of movement—the dark slash of a rifle barrel against the bone white of stone—adrenaline had hit so hard it practically knocked him from his saddle.

Now they would meet. Tyler clutched his Winchester in one hand and lashed his reins to a piece of timber with the other. He stroked the bay's nose. The bay snorted double trails of steam and lowered his head to graze. Tyler thumbed back the hammer on his Winchester.

He crept into the ruins and, low against the wall, he headed after his prey.

50

VIRGINIA PULLED HER BODY through a hole in the rear wall of the church and was free. To the west before her, the mesa dropped into a valley of rolling hills. Her first inclination was to head that direction, the swiftest way out of the mountains, but it would be a deadly mistake. The Standartenführer had been headed that direction. To search for her would be easy and cause him little delay. She would go back. If she could make it through the pueblo ruins without capture, she'd find safety in the forest where she'd wait for Tyler, who might be a mile or two back.

Virginia crept along the north side of the church. At the corner, she peered out. Schmidt, her father's Tommy gun slung over his shoulder, emerged from the ruins, wolfing down a sandwich. A green Hudson sat unoccupied in the little plaza before the church and as Schmidt passed it, he pulled a second, wax-paper-wrapped sandwich from his coat pocket. Virginia's stomach ached with hunger. It grumbled. The noise sounded deafening to Virginia. She pulled back, praying the Nazi hadn't heard her. After an agonizing minute, she peeked back at the car. Schmidt and the sandwich were gone.

Now or never.

Virginia sprinted onto the gravel and ran for her life. She passed the Hudson. If someone heard her and shouted, she'd keep running and hope they'd miss her when they shot, but no one said a word and Virginia hit the road. But the Nazis would be guarding the road. She had to get off it. Virginia dashed into the ruins. She took the first turn she could find and, pausing to get her bearings, continued up a narrow footpath. She kept an eye out for her captors. The footpath twisted and turned like a labyrinth, only to angle her back toward the church. It loomed before her, black and haunted.

Virginia wheeled. She dodged into a dwelling and out of its collapsed rear. She scurried from one toppled stone house to another until the disorienting maze delivered her to a wider lane. She moved onto it, only to lunge for the protection of a wall as this lane fed onto an open flat area enclosed by three high ramparts. Parked against one of these was the truck.

Virginia recoiled. She was running in circles. Panic, carried on the wings of every fear she'd ever known, closed in. She fled back into the crumbling village. A pair of hands shot from the black hole of a ruined doorway to seize her shoulders. Incapacitating pain shot down her left arm, making her incapable of resisting the hands now pulling her in and spinning her round. Virginia stared in terror at the shattered nose and lopsided grin of the Tiger.

"*Guten Abend, Fraulein.* In such a hurry to find me, and now, here we are."

Virginia struggled, but the young soldier's grip was strong. Her pain too intense. The Tiger shoved Virginia against a wall. He pinned her with his body. Virginia writhed beneath him. The Tiger reached into her wrap coat and his hands circled her waist. "Oh, very nice."

Virginia beat at him with her one good fist to no avail. The Tiger thumbed open the large buttons over her chest.

"Excited? Maybe it has been a long time for you, too."

"Please don't do this. Let me go. Please let me go."

The Tiger grinned. He slid his hands over her ribs, stopping them beneath the curve of Virginia's breasts. "You could always cry for help."

Virginia's muscles tightened, body clenching at the horror of her predicament. To cry out now would bring every one of them.

The Tiger's hands crept to her breasts. Virginia leaned in, surprising the Tiger by giving more of herself to him. He moaned as her cheek touched his and she exhaled into his ear an instant before chomping her teeth into it, drawing blood. He threw her onto her back and climbed on top.

TYLER HAD TRACKED GAME SINCE CHILDHOOD. Stealth came second nature to him, his senses as observant as his feet were silent. When he and Gauss suddenly faced each other on opposite sides of the domed waist-high roof of a prayer kiva, surprise came in on Tyler's side. But killing game and killing men are two different sports, and here Gauss had a deadlier advantage. War had made killing men an infection of his blood. For a fraction of a second it took Tyler to funnel moral, ethical, emotional, past experience, and future consideration into the electrical impulse that caused a nerve to flex the three muscles in his forefinger, Tyler lost his surprise.

Gauss didn't have to think or aim. He fired from the hip as Tyler squeezed the trigger and his Winchester spoke over the pistol shot.

HOLDING VIRGINIA between the vice-grips of his legs while his hands opened his fly, the Tiger twisted his upper body at the apparent sound of a single gunshot and, in so doing, partially lifted from her. The weight shifting from her legs, Virginia rammed her knee into the Tiger's groin. The Tiger clutched his crotch, jerking back, the wind knocked out of him. Virginia kneed him again, driving him onto his back. Virginia scrambled to her feet.

The gunshot had come from deep within the pueblo and meant only one thing: Tyler had arrived.

Virginia took off running.

Von Hofmann responded to the gunshot. "You," he thrust a finger at Nestor Cooney. "Get out of here. Now!"

"Our final rendezvous, Standartenführer?"

Von Hofmann shook the orders. "I have it. I'll be there. Go!"

Nestor Cooney ran. Von Hofmann ordered Zundorf to get their hostage. He drew his Luger and strode to the door. He stared into the darkness. Had it been a single shot, or two? No other gunfire followed. If someone was out there, von Hofmann didn't want to give away his position by calling or signaling the Tiger and Gauss. He swept into the plaza and listened.

There would be nothing remarkable were both Tyler's and Gauss's corpses found—they had fired simultaneously. But firing from the hip could only be counted on with a shotgun or into a cluster of targets. Where Gauss's bullet went wide, Tyler's slug hit Gauss half an inch below his right eye and, severing the medulla oblongata, exploded his cerebellum. Gauss didn't register either gunshot: he was that dead that fast.

Virginia clambered over a mound of stone between two pits. She passed under a wide archway into a dark arena surrounded by high walls. A footpath ran between four large stone troughs. Virginia saw the outline of a narrow wooden ladder propped against a wall. She dashed the length of the footpath and threw herself onto the ladder, confident the open field was beyond the wall and beyond that, the forest. She'd climbed three rungs and was putting her weight onto the fourth when it shattered, dropping her to the ground.

The Tiger's voice, goading her in German, was closing in from behind. Virginia leaped onto the first rung. This time it broke too, and the Tiger was upon her.

"You couldn't take it like a woman—had to fight like a man. Now you will see how a man fights." He punched her face, snapping her head to the side.

Virginia backed into the wall. The Tiger wore a brutish grin, clenching his fists and taking a boxer's stance. He would beat her before taking her for his pleasure.

"Move one more inch and I'll be just as happy to shoot you in the back."

The Tiger stiffened his spine. He turned. Virginia sidestepped out of the way.

Tyler stood under the archway. He aimed the Winchester. He intended to use it.

"How's your face, cowboy?" The Tiger's hand went for the gun behind his back, bringing it round in a blur.

Tyler worked the lever and fired.

A million stars exploded white behind the Tiger's eyes like a memory of the Mexican sky. He took one questioning step forward and shot. His bullet blasted through his foot as he crumpled to the earth.

Tyler lowered his gun. He shifted his gaze to Virginia.

Her face white with shock, her mind numb with fear, she sank to a sitting position against the wall.

Tyler rushed toward her and crouched at her side as she convulsed with sobs. His temper flared at the sight of her bloody wrists. Her dislocated shoulder. The men who'd done this—desire boiled to square their accounts with lead, but he had Virginia. That was all that mattered. Tyler brushed a long strand of copper hair from her brow. He tilted her face toward his, finger upon her chin. Her eyes were moist, ready to overflow. Her cheek and her lower eyelid were already bruising from where the Tiger belted her. He forced an amused grin.

"You're doing that on purpose. You know I never could stand the sight of you in tears." Without warning, he yanked her left arm, resetting it in its socket.

"Ow!" She reflexively punched his chest.

"That's the Virginia I remember."

She wrapped her arms around his neck. She held him fiercely.

Tyler embraced her a moment before speaking with total assurance. "Now we get out of here."

"I didn't leave anything behind. Ready?"

"Ready."

Tyler helped her to her feet.

AT THE DISCOVERY of Virginia's escape, von Hofmann ordered Wolters, Schmidt, and Zundorf into a skirmish line. Weapons cocked, they stalked into the darkness. Von Hofmann covered the center of the ruin, moving warily along a passageway between rows of collapsed structures that appeared pounded by artillery. Aside from the distant yap of coyotes, the night had fallen silent after the second pair of shots, and the continued quiet seemed to bear out von Hofmann's earlier guess the gunfire did not represent a concentrated attack by military or law enforcement pursuit. Were that the case, they'd have hit fast and hard with overwhelming firepower.

Luger first, von Hofmann searched the shadows. He looked behind walls, probed each nook of his immediate area of deployment, the opinion growing that whoever had exchanged fire with his men was either a random hunter who'd come into the ruins—perhaps looking for a place to camp—or more likely, Virginia's cowboy whom he'd failed to kill at the ranch. The same cowboy he'd watched ride to the ranch the previous day. The cowboy who'd had the confrontation with the old man . . . For the second time, von Hofmann regretted not having stopped him when he'd passed, and this time it made him angry. He pushed it from his mind. Anger clouded judgment.

DEPLOYED ALONG the southern flank, Feldwebel Schmidt aggressively hunted the ruined pueblo, his mind fueled by his need to remove the stain of humiliation from his honor.

"She escaped, Standartenführer." Zundorf's words echoed in his head alongside the image of the ropes thrown at his feet like a gauntlet.

The Standartenführer had given him the duty of securing the hostage and the bitch had escaped. He'd catch her, he didn't doubt that, but catching her wouldn't give him the satisfaction he required.

Schmidt kicked in a brittle wooden door and spun into an empty room. The next chance he got alone with Zundorf, he would kill him.

51

T HE CESSNA TRAINER had been flying grid searches north of the Torrance-Lincoln and Torrance-Socorro county lines all afternoon. Lieutenant Colonel Marls sat in the student-pilot seat beside Flight Lieutenant Nathan McInerny, chewing his tobacco and alternating his conversation between obscene complaints directed against von Hofmann and a kind of maniacal gloating to a sullen Major Hastings in the rear over the rewards they were sure to reap when they caught up with him.

But for all this searching and swearing, they'd caught up with exactly nothing, and with fuel low and darkness arriving, Marls was left with no doubt that when Agent Cartwright found out what he'd pulled, his ass was going to be used for weather-stripping the men's latrines at Leavenworth. Goddamn, it was killing him. Von Hofmann had to be somewhere below, somewhere tantalizingly just out of sight.

"There!" Hastings said. "Off the port wing: a light!"

Marls stretched his fat neck to see across the pilot as McInerny gave the Cessna full left rudder and banked to port. Sure enough, the major was right.

The plane swept in low. The light revealed itself a campfire, and as Lieutenant McInerny raced overhead, sparks swirled and Marls got an eyeful of two teenage girls on their feet between a campfire and a station wagon, smiling as they each wrapped an arm over their heads to hold their hats, and—"They're Girlie Scouts on a goddamn campout!"

Lieutenant McInerny brought the plane level and swiveled his gaze to Marls. "Sir, we have to turn back now. I am sorry"—he wasn't—"but there's no other way. Look, I'm sure tomorrow—"

Marls seized the pilot's shoulder. "I ain't got no tomorrows!"

Marls's desperation caused the aircraft to plunge. Lieutenant McInerny regained control. He shot Marls's a questioning look. He swallowed. The colonel dropped his fat hand to the butt of his service automatic. Lieutenant McInerny balked. "For Chrissakes, you could have killed us, sir."

Marls's thumb rubbed the ridged edge of the hammer. "We still got one more mesa to cover, flyboy."

Hastings's face was taut. He leaned into the cockpit. "Sir, perhaps the lieutenant is right?"

"Shut up, Hastings. Lieutenant, proceed to that mesa now, or I will put you under military arrest for disobedience to a direct order in the face of the enemy."

Lieutenant McInerny released a deep breath. He angled the aircraft toward the Gran Quivira mesa.

TYLER AND VIRGINIA reached the bay without incident. Tyler freed the reins and swung into the saddle. He grabbed Virginia and easily pulled her up behind him. The horse sensed the trouble in the air, the death huddled around its riders. Its muscles tensed, quivered, and tensed between Tyler's legs. He gave the horse a reassuring pat on the neck. "Easy, boy. Nice and easy."

With a flick of his wrist, he turned the horse and walked it along the broken wall to its end. Once again, Tyler faced the emptiness of the sand scrub field that separated the ruins from the shelter of dark piñon forest. He weighed his options. He could retrace his earlier path along the mesa's northern rim, or cut the time in half and gallop across the field and hope to make the trees before the Nazis saw them.

The bay shook its head and stamped its feet. Extra jittery. That decided it.

"Hang on," Tyler said, and as Virginia's arms locked around his waist, Tyler raked his spurs once and with a kiss-kiss and a "Ha!" plunged into the open field at full hoof-pounding speed.

The first three hundred feet went by in a blur and Tyler figured they'd made it. A surge of exhilaration replaced his anxieties and fears, but their victory died at birth. For one insane moment, Tyler thought the forest come to life to turn against them as the vast breath of a monstrous, primal roar hit them head-on. The bay came to a violent, sliding halt as, blasting dangerously low over the trees, the Cessna whipped straight for them, the sound of its thunder increasing.

Tyler and Virginia struggled to keep seated as the bay reared, bellowing with fright. The plane disappeared over the ruins. The horse twisted and came crashing down. It staggered, almost toppling. Tyler fought to tighten the flapping reins and regain control as the beast spun and galloped back for the perceived safety of the ruins. Vaulting a pile of masonry, the horse entered the stony maze, eyes crazy with fear. Tyler strained at the reins as the bay's churning hooves clattered through the narrow openings between fallen walls and freestanding pinnacles of limestone bricks that jutted like the bleached ribs of a long-dead giant.

This near impassable course allowed Tyler to regain control of his mount. He savagely maneuvered it in a tight circle as automatic weapon fire chased the plane from the mesa.

"Herr Hauptmann!" Wolters cried, eyes catching sight of the horse. His mind flashed to Old Shatterhand—cowboy blood brother to Apache chieftain Winnetou—and his faithful mount

Hatatitla; once again, he felt himself living inside his Karl May novels and this time he grinned crazily.

ZUNDORF PIVOTED from watching the airplane zooming out over the valley. Flame exploded from the barrel of Wolters's shotgun. Zundorf raised his rifle and took aim; both the girl and the cowboy within his sights. He didn't pull the trigger and an instant later, they were gone.

Zundorf was surprised the decision not to kill had come so easy. As he'd stood there, a voice inside his head told him they were not soldiers, which made them not his enemy. There exists a fine line between warrior and murderer. Hauptmann Fritz Zundorf had crossed that line and it had diminished the value of his life. He would never cross it again. If that made his mission for the Fatherland more difficult, so be it.

ITS MOUTH FOAMING around its snaffle bit, the bay carried Tyler and Virginia onto the main road. To their immediate left was the deep, excavated street bridged by wooden planks. Somewhere beyond lay the ancient Spanish church and the far road out. Tyler charged across the bridge.

"You sure you know what you're doing?" Virginia yelled.

"I haven't known what I've been doing for years!"

Twenty yards ahead, von Hofmann took two steps into the middle of the road, materializing from the shadows as he raised his pistol. Tyler saw him. He swerved as von Hofmann triggered the Luger three times. The first bullet dug high into the bay's left shoulder, deflected by the scapula beneath. The other two shots went wild. Tyler released the reins. He lifted his rifle and shot, levered, and shot again. The bullets whiffed past von Hofmann's ear, and he dropped low. Tyler, applying unequal pressure with his spurs, directed the horse across the road into the other half of the ruins as von Hofmann fired a fourth time. The bullet whacked into the saddle's cantle, inches shy of Virginia's spine.

Tyler knew his bay's wounds were bad as soon as they left the road and the horse stumbled. Earlier, he'd considered running alongside the cliff a dangerous risk. Now, with his horse wounded, it would be suicidal. But he had no choice. The bay pulled short at a one-hundred-foot drop, broken only by the occasional cactus, juniper, and boulder clutching precariously to its side. Tyler guided the bay back in the direction of the church and urged it forward at a trot.

SCHMIDT STEPPED into their path. He raised the submachine gun and fired. Hot lead raked a bloody path down the bay's throat and neck. The horse screamed an almost human sound. More bullets buried deep within its breast. Heart pierced, life stopped pumping through the horse's veins, but its spark flickered long enough in his brain for his last act on earth to be an act of grace. Every muscle, every tendon concentrated its final reserve of power, and as its knees buckled, the bay twisted away from the precipice, hurling his riders from its back to safety. The last image to register on its wild brain as his head followed the rest of his body, slamming into the dirt, was Tyler's face. His master was safe. The horse was dead.

THE MEXICAN BITCH had been right as rain. Pushed into a corner, where most men would find themselves battered into submission and defeat, Colonel Lucien G. Marls had once again beaten the odds to find victory and its rewards within his grasp. "I gotcha, you goddamn son-of-a-Berlin-whore!"

"The port engine's hit, sir. I'm losing pressure. We're going to have to put her down quick!" said McInerny, shaken by the machine-gun fire that had raked their belly.

Lieutenant McInerny snatched the radio mike, but Marls grabbed his hand. "Uh-uh, boy. Do yourself a favor and let me make you a hero. Not twenty miles from here's the town of Dutton Butte. We're going set down there and hit von Hofmann when he passes through."

Again, Lieutenant McInerny backed down to his superior.

"Colonel, who's to say he'll go through Dutton Butte?" Hastings asked from the rear.

"I'm saying. Von Hofmann ain't got no other choice. He's not going to go back, and he ain't gonna abandon his wheels and head off on foot. There's only one road out of Gran Quivira and it goes through Dutton Butte."

No sooner did Tyler pull Virginia to her feet at the edge of the cliff than the Nazis converged from the ruin, covering them. Tyler stepped in front of Virginia, waiting for their bullets. No one fired. Von Hofmann addressed his men in German.

Zundorf moved into the open to the unarmed pair of Americans.

Tyler saw conflict in the German's face.

"You're a coward to go along with this," said Tyler.

"I have the power to save one of you, not both," said Zundorf.

Zundorf reached for Virginia's bloodied wrist. Tyler pulled her close with a protective arm.

"I am sorry, but it is war," the German continued. "All I can give you is my word as an officer. I will die before any harm comes to this woman."

"Fuck you, fuck your war, and fuck your word."

Zundorf didn't flinch.

"Don't do this," Virginia said.

"Mach Weiter, Hauptmann!" von Hofmann ordered.

Zundorf locked eyes with Tyler. "If she doesn't come this instant, you both will die."

Tyler hated the man before him. Wished he'd killed him like the others, but this enemy spoke the truth. "Virginia, I came here to save you. Don't make my death a waste."

He watched his words fill her face with anguish as if he'd torn her heart in two. Zundorf pulled her away. She took two dazed steps from Tyler before twisting around and crying, "I love you, Tyler Keyes!"

Tyler called to von Hofmann, "Get on with it, you son of a bitch."

"Schmidt, kill the buckaroo."

He came forward raising the Tommy gun. Tyler would die fighting. He lunged, a war cry on his lips. Schmidt squeezed the trigger and Virginia screamed.

52

The weapon barked. The first slugs hit Tyler as he struck Schmidt with a flying tackle, hurling their bodies onto the side of a large mound of excavated rubble at the cliff's edge. Tyler was in close, between the bullish private's arms, making Schmidt's weapon useless one-handed. Von Hofmann took aim at Tyler's back, but Zundorf leaped in, wrenching Tyler from Schmidt, beating him backward to the mesa's edge with the butt of his rifle. Tyler dropped to his knees and Zundorf swung for his head, sending Tyler over the mesa's edge into blackness.

Tyler tumbled and rolled until his body caught against a boulder. It was the only thing left between him and a one-hundred-foot drop to the valley below. Unconsciousness pressing in, he lifted his head. His eyes focused on Zundorf, silhouetted against the moon, his rifle aimed.

Atop the mesa, Zundorf fired. He lowered his rifle. Von Hofmann, holding Virginia as though she were his, said, "Dead?"

"I don't miss."

Von Hofmann released Virginia to Zundorf. He scrambled up the mound, pushing Schmidt out of his way and peered over the precipice into darkness.

Boulders, some clinging trees, a valley far below—no one could survive that fall—but his ire was raised, and he fired the rest of his clip after Tyler before wheeling on Schmidt. "Wasn't Veit enough of a lesson in disobedience for you? Your next mistake will cost your life."

"*Jawohl*, Standartenführer. I humbly beg for the Standarten-führer's forgiveness."

Von Hofmann stared at Schmidt as he slapped a fresh clip into his pistol. He wanted to put him down with a single shot, but logic and the situation argued against passion. The killing of Schmidt would be impractical. Now that the plane had discovered their position, now that he had his final orders and his objective, von Hofmann needed Schmidt more than ever. He'd come up with a perfect use for his human time bomb.

ZUNDORF STUDIED VON HOFMANN. It would be well within the Standartenführer's nature to shoot Virginia, and he wanted to prevent that. He gave Virginia a brutal shake. "Stupid girl, now you see escape is useless. It only brings the death of fools."

She recoiled from him, cowed.

"You have only yourself to blame for this killing," he said.

ZUNDORF'S OUTBURST STARTLED VON HOFMANN. He hadn't figured the Hauptmann as one to torment a prisoner. Why didn't he grab her from the captain and get it over with?

Kill her!

Because the woman standing before him was already dead. Once. His soul hurt looking at her. He took her from Zundorf.

"You wish you could die, don't you?" von Hofmann said.

Virginia was pale, as if she were about to collapse. Von Hofmann held her up. "He should not have followed."

Agony drained from Virginia's face. She glared at the Standartenführer. "Before this is over, I will watch you die."

Von Hofmann raised a hand and Virginia gave him her face to meet the blow, but the hand struck lightly, a mocking pat on the cheek.

He would kill her, but first, he needed Virginia to get him through the town of Dutton Butte. There was no way to avoid this. In Dutton Butte, he would meet resistance. Even if the aircraft hadn't spotted him, Dutton Butte was the hub of four major highways. The Army or the FBI, possibly both now, would have a roadblock before the town. A frontal assault up the road, guns blazing, would be suicide, but Virginia would throw the Americans off guard. Allow him to get in close. Give the enemy the hesitation he needed. After that, she will have served her purpose.

He tucked his pistol behind his belt, reverting to German with, "It is time we leave this mountain."

"And our mission, Standartenführer?" said Zundorf.

"More than I could have hoped. Our American enemies have an installation not far from here where they are building a uranium bomb. One of their physicists, an agent for the Soviet NKVD, plans to turn over designs for the triggering device to the Russians tomorrow at zero-nine-thirty hours. He will be turning them over to me. Imagine: one bomb for London, one for Moscow, and one for Washington—"

Wolters gasped, astonished.

Von Hofmann remembered Himmler's words: *Whatever the individual task you are asked to perform, know, if it succeeds, it will be no less than a deathblow to our enemies.*

"I promise you, my soldiers, peace will follow on the Führer's terms."

PART THREE

"I know my fate. One day my name will be associated
with the memory of something tremendous—a crisis
without equal on earth, the most profound collision
of conscience, a decision that was conjured up
against everything that has been believed, demanded,
hallowed so far. I am no man, I am dynamite."

— FRIEDRICH NIETZSCHE

53

O F THE TWO TEENAGE GIRLS who eventually dragged Tyler's body, bloody and unconscious, from the granite ledge, it was the one named Rebel—Rebecca really, but no one had called her that since her christening—who was remarkable. Seventeen years old and with secret plans to enlist in the WACs and follow Cody, her father, to England and a town called Middlesex where he was a ball-turret gunner on a B-17, she was the most liberated woman the town of Dutton Butte ever produced. To her mother's chronic embarrassment and her father's terminal pride, Rebel wore her hair short, played hell out of a first base bag, could outrun any challenger at the town picnic's annual footrace, tie a fly and cast a line, change spark plugs and oil, and for the past three years hunting with Cody for the annual Christmas buck, Rebel tracked and killed the animal herself. This, then, was all part of how she and her younger sister Janie came to be camped out two miles from the Gran Quivira mesa when Marls's plane roared overhead and the shadows of the ruin sparkled and popped with gunfire. The idea of not going to investigate would never have occurred to Rebel had Janie not raised a stink, but it certainly did nothing to stop her. She doused their fire, packed up the gear and her sister into the family station wagon, and cautiously approached.

By the time they arrived, the ancient pueblo had all but returned to the silent ghosts of its past, save for the yipping and fighting of four coyotes feeding on the carcass of an empty-saddled horse at the edge of a cliff. If the rider hadn't walked out of the ruins on his own . . . Rebel fired her father's Steyr-Mannlicher rifle into the air, driving off the animals, before trading the weapon for a flashlight. She snapped on the beam. A minute later, she climbed over the mesa's edge and butt-slid to a hollow nest of sage and broken cactus from where her light had picked out the cowboy sprawled on a ledge ten feet below.

The girl winced at the blood that seemed to cover most of the cowboy's face and clothes, then she called in a thick Pecos drawl to her sister. "I told ya' there was people shootin' up here!"

Rebel dropped beside Tyler and touched his cheek. Warm. Tyler moaned.

"He's alive, Janie!" she said.

"So?" Janie answered.

"'So' you wanna jinx Cody by leavin' this cowboy to die?"

JANIE CHEWED her lower lip. She hated how Rebel called their father his first name, but she didn't want to fight. Janie was scared of the night, scared of the ruins, scared of being there alone, but a whole lot braver than she gave herself credit for; she scrambled down to join her sister.

54

Halfway between Gran Quivira and Dutton Butte, the right rear tire shredded. If they hadn't been driving on blacktop, the vehicle would have flipped. As it was, Schmidt needed both lanes to maintain control, slewing back and forth, fighting the truck to a safe stop on the right-hand verge.

Schmidt jumped out. Wolters and Zundorf joined him and the three set about pulling the spare from its bracket beneath the truck, locating the jack and other tools, and getting the tire changed.

Since leaving the ruins, von Hofmann had watched the girl silently weep for her cowboy. He brooded over how two people no more significant to this planet than the rocks and dust and stunted pines of this forsaken land had come so close to settling the future of the Reich. His future. It was surreal. A man alone on horseback, under-gunned—a throwback to another century— had inflicted 50 percent casualties on a team of highly trained, heavily armed Wehrmacht soldiers. Veterans of brutal combat each of them. It made no sense. The cowboy had been to that ranch, had seen the devastation, and still he had followed. What it was about this woman that would drive a man on so suicidal a pursuit?

Agna was that kind of woman.

Von Hofmann admired the curve of Virginia's high cheeks, her eyelashes soft and dewed, the determined line of her jaw. He remembered the warmth of her face when he'd mocked her with a childish pat, how his fingers brushed her tears. He filled with the fire of self-loathing and disgust.

He'd rubbed his fingertips together, guiltily absorbing the moisture of her tears into his skin.

Scheisse!

This shit he wallowed in had nothing to do with Agna. "Get out of the car. I'm tired of looking at you, Virginia."

He'd added her name to reinforce she was only who she was. Virginia did as she was ordered.

VIRGINIA HAD LONG BELIEVED that between men, frustration read as a singular emotion applied to external forces. Either it is alleviated or it runs its course. Men don't bother themselves defining its nuances. It is a uniform reaction to any great number of unwanted and uncalled for annoyances. Experience taught her that male frustration is a reaction to underlying emotions, which are manifold. As she matured and learned the nature of men, she could hear the tones within a man's frustration that communicate decidedly different needs and wants beyond the triggering source. Von Hofmann's frustration was disturbingly amorous, but not in the vile way of the rape-hungry pig Tyler gunned down. It lived in longing, and loneliness, and regret. The need to communicate and commune with Agna who, doubtless, was his wife.

"Thank you." She slid to the driver-side door.

She looked back at him. He was dressed in the civilian clothes the spy had brought him. He appeared less threatening, even handsome. He appeared a man who could have a tender wife who cared for some person inside this monster who wasn't insane with war. Not his frustration, but those emotions behind it would be the weapon she'd use to kill him.

Virginia said, "I gave you my name. Tell me yours?"

TELL HER. *Hear her say it.* His eyes briefly glowed, then darkened.

Agna is dead.

"You address me as Colonel von Hofmann."

Virginia planed her face with patience. She pretended to have trouble climbing out with her hands bound.

"Fall, for all I care." *I know what you're doing.*

Virginia slid her body out and dropped, unsteady, to her feet. Von Hofmann watched her step away in the side-view mirror. He watched her exchange words with Hauptmann Zundorf who, after a brief discussion, allowed her to move into the roadside grass. She squatted. She wrestled with her undergarments. Virginia caught von Hofmann's eyes in the mirror. Held their gaze.

He averted his eyes first. To his wristwatch. 2030 hours.

A little over an hour since the spotter aircraft and the skirmish.

His execution of her foolish cowboy.

If the Americans were flying in troops, von Hofmann could still beat them to Dutton Butte. He switched on the dome light and reread his orders. Virginia returned to the truck and struggled her way back inside. She tried to steal a look at what he was reading. He flipped a page, and she caught sight of some words. She may as well have been staring into a bowl of Campbell's alphabet soup.

Von Hofmann met her eyes over the edge of the paper. "Wish you had studied German?"

"They don't see a need to offer it in our schools."

"They will." The corners of von Hofmann's lips twitched as he buried amusement. "It won't matter. As much as I enjoy your company, I don't think I'll change my plans so you and I can do readings from *Mein Kampf.*"

"Standartenführer!" Wolters called. "Incoming vehicle."

Von Hofmann shifted his gaze to the side mirror. Headlights approached from behind; a vehicle that would have passed through Gran Quivira.

"You will wait for my command, then open fire."

IN ORDERING HIS MEN, von Hofmann lowered his orders into his lap. Virginia's eyes picked out one word decidedly not German: *BRIDGE* and following what looked like *WARNING*—no, that was wrong. It was German again: *WARNERTEA*. Zundorf, Wolters, and Schmidt took positions behind the second truck.

The car slowed as it drew near, and Virginia, keeping an eye on the driver's side mirror, could see its occupants silhouetted in the night. "Please, don't kill them, Colonel. They're not the authorities. It's children. Don't do this."

Von Hofmann shoved his Luger beneath Virginia's ribs. "Try anything and you join them."

ON THE REAR BENCH OF THE STATION WAGON, Tyler knew how lucky he'd been. Hit by two bullets, one through his left forearm, the other had gouged his left shoulder, he'd also fractured three ribs in the fall. His head and face were badly gashed, but the blood had clotted and, like the gunshot wounds, bandaged with the girls' bandannas. The bleeding had stopped.

In the front seat, Rebel drove while Janie sat sullenly beside her.

"A truck's stopped ahead. Maybe they need help." Rebel eased her foot on the accelerator.

"I don't know, Rebel. This cowboy . . ."

Don't stop. Don't— "Stop . . ." Tyler mumbled from the back.

Janie glanced at him, frightened, worried.

"Stop?" said Rebel, her foot moving onto to the brake. "They might need the tow from town."

"Keep . . . going. They'll kill you!" said Tyler.

THE STATION WAGON was ten feet shy of the truck when Rebel floored the gas pedal and von Hofmann shouted, "Fire!"

Bullets exploded from behind the truck, but shots gauged to hit the slow-moving driver's compartment blasted through the windows over Tyler and riddled the cargo compartment behind him as the station wagon surged forward, swerving crazily across the road. Schmidt stepped into the open. He unleashed a hail of fire into the rear of the fleeing vehicle, taking out its back window and its taillights before night swallowed the wagon.

55

Dutton Butte was a dot in the shadow of the Manzano Mountains, clinging to life like a stink bug on a boulder in a windstorm. The town existed to service the fourteen pinto bean farms of this region of the Estancia Valley. It was little more than a Main Street bordered by a post office, a handful of shops, a bank, a service station, a restaurant, and a park with a bandstand that hadn't seen the downbeat of a conductor's baton for twenty years. Main Street ran a quarter of a mile from a stone bridge over a wash, through two intersections, to an adobe church and cemetery that marked the usual way out of town for Dutton Butte's inhabitants. Those who came up Main Street intent on passing through took the road right past the church, past the rusted sidings of the abandoned Santa Fe freight stop, where they were confronted by a bewildering post nailed to which were enough highway numbers and directional arrows to get you out of Dutton Butte in a hurry.

Standing under the shingled roof of the covered sidewalk in front of the post office, Lieutenant Colonel Lucien G. Marls was staking his life von Hofmann would never reach that signpost.

This didn't please the aging mayor of Dutton Butte, Dr. Dexter Colhane, DDS. "Pullin' back our army roadblock," he said, "you're allowin' them Nazzies to drive right into my town. I won't have Main Street become some kind of battle zone, Colonel. Won't do it, won't stand for it."

"Been done and stood for without you, Mayor."

Mayor Colhane sputtered, but Marls kept right on going. "If you'd wanted a choice in the matter, you should've joined the

Army, 'cause this here's a wartime military operation. Now you can either do your duty and get me some volunteers, or you can keep your yap shut."

"I'll tell you what I'm goin' to do. I'm callin' right now the office of the FBI like I was told I was s'posed to. Then I'm calling the sheriff in Estancia. You just wait. We'll see who's in charge, won't we?"

Marls spat a stream of tobacco juice into the gutter. "You'll want to speak to a fellow named Cartwright. He's the big J. Edgar Hoover head-honcho in these parts. Tell him I said hey, and that he can come here for von Hofmann's body any time he wants."

The mayor scratched his little Buffalo Bill goatee. "Fine," he said. "Excuse me." He turned and wrapped his knuckles on the post-office window. A light burned yellow inside. The postmistress, Mrs. Nutter, who, like every other citizen in this town, had been watching the street since that low-flying airplane almost took off the church steeple half an hour earlier, scurried to the door. She unlocked it, peered around the mayor to the fat colonel, and stepped aside. Mayor Colhane entered. He shut the door behind him.

Marls loosened some mucus from his right nostril with a rapid screwing of the knuckle of his right index finger. He pulled out his handkerchief and blew into it. Every goddamn time he missed a meal, he caught a cold. Today he'd missed three. He hoped he wasn't coming down with that flu. Hell with it, anyway. He was about to become a hero and no missed meals, no flu, was going to stand in the way of that. Let the old-goat mayor bleat at Cartwright. Marls had that son of a bitch beat. He could already see the morning's headline: *Army Colonel Foils Escaped Nazis*, and below it: *FBI Arrives to Pick Up Bodies*. Or something like that— bones, pieces, scraps—it didn't matter, this was his victory.

Marls smirked, pleased as Christmas pie. He turned to face the stone bridge as the clouds, gathering since sunset, opened, dripping a timid rain. He guessed it had been Tyler Keyes shooting it out on the mesa. He hoped von Hofmann had saved him the trouble and already killed him. He didn't like the idea this Keyes fellow might now come riding into Dutton Butte. Too many witnesses—but if it had to work that way, he'd make sure to save a bullet or two.

Two jeeps rolled over the wash. That would be Major Hastings bringing in the roadblock. Good. The lead jeep pulled alongside the covered sidewalk. In it sat Hastings, a sergeant, and a corporal. The sergeant was the oldest of the enlisted men and Marls guessed him to be nineteen. Marls waited for salutes before saying, "So what did you bring me, Major?"

"These two and the four recruits in the other jeep, Colonel. How would you like them deployed?"

Marls studied Hastings for a second. Hastings's face drooped like a forlorn cat. The goddamn major was going yellow on him.

Marls turned his attention to the sergeant. "What kind of weapons you carrying, Sergeant?"

"Sir, I got my M1 carbine. There's Corporal Hansen here on the BAR heavy assault rifle. Brenner and O'Toole have the .30 caliber machine gun in the back of the other jeep. The rest have got Springfields, sir."

A .30 caliber machine gun and a Browning Automatic Rifle? *Hot dog! I am going to cut that bastard von Hofmann to bloody red Christmas ribbons.* "What about grenades?"

"I got one, sir."

Marls addressed Hastings. "All right, Major: six fine soldiers plus the two of us . . ." He studied Main Street. Christmas lights ran the length of both sides of the street. Probing their colorful glow with a shrewd eye, Marls planned his ambush. "Here's how we do it," he said, and was about to begin when—"Say, Lyle, where's that dopey flight lieutenant?"

"He's not with you?"

LIEUTENANT MCINERNY declined the jug of corn liquor the old Navajo offered as he sat warming by the Indian's stove. "You drink that stuff?"

"Me, no. Don did, but he's gone now. Quit drinking when he joined the army. Signals Intelligence."

"Signals Intelligence?"

"My people's language is the US military code," the old Navajo said, straightening in his chair with pride.

Although the Indian spoke the truth, Lieutenant McInerny didn't believe him. He simply smiled and nodded, glad to be indoors and away from that maniac Marls.

He'd landed the Cessna in this poor farmer's field and no sooner had he opened the hatch than Colonel Marls pushed his way out and led the lieutenant and the major into town. Well, they'd gotten there. Found the mayor and a bunch of excited folk waiting outside the hotel for them, the mayor's bridge hand still in his liver-spotted grasp.

In the following confusion, McInerny had doubled back to the plane and gotten on the radio. That had been at eight forty-five.

He checked his watch. Nine thirty now. If this storm didn't get worse, he estimated the FBI agent he'd been patched through to would arrive within the hour.

56

S PECIAL AGENT BURLEY'S FIRST INKLING something was wrong came when he'd called Cartwright to report on Marls. The call had been short, the Special Agent in Charge distant and abrupt. Cartwright ordered him to stay put at Clovis Army Airfield, and Burley had sat in the control tower through a long and silent afternoon that drifted into a damp evening. When, at ten past eight, Lieutenant McInerny radioed from some Indian's bean field and gave his story, Burley had the tower patch the flight lieutenant in to Cartwright in Fort Sumner. Events moved rapidly from there.

Once again, Cartwright's handling of the situation appeared out of character. Damn near in opposition to FBI procedure. Cartwright and Burley would fly to Dutton Butte alone. Apparently, the rest of the FBI's New Mexico field office had other things to do that took precedent over apprehending the escaped Nazi killers. Burley didn't buy it. Something was wrong, but Cartwright hung up before Burley could gather the nerve to contradict him, and, well, it wouldn't have been right for Burley to have that conversation with Cartwright with the Army on the line. He'd wait until they were airborne, he decided. Then he'd get some answers.

McInerny's captain, a tough First World War flying vet named Dixon, flew Special Agent Burley in his Beech UC-43 Traveler to an airfield outside of Fort Sumner. There they picked up a sullen, chimney-mouthed Special Agent in Charge Cartwright and went airborne for Dutton Butte.

"There some kind of problem, sir?" said Burley.

"Yeah. I'll fill you in before we land."

Uneasiness crept over Special Agent Burley. He watched Cartwright buckle in. His movements were deliberate, as though his every action weighed heavy with portent.

"Mind if I smoke?" Cartwright called over the whine of the engine.

"No ashtrays on this rig, friend," Dixon replied.

Cartwright didn't take that as a no. He lit up, and with his first exhale, Burley could read in his eyes that Cartwright was gone.

A light rain was steadily falling. Captain Dixon announced they'd be flying into a nasty headwind coming off the Manzano range so to hang on. The flight would take about an hour and a half, and might prove a little bumpy.

While they hadn't yet hit any turbulence, they were now only half an hour out of Dutton Butte, and Cartwright, chain-smoking through a pack of Lucky Strikes, remained lost to the world.

"Sir? Is it just the two of us going against von Hofmann?"

Cartwright squinted at Burley across the dark interior of the stagger-winged trainer. He flicked ash from his cigarette, then blew across its cherry tip. "Looks that way." He gave a humorless chuckle. "Still, we got Marls and whoever he's rustled up."

"What?"

Cartwright stubbed out his cigarette on the metal seat bracket. Changed the subject. "Had a call today. From the director's office. Hoover."

"You spoke to Hoover?"

"By the time I returned it, he was gone. I got his wife."

Special Agent Burley winced. He disliked Tolson, the Ivy League martinet.

"Hoover ordered us to stop the investigation, back off on von Hofmann. He's sending an associate director, a fellow named

Parnell, to take over." Cartwright looked at his watch. "Should be landing in Albuquerque right about now."

"Any reason, chief?"

"'Special circumstances.' Didn't give a damn how many people von Hofmann's butchered, or that he's got a hostage."

"Jesus, what kind of mixed-up swamp sense does that make? Lieutenant McInerny said von Hofmann was trading shots with someone at Gran Quivira."

"Right. And I am under direct orders from the top to do absolutely nothing about it."

The plane lurched, the turbulence making itself known. Special Agent Burley's voice sounded small against the roar of wind. "Us going to Dutton Butte—"

"Goes against Federal authority. And frankly, Burley, to paraphrase Mr. Clark Gable, I don't give a rat's tits. I'm taking von Hofmann tonight and saving that girl. Now you're either with me or you're not—a decision you'll have to make on your own."

Special Agent Burley didn't know what to say, but Cartwright had gone back to his cigarettes and didn't look like he expected his subordinate's answer right that second. *Lay off von Hofmann? What in Christ's name was Hoover thinking?*

THE PLANE HIT a pocket of what must have been nothing because it certainly wasn't atmosphere and it dropped fifty feet onto another rough floor of air. To Cartwright, it was like falling from a horse.

57

FRIDAY, DECEMBER 15, 1916

THERE WAS THE BREATHING OF THE HORSE, the tick of living time beneath him, and then the endless fall and the swirl of yellow, choking dust. Cartwright remembered. He remembered jerking erect on cold, unsteady legs at the gritty sand bottom of the arroyo. Remembered nervously checking himself with rapid patting hands as if afraid he'd come apart. He remembered the bile of fear burning the back of his throat as he tried to catch his horse, knowing if he failed he would die, bones bleached by the merciless Mexican sun and buried in Chihuahuan sand. But he had regained the horse and later, that afternoon in 1916, when the sky turned to sulfur and the air grew hot and thick, and dry as burning paper, he'd caught up with his prey at a Namiquipa whorehouse.

THE STRANDS OF BEADS hanging in place of a front door whipped in the still air, blue tobacco smoke filtering out between them.

Cartwright found the bandits' horses at the broken hitching post. One was a zebra dun, ridden-out and dripping great gobs of lather, its entire body quivering as if receiving a current of electricity. Dying on its feet.

Cartwright parted the beads and led the zebra dun into the building. The horse's hooves clopped on the dirty tiled floor. Four Mexicans seated at the bar pretended they didn't notice. They kept their backs hunched. They stared into their drinks.

Cartwright didn't want to kill the wrong person. "Whose horse?"

No one at the bar answered.

The bartender spoke. "Amigo, put the horse outside. Let me give you a drink. No?"

He poured a shot of tequila, but Cartwright ignored him and said, "You four at the bar. I'll ask one more time. Whose horse is this?"

Their reaction was the same as before.

The Apache knows no pity. We are the enemy. We have already won our fight.

Cartwright drew his .45 and put a bullet through the horse's brain. It slammed to the floor as the men at the bar whirled in their seats.

One of them—stringy, dark hair, long and unwashed—narrowed bloodshot eyes at Cartwright, licked his cracked and scabby lips, and said in a high-pitched sing-song, "Gringo, why you come here an' shoot my horse?"

The Mexican was fast. Even though Cartwright had his pistol covering the men at the bar, this man threw his iron and fired before Cartwright could react. It was a big nickel-plated .44, and it boomed like a howitzer in the close confines of the whorehouse. Cartwright heard the wind of the slug as it passed half an inch from his left ear. Then he triggered his own gun, didn't hear it at all, and knocked the bandit out of his stool.

Cartwright's eyes flashed to the other three men. They raised their hands. Now that they faced him, he could see they weren't revolutionaries. They were vaqueros, plain-old horse cowboys wanting nothing of trouble.

A gun roared behind Cartwright. A bullet tore into his back. Cartwright stumbled forward, turning as the second bandit, fat and shirtless, descended the stairs fanning his pistol, his next two shots, wide.

Cartwright fast-triggered his gun twice. His first bullet buried itself in the bandit's throat. Blood gushed, and the bandit took the rest of the stairs headfirst on his back. When he hit the bottom, he was dead.

Cartwright pivoted to the first bandit. The man, gut-shot and bleeding, was still alive. Cartwright raised his pistol. The bandit's red eyes widened in terror.

"Please, Señor Gringo . . . Mercy, *por Dios* . . . I beg you . . ." But as he choked out his plea, his grubby brown fingers spidered toward his pistol. He couldn't reach it.

"You," Cartwright commanded the shaved head vaquero closest to the bandit: "Give him his gun."

The shaved head vaquero did not move.

"Do it."

The man covered the .44 with the scuffed toe of his boot and slid the gun to the first bandit's fingertips. With remarkable vitality, the Mexican swept up the pistol, cocked and was taking the slack from the trigger when Cartwright let him have it in the face.

"There's more where that came from. Any takers?" Cartwright spoke these words in a rich, smooth voice he didn't recognize as his own. It created the desired effect.

Hands rose higher in fear.

"Good. You, bartender." He jerked his gun at the man. "Where's the girl?"

The bartender lifted his eyes to the top of the stairs.

A kind of calm possessed Cartwright then, as if, surrounded by darkness, he controlled events before him, like photographic images projected through a magic lantern. What he did and decided was fate.

The tequila shot the bartender poured beckoned from the bar. Cartwright took it, threw it back. It burned and told him he was alive and all of this real.

He skirted the dead horse and, stepping over the body of the second bandit, climbed the stairs. Two stairs from the top, he caught sight of the double-black eyes of a scattergun's barrels poking out around the doorframe. Cartwright's free hand shot out, closed on the weapon, wrenching it toward him. The scattergun came free without firing.

Cartwright bound up the last two stairs and through the doorway. He stood face to face with a fat whore. Cartwright pressed the barrel of his pistol into the soft folds of flesh beneath her chin. "Take me to the girl, or so help me God, I'll splatter your brains across the wall and find her myself."

"I didn't want her, señor. They made me buy her!"

"Where?"

"In my room," she whined, pointing to the doorway at the end of the hall. "I made her a bath and gave her perfume. I said someone would come for her. I wanted to take care of her, make her pretty, *entiende usted, señor?*"

Cartwright holstered his .45. He shoved the whore before him, the scattergun aimed at her spine. Frightened eyes of Mexican girls glittered in the cracked doorways they passed. They reached the end of the hall.

Cartwright pushed her into the door. "Open it."

The fat whore opened the door and stepped inside. Cartwright followed, and this is what he would see every day of his life for the next twenty-seven years:

The older of the two kidnapped girls. Age twelve and lying in a white cast iron bathtub. Her eyes fixed on the ceiling. Her naked arms stretched over the edges to hold her body from slipping beneath the soapy water. A bottle of perfume lies broken on the floor, the shards of glass red with the blood from her wrists.

Cartwright's eyes focused on the triangle of glass blood-sticky fixed in the girl's right hand. He couldn't move. *Why'd she lose hope? Why'd she have to kill herself?*

Why hadn't I been faster?

The bloody scatter of glass across the floor was the glistening reminder of each time he'd stopped his horse—

Of holding Galgo up with his complaints—

Of his fall down the arroyo—

The drink at the bar—

His inability to get off a single shot in the firefight . . . The crystal reminders of all his shortcomings and failings.

Cartwright had no recollection of taking the glass from the child's hand. Of gently lifting her body from the water. Of laying it on the bed. He'd rolled her in a sheet and draped her over his shoulder. He must have, for that was how she was when he went back down the stairs.

He paused at the bottom. The barroom had emptied.

Cut out their eyes . . . They do not deserve to find a way to the afterlife.

Cartwright turned the head of the second bandit with the toe of his boot. He aimed the scattergun at the corpse's face and fired one of the barrels. He strode to the bar where the first bandit lay face up among the stools. Flies buzzed around his bloody belly, sucking blood, regurgitating it, eating it. Cartwright disintegrated this man's eyes with the buckshot from the other barrel. He dropped the gun and pushed through the beads. Only his horse remained at the hitching rail. He looked both ways.

The three vaqueros who'd left the bar when he'd gone upstairs covered him with pistols, backed by some citizens of Namiquipa. Cartwright stood motionless.

No one moved. No one spoke.

Cartwright turned his back. He lifted the girl's body from his shoulder and laid it across his saddle. A strand of her golden hair fell free of the sheet. He unhitched the reins and walked toward the crowd. He walked until he was a foot from the line of three vaqueros. They studied the American. He studied them. One of the Mexican cowboys stepped aside. The cowboy removed his hat. The others followed with theirs.

Cartwright passed through the cluster of people. A woman stepped away from her husband and blocked Cartwright's path. Her hand went to her throat. She unclasped a crucifix from around her neck and pressed it into Cartwright's hand. Cartwright nodded. Thanks or something, he didn't really know.

CARTWRIGHT FOUND GALGO where he'd left him. The little girl had made it through the worst of it, and the old Apache pronounced she would live.

After tending to Cartwright's wounded shoulder, Galgo led him back toward the American forces. The little girl slept most of the time, cradled in Galgo's arms. When she woke, it was only to eat and drink. She never said a word, just watched the two men from behind the veil of her soft and golden lashes.

Galgo left in the night before Cartwright rejoined the cavalry at Las Palomas below the border with New Mexico. Cartwright awoke in the gloomy darkness to Galgo singing a prayer over the sheet-wrapped body of the dead older girl. Cartwright watched him. He said nothing. The old Apache finished singing and climbed onto his pony's sway back. He left their creek-side camp and, as Cartwright listened to the pony's hooves splash through the water, he heard Galgo's voice. "Her soul cannot be free until you untie it from your heart. Forgive yourself and let her go."

At dawn, Cartwright rolled and smoked a cigarette. Then he carried the silent little girl and the body of her sister into the camp. He'd been three days AWOL. Soldiers crowded. An officer came forward, took his report. When the little girl was taken from his arms, Cartwright held out the crucifix the Mexican woman had given him.

"It's hers."

Three days later, the US Cavalry withdrew from Mexico, their mission chasing Villa a failure. A week after, on Christmas Day, Tom Cartwright's hitch was up. He mustered out of the cavalry at Camp Furlong, New Mexico.

He was surprised when a handful of reporters ambushed him at the Columbus rail depot. They flashed his photograph, bombarding him with questions, but a young man wearing driving goggles, a tawny topcoat and matching driving cap, who grinned with all his teeth, took Cartwright by the arm and hustled him to a waiting Model T.

"I hope you don't mind, Mr. Cartwright," said the man, settling behind the steering wheel.

"Don't mind? What the hell's going on, buster?"

The driver engaged the gears, and the Ford sputtered jauntily forward. The driver showed his teeth again. He handed Cartwright a newspaper. It was a copy of the previous day's *Washington Post*. The headline read: "President Wilson Calls Trooper Cartwright 'Hero of Our Age.'"

Cartwright rubbed his face with both hands and stared at the headline. "Look, I don't get any of this." Cartwright tossed the paper into the driver's lap. "For starters, who are you and where are you taking me?"

"Work for Senator Eaton."

"Never heard of him."

"Well's he's heard of you. So you and I are getting on a train and heading for San Diego, Californy—if that's okay with you? Gonna visit him with his family. Ring in the New Year."

"Why?"

"'Why?' Because you saved his one niece and killed the three desperadoes what murdered his other. Says it right there: you're an American he-ro, sir."

IN SAN DIEGO, Cartwright spent the weekend with the senator and his family in a Victorian mansion that overlooked the sea. Upon Cartwright's arrival, the mother of the two girls met him at the front door. She thanked him and she broke down and was helped away by a Mexican housekeeper. After supper, the senator took Cartwright into the library and explained. America would soon join the war in Europe. It was inevitable . . . "The military needs a hero, Mr. Cartwright, someone who'll stir the imagination of this country's boys, convince them they too might find the kind of glory you found were they to enlist and go fight the Bosche."

The brandy burned Cartwright's throat. "You telling me, sir, this hero business is a ploy by President Wilson for recruits?"

The senator gave Cartwright a sympathetic smile. "Look, no one likes to be used, but we're going to need men—lots of 'em—if we want to win this thing."

The senator took a long puff from his cigar. He shifted his eyes from Cartwright to the lit end of the cigar that he held upright. He blew his smoke across it and the two men watched the cherry tip glow red between them, the older man passing the mannerism to the younger.

"That doesn't mean you're not the greatest hero I have ever had the honor to meet. No words can express the gratitude and respect with which this family holds you."

Silence hung between them, drifting on the smoke.

"What about the girl? How is she?"

"Stella. She doesn't speak. Doesn't come out of her room . . . She doesn't seem to know who any of us are. The doctors say it's not unexpected; there's a good likelihood it will pass with time. We have faith she'll recover." His tone had gone from formal to strained, and, with his last words ringing false, the senator rose.

Cartwright finished his cigarette. "If she's here, I'd like to see her."

"I don't think that would be good for her. I'm sorry."

The weekend passed with sailing, California summery winter sunshine, a New Year's Eve barbecue. Late Sunday afternoon, while playing croquet on the lawn with the senator's wife and two young sons, Cartwright saw the curtains stir in a high window. He turned to get a better look—*A tiny face? A glimmer of golden hair?*—but the sun reflected harshly off the glass and by the time he shielded his eyes and squinted, the face, if it had been there at all, was gone.

On Monday morning, January 01, 1917, a cable arrived from Washington. President Wilson was offering Cartwright a lieutenancy in the cavalry.

Cartwright declined.

After supper, as Cartwright made his thanks and his good-byes, there was an awkward moment by the front door when the senator tried to present him with a check for five thousand dollars.

"Reward money."

"I couldn't accept it, sir."

"I see—but how will you get by?"

"I've some back pay to collect. It ought to hold me till I find something or other."

Senator Eaton extended his hand. Cartwright gripped it firmly and shook it. As the senator opened the door, the mother of the little girls came forward and touched Cartwright on the arm.

"Write to me. I want to know how you fare, Mr. Cartwright. Please?" Her voice was fragile. Words spoken as if she were afraid they might break and lose their meaning.

Cartwright smiled and caught himself staring at her unmarred white wrist as she pulled her hand away.

The same driver who'd picked up Cartwright outside Camp Furlong waited with the same Model T beneath the portico.

"Ready to go?" He grinned with all his horse teeth.

"Yeah."

As they pulled away from the house, something compelled Cartwright to look back. His eyes sought out the high window. This time, there was no doubt. A child's face. Stella. Her golden hair framed by a halo of electric light. She raised her hand. Cartwright hoped she might wave. All she did was beat a balled hand against the windowpane. Cartwright understood. A few inches below her fist, the silver cross glimmered as it plinked against the glass.

58

"A BOVE THE DEEP and dreamless sleep, the silent stars go by. . ."

Tyler was the spindle and Bing Crosby (or was it Frank Sinatra?) spun a cocoon of vinyl song around him, weightless and dark . . . but the drums were insistent rain, and drums didn't fit, and Tyler's mind took a second step out of the nothing-purity. The rain: wet and outside. He: dry and inside, centrally balanced to a 'Little Town of Bethlehem' universe. His eyes fluttered open. Through a fuzziness resembling consciousness, he faced nothing, not even reckoning of where his mind had gotten to, but he belonged to gravity once again and he fell from one place to land on another, and pain that hurt but didn't necessarily feel, covered him in a landslide of numb.

He wasn't in the back of the girls' station wagon. Not anymore . . . Sepia mouths hovered on a flat white belly of a dry cloud above him . . . He squeezed his eyes shut.

Disjointed images strung like twinkling Christmas lights along a dark night of oblivion flashed across his memory.

The prick of a needle. The end or the beginning?

A doctor. Stitches; his chin, his eyebrow . . .

The station wagon pulling into a town. Voices shouting and indistinct . . . Rough hands reaching in, pulling out, carrying him . . . True pain . . .

Back to the voices; back in the car:

"Don't be an imbecile, Mayor—he's working with von Hofmann!"

A fat, lying soldier.

*Nazis fire at them on the road . . . "Keep . . . going. They'll kill you!"
Probing fingers. ". . . Got some broken ribs, too, I see."*

The fuzziness continued to dissipate and Tyler's brain, like a cold engine coughing to life, sluggishly resumed its job of absorbing patterns of light and shadow through his eyes, trying to give them some kind of meaning. Sight was a backward experience, the understanding of the act taking more importance than the value of what he saw. What did he see . . .? A ceiling, white, not clean, ringed with dozens of water stains—not mouths—in innumerable shades of brown, one inside another inside another. They were beautiful, as if painted on purpose. Tyler stared until the edges of the stains vibrated like quivering lips, once again wide-open mouths.

Tyler's own mouth was dry. He moved his tongue across its roof. He tasted saliva. Was he thirsty, or not thirsty, or thirsting for dry to wet to "peace to men on Earth." Calm.

Tyler turned his head and the world tilted into another balance strangely detached from his being. His own soul spying on him from around a corner. At the same time, he was vitally aware of his every nervous impulse; the electric hum of life inside his skull a constant musical note, every twitch of his every muscle in his every movement—and vision now flip-flopped around: every object, every shade of light, of color, all carrying equal and powerful value—and the physical continuity of . . . the earth . . .? Gravity . . .? It all flowed together. Comfortable.

Tyler's mind jumped like a needle on a phonograph record. He was the guy who just fell off of the wooden bench against the wall. He lay there because people were dead . . . The bench is the color of honey. Mailbags, gray and dirty, the canvas worn and downy— now things were staring at him—piled on the floor beside him. Beside the bench. Boxes of varying sizes. A table covered with pens and pencils, packing materials, and rubber stamps—their ends so black with ink they looked like holes into space.

. . . Virginia . . .

It was a large room halved by a floor-to-ceiling windowed counter. Tyler on one side, the other . . .? Bing Crosby, most certainly, now talking about saving bacon fat for the war effort. Who else?

Tyler focused on the counter. Two workstations framed by drawers. Whoever built it was not good at building things. The edges of the drawers were crooked, uneven in their seat. The drawers were melting . . . and they were not melting. Simultaneous yes-no.

Tyler smiled. Something tugged above his left eye, but behind it, inside, there was a pleasing warmth.

Virginia.

At the end of the counter, a closed door led into Der Bingle's half of the room. Like the counter windows, barred. Although it resembled a bank, and might have been at one time in its past, Tyler suddenly comprehended: he was on the government side of a post office. But this was wrong; he didn't belong inside a post office. Not his choice.

Tyler decided to stand. He lay there picturing standing. And growing. And lay there.

Find Virginia.

That's right. Get up—Must get up, have to get—

The fuzziness closed back in.

Fat soldier shouts in the rain. "Fine. Go ahead. Treat his wounds, but after that, you keep that Nazi traitor locked up and guarded. When I'm finished with von Hofmann, I'll take him off your hands."

Rain splashing his eyes. Carried into a building. The two girls watching from the street, pulled away by their mother. The older one yelling, trying to make someone listen . . .

I'll listen. I'll say thank— Door shut.

Door opened. "Mrs. Nutter? It's Doctor Wilson. Told you got a patient for me." The man with the needles-and-thread. Needles and something cold and warm, yes-and-no . . .

"Come along. I locked him in the postal cage. You be careful, Doc. The colonel says, this fella's a Nazzie."

"I know all about it. He told me to shoot him chock-full of—"

A Nazi with a machine gun blasting from the road. Bullets perforating the back of the wagon . . . A screaming girl . . .

Virginia twisting around. "I love you, Tyler Keyes!"

Tyler lunged to his feet—

Virginia.

He'd failed the woman he loved. His emotions welled, then fuzziness engulfed him in a cyclone swirl. Plaster tape bound tightly around his torso, something wrong with his ribcage, but where there should have been pain, there was only a presence. The same was true for his left arm. He hadn't noticed before, but it lay across his chest in a sling. He could feel the stitches, could feel the hole through the muscles of his forearm, but sensation was cold and meaningless, his body encased in an armor of numbing icy heat.

The prick of a needle. ". . . Something for the pain . . ."

And for the stress and the urgency, and for his ability to concentrate.

Morphine. A heavy dose. Something else to fight. Some cowboy chorus replaced Bing. "Silent night . . . Holy night . . .all is calm, all is bright . . ."

Tyler went to the barred door. He peered into the Roy Rogers' half of the post office. Another bench against the left wall, a high table for addressing mail against the right. A plate-glass window fronted the street, a chair and folding card table set up before it.

Mrs. Nutter, a woman with wiry gray hair alternately blew into and sipped at a mug of coffee. She watched the street. On the table lay a stack of opened Christmas cards, a Motorola radio, and a .22 caliber pistol.

"Ma'am . . ." Tyler was unsure whether he spoke the words anywhere outside his head. "You help me?"

Mrs. Nutter turned. Tyler, he'd never seen so many wrinkles. They furrowed her face like the grain on a windbeaten board.

"What're you at? The colonel ordered Doc Wilson to juice you full enough to keep you out till mornin'."

"Ma'am, please. I gotta get going."

Tyler rattled the door.

"You ain't goin' nowhere. Damn Nazzie."

"What're you talking? I'm not with them."

"Hey! Cut it out with the door—and no, you ain't with 'em no more, I reckon to bet." She bent a shock of gray bristle behind her ear.

Who wears a steel wool wig?

"No, sirree," she said. "Colonel told me all about you, you murderin', treasonous trash. And don't try an' sweet-talk me neither. I happen to be an employee of the Federal Government."

All the drugs in the state of New Mexico wouldn't be enough to get Tyler to sweet-talk the lovely Mrs. Nutter.

From her bedroom window above her parent's restaurant, Rebel watched two of the recruits who'd been at the roadblock the past few days vigorously bob their heads to unheard orders issuing from the fat colonel's mouth. One of the soldiers she recognized was Billy Stevens. He'd played quarterback for Estancia High. His picture had been on the sports page lots of times last year when he took the team to state finals. They stood in the rain in front of the gas station. The boys saluted, and the fat colonel returned the gesture before splashing through the street toward St. Charles Church, where a moment before, Rebel had watched the major set up a machine gun between two headstones.

Rebel looked back at the gas station. Billy Stevens and the other kid huddled in the rain behind the tow truck, arms wrapped around their rifles trying to keep them dry.

"I wish Dad was here," Janie said from the doorway.

Janie, just out of the bath and wrapped in a towel, ran a comb through her long, dark hair. She sniffled between strokes and Rebel saw she was still crying, tears that had started the moment the gunfire had stopped.

"It'll be okay." But would it?

"How come no one listened to us and they locked up that cowboy?" Janie asked.

"'Cause we're girls."

Janie accepted this without understanding the magnitude of the words. Those words were a life sentence.

"Girls, I don't want you by the windows," their mother shouted from downstairs.

"See?"

Janie shrugged. She pushed away from the door. "Those Nazis aren't going to come through town, are they?"

Rebel lied with a shake of her head.

"Why's there gotta be a dumb old war, anyway?"

Rebel didn't have the answer, but Janie hadn't expected her to.

"Bath's free. Still warm," Janie added. She left Rebel alone.

Rebel looked at the empty space vacated by her sister. She dropped her eyes to her father's rifle, lying next to a can of cleaning solvent, a patch, brush, and ramrod on the bed.

59

The truck prowled the highway, the double beams of its headlights etched with heavy rain. After the incident on the road, von Hofmann had ordered Virginia into the driver's seat. If they were stopped, a woman behind the wheel would buy him and his men an edge on law enforcement or military scrutiny. Virginia gripped the steering wheel. Her nervous strain evidenced by her bloodless knuckles, white screams standing out against the night. Von Hofmann had mentioned they might encounter a roadblock before reaching the town, and it's why he had her driving, but now beyond the yellow-white patch of the high beams, Virginia recognized the stone bridge that marked the entry to the town of Dutton Butte stood empty. She risked a sidelong glance at the Standartenführer, who covered her with his pistol pointed at her belly. She could read suspicion in the dull sheen of his eyes.

"Stop right here," he said, shutting off the headlights.

Virginia depressed the brake. The truck splashed to a stop a short distance from the bridge. Past its black shape, a shimmer of electric light provided sparkle enough to outline the shadowy form of the town. With one hand, von Hofmann lifted his binoculars to his eyes while his other jammed the barrel of his Luger into Virginia's side.

Through the binoculars, von Hofmann could differentiate the streetlights from the diffused glow bleeding from storefront windows. He saw the first few buildings lost in a gray web of rain. The rise of the sidewalk. The black shapes of a few cars parked at its curb. He could see the colored dots of Christmas lights, but nowhere did he see people.

"They're waiting for us."

"Can't we go around?"

"There is no way around. Don't do anything foolish. And if there is gunfire, keep driving as fast as you can."

Von Hofmann pounded on the back of the cab and shouted in German.

THE FIRST RECRUIT, a kid from Silver City, had been scared shitless when the truck stopped before the bridge. They flicked off their headlights. He held his helmet to his head, pressed his face into the wet sand of the rapidly filling wash, and waited. The colonel had ordered him to signal with his flashlight as soon as the truck came into view, but the kid from Silver City didn't dare. If he flashed his light, they'd see him. He didn't want to die, and he'd remember this for the rest of his life as the smartest decision he'd ever made.

Presently, the truck rolled forward, a cautious black monster. The kid from Silver City scrunched deeper into the mud.

ON THE ROOF OF THE BANK, the nineteen-year-old sergeant knelt, bracing the barrel of his M1 atop the adobe parapet. His job was to rain fire into the cab and take out the driver. In his mind's eye, the sergeant saw his first bullet hitting that Nazi right between the eyes. *Bingo bango!* He pressed his cheek to cold, wet metal and waited for the signal from the bridge.

ALL ALONG MAIN STREET, the rest of the sergeant's squad were likewise prepared. Private Brenner had a Springfield and the sergeant's grenade. When the shooting started, the colonel had ordered him to roll the grenade under the approaching vehicle. If any of the Nazis survived the blast, Brenner and the rest would take them in a blistering crossfire. Privates Stevens and O'Toole were across and a little way up the street at the gas station. Corporal Hansen was in the park with the BAR. The colonel and the major blocked the end of the street with the machine gun.

The trap was set and perfect.

BACK ON THE BENCH, Tyler sat listening to the radio announcer talk about Dick Haymes's next song as the woman slurped her coffee . . . He found when he didn't move or actively engage his mind, the fuzziness returned. It was trying to surround him now . . .

It was good to sit and do nothing; relaxing to listen to Christmas carols. Listen to the rain . . .

Tyler shook his head. Virginia was out there. Somewhere. He had to escape and find her. He gathered around the drugs inside of him. They would empower him to get through any locked door. Tyler raised a hand full of fingers to his right shoulder. He pushed off the sling. His left arm fell like dead weight. His mind mentioned "pain", but he didn't experience it. Maybe his arm was paralyzed, but it was bending back and forth at the elbow, and Tyler was making it happen. He grinned. He was a mind connected to a machine.

Tyler scanned the floor from corner to corner. He noticed patterns of dirt without wanting to, and then located the carcass of a bloody sheep hanging from a hook on the wall waiting for the butcher. Tyler blinked three times in rapid succession, each a transforming snapshot, the sheep becoming his range coat hanging from a peg. He slipped it on, unsure how he'd gotten to it. As his left arm wormed up the sleeve, he experienced the dull tug and pop of tearing stitches in his shoulder. What did it matter? He was a machine.

Tyler charged across the floor and slammed his other shoulder into the barred door. The pain was immense, but it supercharged him.

Mrs. Nutter turned, fearful. "Cut that out!"

Tyler hurled his body-machine at the door again and the lock smashed. He spun through the door and reeled across the front room to collide with the onrushing front door. He pulled at the knob. Locked.

Pistol on the table.

Mrs. Nutter got it first. She pulled the trigger. The sear spring released the hammer.

60

THE HAILSTORM HIT as Virginia crossed the bridge and entered Dutton Butte.

Von Hofmann spoke, his voice firm. "Keep it steady. This weather will help us. It should keep people off the street and under cover."

Virginia strained to see the church and the end of town. *Just two more blocks . . . No one come out, no one come ou—*

A gunshot snapped from the right. A plate-glass window shattered, Tyler blasting through it, rolling into the street in front of the wheels of the oncoming truck.

Tyler's gaze flashed to the cab.

"Tyler!" Virginia shouted, overjoyed to see him alive, terrified to see him here.

She wrenched the wheel left to avoid him. Von Hofmann slammed into his door, reflexively pulling the Luger's trigger as the weapon jarred from his grasp. The gunshot was deafening in the closeness of the cab. The bullet dug into the upholstery beneath Virginia's thigh.

"OH, SHIT," said the sergeant on top of the bank.

What the hell happened to the signal? It didn't matter. He focused on the cab of the dark, swerving truck and fired his M1 three times. The driver's window and the windshield shattered, two of the sergeant's bullets slicing between Virginia and von Hofmann. Virginia floored the gas pedal, cranking the steering wheel back and forth, swerving the truck in perilous "S"s. The Luger slid on the floor beneath the pedals. Von Hofmann grabbed the wheel.

Tyler pushed to his feet. Gunfire cut through hammering sheets of hail from all directions, but the drugs convinced him it wasn't lethal. Time slowed. Images superimposed themselves over reality.

Endless exploding glass: from the window, from the falling sky. Wet, churning wheels throwing glass beads from the ground. Virginia's face of terrified joy.

One of the Nazis fired a shotgun from the rear of the truck toward the post office. A fantastic tongue of fire carved through the streaking surreality of ice to chase the buckshot from the barrel. The killer swiveled the gun toward Tyler. The barrel made a beautiful, liquid flowing trail. Tyler's legs surprised him, springing him between two parked cars. And the shotgun boomed.

Get Virginia!

Tyler scrabbled onto the sidewalk. The truck careened like a drunken skater across the icy street. Tyler crouched. He ran after the truck, keeping his head low behind parked cars, the world bouncing crazily before his eyes as Schmidt opened fire, ripping a trail of flying glass, splintering wood and searing lead back and forth across the cars.

Hailstones the size of ball bearings battered Marls's head and shoulders. He did his best to ignore them, glad for his hat, glad for the padding of his fat. He'd taken care of Tyler Keyes the best he could when he'd arrived, and now he sat in the wet church graveyard behind the .30 caliber machine gun, waiting to take care of von Hofmann as he zigzagged toward him. Adjacent to Colonel Marls, the miserable Major Hastings held the ammo feed belt that ran into the weapon.

"Ready for the hoe-down, Lyle?"

Hastings didn't answer.

"Toldja. You work with me, we come out of this heroes." Marls clicked his tongue.

He cranked the bolt handle back and let it fly forward. There was the satisfying *clack* of the first cartridge seating in the firing chamber. He had the truck dead in his sights, but he held his fire. He wanted to see that Kraut bastard's face. More than anything, Marls wanted von Hofmann to know who was top dog. Marls savored his fantasy, listening to the opening shots of what would ever be referred to as the Battle of Dutton Butte.

THE BATTLE OF DUTTON BUTTE lasted all of fifty-two seconds. Little time for much in life, it was still enough for four hundred and seventy-eight rounds of ammunition to help increase the number of American dead this World War would claim by seven. For the soldiers under Colonel Marls, everything went wrong right down to ways they fell. Private Brenner, who, at seventeen, needed permission from Mom and Dad to enlist, screwed his eyes shut and fumbled the grenade. It rolled beneath a parked Chrysler. By the time it exploded three seconds later, Brenner, eyes still closed, was jerking to a neatly, red-stitched line of Schmidt's bullets across his chest. The sergeant on the roof of the bank fared no better. Overzealous in his task of killing the driver, he quickly and permanently forgot all he'd learned in Basic Training about cover and concealment. Nor, once shot by Zundorf, did he have the Western grace to totter nobly on the palisade and back flip to the ice-scattered street below; he simply took two bullets to the chest, made a noise like *ohpf,* and fell to his ass, where he'd be found nine hours later, eyes opened and eerily balanced upright in his own defecation. For their part, Billy Stevens and Private O'Toole—bunched like Siamese twins behind the tow truck—did their best to avoid the action and the careening truck as it roared past, but Wolters—accidentally pitched from the rear when the vehicle went out of control—rose to his feet and dashed right up behind them. Rebel saw it all from the hail-cracked panes of her bedroom window: the truck blasting onto the sidewalk, tearing down Christmas lights as it raced straight for the church, colored bulbs popping and sparking across its hood to match the streaks of red tracers zooming in from Marls's gun in the graveyard. From down the hall, she heard Janie's scream and her mother screech, "Rebel! Get in here this instant!" but Rebel remained at the broken window, fingers packing the last of five fresh 11mm cartridges into a clip and slapping them into the magazine as she heard the cowboy yell, "Virginia! Get out!" Then she watched her football hero and Private O'Toole die: the backs of their heads stripped with their helmets by a single blast from Wolters's shotgun. Thirty seconds on the clock, and the Battle of Dutton Butte more than halfway into history. By this point, Marls had already shot off an entire ammo belt—his machine-gun barrel curling smoke, hail hitting its metal instantaneously hissing to vapor—and for those two hundred and fifty rounds he'd expired, only eighteen had hit the truck at all. He screamed at Hastings for another belt and registered the sight of the boy with the BAR, charging from the park, screaming as he tried to fire his weapon from the hip, his expression one of hopeless horror as Schmidt tore him apart. This meant nothing to Marls because the death belonged to someone else. Major Hastings's entire body shook as he pushed the tag of the second ammo belt through the feed block. He pulled it sharply to the right as Marls pulled the bolt handle back as far as it would go, released it, half-loading the gun, and that's when Wolters died. It happened like this:

Tyler yelled for Virginia to get out of the truck. He saw her body tumble from the vehicle, bouncing on the sidewalk across the street as the vehicle roared past, popping lights. And in his haste to reach her side, Tyler rushed straight into the street. He almost collided with Wolters the same moment the German killed the two kids behind the tow truck. It was all Tyler could do to hurl himself to the ground as Wolters tracked him with a second spread of buckshot whooshing over his head. Now the German would kill him. Wolters pumped another shell into the chamber as Tyler struggled, empty-handed, to his feet exactly below Rebel's window.

The report of a Mannlicher rifle once heard is not easily forgotten.

Rebel fired once from her window and took Wolters square in the back, blowing meat and bone through his chest on a boom of thunder that, for its instant, swallowed every other sound in Dutton Butte. Wolters took two graceless steps toward Tyler, his gun still aimed, the ability to kill the cowboy still within his grasp, but he didn't fire. The cowboy wasn't Old Shatterhand; Wolters was not Winnetou and he did not carry *Silberbüchse,* the "Silver Gun", of his Apache hero. A pawn of the Third Reich betrayed by all he followed, betrayer of all he'd ever believed. He twisted as he fell, using his final seconds of mortality to take vengeance for his own life. He fired at the face behind the rifle in the window and only a second afterward understood in abject horror the face belonged to a child, a little girl, and, figuring he'd killed her as he settled into death, he pondered how a shy and gentle boy who'd only ever wanted to be a schoolteacher could have ended here, destroying something so beautiful over something so ugly.

Ten yards from the church, von Hofmann recognized the bloated face of Colonel Marls at the moment the American colonel's fat fingers cranked the bolt handle back a second time on the machine gun.

Marls let it fly forward, ready to fire as von Hofmann arrived at the last possible instant to negotiate a turn past the church. It had always been a contest of wills between these two. A contest von Hofmann would never lose. Von Hofmann skipped the turn and guided the truck over the curb, aiming straight into the churchyard.

Marls tugged the trigger. Nothing. His hand flew to the bolt handle. It wasn't all the way forward. He beat it with the palm of his hand.

"You fool, you've killed us both!" Hastings yelled.

The last thing Marls saw was von Hofmann's implacable gray eyes, then the juggernaut mowed over him, grinding his and Hastings's bones into the ice, spent brass, and graveyard dirt, before smashing through the church doors and plowing inside the old wood and adobe building in a scattering of pews.

The gunfire ended. Tyler raced across the street. Virginia, having pushed herself to her hands and knees, rocked onto her heels as Tyler fell to his knees before her.

"I'm okay, I'm okay. I'm o-kay," she said, surprised more than anything else.

Tyler crushed her to his chest. Maybe it was the drugs, but it was as if electricity rushed through their bodies, melding cells, their molecules, and smashing atoms together with fire until a sun was born inside them, blooming like the opening petals of a magnificent yellow rose, and Tyler believed he was flying.

61

Von Hofmann's eyes blinked open. He pushed off of the steering wheel. His chest ached where the top of the wheel had dug into his sternum. His skull throbbed from slamming into the broken windshield. No blood was evident, and a quick check of his extremities told him he'd miraculously escaped any severe injuries in the crash. Von Hofmann guessed he'd blacked out for only a few moments. Past the buckled hood, steaming water gushed from the radiator. Sparks crackled and danced, threatening fire in the exposed engine compartment.

Von Hofmann kicked open the driver's door and jumped from the cab in a sprinkling of broken glass. A wave of dizziness. He clutched the dangling side mirror. How could it have all gone so wrong? That cowboy. The son of a bitch wouldn't die. Von Hofmann was the best Hitler had to offer—it didn't seem possible some Tom Mix yahoo could, time after time, confound his plans. And over what?

Virginia.

He took a deep breath. Forget her. He would not let Virginia or her cowboy get to him, not allow his men to have died in vain, but instead, he would slough off this disaster with laughter as Nietzsche taught: make the strengths of his enemy his own distinctions and ride them across the abyss. Success still lay within his grasp, and if success were to be anyone's, it would be his.

He found his Luger among glass shards beside the clutch pedal. He snatched it, beat back another bout of vertigo, and lowered into a pew. Zundorf and Schmidt joined him. Schmidt pressed a hand to his scalp to staunch the flow of blood from a mild gash.

"Where's Leutnant Wolters?" said von Hofmann.

"He didn't make it," Zundorf replied without emotion.

Von Hofmann noticed Zundorf's bare calf ran red with blood from a bullet wound. "You all right, Herr Hauptmann?"

"It went through clean, Standartenführer."

Von Hofmann appreciated Zundorf's stoicism. Zundorf unwound the scarf from around his neck. As he bent to tie off his wound, Schmidt brought up his weapon and fired. Both von Hofmann and Zundorf snapped their heads in the direction of the Feldwebel's shots.

An aged priest slumped in a doorway behind the altar. Schmidt grinned.

Zundorf looked sickened, but von Hofmann took it in his stride, adding his own bullet when the old, dying man feebly tried to crawl.

"Feldwebel, find a back way out."

"*Zu befehl*, Standartenführer." And Schmidt left the sanctuary.

"Hauptmann Zundorf, watch the street."

Zundorf didn't meet von Hofmann's gaze.

"Zundorf?" von Hofmann stopped him in his tracks. "Now is not the time to find religion. Remember Nietzsche: 'God is dead.'"

"Standartenführer. He was old and harmless—"

"He was a witness. If you and I are to complete this, it would be a good thing now to make our opponents believe we are dead."

"'You and I'? And the Feldwebel?"

"You and I started this together, and that is how it will finish. You will see what happens to Herr Feldwebel Schmidt—and knowing how you feel about him, you will approve."

Zundorf limped to the broken doors. He cautiously peered into the night. Somewhere in the last few minutes, the frenzied hail had turned into a soft , silent and floating snow. Cars along the street were in disarray. One burned irresolutely. In its flicker of light, Zundorf could just make out the form of Wolters's body.

You and I started this together, and that is how we will finish it.

The Standartenführer's tone bothered Zundorf, and now he put a name to why. For the first time in the nine months of their acquaintance, von Hofmann had spoken to Zundorf as a confidante. A friend. Zundorf's stomach went sour. Friendship implied a bond beyond the relationship between an officer and his superior. Von Hofmann was a sadist and a murderer. A Nazi perversion of everything Zundorf held sacred: duty, honor, country. Zundorf hated him. He hated him with a hatred that went beyond the boundaries of their military, political, and national associations. Zundorf hated von Hofmann with the kind of hatred that develops when a decent human being finds himself acting in collusion with a force of unmitigated evil. Evil on its way to acquiring a weapon of such devastating power—

Von Hofmann yanked the altar cloth to the floor. In the cascade of candles and flowers, the crash of the Gospel onto the floor—

One bomb for London, one for Moscow, one for Washington . . .

Zundorf understood: this mission must end. Duty, honor, country. Zundorf would do this for the best part of himself and for his Germany. He would execute von Hofmann.

Zundorf scanned the snowy street once more. Christmas lights winked at him from the park. Lights timidly flashed on behind frosted windows. People were overcoming fear. He could see their vague outlines as they slinked onto the sidewalks.

"Zundorf, your matches."

Zundorf pivoted from the doors. His leg ached. His spirit felt nothing.

Von Hofmann stood at the truck. The altar cloth trailed from the open gas tank. He held out his hand. Zundorf tossed him his matches.

Schmidt reappeared from within the church.

"A way out, Herr Feldwebel?"

"*Jawohl*, Standartenführer."

"Good. Hoist that body behind the steering wheel, then collect only the ammunition we can use."

Schmidt did as instructed. Von Hofmann lit a match. He touched the flame to the cloth. It instantly blazed. He stepped back from the fire, stepped around the truck and tossed the death's head *Totenkopf* from his officer's cap onto the body inside the cab. "Don't just stand there, Zundorf, we have a train to catch."

62

"SOMEONE FIND DOCTOR WILSON! My Rebel's shot!"

Voices brought Tyler back to the here and now, Virginia in his arms. He heard people running on the sidewalk and in the street. The bang of doors. More shouting. He stared into the turquoise pools of Virginia's eyes and saw within them his eyes as she looked back, seeing her eyes inside of his in the infinite mirror of being alive and in love. A snowflake drifted between their faces to melt in the hollow of Virginia's throat. They helped each other to their feet.

Townspeople surrounded the bodies of the boy soldiers, the wreckage of their town, and the burning car: human fences of grief and horror and American curiosity. The soldier from Silver City wandered in, muddy from the river bank, calling out the names of his comrades. A litany of the dead to the night. Tyler stared and God draped His own white sheet over the face of Dutton Butte.

"I thought you'd died," Virginia said, clutching him.

The truck inside the church sanctuary exploded with the bass-drum hollow *whoomp* characteristic of gasoline ignition. Smoke and fire coiled through the doors and bloomed through the roof in a great orange mushroom tipped black against the snow-falling darkness. Tyler and Virginia moved into the street as ammunition cooked off and a group of men ran for the church.

"They dead, you think?" Virginia said, indicating the church with a glance.

"Hope so . . . Looks that way."

The church burned with flames of taunting laughter. Siren crying, the town fire truck raced from a side street. Virginia and Tyler limped to the sidewalk.

THE WESTBOUND ATCHISON, Topeka, and Santa Fe Railway freight to Santa Fe slowed to pass through Dutton Butte at 10:23 p.m. The engineer was the first to see the flames rising from the town.

"Holy sweet Jesus—you see that, Earl?"

His partner looked from the controls, past the engineer's face, and out the windshield to the yellow flicker of fire. He shook his head. Wet his lips. "Maybe it's them Nazis they been searching for."

"We sure as heck ain't stopping to ask . . . Hope no one got theirselves hurt."

"Mmm."

They watched the fire until they passed back into a world that only came alive inside the spread of their headlamp, lived as they passed, and retreated into darkness as lifeless as the rails they rode. They left Dutton Butte, then, in the belief that nothing had changed with their passage.

They couldn't have been more wrong. As they rolled beneath the ghost of an outdated, unused signal tower, three men fell with the snow onto the back of the twelfth car. Icy snow dust swirled around them as they pried open the ventilation cover at the end of the roof and dropped into a car loaded with dead chickens packed on ice.

TYLER NOTICED the broken second-story window before they'd entered, and now, inside the restaurant, he wanted to find the stairs and see the girl who'd saved him—not once but twice—but the restaurant was untended and Virginia persuaded him it would be better to wait until someone chose to come down. There were two booths and six tables. They took the table closest to the large sheet-iron stove that pleasantly heated the room.

"Want coffee?" Virginia located the fresh pot behind the counter as she helped Tyler from his coat.

"Lots, and strong."

Virginia draped the bloodstained range coat over the back of a chair. She went behind the counter.

"What've they got to eat?" said Tyler.

"I don't know," she said and poured two cups before returning to the table. They sat and sipped. Virginia's hand found Tyler's. She squeezed, then tenderly brushed his hard knuckles with her thumb.

The kitchen door swung open and a woman in her mid-thirties came into the room. Her hair was pinned tightly back, but a few limp strands had fallen loose to frame a face smooth and red, glistening and slightly puffed from spending too much time over heat and steam. She clutched her Santa and Mrs. Claus apron around her waist and looked confused, as if life had recently deserted her and only now come back.

"Your girls . . . They okay, ma'am?" Tyler asked.

"I just don't understand what Rebel was doing. I told her to stay *away* from the windows. Doctor Wilson thought it better I come down here."

"The one at the window saved my life," said Tyler. "Twice."

The woman squinted, unsure whether she was having a conversation. She let her apron fall from her hands. Both Tyler and Virginia saw the blood. Tyler sipped his coffee, and the woman watched the mug move from the table to his lips to the table again. It had a kind of calming effect on her, and she busied her hands with her hair, tucking the loose strands back into place.

"There's meatloaf if y'all'd like supper."

"If it's no trouble, ma'am," said Virginia.

The woman pushed through the kitchen door. Between its swings, Tyler watched her open the oven.

The front door opened. Tyler shifted his gaze at the entrance of Mrs. Nutter from the post office. Mrs. Nutter stared at Tyler for half a minute. When she spoke, she addressed the floor. "Saw you two come in here. Don't rightly know what to say. The colonel told me—told all of us—you were with the Nazzies . . . I tried to kill you . . ."

"You didn't, though."

Her eyes were wide. "But I wanted to."

"It's understandable, ma'am," Virginia said. "He tends to bring out that desire in a woman."

The girls' mother came from the kitchen, a dinner plate in each hand, a bottle of ketchup tucked under her arm. "Mrs. Nutter," she said and came around the counter.

Mrs. Nutter acknowledged her. "Jessica, this young man—"

"I heard."

Jessica put the plates before her guests. She wiped her hands on her blooded apron. "Mrs. Nutter, watch the counter while I check on Rebel?" Her voice quavered. She was barely holding onto her emotions.

Mrs. Nutter agreed, and Jessica hurried back through the kitchen door. Mrs. Nutter helped herself to some coffee, but didn't drink. As Tyler raised his first bite toward his mouth, she spoke again. "Son, I am sorry."

Mrs. Nutter grew more irritating with every word she spoke. "It's really nothing to worry about," said Tyler.

Mrs. Nutter chewed her lip. Tyler's fork hovered near his mouth. She didn't speak until he put his fork inside it.

"At least the other Nazzies—I mean *the* Nazzies, not you—are all dead."

"Is that true?" said Virginia.

Tyler chewed.

"No one came out. Whole place is burnin' . . ." she said, clicked her tongue, tasted her coffee. "I've never shot no one, you know."

Mrs. Nutter stared, then took a seat at the counter, her back to the couple.

Tyler and Virginia ate in silence. They watched the snow through the windows, time passing in a white column, drifting through the beam of an outdoor light. Voices occasionally filtered through the kitchen from the upstairs living quarters. Twice, Rebel yelped in pain. Otherwise, the restaurant was silent.

Mrs. Nutter finished her coffee. She went behind the counter. She wrung out a towel in the sink and wiped surfaces.

Tyler placed his fork beside his plate and waited. When Virginia finished eating, he said, "I'm ready to spend the rest of my life with you."

Virginia folded her hands around her coffee mug. "What about the past?"

"It doesn't matter."

"I know it doesn't, but I owe you an explanation."

Tyler gave her a patient smile. In all things, he followed his heart and he gave it voice when he said, "Faced with losing you these past two days, none of that stuff is important. None of it. Me, you, your father, my time in prison, yours in England."

"My marriage?"

Tyler shook his head. Not even her marriage. "I'm truly sorry he didn't survive," he said.

Virginia gave Tyler an up-from-under look that ended with a soft, sad smile. "I need forgiveness, Tyler."

"I forgive you."

When she didn't respond, he offered, "Came too easy?"

"I'm not asking what you think you're answering."

He drank coffee. "Am I supposed to understand that?"

The front door opened and snow danced across the threshold and twirled into the room. Virginia didn't take any notice of the newcomer who filled the doorway.

"I am not asking your forgiveness for marrying him and not you. I need forgiveness for *me*. I didn't love him like he believed. Like I promised him. I was untrue to you at the same time I was untrue to him."

"Aha, there was someone else."

"Stop it. It was always only you."

"Might have helped you wrote me that once in a while. Or once."

"I wrote a hundred times."

They looked at each other, understanding what that meant, but not caring to put her father's name and machinations between them. Not tonight. Not ever again, if they could have it.

"Only news of you I ever got was O'Hara's visit to show me that British paper—the one with your wedding picture? You two *looked* happy."

"We were."

"But you didn't love him."

"Not in the way he thought—I couldn't let go of loving you."

"You didn't tell him, I hope."

"I never mentioned you once."

"How'd he die?"

"His plane was shot down over Berlin."

Tyler sat back. He watched her emotions play across her face. He'd known her his whole life. He found he could feel her feelings.

A little bit, if he tried. Enough to say, "I don't need to forgive you, Virginia, and you don't need to forgive yourself. You made him happy. He knew love and he felt loved. That's the greatest token a woman can give a man to carry into battle."

VIRGINIA HAD THE ODD IMAGE of a knight receiving his maiden's lace hanky. Funny the way Tyler made her see things, but his words were lifting the weight right off of her. Like always. She leaned forward, reaching for his hands until he gave them to her.

He said, "But if he'd lived and I ever saw you again—"

"I wouldn't have had you and you wouldn't have wanted me."

She squeezed. He squeezed back.

"He did have a kind of look about him. Kind of funny."

"Funny looking?"

Tyler spread his hands.

"Well, he was. He was hilarious."

"For you, and because he made you laugh, I'd have liked him." Tyler lifted his mug. "To Paul: rest in peace. And thank you for lovin' her."

They touched coffee mugs. Their faces matched. Every bit of what Virginia loved about Tyler Keyes reaffirmed itself in that moment; the way Tyler spoke Paul's name without having been told it, spoken with honor, respect, and his easy Western grace.

With that same grace, he swiveled in his seat and addressed the man who'd entered behind him. "Much obliged for letting us have that. You'll be arresting me now?"

"That something you'd let me do this time?" Cartwright's voice cut across the room, clear and cold.

"Seems counterproductive for us to shoot it out again."

The chill the FBI man brought with him shivered Virginia. "Friend of yours?"

Tyler gestured maybe-maybe not.

"Miss Hendricks." Cartwright touched two fingers to the brim of his snow-flaked fedora. "I'm glad to see you safe."

He crossed to their table.

"Handcuffs or 'Have a seat'?" Tyler said.

Cartwright pulled out a chair. He unbuttoned the top two buttons of his trench coat and searched out his Lucky Strikes. He tapped out a cigarette, the pack against his knuckle. Asked Virginia: "Mind if I smoke? It helps me listen."

"Who are you?"

"Tom Cartwright," he said plugging his mouth with the cigarette, then talking around it in a quiet voice, each word specific in its threatening heat, "Special Agent in Charge, Federal Bureau of Investigation, Santa Fe. I'll listen to all you two have to say. Then, Miss Hendricks, I get to decide whether we can be friends, or I arrest Tyler for murder and treason against the United States."

63

AT HALF PAST ELEVEN, Nestor Cooney let himself inside his house. All was dark and quiet. Nestor leaned his shoulders against the door and took slow, measured swallows of air as he listened to the beautiful silence. He'd never experienced such an intoxication of fear and excitement.

He reflected back on his evening. The meeting. The raw power and magnificence of the Standartenführer. His escape from the mesa—he'd passed through Dutton Butte, smiled and chatted with the boy soldiers manning the roadblock, peering into their faces, looking for that hint of death that was surely theirs if they planned to tangle with the Standartenführer.

Nestor Cooney had no doubts von Hofmann would complete his mission in triumph.

Triumph for the Third Reich.

Triumph shared with Nestor Cooney.

Grinning, Nestor Cooney made his way to the basement stairs and descended into the cold, black room. Per his instructions, he would now confirm the first part of his mission had gone off without a hitch. He was too confident to mention anything about the gunfire out in the ruins. Besides, the Standartenführer had said he'd be at the final rendezvous. He was Nestor's commanding officer now, and the Standartenführer wouldn't want him injecting worry into the mind of some radio operator hidden away in a Mexico relay station.

Five paces right, eight paces forward, reach up . . .

Nestor Cooney pulled the light string. On his workbench, illuminated in the pale cast of yellow, the piece of loose mortar lay on the counter like a piece of Nestor's heart.

64

CARTWRIGHT STUDIED the blackened, fire-distorted Toten-kopf from von Hofmann's officer's cap and, turning his attention from Tyler and Virginia to Special Agent Burley, said, "So he burned?"

The death's head appeared to be grinning.

For the past forty-five minutes, Cartwright had listened to Tyler and Virginia tell their stories. He had heard enough liars in the last seventeen years to recognize the truth when it came his way, and he had to admit that in the actions of Tyler Keyes over these the past two days, he saw more than a glimmer of himself and found he had no condemnation for this young man's decision to take the law into his own hands and rescue the woman he loved.

Cartwright had been concluding the interview with a handful of questions, probing Virginia's observations of von Hofmann's behavior, when Special Agent Burley came inside to report the church fire extinguished and that a charred body had been discovered in the burned hulk of the truck's cab, the silver death's head in its lap.

"No sign of escape, sir," Burley answered.

"You searched the grounds again?"

Cartwright had walked the church's perimeter twice before coming to the restaurant. He'd found no footprints in the snow and, although the townspeople insisted there was no way von Hofmann or anyone else could have survived the explosion they'd witnessed, he'd instructed Burley to check it again while he went for Tyler Keyes and the girl.

Burley had checked it again in three ever-widening circles. There hadn't been a thing. "Of course, the snow's been falling pretty hard. Tracks might have been covered already."

"What is it with this guy and the weather? It's like he gets it to help him," Cartwright said.

He sighed, then lifted his chin toward Tyler and Virginia. "You two see anything after the truck crashed into the church?"

Tyler answered. "Nothing happened for a minute or two. Then the explosion. That's it."

Cartwright mulled it over. "And you only found the one body?" he said to Burley.

Burley nodded.

"Because from what Miss Hendricks tells me, there should have been two more of the Nazis with von Hofmann. Rear of the truck."

"If they were, sir, we'd never know. That half of the vehicle disintegrated in the blast."

Jessica had returned to the counter during Cartwright's questioning of Tyler and Virginia. She and Mrs. Nutter sat facing each other across the counter, posed as if in conversation, but neither had spoken a word the entire time. Now she leaned toward them. "Excuse me for eavesdropping, but there would be *three* other bodies inside the church."

"How so ma'am?" Cartwright said.

"Father Lapidus, he has a house a little way out of town, but tonight he ate supper here. The meatloaf same as I served them. We talked a little. He was headed to the church to write his Christmas sermon."

Cartwright blew smoke, narrowed his eyes and searched the misty coils. "One body, three missing. Three Nazis, one priest . . . Hmm." He shifted his attention back to the girls' mother behind the counter. "I noticed your Santa Fe depot's shut down. Any trains ever pass through here?"

"Sometimes I hear them pass. Don't pay much attention though."

"Jessica, Rebel and I are finished," the doctor called from within. He poked his head through the kitchen door. "If I could have a word with you about these dressings?"

The woman looked like she might cry, and her voice broke as she excused herself from the restaurant.

Mrs. Nutter answered Cartwright from her counter stool. "I know when they come through, mister. I should. Since they don't stop no more, I gotta drive the post into Estancia every day—and they don't give me an extra gas ration neither."

"When do they come through?"

"There's a daily ten a.m. And every other Thursday night round ten thirty-ish there's a special limited freight to Santa Fe. It'll be this week."

"Today's Thursday," Cartwright said.

"Oh. You're right. In all the confusion, I plumb forgot. But we got Christmas in two days and I always think of Christmas as a Sunday."

Cartwright and Burley exchanged a look.

"We could beat that train to Santa Fe," Burley said.

"Santa Fe? Hell, we're going to stop it in Albuquerque."

Cartwright rose and stalked behind the counter to the telephone.

"What are you doing?" Mrs. Nutter said. "Jessica's got enough bills without you running one up on her phone. There's a payphone right there beside the door."

Cartwright lifted the receiver and stuck a finger in the dial. He locked eyes with Mrs. Nutter. "Burley, tell the lady to shut her yap."

"Ma'am?" Special Agent Burley nudged.

Mrs. Nutter snorted.

"Chief?" Burley stepped to the counter. He lowered his voice. "What if you get that associate director from Washington? It'd be one thing if we'd gotten here and caught von Hofmann, but, you know, he might not be too pleased to hear from you . . ."

Cartwright placed the receiver on his shoulder, dark where the snow had melted. He scowled at his subordinate. "I don't give a damn what pleases him. Five high-schoolers playing at army, plus those two nitwits from Camp Santa Rosa, and a priest are dead. If we're to stop that train, I'm going to need men. Besides, I'm dialing Torres in Fort Sumner."

A tone hummed in Cartwright's ear. He dialed direct. The phone at the other end of the line was answered after one ring. "Cartwright here. I want Torres."

"He went back to Santa Fe, sir." Cartwright recognized Agent Dunlap's voice.

"What? Why?"

"Everyone did. Associate Director Parnell came in, ordered all of us back. I was left here to wait for your call, sir."

A lead weight dropped in Cartwright's chest. "Where does Associate Director Parnell suspect I am?"

"He knows where you are, sir. Knows you're still chasing the escaped PWs. He's anxious to hear from you."

"Yeah, I'll bet."

"You catch 'em, Tom?"

Cartwright disconnected the call. He dialed his office in Santa Fe. Associate Director Parnell took the call, but Cartwright was ready for him. He skipped all formalities and went on the offensive, shooting off point-by-point, where he was, who he was with, and all that had transpired. Parnell didn't interrupt, and Cartwright was surprised when he didn't argue. Parnell was brief and to the point, and a moment later, Cartwright replaced the receiver and faced the room. His expression was one of total shock.

They all stared as if waiting for him to make some kind of transformation.

He allowed a sardonic smile and held up his cigarette. He blew across the tip until he saw the cherry glow. "We're headed back to Santa Fe. You two are coming with us."

Tyler stood. "Under arrest?"

"No. Just need official statements."

Cartwright came out from around the counter.

"Sir? I don't get it: what about Albuquerque? The train?" said Burley.

"It's already been stopped. Von Hofmann and the others are in custody."

"How? It only passed through here a little over an hour ago. How did they know?" Burley said.

"Apparently, Washington knows a lot more about von Hofmann and his plans than they've let on. Parnell said his men were waiting."

Virginia caught her breath. "But if they've known so much all this time, why didn't they stop him earlier?"

Cartwright met Virginia's gaze. She wore her exhaustion and the effects of the incredible horror she'd been through with dignity. Cartwright would never see a woman as beautiful and sad as this woman at this moment. He held her gaze perhaps longer than comfortable for her, but she meant so much more in the context of his life than anyone else, and even though he'd sacrificed his career for this young woman, his answer to her question would be painfully inadequate. "I'm asking myself that same disgusting question, Miss Hendricks, and believe me I'm going to find out."

Virginia rose and leaned toward Tyler. He offered her the protective circle of his good arm and held her tight.

It was over. The Nazis captured. They'd pay in court for what they'd done.

Cartwright flicked his cigarette butt out the door, but it blew right back inside. Burying his hands in his pockets, he stepped into the soundless snow.

PART FOUR

"Ultimately, it is the desire, not the desired, that we love."

— FRIEDRICH NIETZSCHE

FRIDAY, DECEMBER 24, 1943

CARTWRIGHT FOUND SHERIFF FARNUM who, having driven in from the county seat at Estancia, stood with his deputy, the fire chief, and a group of citizens at the wet, smoldering ruins of the church. Cartwright informed him the remains were the priest's and that the Nazi fugitives had been apprehended. Sheriff Farnum accepted this. He'd also spoken to the Army. They'd be coming in the morning to collect their dead. He didn't understand since the families lived closer. With little more than the arch of an eyebrow, he inquired about Tyler and Virginia, and Cartwright told him they were the concern of the federal government. Beyond that, there was nothing to say.

The sheriff drove the FBI agents, Tyler, and Virginia out to the Navajo farmer's adobe on the edge of town. At midnight, he said goodbye and drove off, all but the sound of his Chevrolet quickly swallowed by the snow.

They found Captain Dixon and Flight Lieutenant McInerny playing poker with the old man, dried pinto beans their chips. The Indian raked in a pot the size of a hearty dinner as Cartwright stepped to the table.

"One of you needs to fly us back to Santa Fe."

Dixon's lizard eyes blinked. "Taking off from that field's just asking for disaster."

"Then that's what I'm asking for, because we're going back to Santa Fe. Now."

IT HAD BEEN LIKE FLYING A KITE in a tornado and had more than doubled their time aloft, but two hours later, they landed at the municipal airport outside of Agua Fría Ranches where Agua Fría Road followed the Rio Santa Fe five miles into town. Cartwright led their party from Dixon's UC-43 Traveler, past a large unmarked transport plane receiving fuel, to the low adobe terminal. The rim of its flat roof and the ends of the outcropping vigas were mantled by the fresh falling snow. Seven trench-coated men, agents from out of state, waited to depart on three benches inside the terminal.

"Special Agent Cartwright?" A hatless, gray brush-cut agent inquired across the top of the paper cup of coffee he cradled in both his hands like something precious.

"I'm Cartwright."

"There's a couple cars waiting to take you in."

Cartwright and Burley traded a cautious look. Cartwright said, "Fine. Let's go, people."

Two black Packards from the Santa Fe pool idled in early-morning darkness at the curb. Snow had collected on fenders and roofs, but not so much on the hoods where the engines' heat melted most as it settled. They hadn't been there long. Two agents stepped from the cars and onto the curb, brackets closing in on a set made finite by their presence.

The agent from the first car spoke. "I'm Special Agent Lascomb and this is Special Agent DeGrey. We're out of the DC office, sir. Came in with Associate Director Parnell."

Cartwright took their measure with his gaze. They came up short.

"If you and Special Agent Burley will accompany me in this vehicle, the others will follow with Special Agent DeGrey."

"No. I'll ride with you. Lascomb and Special Agent Burley will ride with Mr. Keyes and Miss Hendricks."

"That's not according to Associate Director Parnell's wishes, sir," said Special Agent Lascomb.

"Fairies and Santa Claus grant wishes, not me. So unless Associate Director Parnell wrote these orders out, I'm in charge here. Got it?"

The agents shared a dubious glance. Lascomb shrugged. He marked Tyler with an abrupt nod. "He'll have to surrender his weapons."

"What for?" said Cartwright.

"Does he have any weapons, sir?"

Cartwright looked to Tyler. "Mr. Keyes?"

"Nope."

"There. Easy."

Cartwright moved with the others to Special Agent DeGrey's car. Burley climbed into the front passenger seat. Cartwright helped Virginia, then Tyler into the rear.

"They plan to arrest me, don't they?" said Tyler.

"Don't worry, Keyes. Whatever they plan, I promise I'll see you treated fairly." He caught Virginia's glance as he shut the door.

Cartwright joined Special Agent Lascomb. He lit a Lucky Strike and climbed into the Packard. Special Agent Lascomb drove and didn't speak, and Cartwright was glad for it. He needed time to think.

A plane prepared on the runway. Agents waiting on it in the terminal. And where were his own men? Why didn't Torres meet them at the airport instead of this pair of insubordinate junior G-men? Keyes was on the money about their intentions. But why would Parnell arrest Tyler? Cartwright had cleared him for Hendricks and the men at his ranch. The German, Mesmer, was in self-defense. There was, of course, the incidence of Cartwright's ambush in the Cibola, but Cartwright had minimized that, covered for him. He was the only witness and his testimony would play in Keyes's favor—let alone the fact that Keyes had rescued Virginia, whose testimony on his behalf would be even stronger. As it stood, arresting Keyes would be terrible for Hoover and his FBI. Cartwright almost laughed at the idea of von Hofmann implicating Keyes just for the hell of it . . .

So what phony grounds, testimony, or other circumstantial evidence did Parnell have? What was the point of it, and what was it buying him?

Cartwright tapped the ash from his cigarette, its fall into the ashtray, mirroring in miniature the snow outside.

The whole thing stunk like stirred shit.

Cartwright stared into the snowstorm.

Hell, maybe he was paranoid. The agents at the terminal were from out of state. With von Hofmann captured, they're headed home.

Cartwright sucked in soothing smoke. But the nicotine roared inside him. *Billy-be-damned and screwed sideways if I'm being paranoid. No one flies home on a night like this. No way.*

Those agents in that terminal weren't risking their lives to fly tonight somewhere they could as easily fly tomorrow. They were there under orders. They were going to fly because they had no choice.

Maybe Parnell planned to ship von Hofmann out that evening?

Where? The White House. Hoover's living room? He couldn't find sense in any of it . . . Well, he wouldn't chase it and settle for something wrong. He'd rest his mind. See what answers came when he left the questions alone.

Cartwright concentrated on the passing road, the veiling snow. He tilted his head against the window glass, watched the headlights illuminate the occasional mailboxes, old and rusted, on leaning mesquite poles. He smoked and tried to relax. Cartwright was familiar with Agua Fría Road. He recognized these mail-boxes, each emblazoned with a Spanish surname.

Gallego . . . de Vargas . . . Fonseca . . . Ruiz . . . Muñoz. Great families whose lineage traced straight and steeled, like the barrel of a Spanish musket, back to the pride of the conquistadors. These letterboxes were the only escutcheons left them. Their once great ranchos, a scatter of dark and dilapidated farmhouses. All because of a robbery.

The first case of any import Tom Cartwright had as Special Agent in Charge began and ended on an afternoon in October on this same old road. A boy from one of the families had taken his father's pistol, left his withering farm, and robbed the First Western Bank of Santa Fe on Buena Vista Street. He'd done it alone and taken the money in a burlap feed bag and rode on his bicycle back to his family home. He'd shot a teller in the eye and she had died. The police took a few hours to discover the boy's identity, follow, and surround him in the cow shed out the back of his house. When the boy wouldn't surrender, they'd waited for the FBI. Cartwright remembered driving to the house. The heat. The dust. The smell of creosote in the air because his windows were down. Before he'd stopped caring about smoking up his official car.

He remembered meeting the father. A proud and somber man. He'd told him he thought he could talk the boy out, but had never learned Spanish too well, and the father had said Cartwright was young and there was still time. Cartwright said there wasn't time today, and the father volunteered to translate. So they walked to the barn, gravel crunching underfoot like a dim memory of soldiers marching after Pancho Villa, and Cartwright spoke the lies he'd trained to speak in Washington DC, telling the New Mexican boy it would all be okay if he'd just toss out his gun and give himself up. The father repeated his words in Spanish. His tone and the beauty of the language made it sound like a prayer. It didn't make the words any truer.

Three feet from the door, Cartwright could see the boy through a crack in the wood. He allowed the boy to push open the door with the end of a pitchfork. The boy sat on the ground, the money spread about him, the pistol in his lap, and he wept. The gunshot made Cartwright jump. He jumped a foot to his left, and now in his memory he saw the impossible: the bullet frozen in space an inch before the boy's heart. He didn't remember seeing it hit. All he'd seen that day in October was the body slump and the blood pool over the money, soaking into it, through it, making it worthless, and the father dropping to his knees, the other pistol he owned hanging from his finger by the trigger guard upside-down. Smoke rolled lazily from its barrel. He mentioned to Cartwright something about a family's name, its honor, and its place in history that could not be erased. He said a son should understand this. Should not allow the stain of murder over a matter of stolen water.

Stolen water. The real robbery. It had happened two years before the boy was born. Fifteen years before the boy walked into the bank with his burlap sack. It happened when the people of Santa Fe diverted the irrigation water from the ranchos on Agua Fría Road and condemned to a lingering death all the families of the men and woman who had founded their state. And a boy, descended of princes of Spain, died impoverished and desperate on his knees in a barn in a pile of other people's bloody money.

Cartwright remembered. A father had killed his son and wanted to die. The citizens of the state of New Mexico granted his wish on Christmas Eve, 1929. How could he forget? Fifteen years ago, this holiest of nights, Cartwright had visited that father in his cell at the New Mexico State Penitentiary off Cerrillos Road a quarter mile southwest of the plaza. Cartwright had witnessed the crime, had attended the sentencing, had testified, and been cross-examined.

He learned about the water, and the history of this family and all the others. He learned that two of this man's great-grandfathers had been governors of the state. Cartwright listened as the father related to the court how he heard the boy tell his mother he was bike-riding into town, and it was a matter of record the father watched the boy take the gun from his dresser, and the burlap sack from the back of their broken-down truck where his speckled hound slept.

The facts of the case were plain, simple, and enough to authorize the penitentiary to purchase twelve feet of thirteen-strand hemp rope. But they weren't enough for Cartwright. He'd gone to the man's cell the night before his execution, hoping for the gift of an answer.

"You could have prevented it."

The father chuckled, hollow and pensive. "*Lo es Nueve Mexico, nada mas*—she promises to give you everything and you take it from her and she gives it with much beauty and willingness. She doesn't tell you that tomorrow she will promise all of it to someone else and they will come along and take it from you. You will believe this is just men stealing from men, as the native Indians believed it was us, and we believed it was you . . . but it is her." He slapped the stone wall twice with his open palm. "She is a whore and we love her and we make her our bride and we die fools."

Cartwright witnessed the hanging as representative of the federal government. It was a quiet, pitiful affair behind the penitentiary orchard. The father asked God His forgiveness. He declared he loved his son and the whore that was mother to them both and no one but Cartwright understood what he meant as the father dropped and choked and died.

Cartwright lit another Lucky Strike.

What has the whore promised J. Edgar Hoover? Publicity? The glory of capturing von Hofmann?

If that were true, Hoover would be here. He'd want his picture with von Hofmann in every paper. He'd want to wave it in front of Tolson over soft-boiled eggs. He sent Parnell instead. So what has Parnell stolen?

Cartwright understood. The theft was still in progress. He'd been played for the biggest fool since Coronado was lured into New Mexico to claim the Seven Cities of Gold.

Inside the second Packard, Special Agent Burley sat beside Special Agent DeGrey, scribbling notes inside his black book. He and Cartwright were in trouble and he wanted to write down their actions and decisions before he forgot, as much for his own protection as his superior's, because Cartwright wouldn't write a word.

Tyler sat behind him, legs wide, leaning back, eyes closed and face tilted toward the headliner in surrender to exhaustion and pain. The vehicle th-thudded over the tracks of the Denver & Rio Grande Western and he fiercely gripped Virginia's hand.

She wished she could do something for his pain. They entered Santa Fe proper, crossing the river and turning right on Water Street. Virginia couldn't shake her dread that Tyler headed into something worse than any of them had yet experienced. It was quarter to three in the morning. Cars parked at the curbs were busy disguising themselves as snow banks. Otherwise, the street was empty. They approached Don Gaspar Avenue and Virginia looked across the corner as the first Packard swung left.

The road leading into the plaza was pristine white, like a Christmas card waiting for Old Dobbin's sleigh, but the snow churned under the tires of the lead car, sucking up the grime beneath, and, in defiance of the one-way arrows sprouting law from the curb, they drove a counterclockwise circuit of the plaza. A Christmas processional, lonely and backward, silent and abused, past empty sidewalks, the *portales* festooned with red glass Christmas balls and paper flowers beaten by the wind scudding in from the north. Virginia's tired eyes pleaded with the decorations, trying to find in them the kind of succor sweet in Christmas. Some of that glory to sustain and uplift them all, but as they drove on, she noticed the beating wind had shattered most of the balls. Their half-globes dangled rude and jagged from their wires. When she turned away to look into the square, the brightly painted tin angels hanging from the branches of the smaller trees spun and fluttered in the rapid jerks of the executed, unable to mount to heaven as limbs bowed by snow pressed them closer and closer to earth and an icy burial abandoned by God.

The Packards veered onto Washington Avenue. They angled onto Lincoln. The pre-Civil War Federal Building came into view. Virginia vowed whatever happened, she would see Tyler free.

66

Associate Director Parnell stood in dim light at the top of the stairs on the second-floor landing as Cartwright and the others trudged from the ground floor where the district court and its attending chambers and counsel rooms lay chill and empty. Cartwright studied the man as he climbed toward him. He took small satisfaction in noting that Associate Director Parnell appeared much as he'd imagined. Under six feet, he wore a gray flannel Brooks Brothers suit that fit him so well it suggested the tailor had known his shape and the size of his temperament since before Parnell could take the silver spoon out of his mouth by himself. Pale blue eyes shone behind the type of tortoiseshell glasses given by Connecticut mothers upon sending sons to papa's university, and Parnell's wavy blond hair, plied with half a tin of Murray's pomade, shimmered with such incandescence that when he looked in the mirror, he probably thought his mind electric. Mid- to late-thirties, Parnell was no shrinking violet, but Cartwright didn't see in him a man who ever acted on anything out of virtue, which made him a man of ambition, who would do anything to get what he wanted.

Parnell would be dangerous.

Agent Torres stood a few paces behind him, busy counting scuffmarks on the floor. Cartwright and the others stopped before the final step. Parnell studied Tom Cartwright. Lascomb and DeGrey stepped around him and disappeared into the corridor.

"So you're Cartwright," Parnell said as though warned it was something horrid to step in, but now scraping the sole of his shoe found he could wipe him off without much concern.

"You got von Hofmann? I want to see him," Cartwright said, knowing his demand could not be met.

Parnell stepped backward. Smirked. "Special Agent Torres, place Mr. Keyes under arrest."

Virginia firmed her grip on Tyler's arm.

"I don't know what you're up to, Torres," Cartwright said, "but to do that you got to step past me. You ready for that?"

Torres looked to Parnell.

"For your information, Mister Cartwright, Special Agent Torres found German documents and a short-wave radio hidden on Mr. Keyes's farm."

"What the hell—?" said Tyler.

"Torres?"

Torres glared at Cartwright with too much emotion, and Cartwright understood the truth.

"Torres," Cartwright repeated his name as though reading it from the blade of a knife he'd pulled from his own back.

"Agent Torres, you *will* take the suspect into custody." Parnell crooked a finger impatiently. Torres grabbed Tyler.

"Get your hands off me, you lying son of a bitch!" Tyler hooked Torres across the jaw.

Torres crumpled to his seat as Tyler doubled over, clutching his broken ribs. Parnell stepped in with handcuffs. He slapped them over Tyler's wrists.

"I am placing you under arrest for treason against the United States of America."

"You're insane! He hasn't done anything! Ask me! You got von Hofmann prisoner, ask him!" Virginia tried to push forward, but Burley held her back.

Cartwright said, "I'm sorry, Miss Hendricks, Mr. Keyes. We've been lied to. There's no von Hofmann to ask."

Parnell held Tyler by the cuffs behind his back. "That's right, von Hofmann's still at large. Only way to get you back, Cartwright."

Cartwright said nothing.

"Take him and book him, Torres." Parnell propelled Tyler into Torres's arms as the Hispanic agent rose to his feet.

Tyler tried to fight, but Cartwright placed a hand on his shoulder. "Take it easy, Keyes. I made you a promise and I'm a man of my word. They won't hold you for long."

"Where you from, Cartwright?"

"Hereabouts. Same as you."

It meant something to Tyler.

"Move it." Torres pushed on Tyler's wounded shoulder, but he didn't budge.

Virginia tried again to go to him, but Burley continued to restrain her.

Tyler narrowed his eyes at Cartwright. "I'll count on you to keep an eye on Virginia for me."

"What about Miss Hendricks?" Cartwright asked Parnell. "You arresting her too?"

"Not at this time."

Tyler visibly relaxed. Torres moved him down the hall.

Associate Director Parnell turned Virginia over to an agent from Denver named Reid. She followed him, silently defiant, to an interrogation room.

Cartwright and Burley followed Parnell to Cartwright's office. Parnell instructed Burley to wait outside the door. He gestured for Cartwright to enter. He closed the door. Cartwright watched him, disgusted as Parnell went around his desk and sat behind it as though it were his own. Parnell gestured to a chair.

"I won't sit for you."

"Suit yourself."

Cartwright turned to the window. The reflection from the desk lamp on the glass behind the Venetian blinds prevented him from seeing what lay beyond. Parnell leaned forward, placing his elbows on the blotter and pressing his fingertips together.

"You don't have a very high opinion of those of us at the Seat of Government, do you, Cartwright?"

"At least cockroaches and rats don't pretend to be anything other than dirty vermin."

Parnell's right cheek twitched.

Cartwright pressed his attack. "What I'd like to know is if you're not trying to catch von Hofmann, why'd you come here?"

"It might surprise you, but while you've been out there treating this as cops and robbers, the rest of us are trying to win a war."

"Spare me the flag. I can't see it over the bodies."

Cartwright's hand went for his cigarettes. He gave the pack a shake. His lips pulled out the tallest butt.

"Don't. I don't like it."

Cartwright's Zippo appeared. He flicked the lid but didn't strike the flint. He held the lighter before the tip of his cigarette. "You didn't answer my question." He gave his head a mocking shake. "You don't know what you're doing, do you, Parnell? A pair of wingtips stuck in the snow with only a pencil to shoot with."

"I know exactly what I'm doing, because I know exactly where von Hofmann is headed. For reasons of national security, the director plans for me to apprehend him there and not before."

"And where's that?"

Parnell gave him an enigmatic smirk.

Cartwright shrugged. He lit his cigarette. "Meanwhile von Hofmann gets to murder whomever he wants."

"It's not our place to question the director. We're team players and Mr. Hoover is our captain. Too bad you never learned the rules."

Parnell's words brought an image to Cartwright's mind of Hoover, Tolson, Parnell, and all the rest of the Washington boys dressed in baseball jerseys and knickers, posing for a brownie-box team photo over the bodies at the Hendricks ranch. The boy soldiers out at Dutton Butte. It was more than he could take. "This isn't a fucking game, Parnell."

Parnell rose from his seat. "Don't use coarse language with me, Cartwright. I won't stand for it."

"Fuck you sitting then."

Cartwright glared and in Parnell's face, he saw his contempt reflected. Parnell withdrew a document from his breast pocket. Smacked it on the desk. "You're out of the game, mister. You're to sign this letter of resignation prepared for you by Assistant Director Tolson, at the director's approval, and you are going to take a walk."

"And if I don't?" A puff of smoke.

"You'll stay on: restricted to this building for the duration of the operation, at the end of which, I guarantee, you will take the fall right alongside that cowboy friend of yours from 'here 'bouts.'"

"What'll you do? Plant a U-boat on me?"

"Mr. Cartwright, there's nothing you can prove. If you didn't want Keyes uncovered, you shouldn't have sent Special Agent Torres out to his place."

At the mention of Torres, Cartwright's blood burned hot.

"Beside the physical evidence at his place, we can prove he masterminded the escape from the outside. It will be his word against Hoover's," said Parnell.

"How's that play against Keyes killing von Hofmann's squad one after another?"

"Oldest motive in the book. Jealousy. Over the Hendricks girl—he's raped her once before—expected her as a prize. When that went sideways, when von Hofmann protected her, the young man went trigger-happy. Suicide run—burned his own place down."

"What're you talking about?"

"Set his prison cell on fire last time he murdered someone. Ex-con psychological pattern, I'm afraid. But juries love that."

Cartwright flared smoke through his nostrils like a warming dragon. "And you think Miss Hendricks will just go along with that."

"She went along with it before—spoiled brat like her, standing to lose everything Daddy built, lifestyle she's led—not a lot of fortitude, woman like that up against the power of Hoover."

Cartwright fought the urge to take Parnell, hammer his face, and be done with him. Instead, he blew a smoke ring at the associate director. "Parnell, you talk like a guy who's in love with the smell of Hoover's shit on your dick."

Parnell didn't flinch. He took a Parker fountain pen from his shirt pocket. He placed it atop the document. Pushed them both toward Cartwright.

Cartwright picked up the pen. He unscrewed the cap. His hand hovered over the line for his signature. His eyes caught sight of Parnell's briefcase in the corner. "After I sign this, I'd like to have a few minutes in here to collect my personal things from the desk."

"A box has already been filled. It's waiting by the door."

Cartwright signed.

Parnell smiled faintly. He held out his hand.

"What? You need to borrow some money?" said Cartwright.

"I need your keys, your identification, and your weapon," said Parnell.

Cartwright fished out his keys. He removed one from the ring. Next, he found his black leather ID case, so familiar its feeling in his fingers.

Just things. Useless junk.

He dropped them into Parnell's hand.

The hand remained. "Your weapon."

"I own my weapon."

"Your permit to carry it has been revoked."

Cartwright pulled himself to his full height. He dropped his arms to his side so that his hands hung loose. He raised his chin. *He was a big man, muscular and well-proportioned, with the rough comportment and hard-edged countenance of man poured from iron instead of flesh and bone.* "Take it from me."

Parnell looked at him hard. "Get out of here. I have an operation to plan."

Cartwright left.

As he passed Burley, he wanted to say something, but couldn't find the right words. He settled for, "Boy, I sure torpedoed your career."

"This isn't any organization I'd keep sailing with, Tom."

Cartwright found a piece of a thankful smile. "See you soon."

Burley considered him with a suspicious look. "You're not giving up, are you?"

"I'll take the fifth on that. For both our sakes."

"I'd like you to wait for me."

Cartwright didn't answer. Burley went inside with Parnell.

CARTWRIGHT FOUND HIS BOX in the main duty room. It was half past three in the morning, but four of his special agents sat spread out between the ten desks, folding and tossing paper airplanes like students in detention. Cartwright found his box beside the water cooler.

"Hey, sir." Special Agent Dunlap held some envelopes. "Your mail from the past couple days."

Cartwright went over. Took it. The others watched expectantly. "Parnell's not making you guys sign anything . . ."

"No. Those of us most involved . . ." He paused. ". . . with you—we're deskbound till after the case. The others were sent home. The associate director's only utilizing agents from out of state."

"What's going on, sir?" said another agent.

"You don't want to know."

Special Agent Dunlap nodded. Sage advice. Cartwright examined his mail. Four Christmas cards. He looked at the return addresses. He recognized three without tearing their envelopes: the mayor, the governor, and the post office. The fourth one puzzled him.

San Pedro, California.

No name, but the return address was the naval station. Who'd he know shipping out from there? Someone's son maybe? He shoved the envelope in his pocket. Cartwright looked at the box of his belongings and heaved a sigh. Desk supplies, his name plaque, a couple of framed certificates and his graduation diploma from the academy. A commendation from Hoover—every agent in charge got one and was required to hang it. Fixing the angle of his hat, Cartwright strode to the door.

"Sir, your stuff?"

"Parnell can toss it in the incinerator and jump right in behind it."

67

S PECIAL AGENT REID could type while he talked.
"After you stopped to leave the wounded PW and the damaged vehicle, you say you and the fugitive von Hofmann had a conversation. Please repeat that conversation to the best of your ability, Miss Hendricks." The keys of his Underwood clattered out the words.

He poised his fingers over the keyboard, awaiting Virginia's answer. He hadn't once looked at her as the interview stretched toward its second hour. Virginia was glad. She didn't want him to see her disdain.

"Miss?" (Forefinger right hand, middle finger right hand, ring finger left twice. Pinkie right.)

Virginia answered, making her voice a monotone of resignation. The agent's fingers tap-danced clattering keys. She told the FBI agent all that she remembered, knowing that what she said was not going to make a bit of difference. These were the "good guys." These were the people who were supposed to protect her, sworn to it, and yet she felt a worse kind of danger here than she had experienced as von Hofmann's prisoner. Like every kid in America, Virginia grew up believing J. Edgar Hoover and his FBI the nation's greatest heroes, bastions of unimpeachable honor and justice. She was Alice shoved through the looking glass. Everything was backwards. Topsy-turvy. Tyler arrested, von Hofmann set free.

Agent Reid asked another question. Virginia replied, and each keystroke cracked like von Hofmann's gun firing at Tyler when she'd thought the Nazi had killed him.

"The orders von Hofmann received at Gran Quivira: did you read them? Did you see anything at all?"

"Why? What do you care? If you believed anything I've said, you'd be setting Tyler free instead of carrying on this charade. Agent Cartwright knew where von Hofmann was and you people lied to him. Really, what does any of this matter?"

Agent Reid typed it out, and Virginia groaned.

"Answer the question, miss. Did you see the order von Hofmann received?"

Virginia saw herself with von Hofmann at the side of the road.

He met her eyes over the edge of the paper.

"Don't you wish you had studied German..?"

The bald Nazi shouted a car was approaching, and when von Hofmann responded, he lowered his orders into his lap. Virginia's eyes picked out two words, one in English, one in German: BRIDGE and . . . WARNERTEA.

Virginia's body tensed with the intensity of her surprise. It wasn't two words she'd seen, but three. *BRIDGE, WARNER,* and *TEA.* Virginia knew where von Hofmann was going. She bounced a knuckle against her lips. She couldn't tell them. She wouldn't. Von Hofmann was her only link to Tyler; his, the only words that could exonerate Tyler from these false charges. If the FBI caught him first, those words would never be heard. Tyler would pay with his freedom and possibly his life.

Agent Reid cleared his throat. "Miss Hendricks, it's going on four. We can stay here as long as you like . . ."

"I can't concentrate."

"Well, you must concentrate."

"Well, Mac, I can't."

Agent Reid sighed. He leaned back. He looked her way, but his fingers still clattered their tappity-tap duty. "Why?"

"Because no one's let me use a bathroom since I was brought here. Unless you want me to embarrass both of us, you'll be a gentleman and offer me the use of the facilities."

Agent Reid considered her request.

"I'm not a prisoner, am I..?"

He rubbed his chin. "There's a men's room right around the corner. It's easier than going across the building."

Across the building? "Beg your pardon? I won't use a room with urinals!" He'd never guess she'd squatted in a field the last time. Reid was a fool, and she'd play him for all that was worth.

THE WORDS FEDERAL BUREAU OF INVESTIGATION were painted across the pebbled glass of the door Agent Reid closed behind him as he ushered Virginia into the dim corridor. The only sound between them was the echo of their footsteps on the Saltillo floor tiles as they proceeded to the opposite end of the building.

They stood before a wooden swinging door; *Ladies* marked in gold letters on a piece of black-painted tin. Keys jangled in Agent Reid's hand as he went through three before he found the correct one. He unlocked the door. Pushed it open. Found the lights. Holding the door with an outstretched hand, he motioned Virginia inside.

Virginia entered past white sinks on metal legs and stepped to the second of three wooden stalls. She placed a hand on the door. Agent Reid stood in the open doorway. "Feel free to come inside and hand me the tissue if you want."

"Miss, I am only doing my job."

Virginia derided him with a mean smile.

"Christ a'mighty." He left.

Virginia studied the room. Inside the doors were two chairs upholstered in butter-yellow vinyl, a small sofa in aqua. An ashtray on a metal stand stood beside them. The sinks, the three stalls, and most importantly, a window, its glass pane painted white.

Virginia went to the window. It opened easily. A blast of frigid air invigorated her face. She peered outside. She was two stories high without a ledge. Still, her plan would work.

68

Zundorf watched Schmidt's eyes slide shut. For the last two hours, he and the Feldwebel had sat clutching their weapons, staring at each other with unguarded malice, both awaiting their chance. Zundorf had no illusions Schmidt would murder him if he drifted off first, but now it was Schmidt who slept. Zundorf looked at the Standartenführer behind him. Von Hofmann's eyes moved rapidly behind their lids.

He's dreaming.

A burst of adrenaline shot through Zundorf's veins.

Do it now! Be done with it!

Zundorf rose to his feet, his rifle in his grip. How would he do it? To kill von Hofmann without alerting Schmidt . . . He didn't want to die. It would have to be done silently. Von Hofmann first, then Schmidt.

Von Hofmann was dreaming—back in his boyhood Stettin—his first encounter with a woman. He thirteen, she from Danzig, thirty-two, and shapely. His tutor since he was six. She had crept into his bedroom and climbed on top of him. His fright gave way to pleasure as she brought him to the point of climax, only to climb off, leaving him alone on the threshold. His tutor turned her body around. Positioned her sex over his face. She did to him with her mouth what she wanted from him for herself, that which he gave her well and frantic and wet, only this time it did not end with her tears of guilt, her confession to his father followed by her termination, because this time it wasn't her at all.

Von Hofmann had relived this encounter in his dreams numerous times, always fantasizing Agna's sex and Agna's mouth.

This time it was Virginia. She hadn't escaped from the truck, but was with him in the ruins—not Gran Quivira, but Berlin—doing these things to him, making him her prisoner, making him build toward climax as he broke her willpower, taking her surrender with his mouth and with his tongue. Out of the corner of his eye, von Hofmann noticed his son, Martin. He was riding his bouncy ball, the globe painted around it. Confusion and horror filled his eyes at the sight of his father eating of and eaten by this stranger who wasn't his mother. Von Hofmann tried to push away from Virginia but could not. The globe burst into flames that traveled upward, consuming his child—

Von Hofmann yelled, lashing with his arms. He twisted awake, staring at Zundorf's rifle rushing in horizontally between his captain's hands. It missed von Hofmann's wind pipe to smash into chicken crates above the Standartenführer's head. Scrambling backward, von Hofmann went for his gun. Zundorf shifted his grip on the rifle. Von Hofmann freed the pistol. Zundorf swung the rifle before von Hofmann could fire. The Luger spun from von Hofmann's grip. Von Hofmann met Zundorf's murderous glare, his eyes great circles of shock.

Neither man spoke. True betrayal leaves nothing for words.

Zundorf's finger found his trigger as Schmidt leaped on him from behind. The gun went off. Von Hofmann felt the bullet fly through the inch of space between his left arm and his chest, and then Schmidt was propelling Zundorf headfirst into a wall of slat-pine, feathers, and ice. They reeled backward. Zundorf tried to turn and fire the weapon into von Hofmann. Schmidt gripped Zundorf's chin with the palm of one hand and the back of his head with the other. He jerked down, around, and back in a single violent motion.

He released Zundorf to the floor of the moving freight car. He stood over him, panting like a dog. Von Hofmann stepped beside him, unhurt. Zundorf could see this. He lay on his back, neck broken. Paralyzed. Dying.

"Pistol, Herr Feldwebel."

"*Zu befehl,* Standartenführer."

Zundorf's eyes watched the hand-off. Stared into the Luger's barrel. The gunshot, and the floor of white feathers splattered red.

Schmidt spit on the corpse. "I would say to the Standartenführer I always considered him—"

"Your opinion of Hauptmann Zundorf is of no interest to me. Do you understand?"

Von Hofmann's frame vibrated with weak, pathetic emotions he willed himself to ignore. The whistle sounded. The train slowed.

"*Jawohl,* Standartenführer."

The train clattered over switches. It continued to slow, preparing to stop. Von Hofmann checked his watch: 04:18. Five hours and twelve minutes left before his nine thirty rendezvous with the Soviet spy. That he had awoken when he did clearly showed the inevitability of his success, and it was here he took his comfort, telling himself Zundorf's betrayal was a setback of little importance. He only needed Schmidt, his time bomb, to complete Operation Steppenfeuer.

Von Hofmann stepped to the door and levered the bolt. He grabbed one handle and strained to open the door. "Help me with this, Schmidt."

Together, they slid the door open, revealing their arrival in a marshaling yard. Untended rolling stock waited for freight, collecting snow on the abounding tracks. There were engines, old and new, and ahead, the Santa Fe station. Its outside traced in unevenly spaced lights of halfhearted luminance, its interior hoarding the power, the high banks of white-painted checkered panes glowed like a summer noon in a country far from war's dark reach.

"There isn't much time, Feldwebel. As I enter the final stage of my operation, I must ensure its success. I am glad it is you, Herr Schmidt, who will be there to see it with me."

Schmidt lowered his head submissively.

"Since the Americans have been onto us since the beginning, we must assume they remain close. By now, they will have guessed something of my intentions and shall be waiting. Feldwebel Schmidt, you will meet them for the Reich and divert them long enough for me to achieve my goal."

"The Standartenführer suggests we split up?"

"I never suggest. Your job will to be to kill as many important Americans as you can. Believe me, the place I have chosen for you will provide you with enough to satisfy your needs."

Schmidt brightened. Von Hofmann peered out the door. The train crawled forward at a snail's pace. There was still time. He took out his map and unfolded it.

"This is where we are. Santa Fe. You will acquire a vehicle and proceed from here to here—Los Alamos—where the American military has a scientific installation. Get there as quickly as possible and create as much havoc as you can. It is small. It will give you no trouble."

"Afterward?"

"You will rendezvous with me at this bridge outside the installation at eleven hundred hours," he said, picking the time arbitrarily.

Schmidt took the map.

Von Hofmann lifted his hand. "Heil Hitler!"

"Heil Hitler," Schmidt echoed.

Von Hofmann stepped away from the open door. He found Schmidt's Tommy gun and handed it to him.

"You have enough ammo?"

Schmidt patted one of the deep pockets in his duster. "More than enough."

Von Hofmann checked his own ammunition. Seven cartridges left in his weapon. Another eight in the spare clip in his pocket. He and Schmidt shared a look before the Feldwebel jumped from the train.

Von Hofmann watched Schmidt run until he vanished into snow and darkness. Von Hofmann didn't know if Schmidt would make it all the way to Los Alamos, but the Feldwebel was a tough son of a bitch, a psychotic killer, and a survivor. Only the forces von Hofmann intended for him to engage would stop him, and in that, the job would be done.

69

AGENT REID CHECKED HIS WATCH. Four minutes since Virginia had gone into the bathroom. Her statement, once finished, would go directly to Hoover's office in Washington where Helen Gandy would place it in a folder with the heading *HENDRICKS, VIRGINIA*, and file it in Hoover's Official/ Confidential file kept under lock and key behind Miss Gandy's desk in her office. Like the rest of the files in those cabinets, it would never see the light of day. A pointless exercise and he wanted to be finished. He waited. Four minutes . . . He knocked on the door. "Miss Hendricks, you need to come out of there."

She didn't answer. He pushed open the door. His breath came out as vapor. His eyes leaped to the open window. Snow blew across the sill.

"Doubling bitch."

Agent Reid took two steps into the icy room. Sensing movement behind him, he turned into the swing of the ashtray. Aimed for the back of Agent Reid's skull, it connected with his face, destroying his nose in a blast of bloody cartilage.

VIRGINIA WATCHED him fall backward in sick fascination. His panicked eyes found hers as his hand went inside his coat toward his pistol. His head hit the back of the first sink. His eyes rolled, and his body went limp to meet the floor.

Virginia stood the ashtray behind her. She crouched over the body and stared. No guilt, no sorrow, no triumph. Blood flowed from the man's nose and into his mouth. Virginia didn't want him to drown. She turned his face. Blood dripped out of his mouth and across the white-and-black octagonal tiles. With two fingers, she pulled open his jacket. His hand was closed around the butt of his .38 and the gun was free of its holster. If his head hadn't hit the sink, Agent Reid would have killed her.

She took the pistol and shoved it into her raincoat pocket, lancing her finger on the point of the four-inch hatpin of the mourning rosette. She sucked the blood from her fingertip, walked to the window, and closed it. She went to the door. The hall was empty. Fighting back fatigue, Virginia walked quickly to the stairs and descended to the street.

70

A T FOUR THIRTY on the morning before Christmas, Burley stood on the sidewalk staring at a set of fresh footprints trailing south across the snow-swept street. They were a woman's footprints and Burley didn't have to guess who they belonged to—all he had to do was decide whether to follow Virginia or continue hunting for Cartwright.

Only a short while earlier, Parnell had presented him his letter of resignation. Burley made no remark and signed it. Without complaint, he handed over his keys, his ID, and his sidearm—proud he'd never fired the weapon in the line of duty or out of it—then left to locate Cartwright. Out back in the dirt lot of the motor pool, Burley located Cartwright's Chrysler. Hoover didn't approve of his agents using their personal automobiles for Bureau business, and the same was true in reverse for the Bureau Packards. Rectangular slabs of snow balanced on the sedan's hood, roof, and trunk while rivulets of cayenne-pepper-colored dirt streaked its brown sides, giving the whole thing the appearance of some kind of Chrysler sandwich and Burley was certain the car hadn't been touched since Tuesday morning, before he and Cartwright had ever heard of von Hofmann. Burley's own Ford sat a few empty spaces away.

That Cartwright wasn't at his car, or in the lot, puzzled Burley. On his way out of the building, he'd passed Agent Dunlap and the others in the main duty room. After offering Burley their muted condolences, they'd told him Cartwright had come through some time back, said his own goodbyes, and had gone.

Where the hell is he?

Burley went to the front of the building but came up empty-handed. Like Cartwright, Burley intended to see this case to its end. Deep down, he kept alive a faint ember of a hope that if he and Cartwright brought in von Hofmann, their careers could be resurrected.

The trail of footsteps beckoned.

If Cartwright wanted me to know where he was, I'd know.

He lifted his trench coat collar and took off after Virginia into the snow.

"TELEX FROM THE DIRECTOR, SIR." Special Agent Lascomb handed the flimsy to Parnell.

Operation approved at all levels. Full speed ahead. Edgar.

Parnell smiled, satisfied. The approval they'd waited on was from General Groves and Boris Pash, the men officially in charge of Project Y intelligence. Hoover had twisted Roosevelt's arm until he'd gotten it, which meant until von Hofmann was taken into FBI custody and the Soviet spy on the inside exposed, all security for the Los Alamos facility would be turned over to the Bureau.

"The agents there yet?" Parnell said.

Lascomb glanced at his watch. "The plane should be landing any minute."

"What about the roads? We going to have to fly, or can we get there by car?"

"The roads are still open, sir, and the pilot I have standing by at Agua Fría says with weather like this, the wind coming down from the north, it's a toss-up between which way would be faster. The plane is ready, though."

"We'll drive . . . Probably pass von Hofmann on the road."

Cartwright heard Parnell and Lascomb conversing as they passed the janitor's storeroom.

"And our fall guy?"

"Spic agent booked and printed him. Took him down to the holding cells. He's keeping an eye on Keyes till it's over. I figure let him handle the whole thing. That way, in case something goes wrong, we can point the finger at this Torres and no one else has to be involved."

"Nothing's going wrong, Lascomb."

"Of course, sir. Sorry."

"What about Reid?"

"Must be still taking the girl's statement."

Cartwright listened as they headed for the stairs. A minute later, Cartwright heard the sound of an automobile engine turning over. He waited until it disappeared from earshot before he emerged from the storeroom. He quickly walked down the darkened hall toward his old office. He could hear the rhythmic sound of snoring wafting around the corner from the main duty room.

He fished his keys from his pocket. As he unlocked the door, Cartwright amused himself with the memory of Parnell's shit-eating expression when he'd taken possession of the key to Cartwright's yard shed.

Cartwright slipped inside, locking the door behind him. Parnell's briefcase was gone. He quickly searched the desk and wastebasket. Nothing.

Even before he'd snuck back inside, up the fire stairs to his hiding place, Cartwright had devised a plan to take care of von Hofmann and do it with immunity. But the plan was worthless if he didn't know how to find him. Torres would know. Maybe not everything, but something. Enough to make fabricating evidence and false arrest seem worthwhile propositions.

Cartwright stepped into the corridor. The Santa Fe Federal Building contained three holding cells originally built for use by the district court, but shared with the FBI. Cartwright went to the fire door at the end of the hall and descended to the first floor. He made his way past the courtrooms, turned toward the back of the building to the bailiff's office. He tried the door. Locked.

Tyler Keyes was fast asleep, lying on the cot behind the bars of the second cell. Torres tried to ignore the cowboy's painful moaning by concocting daydreams about Chicago. About this New Year's Eve to come, pressing against the soft curves of his beautiful wife and dancing in 1944 at the Drake. The knock startled him from his reverie. He lifted his feet from the desk he sat behind, went and opened the door.

Cartwright filled the doorway.

"You shouldn't be here," Torres said, failing to sound threatening.

"Let's talk, Torres, like friends. Maybe I can help you out of this mess," said Cartwright.

Torres gave a short, scornful laugh, almost a bark. "I'm not the one who needs help. Not anymore. And if you don't blow right now, I'll—"

Cartwright's hands grabbed Torres by his lapels. He ripped the jacket open and pulled it down, pinning Torres's arms before laying into him with a sledgehammer right to his gut and a fast left cross to the jaw that sent Torres once more to the floor. Before Torres could rise, Cartwright shoved his own Colt .38 in his face.

"Sorry to interrupt. What is it you're going to do?"

Torres spit blood-bubbly saliva onto the floor. He turned his contemptuous gaze to Cartwright, looking past the pistol to his clear eyes. "You don't get it. These are the director's orders, Cartwright. It's the way the nation wants it."

"It's the way Hoover wants it."

"Sure, and guess what? He's the highest law in the land."

"No, he's not. He's just sworn to uphold it, and you and he, and everyone else involved in this bullshit deal know what you're doing is wrong."

"Sorry, I don't see it that way. Come next week, while you're out freezing your ass without a job, I'll be back in Chicago, continuing my service to the Bureau. Maybe then we'll talk."

"And what about him?" Cartwright jerked his head toward the cell where Tyler Keyes slept.

"Look, if one innocent man falls to protect the security of this country, that's jake with me. All I did was follow orders and protect my job."

"Your job is to protect the Constitution, you son of a bitch."

Torres scrunched his face in anger. "Cartwright, holster your weapon, turn around, and get out of here. I'll pretend this didn't happen."

"I got a better idea." Cartwright thumbed back the hammer. "Tell me what Parnell's got planned, or you die."

Cartwright's tone was unmistakable. Fear gnawed its way along Torres's spine. "Fuck you. I'm not afraid of you."

"Really. Don't believe I'd do it?" Cartwright grabbed Torres by the face. He squeezed open his mouth. He shoved the gun inside. "Five seconds."

Torres tasted metal. Gun oil assailed his nostrils. "E-wen ih I tow you—Thehs nu-hing you khan do! Gah dhammit!"

"Three, two—"

"*Okay!* Lohs Awamos! Lohs Awamos!"

Cartwright kept the pistol in his mouth. "Los Alamos?"

Torres nodded vigorously, his teeth clicking on the .38's short barrel.

"Why? What's there?"

"I dohn know—I swhear ih! Aww I know ihs thhey're tay-king von Hoh-man away frum therh a-life."

Cartwright pulled his gun from Torres's mouth. He eased down the hammer and narrowed his eyes. Torres cowered, frightened, humiliated, gasping to catch his breath.

"Fuck it. You're lying. Los Alamos is an old Boy Scout camp."

"No! I swear it! The Army controls it—"

"Nice try, Torres, but Hoover sent me a memo last year. All the Army does is train engineers there. What's von Hofmann gonna do, steal a tractor?"

"It's a secret base."

"Uh-huh. I don't buy it. I'm done with you."

He cocked the pistol once more.

Tears welled in Torres's eyes. "Damn you, Cartwright, it's all I know: von Hofmann goes back to Washington!"

But Cartwright brought the gun back up. Torres raised his hands as Cartwright struck him on the side of the head with the pistol butt.

Torres sprawled on his side, unconscious.

"Chickenshit bastard." Cartwright had only contempt for the man he'd once considered his friend. He rolled him onto his back and took his gun. He went to the desk and found the keys to Tyler's cell. He unlocked the cage.

"Get up, Keyes. Time to go."

Tyler jolted from sleep, disoriented, looking around. His eyes found Cartwright.

"Jail, remember?"

Tyler rubbed his face, only to wince when his fingers hit stitches. "Years of memories, thanks. What's happening?"

"I'm breaking you out. You and me are going to go find your Miss Hendricks. Then I'll stash you two somewhere till your name's cleared and I have a way to bring in von Hofmann."

Tyler looked from Cartwright to Torres sprawled across the floor. "You sure you can do that? You know someone willing to step into the ring against J. Edgar Hoover?"

Cartwright picked up the telephone. "I'll know him in a few minutes," he said, and placed a call to the OSS.

"Mr. Larkin briefed me on your operation, Agent Cartwright," said Colonel Bill Donovan from the Office of Strategic Services in the National Institutes of Health Building in Washington, DC.

"It's not 'Agent' anymore. And it's not my operation."

"I'm sorry to hear that, but I assume you're not calling to wish me Merry Christmas. What can I do for you, Mr. Cartwright?"

Cartwright had lit a cigarette and now he exhaled smoke. "It's what I can do for you, Colonel Donovan."

"Please? I don't follow."

"I plan on taking von Hofmann away from the FBI."

Donovan chuckled. "Why would you want to do that?"

"Because I want to see him brought to justice."

"That's not what Hoover wants?"

"Fancy that, Colonel, it is not. As soon as he captures von Hofmann, Hoover plans to illegally extradite him from the state of New Mexico all the way to your fair city. He's already set up an innocent man on false charges of treason to take the fall for the murders." Cartwright glanced at Tyler. "Once he's got von Hofmann out of here, that's the last anyone will hear of our friend from the SD."

There was a pause at the other end of the line. Cartwright could hear the miles crackling with static.

"How do I know you're telling me the truth?"

"Does it matter, Colonel? In principle, you agree with me—you'd like to see von Hofmann impaled on the Washington Monument—I'm offering you that and with it a chance to give J. Edgar Hoover a kick in the ass."

"Now I've got to ask you, why would *I* want to do that?" said Donovan.

Cartwright blew across the tip of his cigarette. "Let's not jerk each other off, Colonel. It's late and we've both got presents to wrap. I'm going to get von Hofmann, but I need someone to give him to who won't just turn him right back over to Hoover. You want him under your tree, you work with me."

Donovan paused a good five seconds before responding. "There is, of course, the question of jurisdiction."

"Yes, there is. But say I turn him over to the OSS in public, make an event out of it in the press, Hoover will have to think twice about whether he can keep all his loose ends secure if there's a congressional investigation. Which I'm sure you'd insist upon."

This time, Donovan laughed outright. "Mr. Cartwright, I like you."

"I'm flattered. In or out?"

"Call me when you have von Hofmann."

71

"You'll be needing a hat." Cartwright handed one of the bailiff's tan Stetsons from the peg by the door to Tyler Keyes. "Fit?"

"Little snug."

"Small thinkers here. Good for moving fast."

"Reckon so," said Tyler and stepped over Torres to follow Cartwright through the door, eager to find Virginia and something resembling safety.

That his escape might further implicate him didn't matter to Tyler Keyes one bit. What was the point of playing by the rules? The "how"s and "why"s—the truth—about his incarceration and actual involvement with the Nazis clearly did not matter to the FBI and would not amount to squat in a courtroom. The FBI had set him up, and sure as Saturday follows Friday, his word against theirs, they would get him convicted fast as double-geared lightning.

Tyler followed Cartwright up the stairs to the FBI wing. As they made their way to the interrogation rooms, Tyler realized his life lay in Cartwright's hands. He'd listened to Cartwright's side of the phone conversation. How ironic it had become that truth, and with it his and Virginia's, Cartwright's, and the other agent—ex-agent—Burley's fate and future rested with the Nazi von Hofmann coming through this alive and in Cartwright's custody. But what if Cartwright failed? Sure, from what he'd seen, Cartwright seemed a capable man, but going against von Hofmann and the FBI alone? Tyler figured he might be looking at the world's quickest trip to the electric chair.

Light bled from the transom window above the second inter-rogation room's door. The other three were dark. Cartwright drew his Colt.

"I'll open the door and cover the agent, you go in, grab Miss Hendricks, and get out of the building. I got a brown Chrysler out back. We'll meet there."

"I'm going after von Hofmann with you."

Cartwright met his steady gaze. "You've already done more than any of us, Keyes. Your girl's safe. You two should be together."

Before Keyes could argue, Cartwright threw open the door and went in gun leveled.

Paper still encircled the typewriter's spindle, the page only half-filled. The room was otherwise empty.

"Sure this is the right place?" said Tyler.

Cartwright riffled the pages of already completed statement. "Yeah. This is the room."

He pulled the last sheet from the typewriter and read it. He checked his watch then handed the page to Tyler.

V. HENDRICKS: Why? What do you care? If you believed anything I've said, you'd be setting Tyler free instead of carrying on this charade. Agent Cartwright knew where von Hofmann was and you people lied to him. Really, what does any of this matter?

FBI: Answer the question, miss. Did you see the order von Hofmann received? . . . Miss Hendricks, it's going on four. We can stay here as long as you like.

V. HENDRICKS: I can't concentrate.

FBI: Well, you have to concentrate.

V. HENDRICKS: Well, Mac, I can't.

FBI: Why?

V. HENDRICKS: Because no one's let me use a bathroom since I was brought here. Unless you want me to embarrass both of us, you'll be a gentleman and offer me the use of the facilities. I'm not a prisoner, am I?

FBI: There's a men's room right around the corner. It's easier than going across the building.

V. HENDRICKS: Beg your pardon? I won't use a room with urinals.

"What time do you have?" Tyler said.

"Four fifty-one," Cartwright answered, waiting for Tyler's reaction.

Tyler placed the sheet of paper on the desk. "She's gone after him."

"She didn't tell me what she saw in von Hofmann's orders? She tell you?"

"First of anything I heard, I heard with you. She said they were in German."

"What she said . . ." Cartwright glanced at the rest of the interview pages. "These questions must have jogged some other memory."

THEY FOUND AGENT REID'S BODY where Virginia left it on the other side of the ladies' room door. Cartwright checked the agent's neck for a pulse. "He's alive."

"I ain't asking now, Cartwright, I'm telling: I'm going with you."

"Your wounds are going to open up. You'll probably bleed all over my car, ruin the upholstery," he said, but he pulled Torres's pistol from his belt and handed it to the cowboy.

"How will I know the white hats from the black hats?"

"At this point, anyone in a hat is fair game."

"Except von Hofmann?"

Cartwright gave him a sober look. "I'm the only one who made that promise."

72

B URLEY CAUGHT SIGHT OF VIRGINIA as she crossed the snow-drifted flagstones of the plaza. For a split second, he considered calling out to her, but his Bureau instinct rejected the impulse. Observe and analyze. Decide, and then act. He stopped outside the Spitz jewelry store in the shadow of the large Spitz clock and observed her passage. The young woman's stride was swift and confident. She passed the pair of white-shrouded black iron cannons. Her square-shouldered, chin-up, eyes-front bearing reminded Burley of a soldier headed into battle. Yet, continuing to study her, watching the snow and wind dance with her copper hair and her wrap coat rhythmically billow behind her as Virginia passed beneath a swinging string of shattered ornaments west onto San Francisco Street, his impression of her became that of an avenging angel come to earth. Pure imagination on Burley's part, but it provided a kind of visual text that years of investigative experience converted into what Cartwright had always said was an agent's greatest asset: the gut feeling. Virginia was heading back into the fray, headed for von Hofmann, and Burley's gut told him that Virginia would find von Hofmann first.

Burley jogged after her. At the corner, he waited until he saw Virginia turn down Galisteo Street. He cautiously continued. He maintained at least a block between them. Even then, he was forced to duck behind parked cars when, twice, she turned around, responding to her own gut suspicions. He was quick to cover, and she did not see him. Burley tailed her over the bridge across the frozen Santa Fe River where the bare, broad arms of the cottonwoods clutched at each other from bank to bank and onto De Vargas Street where dogs, behind brown adobe walls of ancient houses, barked and howled at her passage.

Two blocks later, Virginia crossed Guadalupe Street. She headed for a crowd of Zia Indians in front of number 432 organizing the baskets and boxes of tribal souvenir trinkets they sold year-round at the plaza. 432 Guadalupe: the Denver & Rio Grande Western railroad station. Virginia shouldered the door and disappeared inside. Afraid to risk discovery inside the small stationhouse, Burley ducked into the shadows of the adobe-arched gates of the Guadalupe church across the street and waited for more people to enter the station.

Although the five thirty train to Antonito, Colorado, carried few passengers on weekdays, this was the morning of Christmas Eve. The train would be filled to capacity with people who worked the week in Santa Fe returning to homes, pueblos, village churches, and the reservations for the holiday. Burley would wait until the Zia family—perhaps a few more people—went inside before he moved. While the Indians continued sorting their goods, four Mexican farm workers arrived on foot from south of the station and entered. The Zia Indians made their way to the door. A truck pulled to the curb and two Hispanic families, complete with crying babies, piled out. Along with their children and luggage came a crate of chickens and a pair of black-and-white spotted goats on rope leads. The goats jumped, bleating, to the sidewalk.

Burley headed into the street. Before he'd crossed, the truck pulled away, immediately replaced by an Oldsmobile coupé. Two prosperous Anglo ranchers climbed out. They grabbed suitcases from the back seat. Burley negotiated around them, then slowed on the steps. He pretended to tie his shoelace while the Olds was locked, then he walked into the station, close behind the two men as though he belonged with them.

He couldn't have timed his entrance better. Two polished lime-stone steps led onto the tightly packed, yellow-tiled floor of the one-room station. Burley caught sight of Virginia fourth in a line facing a pair of sliding doors that opened to the platform and the train beyond. Virginia's attention was focused on the doors as the Hispanic stationmaster pulled them wide and entered the room. Two empty passenger cars waited beyond. The uniformed man produced a paper punch from his vest pocket. He announced in Spanish, boarding would now begin.

Burley joined the crowd. The pungent aroma of humanity mixed with the piñon smoke filtering hazy and blue from the corner fireplace. At one end of the room, men and women waited to purchase tickets, while at the other stood an unattended news-paper stand, shoeshine, and telephone. Two boys played with the goats, laughing as one of the animals tried to eat the hair from a small Zia girl's head.

Burley bought the morning edition of the *Santa Fe New Mexican.* He situated himself to give an unobstructed line of sight over the top edge of the paper to Virginia. She stepped to the stationmaster and offered her ticket. The stationmaster exam-ined it, looked to Virginia, then punched the slip. Burley waited until Virginia was out the door before folding the newspaper and moving to the front of the line.

"*Con permiso, señor?*" He excused himself to the first man in line.

Burley watched Virginia board the first car as the station-master narrowed his eyes. He flashed an embarrassed smile.

"*Por favor, señor,* the *señorita* with the *pelo rojo—tu sabes a donde va?*"

"I can't tell you that."

"Oh, great, you speak English." Burley rubbed his hands together. "I got a real problem, mister. See, she's my wife—I mean we're newlyweds—from Iowa? This is our, how do you say . . . *miel de la luna?*" Honey of the moon. He hoped he wasn't pouring it on too thick. "We've had a fight. Please if you could tell me? Tomorrow's Christmas."

The stationmaster looked at Burley's hands. He didn't see a ring. He frowned. "How do I know she's your wife? Show me a picture or something then, maybe . . ." He spread his hands to show that the matter wasn't necessarily in them.

Burley closed his eyes for a moment. Sympathy wasn't this man's strong suit. He opened his eyes, made a quick reassessment. "I can't show you a picture of me and her, but I can show you a family picture."

He pulled out his wallet. He slid out a five-dollar bill. "This could be the spitting image of her father." He pointed to Lincoln.

"Hey, what's the hold-up? There're people with a train to catch back here," shouted one of the ranchers near the end of the line.

The stationmaster murmured, "Perhaps if you can show me more of her family, eh?"

Burley thumbed free a ten-spot. "Uncle Hamilton."

The stationmaster took the money. "One way. Otowi station."

"*Gracias*," said Burley, and retreated.

The stationmaster addressed the line. "*Quién es el turno?*" Who's turn is next?

The line surged forward.

Burley went to the telephone. He found a nickel, lifted the receiver, and dialed Cartwright's house. The telephone at the other end rang. He watched the last person at the ticket window purchase his fare and leave the counter. Burley glanced at the clock above the front door. 5:18. Cartwright's line continued to ring. He hung up after the eleventh bell. The nickel plinked into the coin return. He fished it out and held it at the slot. One other place to try . . . He hesitated. The men in the duty room were his friends, but they were also still Special Agents. What if Torres answered? Or one of Parnell's people who'd stayed behind?

Did he have a choice? He dropped the nickel and dialed the Bureau offices.

"Special Agent Dunlap, Federal Bureau of Investigation," came the sleepy answer after the second ring.

"Dunlap, it's Burley. I need Cartwright. He's there someplace. It's urgent."

"Burley, I told you before, Agent in—Mr. Cartwright left before you did. Is this something you should tell me?"

The last two passengers got their tickets punched and shuffled with their luggage onto the crowded platform.

"Listen to me, Dunlap. Cartwright's there. I know it. If you go to the window, you'll see his car."

From the platform came the call of the conductor. "*Pasajeros al tren.*" All aboard.

"What was that? Where are you?"

"I can't answer that. We've been friends a long time . . . Can you do what I ask or not?"

"And if his car is here?"

"Maybe he's in it, maybe he's in the building—I don't know, shout for him for Chrissakes."

A man wearing a black leather coat over a gray suit entered the station.

"Okay, I'll look. Hold on."

A tall man, broad shouldered, with the loose, predatory movements of a wolf. Burley followed this late arrival with his eyes as he crossed the empty room toward the stationmaster. Burley noticed his shoes and trouser cuffs were as wet as his own.

He's crossed through thick snow . . . Off the beaten track . . .

The man produced a ticket from his inner breast pocket. He handed it to the stationmaster, along with an exchange of pleasantries. As the stationmaster punched the ticket, the man, still smiling, glanced in Burley's direction.

Burley recognized the face. Standartenführer Jürgen von Hofmann.

Their eyes met and held. Burley fought the impulse to drop his gaze. He sensed if he did, it would cost him his life. Burley gave a respectful nod.

Von Hofmann dipped his chin. He took his ticket and left the station for the platform without a second glance.

Where was Dunlap? He checked the clock once more. 5:24.

"Pasajeros al tren!"

"You coming or not?" the stationmaster called over. "We don't wait."

Burley raised an open hand. Wait. At his ear, the line remained quiet as the grave.

SPECIAL AGENT DUNLAP raised the venetian blinds and peered through the snowfall to the lot below. He located Cartwright's car, but not the man. If he'd been wearing his glasses and it was daylight, the weather clear, he might have noticed the trail of exhaust coming from the Chrysler's tailpipe. As it was, Dunlap dropped the blinds and turned to the telephone, ready to tell Burley it was for the better.

Dunlap reached his desk. He lifted the receiver. He knew Cartwright and Burley enough to know they were taking the law into their own hands. They were potentially obstructing justice and committing a federal offense. But what of Parnell? Did he represent justice, he with his casual disregard for murder, coming in, seizing their evidence of the Hendricks massacre and shutting down the investigation under the auspices of "national security?" Something didn't jive, and God dammit, Cartwright was one of the good guys. Dunlap glanced back at the window. A tiny stripe of yellow light warmed the three lowest slats.

Headlights.

CARTWRIGHT AND TYLER sat silently inside the cold Chrysler as Cartwright turned out of the Federal lot onto Lincoln. He lit a cigarette. Activated the wipers. After three passes, the windshield was clear. Special Agent Dunlap stood framed in his headlights.

Cartwright stomped the brake.

"This a good idea?" asked Tyler.

"Better than denting the hood." Cartwright reached for the door handle. "Don't shoot him."

VIRGINIA SAT by a window in the first car. She'd examined each of the two dozen passengers who'd come onto the platform, hoping—and frightened—she'd catch sight of von Hofmann or one of his men. Maybe Zundorf? But the crowd on the platform had dispersed into the two cars and there had been no one else since the last call for passengers.

Virginia flinched at a sudden pressure against her thigh. One of the goats, having slipped its lead, snuffled at her, smelling the sheep scent she had picked up in the truck. A man ordered a boy after the goat. Virginia held the animal by the horns until the boy claimed it.

She never saw von Hofmann step onto the platform.

THE FIRST CAR was full. The conductor signaled von Hofmann to the second. Von Hofmann indicated he understood, but stopped. He looked right, along the length of the train. The first passenger car connected to a baggage car. In front of it sat an engine that, like the rest of the train, must have been sixty years old. Steam curled from between the wheels and the drivers. The train's name, *Apache Flyer*, was painted in white along its coal tender. It reminded von Hofmann of the quaint antiques run by the Reich in Poland. He looked back along the two crowded passenger cars packed with their subhuman species, back to the dark shapes of the three freight cars that completed the train. His mind's eye superimposed an image of a string of cattle cars. A cargo of Jews, dirty faces peering through slats. Groping hands. Guttural prayers. The pathetic whimpering . . . He'd had the honor of seeing off the first train to the *Sonderbehandlung* "Special Treatment" program at Warthegau.

Von Hofmann smiled, then, as quickly, shuddered. Why had he allowed the thought? He had to ride this train.

BURLEY WATCHED the minute hand click to 5:28. He shifted his glance to the ticket booth. The white-haired ticket seller lifted a piece of white-painted plywood cut in the shape of the window's hole.

"Wait!"

The ticket seller peered at Burley and pointed to himself.

"Yeah, you. I need a ticket to Otowi."

The ticket seller tapped his pocket watch.

Burley pointed at the station clock. "Three minutes. I still have three minutes."

The ticket seller shrugged. Burley released the receiver and dashed to the window. He pulled out his wallet and found another ten.

"Otowi, you say?" the ticket seller said, taking the bill.

Burley glanced at the dangling telephone. The stationmaster also looked at it. He approached it.

"Don't touch that phone," said Burley.

The stationmaster spread his hands.

The ticket seller finished filling in Burley's ticket. He slid it to him. "Only thing in this life a close shave is good fer is yer face."

"I'll try to remember." Burley snatched his ticket and his change.

Crossing back to the telephone, he glanced at the clock. 5:29. He grabbed the receiver. "Hello, Cartwright? Dunlap?"

The call remained connected, but the line was an empty hole through space. Burley dropped in the ticket change.

Out came his notebook and pen. He wrote: *Otowi Station— von Hofmann. Virginia.* He tore out the sheet, folded it down the middle, and placed it sticking from the coin return. He glanced at the stationmaster. The man stared at him, looked away. Burley blocked the telephone with his body as he hung the receiver. He joined the stationmaster. Burley handed him his ticket, took it back, punched, and ran for the train.

The stationmaster glanced at the ticket seller, who shrugged a second time and shut his window. He shifted his gaze to the telephone. The man had saved him the trouble and hung it up after all. The stationmaster turned to the doors, not noticing Burley's pen wedged sideways into the slot beneath the disconnect lever, keeping the line alive.

Von Hofmann took a seat alone at the back of the second car beside the door to the observation deck. Although the vintage Pullmans had electric lights, these were dark, the car illuminated for the holiday season by the flicker of fancy oil lamps hanging above the center aisle. The temperature steadily dropping and the only heat source a coal stove at the far end of the car, saw passengers eager to sit bundled close beside strangers. Von Hofmann pulled his leather coat tight and set his face to disabuse even the most dense of humans from nearing him. In this manner, he remained alone in the crowded car and observant. Upon boarding, a warning flashed from his subconscious and von Hofmann scrutinized the other passengers, curious as to why.

Mostly Native Americans and Hispanics, von Hofmann's traveling companions gave him no cause for alarm. Members of the inferior races would never be entrusted with his pursuit. An American businessman and his wife had also found seats in this car, but von Hofmann was confident he could take them at face value. He searched his mind for what bothered him. Perhaps the two men in cowboy hats he'd seen smoking on the landing between the two cars. But they would have seized him when he pushed past. They posed no threat. It was the other man. The man from the telephone. The shoulders of his trench coat had been soaked by melting snow as had the cuffs of his trousers, which meant he hadn't come off the train when it had arrived, or driven in, but had walked through darkness and the weather to the station.

If he doesn't board, he's FBI and is calling reinforcements. Von Hofmann checked his watch. *5:30. Why isn't the train leaving?*

Burley climbed aboard. He found a seat beside a Mexican farmworker four rows ahead and facing von Hofmann. Von Hofmann waited for eye contact, but Burley simply said something to the Mexican, then opened his newspaper.

A bell rang. Von Hofmann listened as the engine blasted steam.

THIS TIME, Burley hadn't made eye contact, but that didn't mean he hadn't seen von Hofmann. He considered whether von Hofmann had marked him as FBI, and if so, was already planning to neutralize him. He lowered half the paper and commented to the young man beside him. The Mexican grinned. Out of the corner of his eye, Burley watched von Hofmann lower his hand. The Nazi faced the window, feigning preoccupation with something outside.

Von Hofmann transferred his pistol to his lap. He cocked it.

Burley turned to the sports page. The steam whistle blew. He wished he hadn't relinquished his pistol to Parnell.

"Burley . . .? C'mon, Burley—where the hell are you..? Pick up the phone!" Cartwright had been holding Dunlap's receiver to his ear a full minute, unable to raise Burley, but agonizing at the knowledge Burley had left the line connected—Cartwright could hear a symphony of unidentifiable sounds. Had he gotten into some kind of trouble? Was he lying dead beneath the phone? *Yeah, and he'd spelled out the killer's name in his own blood—Shit, that's the stuff of Ellery Queen.* "Burley, answer this goddamned phone right now!"

That's when the steam whistle blew which for Cartwright, was as good as Burley's voice. "I know where he's calling from. Only steam train left in the state's the D and RGW."

"The Chili Express?" said Dunlap.

"*Apache Flyer* does the morning run," Tyler corrected before he and Cartwright bolted for the door.

73

"'Otowi Station—von Hofmann and Virginia.'" Cartwright read the note as he pocketed Burley's fountain pen. The stationmaster, who'd been sweeping the floor when Cartwright and Tyler arrived, leaned on his broom and stared. He didn't like their looks.

"When's the train make Otowi?" Tyler called to the man.

"You missed the train," the stationmaster said, remembering the call he'd gotten earlier in the week from the FBI about escaped Nazi prisoners. He speculated this pair could be them. "Gets in nine, maybe nine thirty today depending what the storm dropped up that way."

"We could beat it in the car," said Tyler.

"Cars don't pull freight by steam, do they?" the stationmaster said and quickly left the room.

From out on the platform, he watched the pair hasten off. No mistake, whoever they were, they were bad news. One of them, his clothes torn and bloodstained, his face etched with stitches, looked like he'd recently lost a fight with a meat grinder. The stationmaster considered placing a call to the authorities, then decided against it. He didn't want any trouble. It's what he'd get if he stuck his nose in this one. It wasn't his war. Or his people's. His people lived down in Sonora. He was only here for the Yankee dollar.

FELDWEBEL SCHMIDT had been enjoyably active. Three quarters of an hour ahead of Associate Director Parnell, he gripped the steering wheel of his newly acquired wrecker and angled west onto the layer of untouched snow covering the road marked NM 4 on the map the Standartenführer had supplied him. Exulting in his triumph over *Herr Hauptmann* Zundorf, Schmidt had left the rail yard by climbing the low cyclone fencing where the sidings ended perpendicular to Hickox Street. The street was empty and unlit. The falling snow, hushed and gray-shadowed. Schmidt trudged through the flurries, heading in the direction of the dimly glowing town, hoping he would find a vehicle before reaching civilization.

Schmidt was not to be disappointed. Where Hickox intersected with Cerrillos Road, a bakery truck had foundered in a ditch. Schmidt stopped outside the beam of headlights that belonged to the wrecker, arrived to pull the truck free.

Schmidt set the Thompson gun on semiautomatic and waited.

The snowy embankment fought to keep its prize, but found itself no match for the power of the wrecker. Schmidt stood in the shadow of a cottonwood stroking the walnut foregrip of his gun. He waited until the wrecker driver climbed from his cab and set about unhitching his chains. The wrecker driver worked until finished, when he poured a cup of coffee from a thermos. The baker offered him a donut.

Schmidt approached.

The two men saw him like a phantom taking figure from the snow itself. The wrecker driver scowled, suspicious, but the baker man smiled, waving a donut and greeting him in Spanish. Schmidt's hand emerged from his slicker, bringing the Tommy gun out of the folds of fabric. He fired two quick shots and the men dropped dead as if they'd never had any business being alive.

Schmidt dragged both bodies into the ditch, where he took the wrecker driver's wristwatch.

Now, from the light spreading like the faintest of dyes into the thick black cotton of clouds pressing from overhead, Schmidt could distinguish the shadowed outline of a high and isolated plateau rising above the ragged hills some miles in the foreground. Killing the two men in the road had been rewarding. He'd gotten a truck, some breakfast, and hot coffee to go with it, but it hardly compared to what he'd done to Zundorf. The sweet snap of his neck beneath his hands . . .

What had the Standartenführer said? *I am glad it is you, Herr Schmidt, who will be there to see it with me.* As if there had ever been any doubt Schmidt would make it? He laughed aloud.

Schmidt turned on the light. He checked his map for the fifth time. He found the bridge at Otowi where later he would meet the Standartenführer, the bridge and the main highway onto the plateau. It appeared the only way into Los Alamos. Anxious to trace a path from where he'd turned onto NM 4 and the bridge he was approaching, he alternated his view between his thumb tracing the page and the road. That's how Feldwebel Schmidt found the crossing at Buckman. Looking from the highway to the map, he caught his thumb as it slid over the symbol of a smaller bridge with the name *Buckman* beside it. The bridge spanned the Rio Grande three kilometers below Otowi. Beyond it, a faint dotted line denoted the unimproved road that shot straight out of the valley and up the side of the plateau until, meandering for a while below the crest, it petered out just before the top.

Schmidt had no idea how lucky he'd been to find the Buckman Bridge and road. The map Nestor Cooney had provided von Hofmann was printed from the survey drawn in '26, already five years after the road and bridge had been abandoned from use. New Mexican road maps printed after '28 didn't bother to mark it. In fact, no one working for the US Army at the laboratories on the plateau had any idea it existed at all.

THE APACHE FLYER puffed north from Santa Fe perpendicular to the weak dawn that hadn't decided if it would be anything more today than a memory of light. The car had settled in, as much as the goats were contained and the other passengers managed to stay in their seats, but a baby cried, his mother easing her nipple into his mouth, and Virginia leaned her head against the window, watching sparks whisk and spiral like summer fireflies past the frosted glass. She was exhausted, but sleep was slow to come, held at bay by increasing worry. She listened to the wheels clattering on the track repeating the words: *what to do, what to do, what to do . . .*

Virginia hadn't had time to plan anything since deciphering what she'd seen in von Hofmann's orders. She'd acted solely on impulse. Acted toward a goal without concern for the steps it might take to get there. She had been to the Warner Tea House at the Otowi Bridge crossing only once. A dozen years ago, a rare trip with her father and Señora Gúzman, they had stopped for tea and some of the chocolate cake Edith Warner made famous. The tearoom was actually the adobe dining room of Miss Warner's home. It was not a large place, and Virginia feared if von Hofmann were there and she walked inside, he would kill her out of hand.

Virginia tried to remember other details of the place . . . The porch . . . wisteria vines . . . wooden floorboards inside the sitting room and the general store that shared the front of the house with the dining room. She'd gone out to the privy, by the river, out through the kitchen.

The kitchen was behind the tearoom. She would enter there, through the back door.

And what? Shoot him?

As much as she wanted to kill von Hofmann, he would be no help to Tyler dead. She couldn't overpower him—and what about his men?

I'm a fool to try this.

No. This was the right thing. The only thing. She'd acted on impulse this far and it had gotten her by. Virginia would figure it out when she got there. Opportunity would present itself. It had to.

But the wheels kept clattering in the dark—*what to do, what to do, what to do*—and Virginia drifted into a troubled sleep.

74

Grease spattered the counter. Myra went after it with a rag. Every drop. Myra Cooney lifted six strips of bacon from the frying pan and laid them on a piece of newspaper to soak the grease. She cracked three eggs on the edge of the pan and watched them sizzle, turning white. It would be Nestor's last breakfast in her home. Cooking breakfast was all she could do to keep from screaming. It would soon be over. Nestor was awake and about, and whistling the tune he always whistled that wasn't anything melodic. For the past half hour, Myra had listened to him scooting between his bedroom and his bathroom. Any moment he'd emerge, take his chair, fold his hands over his place mat, and wait for Myra to serve him as he had done practically every day of his life.

Myra flipped the eggs. She noticed a tremor run through her hand. She decided it was more a matter of fatigue than of worry. Although she'd gone to bed shortly after eight the night before, she hadn't slept a wink. When, sometime after ten, Nestor had returned, she'd written her letter, now waiting for the postman, and had lain there listening, curious as to where he'd been, concerned if she should be afraid. Myra listened, holding her breath as he'd flitted to the basement door and down the stairs. He was there a long time. The house was silent. Myra repeated to herself over and again she'd left his secret radio as she'd found it. He couldn't possibly know she was onto him, but as his footsteps scratched their way upstairs, she had a sudden picture of him throwing open her bedroom door and swooping inside to . . .

What? Strangle me? A cynical smile forced its way onto her face. *Not that chicken.* A moment later, she'd heard the water running in his bathroom, then the sound of him nesting into his feather bed. At six-fifteen, she'd dragged herself to the kitchen and began preparing breakfast. She finished the eggs at six-thirty and set the coffee percolating on the stove.

Nestor Cooney entered, lured by the aroma. He sat in his chair and folded his hands over his place mat. Myra took plates from the cupboard. It surprised her to see him dressed in his blue coveralls, snow boots, and leather jacket.

"You're not flying in this weather, are you?"

"Snow's stopped. I certainly am indeed."

Myra scooped his two eggs onto his plate. "How many pieces of bacon would you like?"

"Four, please."

Myra tonged them from the newspaper. She served his plate. "Coffee will be done in a minute."

Nestor Cooney waited for his sister to sit before he ate. Myra watched him cut into his egg. As always, he took care not to break the yolk. 'The white is nutrition for the growing bird, while the yellow is the bird itself. I choose to swallow that part whole.'

She watched him chew. She wanted to speak now, but didn't know how to begin. Myra picked up her fork. She popped her yolk and watched it ooze toward the bacon. She couldn't eat. She set down her fork and stared at the yellow fluid.

"I'm going to give you a chance to help yourself, Nestor."

Nestor cut around the yolk again and took another bite of the white. He chewed.

Myra forced herself to look at him. "I know about the radio."

"The radio? Is something wrong with the radio?"

"Nestor. Your radio. In the basement."

Nestor smiled. He forked the yolk of the first egg whole and dripping grease into his mouth. He swallowed it. Dabbed at his lips with his napkin. "I see." His teeth were gooey yellow. "You know, radio has always been my hobby."

"You dare call spying a hobby?"

"Spying? Oh, dear."

Myra clenched and unclenched her jaw. "Don't play dumb with me. I know about the German radio, about the Minox camera—you're a spy for the enemy."

Nestor Cooney stared blandly. "They're not my enemies," he said.

He attacked the other egg. Myra watched, filled with disgust. He didn't seem human, perched at the edge of his chair his eyes magnified by his spectacles, his elbows pressed to his sides like wings as his little hands rose over the edge of the table to work his utensils. Like some kind of soulless vulture.

"It's treason."

"I don't see it that way. I see it as patriotism to my Führer."

His smile became a smirk. Myra lunged across the table and slapped it off his face. Nestor's spectacles fell to the floor.

They stared at each other, the strangers they'd been their entire lives, then Nestor Cooney spoke. "So, Myra, tell me, if it means so much to you, why haven't you called the police?"

"Because you're my brother. Nestor, I want you to turn yourself in. If you work with the government, expose this ring, or whatever it is, they might go easy on you."

"Sister, sister, sister. They won't go easy on me." He retrieved his spectacles from the floor.

"Easier than if I turn you in." Myra noticed Nestor's expression change. *Finally, he understands I'm serious.*

"Look, maybe we can find a compromise."

"Compromise? Nestor, there is no compromise. You're always like this— Why are you like this? Sometimes I wish I'd followed mother and father out the door," she said, not understanding that essentially, when she'd locked his bedroom and left him, a baby, alone every night for three years, she had. "I deserve better than this, Nestor," said Myra.

Nestor looked down at his plate. The coffee finished percolating. Steam whispered into the air. Myra sighed, about to rise, but Nestor beat her to her feet. She heard a note of surrender as he said, "Sit, I will get it."

Myra followed him with her eyes as he stepped to the stove. He tended to the coffee. His cup and saucer. He poured.

"You don't leave me with much of a choice." He placed his cup on the table. "Have you called anyone yet?" said Nestor Cooney.

"Who, the FBI?" said Myra.

Nestor nodded. He picked up her cup and saucer.

"No."

"Then I guess I better do it when we've finished eating."

A bud of hope blossomed for Myra, and she allowed its perfume to cloud her judgment. She had no desire for Nestor to suffer, but this was the right thing to do. "They have an office in Santa Fe."

"I am aware."

Nestor Cooney took his key chain from his pocket and swung the keys like bodies hanging from the ends of ropes. "I can drive myself over, but I'd prefer you come along. I've always relied on your support."

Myra didn't see his thumb apply pressure to the center of the key-chain medallion.

"Of course I'll go with you," she said.

Nestor Cooney handed Myra her coffee.

She took it and tried to smile.

Nestor Cooney watched her sip.

Her expression changed, her taste buds reacting to the bitterness of the cyanide she swallowed.

SHE KNOWS, *and knows it's too late.*

Nestor Cooney saw it in her eyes. The steaming cup dropped into her lap. Myra pitched sideways from her chair. He stood over her and watched saliva froth out the corners of her mouth. Her hands grabbed for her throat, fingers curling into claws before they got there. He'd poisoned rats before and their paws did the same curling. A twitching sort of thing as the poison did its steady work. It delighted Nestor Cooney to watch his sister suffer and die.

Nestor Cooney picked up the cup. A faint residue of the partially dissolved cyanide tablet remained in the bottom. He stepped to the sink. Rinsed it clean. He'd found it overly theatrical and somewhat insulting his Abwehr trainers had given him the poison capsule and the secret keychain with the instructions to use it were he caught. As if he, Nestor Cooney, would ever stoop to a coward's way out. Didn't they know? He'd marched with Hitler. Would the Führer ever contemplate suicide? How silly, of course not.

"Use it if you are caught." Well, I certainly have, buster, haven't I?

He stared at his sister's body sprawled across the floor in the graceless obscenity of execution. He imagined the freedom of the wind beneath his airplane's wings.

Nestor Cooney crossed the living room. He closed the draperies. He headed for the door. Although he would not be coming back, he wanted to make sure nothing was visible to arouse suspicion. A stack of letters waited by the front door to go out for the postman. Nestor Cooney took them as he let himself out into the icy morning air. He wedged the envelopes into the mail slot for the postman, who would expect to find them there. He got into his Hudson, started it, and drove away.

Five minutes later, going over his preflight check in his mind, Nestor Cooney passed the post office and something clicked inside his head. The letters: he'd only looked at the one on top. *What if. . .?*

Nestor Cooney threw a U-turn in the middle of Lamy Street and raced back home. He pulled into the driveway. He hit the brakes, and his car rode on the ice to collide softly into the garage door, where it stopped. Nestor Cooney flew from the car. He could see the mail slot from the driveway.

The letters were gone.

Nestor Cooney's world crashed out of control. He couldn't believe it. Since when did the postman come at the crack of dawn? He hurled his little body forward, plowing across the snow-banked lawn to the front porch.

They were there. The envelopes had simply fallen loose. A wave of release, almost sexual in its pleasure, washed over Nestor Cooney. He whistled happily as he gathered the letters and rifled through them. The first three were bills. The fourth—yeppi-ty-do—was addressed to the Federal Bureau of Investigation, Santa Fe. Nestor Cooney stopped whistling but only so he could laugh. He shoved Myra's feeble attempt at justice into the pocket of his flight suit and, unable to control his laughter, went back to his car, kicking his boots through the snow like a little boy.

75

IN ROOM 17, Dormitory T-102, in the new barracks town of Los Alamos, Dr. Klaus Fuchs dragged the straight razor down his throat, clearing soapy, faint whiskers in its swath. He swished the razor clean in his sink basin then lifted it to his chin, watching his neck in the mirror as he brought the blade down again, and then once more. Finished shaving, Klaus toweled off his narrow, sallow face, ran a black comb through his balding reddish hair, then hooked the circular spring temples of his wire-rimmed glasses over his ears and studied what thirty-two years on this planet had made him. He saw two people, really. Long ago, he'd used his Marxist philosophy to establish in his mind two separate compartments for himself. In one, he held friendships and associations; the social model of his life where he could be the kind of man he wanted to be. The Klaus Fuchs the people here at Los Alamos experienced as the shy bachelor who danced so well, the pleasant fellow who helped babysitting for some of the other physicists' wives. The Klaus Fuchs of compartment two was the free man: a being independent of the surrounding forces of society. This Fuchs lived the letter of the Communist Party doctrine. He viewed his espionage in terms of historical determinism. That he was suffering from a kind of self-controlled schizophrenia never entered his mind, but if it had, he had come too far to care.

The T-1 Group: Implosion Dynamics, Los Alamos, New Mexico. A long way from the German Communist Party cell at the University of Kiel.

He buttoned his shirt to the collar. From the son of a socialist Quaker minister working for peace and equality for the lives of all German people, to an architect of the atomic bomb working for death, the path of Fuchs's life, and that of his family, had been unnecessarily grim under the winged shadow of the Nazi eagle.

His mother's suicide.

His father's imprisonment and torture by the Gestapo.

The arrest and imprisonment of his sister Elisabeth and her husband, Klaus Kittowski. Kittowski went into a concentration camp and Elisabeth threw herself from a bridge into the path of an onrushing train, its engine waving swastikas.

Klaus selected a dark necktie. He knotted it around his throat. The Nazis had a standing warrant for his arrest and execution since 1933. He still had nightmares of hiding in a Berlin alley, listening to the sound of the storm troopers' jackboots pounding past him across the paving stones, hunting him like his namesake, the fox. In his dreams, he never escaped.

But Klaus Fuchs had escaped. A brilliant student in physics and a hardened communist, he'd been ordered out of Germany by the KDP until such a time that the war was won and Germany had become a communist nation.

He finished dressing, experiencing a rush of proud satisfaction for the service he'd provided his Soviet comrades. Since the autumn of '41, when he'd presented himself at the Soviet embassy in London and offered to share with them the information he had access to regarding the Anglo-American atomic weapons programs, he'd given the Soviet Union a steady flow of the most top secret intelligence on the planet. His last batch, in early June, had been microfilm copies of all the reports on the K-25 Oak Ridge plant, including the details of its valves, pumps, and control barriers. He gave them the equations he and the others had developed to calculate the effects of fluctuations on the production rate of uranium-235, and his own mathematical theory of control, emphasizing the mathematical hydrodynamics that explained the flow of uranium hexafluoride through the metal barriers of the Oak Ridge gaseous diffusion plant that was producing the fissionable material. All of it he'd routed out of Tennessee and he assumed it had gotten to his NKVD control agent in London known only to him as "Sonia."

Up until that time, getting information to the Russians had been easy. But as Britain and America decided to cooperate on the bomb, security increased around Project Y in general, and around Klaus specifically. He'd been forced to change the method with which he passed his secrets. Direct contact from his Soviet masters could no longer be risked. Instead, he advised them, he would control both meeting time and place. These he had set within the text of his last message routed through Zurich back in June.

And today was that day. The meeting time set for 9:30 a.m.

Klaus found the gold tie-clip set with garnets, which would identify him to his contact—red and gold: the colors of the communist flag—then he reached under his mattress and withdrew the three notebooks. He shoved them into his overcoat pocket and headed for the door. Klaus Fuchs would have been shocked to know that no one in the Soviet Union or its employ had any idea he was in New Mexico.

76

Halfway across the Rio Grande, Feldwebel Gunter Schmidt heard the timbers of the bridge crack beneath the weight of the wrecker. Schmidt pressed the gas pedal to the floor as brittle pieces of gray wood fell to the mud-brown, ice-frothing waters below. The wrecker lurched forward.

Almost there, almost there—

His rear right wheel crashed through the boards.

Schmidt downshifted. The tire spun. The rhythmic motion of the bridge's death throes increased. Huge chunks of wood jettisoned into the water. The wrecker clawed forward, the trapped wheel eating a furrow as the three other tires wrenched it along, but presently Schmidt guided his vehicle into the snow on the other side.

He continued forward, guessing where the road might be beneath the snow. He kept his eyes fixed on the plateau that rose before him, windswept of snow, purple and rose and pink, its grooved canyons spread outward like a lady's fan upon a table of white. A border of pines marked the edge of the plateau's base, a lace of white-speckled green, and here Schmidt relocated the road and wended his way up the mountain's side. He estimated he was almost to the top when black clouds coiled in beneath the gray, foggy snakes to loose their breath of snow once more.

Visibility decreased as Schmidt drove into the clouds. Schmidt cut his speed to a crawl, leaning in close to the windshield, trying to X-ray the snowy mist with his eyes as, ever-rising, the road meandered through a series of tumbling cliffs and step-like mesas before petering out among pine-canopied boulders.

Schmidt parked the wrecker between two stones the size of houses. He faced the vehicle back the way he'd come in preparation for his escape. He took the time to finish his bread and empty the thermos of coffee, then he attended to the Thompson. He fieldstripped the weapon. He removed the oilcan from the stock and oiled it. Reassembled it. A matter of minutes. He packed the last of his ammo into his two magazines. He put one in his pocket, loaded the other, and charged the gun.

Schmidt stepped into the freezing air. Needles of ice intermingled with the snowflakes stung his cheeks.

In the rear of the wrecker, he found a pair of bolt cutters and a jerrican of gasoline. Both would come in handy. He set them aside.

He'd just set off among the rocks when something drew his attention to the stone beside him. Etched into the lichen-speckled side of one of the boulders was a pair of Indian hieroglyphs. A plumed serpent rising in the air, lightning zigzagging from its mouth, and beside it, a backward swastika. Schmidt touched the ancient drawings for luck before continuing.

Five minutes later, Schmidt came out around the wall of rock, ten meters from a military policeman astride a horse, who'd stopped alongside a fence to light his pipe.

Schmidt raised the Tommy gun. The pipe dropped from the soldier's mouth. He didn't reach for the 12-gauge shotgun hanging by its leather sling to the saddle horn. He just whimpered. "No, don't, please."

Schmidt shot him once in the chest.

Steller's jays leaped, screeching into the air. The horse rushed forward, pitching the body and shotgun into the snow. Schmidt stepped to intercept the mount, but he was unable to grab the dangling reins. It trotted past. Schmidt watched it stop twenty meters away. He clicked his tongue. The horse looked back, but didn't move.

The dead American was only slightly taller than Schmidt, but his uniform would fit. He traded his duster for the US Army cold-weather parka. He took the dead man's thick woolen socks and boots. They were still warm as he put them on. Schmidt took the American's Sam Browne belt with its holstered .45 and two grenades. He picked up the shotgun and slung it muzzle down over his right shoulder. Then he strapped on the man's white-painted helmet emblazoned with the letters: *MP*. He claimed the lighter from the hole it had melted in the snow.

The horse shook its head and quivered at Schmidt's approach. As the Nazi reached for the animal's reins, it took three steps backward. Fog blew from its nostrils. Schmidt's hand closed around the leather traces. He held the beast steady, speaking to it softly in German. He waited until the horse accepted his dominance, then lifted the jerrican of gasoline from the snow and strapped it behind the saddle.

Schmidt mounted. He hadn't been on a horse since he'd served as a groom for a petty bastard of an Oberst in Berlin the year before the Great War thirty years ago. It wouldn't matter. He had no plans for any hard riding. He simply guided the horse to the fence and, looking at the hoofprints in the snow, turned it back the way it had come. As horses do, it headed for home.

Ten minutes later, the horse stopped at a locked gate. A red sign announced in white letters: *DANGER! PELIGROSO!* Schmidt snapped the lock with the bolt cutters. He kicked the gate open and entered the Los Alamos compound.

77

Klaus Fuchs exited the two-story tar-paper-sided dormitory by the back door. The night's storm had dropped almost a foot of snow. Clustered puffball flakes were falling and Klaus, standing beneath the protective wooden shell of the awning, watched them, thinking about a different snow entirely.

The invisible snow of radioactive fallout.

He stepped into the weather, the world, his future. A push broom leaned against the building's wall beside three trashcans. Klaus carried it to his battered blue Buick. He worked its bristles across the windshield, clearing the glass. He put the broom aside. Klaus opened the passenger door and groped under the dashboard to open the secret compartment. From behind, came a voice in German. "*Frohe Weinachten*, Klaus." Merry Christmas.

Klaus Fuchs shoved the first notebook into the compartment, stood and identified Dr. Hans Bethe and Mrs. Bethe taking their morning walk, gauging whether the physicist had seen the notebook.

"Dr. Bethe. Good morning and merry Christmas to you. And you, Mrs. Bethe."

"You're up early for a holiday," Dr. Bethe said. "Are you leaving the mountain?"

"Some last-minute errands."

"We will see you this evening at our party, yes?" Mrs. Bethe encouraged, friendly.

"Of course, Mrs. Bethe," said Klaus Fuchs.

He waited until they had continued a short distance away before adding the second two notebooks to the compartment and securing it closed.

Klaus adjusted the choke and let the engine warm. He eased out of his parking space. On his way to turn over secrets, he entered the current of history. He maneuvered past a row of apartment buildings still under construction and noticed a civilian sitting in a car parked at the edge of the civilian housing area. The man watched him. Klaus waved, but the man didn't return the gesture.

Each day Klaus drove through the civilian housing area and each day the dusty dirt roads and muddy yards, the maze of expansible government trailers and Pacific hutments reminded him of a military internment camp. Klaus noted few people about, but this was Christmas Eve and civilians had the day off. He saw another lone man, this one wearing a hat and trench coat, standing on a corner smoking a cigarette, as if he were waiting for a bus at Picadilly Circus instead of lurking in the middle of nowhere in a heavy snow. It made him uneasy.

This time, he didn't wave.

Klaus turned east onto Trinity Drive. Rolled past the PX. Joined a line of cars entering the barbed-wire corridor that separated the two dozen buildings of the main Technical Area on his right, with the University of California's Building P and the Gamma building on the left. A few WACs and some of the "engineers"—as security rules classified all the physicists—hurried along the sidewalks and between buildings, clutching coats against the cold and falling snow. Klaus didn't recognize any of them and no one looked his way. As he approached the intersection at Twentieth Street, the light changed red. Klaus stopped fifth in line behind a pair of army trucks and two civilian cars. Above him, a covered walkway extended over the road between building P and building A.

Klaus glanced upward. Two more of them—severe men, trench coats and hats—stood at the window, staring down. Eye contact made and unnaturally held. Klaus's heart beat faster.

The traffic light turned green.

Klaus accelerated beneath the walkway. Past the pass office and cleaners, toward the first of the two gates that led off the plateau. He was queasy. It was as if from the moment he'd left the dormitory porch, he was being funneled into a gigantic kind of trap.

The cars moved forward.

His turn came. Klaus unrolled his window to show his ID and answer the MP's questions. He heard himself tell the man he was going into Santa Fe for some last-minute shopping. He listened to a warning against talking to strangers or attempting to make contact with anyone via telephone, telegram, or letter. He watched his name logged in the book. The guard waved him forward.

Business as usual. Nothing to worry about.

At the second checkpoint, Klaus noticed the presence of three more trench-coated civilians gathered at the guard shack. One stood speaking with the officer of the day. The other two lingered behind the MP gate guards as they questioned the occupants of the civilian cars in front of him. These men were FBI agents. Every member of the British mission he was part of had been interviewed by the FBI when they'd arrived in New York. That was routine. It wasn't routine to see them here. He never had. Were they onto him? Impossible. Their presence couldn't have anything to do with him. How could they know? He was too careful. Too smart.

His heart pounded.

The passenger of the first car, a young lady, was directed out of the vehicle. From her guilty expression, it was clear she'd been denied exit from the plateau. She exchanged a few words with the driver, whom Klaus assumed was her husband, then she stepped back and waved as he drove off. Klaus watched her escorted to a covered jeep that would return her to where she lived.

The line crept forward.

The second car fared worse than the first. The barrier was raised, but only long enough for the driver to execute a U-turn and head back into the camp. The army trucks were next. Klaus swallowed as guards opened their canvas back flaps and searched them.

Klaus Fuchs stared at the dashboard, picturing the three notebooks in their amateurish secret compartment. He contemplated shoving them back into his overcoat. Found on his person, they'd be much easier to explain as a sloppy mistake than were they found hidden in the compartment. What would that buy him? An hour? Two? Under scrutiny, their explicit contents would in no way come off as a scientist's personal notes, an absentminded oversight. The information they contained was too sensitive, too complete, too instructional.

The three notebooks hidden in Klaus Fuchs's car were nothing less than a detailed manual of how to achieve a critical mass of plutonium-239. The design concept for the implosion bomb. The implosion bomb would have a solid plutonium core, detonated by a complex system of polonium initiators (a neutron source), a tamper, an aluminum shell, and a set of high-explosive lenses assembled in a uniformed manner around a sphere which upon detonation would compress the plutonium core to critical mass size.

Klaus guided the Buick alongside the next set of MP guards. He showed his pass, his ID, and told the same lie about going to Santa Fe. Sweat trickled down the back of his neck and along his sideburns. He prayed the MP didn't notice.

"Excuse me, sir," the MP said, taking his ID and pass and stepping over to the officer of the day and the trench-coated man beside him.

He hadn't done that with the others.

Klaus held his breath. He stared at the barrier ten feet ahead of him. He stared at the MPs with rifles who guarded it. He'd run the gate if he had to. The MP returned with his ID and gate pass.

"Dr. Fuchs," he said, handing him his papers, "seeing as you're one of our engineers, is it possible for you to reconsider the necessity of today's trip?"

"I don't understand. Am I cleared or not?"

"You are cleared, sir. Yes. But would you reconsider?"

Klaus snuck a glance past the soldier to the FBI agents. They watched him. Their faces betrayed nothing.

He foisted a smile onto the MP who awaited his answer. "The necessity is overwhelming. Sure, the world's at war, but that doesn't hold back Father Christmas. There are six families here without passes who are counting on my being Saint Nicholas tonight. It's hard enough on the children as it is . . ."

The MP studied him a full thirty seconds. "You'll check whatever packages you bring from town with us at the gate when you return?"

"Certainly."

"All right," he said, then ran down the list of do's and don'ts Klaus had gotten at the last checkpoint. Stepping back from the car, the MP waved for the gate guards to raise the barrier.

"Merry Christmas," Klaus called before he rolled up his window. He was glad to see the FBI weren't immune to a seasonal greeting.

Klaus Fuchs left Los Alamos, driving at a careful pace down the treacherous mountain road. Forty minutes remained before his rendezvous and he didn't want to risk an accident in this weather, now having accomplished the difficult task of clearing the camp.

In the race for the atomic bomb, the Anglo-American effort led the world with both the reactors to separate the fissionable material from the uranium and plutonium, and two different designs for using this substance in a weapon. Nazi Germany followed close behind with supplies of both uranium and plutonium, a reactor under construction, but no plans yet for constructing a bomb once their U-235 and plutonium were produced. Klaus's beloved Soviet Union, on the other hand, had neither the uranium, the separation plant, nor a working plan for building a bomb. It wasn't fair. Churchill and Roosevelt had excluded Stalin from their meeting in Quebec in August, and the subsequent Quebec Agreement for the full exchange of information and ideas in the construction of the atomic bomb was made without him. The Soviets were *allies* with the British and Americans. So far, the Russians had carried most of the burden of fighting the Nazis . . . Well, with what he was providing them, the Soviet Union would have what was rightly theirs, and all they would soon need was a small quantity of Pu-239.

As Klaus wound down the plateau, headed for Edith Warner's Tea House on the far side of the Otowi Bridge, he correctly assumed he rode to a moment that could completely change the outcome of the war.

Associate Director Parnell saw the slight, narrow-faced man get out of a blue Buick and enter the adobe house when DeGrey slowed to make his turn onto the Otowi Bridge. He didn't give the man much thought. Once over the bridge, he passed the Otowi railway station and freight house. He headed up the Parajito Plateau for Project Y.

78

Nestor Cooney parked his pea-green Hudson outside his hangar on the outskirts of Albuquerque. With the help of the two old mechanics he'd hired to maintain and prepare the aircraft, they guided the Twin Beech out of the hangar and onto the taxiway. Nestor Cooney initiated his preflight checks.

"Don't you think it might be safer not to go up today, Mr. Cooney?"

"Don't I pay you to mind your own business, grandpa?"

Twenty minutes later, Nestor Cooney taxied onto the runway and requested a take-off from the tower.

The two mechanics watched him go airborne, wings wobbling, five minutes after that.

"The guy's a fool to fly in this weather," said the mechanic Nestor Cooney called grandpa.

"How's he gets all his fuel, anyway?"

"Hell, Vic, you've seen his gas ration card."

"Sure, I seen it. Jus' wanna know why."

"Shit, the little creep's a spy, didn't you know?"

Laughing, the pair retreated back into the hangar.

79

SS-Brigadeführer Walter Schellenberg had not been invited to Wewelsburg castle since the last of the Loki interviews in the fall of '41. It was Christmas Eve, or as officially changed by Himmler in 1936, Yuletide of the Winter Solstice Celebration. Schellenberg's staff car pulled to a stop in the snow-patched, cobbled courtyard. Tongues of gas-fueled fire still flickered in the wall-mounted braziers, and the two iron torches still burned vigilantly beside the massive doors, but as Schellenberg exited the car, the platoon of SS honor guards who had once snapped to attention, their boots throwing sparks across the stones, were gone to feed their blood to the battlefields in the east. In their place waited five Waffen-SS, extraordinary men, each over six foot and 190 pounds, turned out not for ceremony, but armed to the teeth for battle. Himmler's current bodyguard. They came to attention and saluted as Schellenberg strode to the door.

A Hauptsturmführer escorted Schellenberg into a reception room, asking him to wait before closing the double doors behind him. Schellenberg considered his surroundings. The room was large with high, rounded ceilings ribbed with swastika-stenciled beams of Black Forest timber. Two busts of Hitler flanked the doors while directly opposite blood-red draperies cloaked a window. Two massive oil paintings faced each other from the flanking walls. Schellenberg studied them. The first was a Rubens depicting the rape of the Sabine women. The other, a Titian portraying a glorious and bloody battle filled with half-naked men and women, flashing steel, foaming steeds . . . He'd seen it once in Paris. Schellenberg approached a gold-plated liquor cart.

He helped himself to a glass of chilled Dom Pérignon champagne and cracker onto which he heaped Beluga caviar. To the victors go the spoils. He popped the hors d'oeuvre into his mouth.

But that's not the case anymore, is it? This caviar hadn't come out of Russia any time in the recent past, and unless things changed quickly, the Reichsführer might be advised to leave the art appreciation to the scholars and convert these assets into gold. Schellenberg had already made one trip to Switzerland to negotiate the confidential transfer of his own gold to the Bank of International Settlements in Basel. He would soon make another.

Regardless of how the Führer viewed the progress of the war, the last eight months had been one setback after another. On the Eastern Front, the Russians piled victory on top of victory. Schellenberg had read today's radio dispatches from von Manstein's *Heeresgruppe Süd.* At five this morning, the Russians had thrown six armies and three assault groups against von Manstein along a center line between Kiev and Zhitomir. If the Dnieper line fell, the Eastern Front was lost, unless . . . Schellenberg still ardently believed that, one way or another, if they could force the British and American Allies out of the war . . . But that's what this was about, his visit here tonight.

The ten Loki.

Operation Steppenfeuer.

The doors swung open. The Hauptsturmführer said, "Please follow me, Brigadeführer."

The Hauptsturmführer led Schellenberg deep into the castle. He pulled open a heavy wooden door to reveal a circular stone stairway lit by oil-burning torches. He gestured into the smoky tower. "The Reichsführer awaits."

More theatrics. Too much for his personal taste. Schellenberg stepped past the Hauptsturmführer.

Operation Steppenfeuer. Prairie Fire. Activated four days prior, Standartenführer von Hofmann was less than an hour away from acquiring the intelligence that would save the Reich. That and a quick flight to Mexico; Schellenberg had heard this morning from Admiral Dönitz *Oberbefehlshaber der Marine*, Commander-in-Chief of the Navy that a U-boat was in place one mile off the coast of Veracruz. He climbed the stairs remembering Himmler's words: *Whatever the individual task you are asked to perform, know, if it succeeds, it will be no less than a deathblow to our enemies.*

He'd said this to each of them. The ten men inserted into America, but of the ten, seven had been killed before capture, one was missing, and only two had made it. The first and the last. Von Hofmann, and the young doctor, Kurt Behr, interned only last month in an American camp in North Carolina.

Schellenberg stood before another wooden door. He knocked.

"Come in, Walter," Himmler said from within.

Schellenberg pulled open the heavy door and entered. The austerity of the circular room stuck him immediately. Spaced along the stone wall were twelve pedestals. Above each of these, a window angled through the five feet of wall in such a way that the faint moon glow coming through lit the opposite pedestals with mystical light. On one of the pedestals sat an unadorned urn. The center of the room was inscribed by a sunken circle. About ten feet across, three steps led into this circle where at its center lay another, lower circle, only a few feet in diameter and blackened by fire. High above, an ornate swastika capped the ceiling dome. Himmler stood at the edge of the fire pit.

"Herr Reichsführer, *Fröhlich Julfest*," Schellenberg wished him a happy yuletide and saluted.

"We shall see . . ." said Himmler, staring into the pit. "Do you know what this room is?"

"I cannot say I've heard you speak of it," said Schellenberg.

Himmler smiled faintly beneath his mustache. "This is my Supreme Leaders' Hall. My researchers have drawn back the curtain to our past and have found the authentic Teutonic coats of arms for those of us who have brought the Reich to its present greatness. When, in the course of time, one of our leaders falls, here is where I burn his coat of arms. I put the ashes in an urn and seat it in a place of honor."

Schellenberg indicated the single urn. "And whose coat of arms is in that?"

"Our friend Heydrich's." Himmler met Schellenberg's glance. "If Operation Steppenfeuer succeeds, I shall accord you a place of honor in this room."

"I am honored, Reichsführer," although he couldn't care less.

Himmler nodded like a priest bestowing salvation. "And von Hofmann," he said. "When he returns, how long will it take us to assemble an atomic weapon?"

"Not long, Reichsführer. Herr Doktor Heisenberg at the Kaiser Wilhelm Institute in Berlin has enough heavy water from the Norsk Hydro plant in Norway for his 'uranium burner,' the separation system he will use to draw the isotope U-235 from U-238. U-235, I am told, is the substance that will create the explosion. In August, we received two thousand sacks of coffee beans I had the Swiss purchase from the Congo."

"Coffee beans? Walter, you are not making sense."

"That is what the Swiss shipped—at least what their *certificat de garantie* said when they passed through the Allied blockade. Those two thousand sacks contained two hundred tons of uranium ore I purchased from the Union Minière's mines in Upper Katanguin. When von Hofmann returns, an atomic bomb will only be a matter of following the recipe he brings us."

Himmler nodded, his eyes bright with anticipation behind his glasses. Schellenberg took the opportunity to produce a sterling flask from inside his black leather officer's coat. He opened it, poured golden schnapps into the jigger lid and offered it to the head of the SS.

"A toast to von Hofmann and the success of Operation Steppenfeuer."

Himmler raised his drink. "And to the Führer on this momentous eve."

"*Prost!*"

80

"I HAVE A DETACHMENT of two hundred and nighty-five men divided into four six-hour patrols of approximately seventy men each. I've posted half of each patrol within Technical Area 1. The rest are divided into gate security, motor patrols roaming the site, foot patrols along the fence, and six mounted patrols outside the perimeter wire," the Los Alamos Provost Marshal said, escorting Associate Director Parnell and Agents Lascomb and DeGrey into the military police radio and operations center, inside Administration Building T-1, two blocks north of Tech Area 1.

"And communications with your men? How good are they?" Parnell asked.

"I have a staff sergeant equipped with a radio jeep assigned to each section of patrol. Unless something comes up, they check in on the hour."

"What about communications with my men on surveillance?"

"Each has been given access to a field radio. Anything happens, we'll know about it here." He indicated a corporal sitting at a radio, headphones covering his ears.

"Good." Parnell crossed to a counter on which sat a thermos. "Cups?"

"Cupboard below."

Parnell found a ceramic mug. He poured some coffee. "Your men aren't trigger-happy, are they? They've been briefed on what to do? I won't tolerate mistakes."

The provost marshal's back stiffened. "They are to identify suspects and await your orders."

"And they're not to engage or be seen if they can help it."

"Unless you'd like us to do something different."

Parnell frowned. He didn't like the man's tone and was about to remind him of the serious nature of today's mission when the radio operator swiveled in his chair.

"Sir, mounted patrol four checking in, sir. Private Bains is missing."

"Missing?"

"Von Hofmann's calling card. Where is mounted patrol four located?" Parnell gestured at the wall-mounted map of the plateau.

The provost marshal ignored Parnell's question long enough to get on the radio and advise the staff sergeant to use extreme caution in searching for the missing soldier.

He stepped to the map. "That patrol works this slope of the southern canyon directly below the foundry and uranium and normal machine shops at the western end of the tech area," said the provost marshal.

"Fine. Put the men on alert for a likely incursion, move in some more assets, and see what von Hofmann does," said Parnell.

Here, where the pines grew all the way to the fence, Schmidt lay into the woven-wire fence with the bolt cutters. This interior fence stood as further security for the Technical Area, visible to Schmidt beyond. He finished with the fence, tossed the bolt cutters into the snow. He pulled back the wires and led the horse by its reins past an incongruous log cabin toward the rear wall of a foundry. Past the foundry stood some warehouses. Past them, was a wide, empty space of almost seventy meters, an iced-over pond at its center, protected only by the falling snow. It stretched east toward a dense grouping of about twenty buildings.

Schmidt studied his target area. He noticed guards posted at some of these buildings, unprepared for him as they stamped their feet and smacked hands in the numbing weather. Typical stupid Amis standing around. There were also three guard towers he could see, the closest situated at the edge of the open space. It would have to be distracted.

In the guard tower above Building X, which housed the cyclotron, Private Keilly blew through his hands and scanned the snow-hazy far buildings of the tech area. Orders that morning had been strange. Ominous in their warning of a suspected infiltration. The standing rule on the plateau to shoot first, answer questions later, had changed. Today they were to observe, report, but only fire if fired upon. Maybe it was part of some new drill concocted by the general and the provost marshal.

Keilly was wiping frost from the barrel of his .30 caliber Browning machine gun when he noticed a horse poke its head around the back of the foundry. Its reins dangled into the snow. A loose horse—was this all the feared infiltration amounted to? Keilly activated his radio and called it in.

The horse bounced its head in distress.

It had worked with the truck. It would do the same kind of job on a horse. Schmidt lit the gasoline soaked MP armband that trailed from the jerrican. Smelling smoke, the horse screamed and bucked. It shot out into the compound, terrified by the fire attached to its back.

Private Keilly was on the radio to the corporal in the radio and operations center when the horse bolted between two warehouses into the open space in front of Building Delta. Keilly stared, aghast at the cruelty but too mesmerized to look away as the animal exploded. It tore in half in a shower of fire, gore, and bone.

Schmidt sprinted along the southern fence. As he neared the medicine lab, a jeep carrying two MPs materialized through the snow, heading toward him along the other side of the perimeter fence. Schmidt and the MPs saw one another at the same time. The jeep driver hit the brakes as Schmidt fired on the run, raining the vehicle with lead. Schmidt threw himself around the corner and against the med lab's wall, ducking beneath a window. He'd caught a glimpse of the driver slamming back into his seat. He didn't know if he'd hit the passenger. He didn't have time to worry about it.

Sirens wailed across the compound. One hundred and fifty-nine 1500-watt floodlights rippled on, illuminating the gray, freezing day as if it were the middle of summer.

Private Keilly tore his eyes from the mangled horse at the sound of gunfire. In the time it took him to throw off his safety and swivel his gun, all he saw was the aftermath: the passenger of a patrol jeep going to the aid of the bloody driver. He hunkered behind his gun and swept the buildings for the enemy.

Schmidt caught his breath. The high altitude was working against him. He listened to a weepy voice over at the jeep as the passenger tended to his partner. Schmidt considered spinning out and killing him too, when above his head came a rap on the glass. In the window, a worried man in a lab coat tried to communicate something to Schmidt.

Schmidt triggered the Tommy gun once, knocking the worried man back in a spatter of blood. He raised the weapon over his head, shoved its barrel through the broken glass. He sprayed a burst blindly into the room. Screams answered the shots for which Schmidt was glad.

He darted toward a cluster of small laboratory buildings, smashed a window at random, and pulled a grenade from his belt.

PARNELL'S EXCITEMENT became suspicion something was going wrong with his plan when he heard the horse blow up. This didn't fit with the scenario Hoover envisioned. Gunfire followed shortly after. They headed for Technical Area 1. Nickel-plated Colt .38 revolver firmly in his grip, he leaped from the Provost Marshal's jeep into the snow, slipped, fell on his ass, pulled himself to his feet, and led the others against the tide of frightened men and women streaming from the tech area.

An explosion rent the air. Smoke billowed from behind a building to their right, while ahead and across the compound, three patrol jeeps rolled into view, disgorging men.

"Provost Marshal, see to your troops. Remember, von Hofmann could have men with him—I don't give a damn about them—but I must take von Hofmann alive!"

The provost marshal gave Parnell a dubious look, then headed for his men. Parnell faced Lascomb and DeGrey. Directed them around the building's right side while he moved around it to the left.

AFTER THROWING THE GRENADE, Schmidt crossed a loading dock, sprayed a group of men inside a garage, and continued to move, changing clips before reaching the corner. Peering out, he could see a full platoon of men organizing around three jeeps. There were three more guard towers, each sporting machine guns, their gunners ready. He could hear the shouts and sounds of equipment as more soldiers poured in behind him. It hit Schmidt like an officer's slap in the face that his situation was hopeless.

It is small—it should give you no trouble.

The Standartenführer's words taunted him with their lies. This Los Alamos, this secret installation, was vastly larger and more heavily secured than Camp Santa Rosa had ever been. The Standartenführer must have known this.

A wide walkway separated Schmidt's position from a large three-story structure identified by the sign nailed to its corner as Building V. Schmidt ran for it, crossing the walkway under a shower of bullets from the guard tower that had been tracking him from the start. As Schmidt kicked in the door to Building V and tossed in a second grenade, Private Keilly caught him with a burst that knocked him off his feet.

At the other end of Building V, Parnell watched Schmidt fall. A second after that, the grenade went off in a blast of fire, smoke, shrapnel. Schmidt rose again. Halfway. He plunged through the door.

Machine-gun bullets had made spongework of Schmidt's right leg. Blood poured between his fingers. There was too much wound to hold. He pushed to his feet on the strength of his rage. The Standartenführer had sent him on a suicide mission. In the end, von Hofmann was every officer Schmidt had served under: a conceited liar who thought himself better, thought his men fodder for the big guns they themselves were too afraid to face.

Schmidt slumped against the wall inside a long corridor. His grenade had killed two people and wounded another. He put a wounded, whimpering woman in uniform out of his misery. Schmidt clawed his way along the wall to a staircase at the center of the building.

A Mexican janitor huddled at the bottom of the steps. Schmidt did him with the Tommy gun, did a doctor wearing a pencil behind his ear with the rest of the clip, then dropped the Thompson and raised the shotgun as he lurched onto the second floor.

He stopped to catch his breath. He looked back at the slimy red trail he'd left behind. *That's me. The part the Standartenführer's already killed.*

Across from the stairs, a laboratory door was ajar. The lights were on. Schmidt lurched toward it and pumped four shells into a room full of equipment. Chemicals flew and ignited. Papers and books spread across the counter quickly caught and burned. But there was no one here to kill. In the hallway, the fire alarm and sprinklers came alive. Schmidt moved to the next room.

At the opposite end of Building V, Parnell climbed the fire stairs toward the sound of shotgun blasts. Here, the fire sprinklers hissed before finding water. Parnell slammed open the second-floor fire door and thrust out his handgun, ready. A Navajo cleaning woman rushed toward him. She screamed and Parnell shoved her out of his path as he lunged into an empty corridor filling with smoke.

Parnell heard the guttural sound of shouted German issuing through an open door. He jogged to the door, gripped his pistol two-handed, and spun inside. Parnell registered everything in an instant. A laboratory Christmas party. Decorations, cheese ball, cider, cookies. Four lab workers faced a blackboard, hands raised. A Nazi dressed like an MP shouting at them as he reloaded a shotgun for execution.

"FBI! Drop your weapon! Hands on your head!"

Schmidt swung around, turning the shotgun in his hands as he saw the flash and felt the fire dig into his shoulder. The shotgun left his hands as he collapsed. The trench-coated man who'd shot him remained where he was, covering him with his smoking pistol as American soldiers rushed into the room, then Schmidt lost focus and with the sensation of falling down a well, light became a circle growing smaller and smaller until it was gone.

The Nazi looked dead to Associate Director Parnell, but the soldiers checking him called for a stretcher and Special Agent Lascomb was beside him, telling Parnell the wounds weren't life threatening to von Hofmann.

"It's not von Hofmann," Parnell said.

The man was too short and too old to be the Standartenführer.

"Yes, sir," Lascomb said. "Anything else you want me and Special Agent DeGrey to do?"

Parnell looked askance at him. "Get on the horn and check in with the surveillance men. See if anything else happened while this was going on."

Parnell was furious. He'd fallen for a diversion, concentrating the entire force at his disposal on this one-man killing machine, and now von Hofmann could be anywhere. The provost marshal led in the team of medics with the stretcher. They set the stretcher beside the body. One of them pulled out a syringe.

"What is that?" Parnell challenged.

"Morphine, sir."

"He gets none of that. Pump him up with Dexedrine. I need him wide-eyed and ready to talk in five minutes."

The medics looked at the provost marshal.

"Listen, Mr. Parnell, you feds had your chance, but now this is a prisoner of war and his treatment is governed by the Geneva—"

"The son of a bitch is a fugitive from federal authority, and dressed in that American uniform is not a prisoner of war. He's a spy. Before I have him shot, he's going to answer some questions. Lascomb, DeGrey, escort these medics and our spy to a quiet room. And you"—he jabbed a finger at the Provost Marshal—"You get some rope and a desk lamp."

Feldwebel Gunter Schmidt returned to consciousness at the combination of an injection of dextroamphetamine and a half dozen slaps to his face. He found himself tied to a heavy wooden chair centered in a beam of overhead light. His wounds were wrapped and the pain bearable. Schmidt's heart pumped strong and steady, his being imbued with energy. Not terrible, considering he was still alive.

Schmidt was naked from the waist down. On the floor next to his feet, a lamp lay on its side. Its shade was off. It was unplugged. The man who'd shot him had done the slapping. Arranged behind that son of a bitch stood two other trench coats and an Army officer. The officer looked worried. Schmidt squinted to make out a wall clock. 8:52.

"Lucky you," Parnell said, "you're going to live."

"Fuck you."

"Please, I don't appreciate that kind of language. Sergeant Schmidt, is it? How about instead you tell me where I can find Standartenführer von Hofmann."

"How about I suck out your mother's mouse?"

Parnell grinned like he'd just heard the best of jokes. He held an open palm toward the men behind him. "Wire strippers."

Schmidt watched Parnell's hand close around the wire strippers. He watched Parnell stoop for the lamp. His foot twitched at its bonds as he tried to kick the Ami motherfucker in the face.

Parnell broke the ceramic body of the lamp on the edge of a desk. He wrapped the plug end around his fist and tore the cord free from its connectors. He pulled the two plastic insulated wires apart at their seam and then used the wire strippers to clear the insulation from the ends. These he twisted into points. Keeping the ends away from each other, Parnell inserted the plug into a wall socket. He brought the ends together, ever so briefly. Sparks flew and the lights dimmed. He hovered the wires near Schmidt's hair-matted testicles. "Want to reconsider? Tell me where I can find von Hofmann."

"You don't frighten me."

Parnell jabbed the wires into Schmidt's scrotum. Schmidt didn't have time to scream, as his body surged with electricity. Parnell pulled the wires away before the flesh burned. Schmidt's bowels automatically released, and the grown man cried.

"Christ! You said you were only going to scare him! Are you out of your mind?!" the provost marshal shouted, pushing forward, but Special Agents Lascomb and DeGrey grabbed him from each side. "You'll answer to General Groves for this! All of it!"

"No, I only answer to J. Edgar Hoover. Even the president answers to him. Get this turkey out of here."

His men hauled the provost marshal from the room. Parnell returned his attention to Schmidt. "Where's von Hofmann?"

Schmidt muttered something in German.

"Not good enough."

In came the wires. The lights dimmed. Schmidt's body writhed. Smoke rose and added to the shit stink as the German's pubic hair melted. Parnell removed the wires and Schmidt, who'd gone unconscious was brought back screaming by the power of the chemicals inside him. He screamed in agony he had never known.

"Where is he?"

"I don't know!"

"Not good enough." Parnell zapped him.

"I'll tell you!"

But Parnell charged him again, saying, "You said you don't know."

Schmidt could bear no more. His head lolled. He couldn't lift it any longer and his eyes were forced to stare at his humiliation. The shit and piss all over him. The ruination of his manhood. *I'm glad it is you, Herr Schmidt . . .*

Parnell touched his wires together under Schmidt's eyes. He saw the sparks. "Where, Sergeant?"

Schmidt licked his lips. The wires descended toward his blistered, bloody balls. The Standartenführer had betrayed him, given him up to the enemy. Fuck him anyway. The Standartenführer deserved death, not Gunter Schmidt. He would do anything to stop the pain.

". . . Otowi Bridge . . . Meet . . . there . . ."

Parnell brushed Schmidt's penis with the ends of the wires. "You sure?"

Schmidt's head jerked and flopped. Parnell, however, wasn't willing to take that for a confirmation.

"I can't believe you."

Parnell gave him half a dose of juice. It was enough to turn Schmidt's brain to jelly. He repeated two words over and over again. Parnell grabbed Schmidt's head by the hair and put his ear close to the Nazi's mouth.

"Otowi Bridge . . . Otowi Bridge . . . Otowi Bridge . . ."

Parnell smiled. He dropped his wires and drew his revolver.

In the hallway, the provost marshal locked eyes with Special Agents Lascomb and DeGrey at the sound of the Parnell delivering the coup de grâce.

81

VIRGINIA AWOKE as the train pulled past the Otowi freight house and alongside the station platform. She checked her watch. 9:35. A pair of Tewa Tribe station attendants waited on the platform. Beneath cowboy hats, their long black hair ran in braids down the fronts of the shoulders and their jackets were made of thick woven and geometric-patterned Native American blanketing. The conductor jumped off the moving train to speak with them. He was back aboard a moment later as the *Apache Flyer* ground to a complete stop. He announced in Spanish and English that the usual ten-minute freight stop would be delayed. Four miles ahead, at the upgrade into the Rio Grande Canyon, the track was blocked by snow. It was in the process of being cleared. The passengers were advised to disembark and wait in the comfort of Edith Warner's Tea House across the river.

The announcement was repeated in English.

Only half the passengers from Virginia's car bothered to rise, most of them too poor to enter something as frivolous as a tearoom.

Virginia studied the snowy platform and peered into the freight building beyond. Passengers disembarked from both cars. She didn't see von Hofmann among them or on the platform. She left her seat.

THERE WAS MOVEMENT IN THE SECOND CAR as half the passengers decided to head across the bridge. Von Hofmann remained seated, watching the man from the station telephone. He couldn't quiet the warning voice in his brain. He waited to see what the man would do.

Burley rose and folded his newspaper. He hadn't looked at von Hofmann more than twice in the past four hours. He stepped into the aisle as von Hofmann came at him. The two men collided. Von Hofmann grabbed Burley as if to steady him.

"Excuse me, my fault," von Hofmann said in unaccented American English. He headed to the doors.

Burley took a second to let his nerves settle. Von Hofmann had just expertly frisked him with one hand while the other had been ready to kill him with his pistol.

Von Hofmann stepped onto the platform. The man wasn't armed. As the weather refreshed him, he put the whole episode off to excitement. Almost two and a half years he'd waited for this day. Since that fantastic meeting with Himmler, Heydrich, and Schellenberg at Wewelsburg. Excitement. All it was. It made no sense any other way.

Virginia almost didn't see him, but as she descended the steps from the passenger car, a flash of black leather already halfway down the platform caught her eye and she froze in place. He'd been on the train all along. Did he know she was there and already had a plan for dealing with her? She felt the pistol she'd stolen heavy in her pocket beside the black rosette.

"*Pase, pase.*" Someone urged her forward from behind.

Virginia moved onto the frosted platform. She watched von Hofmann trek into the obscuring snow until the black faded into gray, and the white swallowed him entirely before he reached the bridge.

82

Klaus Fuchs sat in the privacy of the dining room facing the door to the sitting room and general store where the only two other customers, a rancher and his young son sat—the rancher, drinking coffee and chatting with the diminutive Edith Warner, the boy concentrating on a huge piece of chocolate cake. Klaus's overcoat was off, draped across the back of the opposite chair, reserving the seat. It was 9:38. His contact was late, almost ten minutes overdue. This had never happened before. Klaus's mind went back to the FBI agents he'd seen on the plateau. He was getting nervous.

His leg jigged below the table. *It's the weather. Only the weather.*

Edith Warner glanced out the window. "Train's finally arrived. Let's put some more tea and coffee on, María." The young girl from the San Ildefonso Pueblo put down the silverware she was polishing and moved silently into the kitchen.

The first passengers from the train wandered in from the cold. A Hispanic family . . . A pair of ranchers . . . A man and his wife . . . Klaus Fuchs adjusted his tie clip.

Von Hofmann entered Edith Warner's home behind a pair of Mexican farm workers. He scanned the sitting room and general store. The tables were mostly filled. An American woman and a native girl were busy serving tea and coffee. Von Hofmann shifted his gaze through the doorway to the separate dining room and saw what he was looking for. The lone man wearing a gold tie clip with red stones. This would be the crucial moment. Either Klaus Fuchs—German traitor—would fall for von Hofmann's false flag and foolishly hand over the notebooks, or von Hofmann would have to kill him, take the books, and make his rendezvous with the airplane eighteen kilometers up the tracks under pursuit. Von Hofmann approached.

"I couldn't help but notice your tie clip. Did you buy it in London or Vienna?"

The signal Klaus had provided in his last communication with Russia. He smiled. "Please. Sit." He gestured at the chair.

Von Hofmann did as instructed. He didn't say a word.

Klaus Fuchs studied his contact. A formidable man, more like a soldier than a spy. He noted his implacable, wolfish eyes. His skin crawled. Something wasn't right. "You're late. I was worried."

"So was I."

Their eyes locked and in von Hofmann's cold gray spheres, Klaus saw death. *Just nerves. Just nerves . . .* Klaus broke the gaze and looked around. There was no one else in the dining room. He needed more from this man before he handed over the notebooks. "You're not my usual contact."

"And you are violating procedure. Remember carefully, my friend who you serve and who we fight."

Before he could continue, the girl, María, stepped to their table. "Coffee or tea, *señor?*"

Von Hofmann said, "Tea, please" and smiled. Pleasantly.

She poured and left.

"I will say only this, Doctor: you have been removed far from us. By this government, and by your own choice. We follow your instructions, but out here in this remote land you must let us consider our own methods of security for intelligence as important as yours."

Relief. It made sense. The notebooks were important and would have to travel far before reaching the Soviet Union. Looking at the man seated opposite him, his fear became respect. This man could do that job.

Klaus lifted his teacup and spoke over the rim. "You will find my Christmas gift to the Party in the right-side pocket of my overcoat."

Virginia tramped through the snow to the back of the adobe house, feet numbed and aching with penetrating cold. She climbed the steps and tried the door. Unlocked. She pushed it open. María turned from cutting a chocolate cake.

"*Está frío afuera*," Virginia commented on the outside cold, positioning in front of the oven to get warm, playing it like she belonged.

The girl nodded. A moment later, she left the room to serve the cake. Two doors led from the kitchen, one directly into the sitting room and general store, the other a swinging door that opened into the separate dining room beyond. Virginia opened the swinging door and peeked through the crack. Von Hofmann and another man were the only two occupants in the dining room. The Nazi's back was three quarters facing her. She pulled away. This is what she'd come for. The decisive moment was upon her.

Virginia's only chance of success was to incapacitate von Hofmann. She'd hold him until local authorities arrived, then maybe Tyler would have a chance with the FBI. She reached for the stolen pistol. She cocked the weapon. Again, she cracked open the door. She slipped the gun between the door and its frame. Wound him, rush in, disarm him. She prayed to God it would work. Virginia aimed at the Nazi's back. Hands seized her from behind. They spun her into the kitchen, expertly relieving her of the gun.

"Not that way," said Agent Burley.

"You're one to talk, after all that you people have done," said Virginia.

"Look, Miss Hendricks, your killing von Hofmann isn't going to help anyone."

"I wasn't planning on killing him."

"Then you wouldn't have left this house alive."

The confidence she'd worked so hard to build crumbled into a thousand uncertainties. "All right. What do you suggest?"

"Cartwright's on his way. Between the two of us, we'll get the job done."

"And what do I do? Wait? Hide?"

"Isn't it what your fiancée would want?"

In referring to Tyler as her fiancée, Burley made an honest mistake based on what he'd seen between them, but it caught Virginia off guard. Burley said, "We wait here. There's no reason for von Hofmann to enter this room."

"When's Cartwright going to arrive?"

Burley moved to the sink and pulled back the yellow curtain. He leaned forward, angling his head so he could get a faint view of the highway. "Any minute, I'm hoping."

"And if he doesn't?"

"Then he is not the man I have worked beside for the past three years."

SPECIAL AGENT DEGREY drove while Associate Director Parnell sat beside him poring over the Los Alamos main-gate pass sheet for the last forty-eight hours, trying to see if he could spot a Russian agent unwittingly headed for a meeting with a false-flag von Hofmann at the Otowi Bridge. Parnell had never killed a man before, and his ego was still amped from his experience with Schmidt. He was on top of the world, the dread he might fail the director gone from his mind. Soon, von Hofmann would be his. His future assured. Parnell smiled, then focused back on the pass sheet. So far he'd found six "engineers" who'd left the mountain under white passes, and white passes, he'd been told, meant physicists.

Special Agent Lascomb spoke from the back seat. "Sir, how would the Russian spy know to meet von Hofmann. Why would he want to? Von Hofmann's his enemy."

Parnell answered without looking from the pass sheet. "He doesn't know that. He believes he's meeting one of his own people. Come on, Lascomb, use your head. It fits Hoover's model perfectly.

"The Nazis are playing this real smart. Not only did they uncover the Russian agent, but they also got their hands on his plans to turn over material. For all I know, someone's going to find a body in the next few days and it'll turn out to be the dead Russian courier they've substituted von Hofmann . . . for . . ."

His voice faded to nothing as his mind focused on the word "Buick." *On the way up, the slight man getting out of his car in the snow* . . . At 8:15, one Dr. Klaus Fuchs had left the plateau in his Buick ostensibly to buy Christmas presents in Santa Fe. Parnell had seen him getting out of his car at the house beyond the bridge.

The notebooks weighed heavily inside von Hofmann's pocket. He sipped his tea. All that he'd overcome to get here. His men and how they'd paid for his victory, Germany's triumph, with their lives. Even the traitor Zundorf he could mourn. Now all he had to do was meet his plane. The front door opened and the conductor from the train entered.

He announced something in Spanish. He repeated it in English. "Passengers on the D and RGW. A bike messenger has arrived with word that the tracks ahead are clear. We will be departing Otowi Station in ten minutes."

"You better go," von Hofmann suggested.

Klaus Fuchs finished his tea. "I hope the road into Santa Fe isn't too bad. I'm supposed to be buying presents. It would look strange if I returned without any."

"Yes, well, that's up to you. *S Rozhdestvom, tovarishch.*"

Klaus Fuchs smiled at the Russian. He repeated it in English. "Merry Christmas to you, comrade."

KLAUS FUCHS STEPPED onto the porch and into a curtain of snow. He noticed the flakes on his shoulders. Hard and small, they were in perfect hexagons with symmetrical dendrites and tiny holes in their centers. Perfect, like confectioners' candy. He was joyful. Relieved. A burden lifted from his snow-sprinkled shoulders. America and Britain wouldn't be the only nations to have the bomb.

VON HOFMANN WAITED until he heard Klaus Fuchs's automobile cough to life. He stood. Pulled out the wad of bills his American contact had given him. He thumbed through it until he found a one-dollar bill. He placed it on the table. The tearoom was all but empty as he stepped toward the sitting room, his mind already racing toward the train ride ahead and his rendezvous. A shaft of light from a door cautiously opened behind spread before him.

Von Hofmann's hand was already drawing his pistol when Burley said, "It's over von Hofmann. Raise your hands slowly and turn around."

AS FORMER LAW ENFORCEMENT, those words were a living part of Burley as much as the beat of his heart. Training dies hard and Burley died harder. Von Hofmann spun and fired as Burley squeezed a round from Agent Reid's .38. It was perfectly aimed where the Nazi's heart would have been had von Hofmann not dropped into a crouch when coming around. Burley's slug zipped over von Hofmann's shoulder as the Standartenführer's bullet drove home between the FBI agent's eyes.

VIRGINIA WATCHED the ex-FBI man fall. She lunged for the back door, but von Hofmann snagged her around the belly before she could open it. He threw her. She caromed off the stove onto the Pine-Sol-fragrant floor. Von Hofmann scooped up Burley's weapon. He couldn't understand how the man had gotten it. Was he losing his touch?

If he was, he had it back now. And he had Virginia.

Von Hofmann shoved his Luger beneath his jacket at the small of his back, opting for the more concealable .38 for his hand. He wrenched her to her feet by her thick copper hair. She struggled and cried out.

"Ah, ah, ah. Why fight it, Ginny? We are meant to be together."

Von Hofmann dragged her through the sitting room to the door. The Indian girl stood dumbfounded behind the general-store counter, but Edith Warner blocked the Standartenführer's path.

"I don't know who you are, but I demand you release this young lady."

Von Hofmann detected a German inflection to her words. Her ancestry accounted for her bravery. He pressed the barrel of the .38 into Virginia's temple. "Tell her to get out of the way. or I will kill all of you."

"Please, Miss Warner. He will."

Edith Warner reluctantly stepped aside.

Von Hofmann grasped the doorknob. Keeping cover, he pushed Virginia through the door. She went sprawling across the porch and into the snow. There was no gunfire. Von Hofmann cautiously came after her, scanning the property for any sign of movement. There was nothing but the snow. He was safe. All he had to do was get the train out of the station.

83

CARTWRIGHT DIDN'T NEED TO BE TOLD why Edith Warner stood at the side of the road waving them down. Tyler braced against the dashboard of the smoke-filled car as the ex-FBI man sped past her, turning off the highway into her drive to make a sliding stop before her house. Both men threw open their doors.

María sat on the porch pressing her apron to her face, sobbing. "*Muerto, muerto, muerto.*"

"Virginia!" Tyler drew his pistol and rushed inside.

Cartwright didn't follow. "Muerto" meant dead. No one was alive inside that house. Cartwright fastened his eyes on the Indian.

"Where did he go?"

She pointed across the bridge.

Cartwright heard Tyler call Virginia's name one more time before he got back into his car. If she was inside, Cartwright had no business going in there. If not . . . this time around, he wouldn't be too late.

Tom Cartwright spun his car in a shower of snow and sped toward the bridge.

AS THEY DROPPED OUT OF THE LAST CANYON and onto the flat beyond the Parajito Plateau, Special Agent DeGrey watched a brown Chrysler streak across the bridge and slide halfway around as it stopped behind the freight house.

"You see that, sir?"

"I saw it," Parnell answered. It was then he remembered to reload his pistol.

"Everyone off the train!" von Hofmann shouted. "Everyone off! Now!" He fired the revolver once into the air. "Move! Move! Move!" And fired it again as he maneuvered his hostage toward the engine.

The pandemonium was instantaneous as passengers fought one another to clear the cars and flee. Von Hofmann and Virginia reached the engine.

Cartwright mounted the platform at the other end. He drew his pistol. The people running toward him saw it and parted.

Von Hofmann clenched his forearm around Virginia's throat as he pointed his gun at the gray-haired engineer and middle-aged fireman inside the engine compartment.

"I'm taking your train."

The instant von Hofmann's gun moved from Virginia's head, Cartwright drew a bead and fired. The bullet struck von Hofmann in the forearm. The muscles spasmed and his hand involuntarily released the revolver. It clattered beneath the wheels of the train. Von Hofmann pulled Virginia into his body as a shield.

He shouted into the engine, "If you move this train, I break her neck." He faced his attacker. "Now you, put down your weapon, or she dies."

Cartwright sidled toward him two steps, his pistol gripped two-handed, steady on the Nazi's forehead. "So she'll be dead. Then what . . .?"

They were a dozen feet apart.

As soon as he'd seen Cartwright clamber out of his car, Parnell ordered DeGrey off the road. The Packard plowed through snow that broke across its hood like sea-foam across a black ship's bow, and sped down the far side of the train—the blind side to both Cartwright and von Hofmann. Parnell ordered Special Agents Lascomb and DeGrey around the back of the train. He moved in from around the engine. Parnell stepped carefully over the cowcatcher. He stood on the tracks below and behind von Hofmann when Cartwright fired his pistol.

"Put down your weapon, or I break her neck," he heard von Hofmann say.

"So she'll be dead. Then what . . .?" Cartwright replied in a low, steady voice as he came within a dozen feet of von Hofmann.

Parnell raised his weapon.

"I blow you away?" Cartwright said, his voice so soft as to almost be inaudible.

Parnell's gun exploded with fire and smoke. The .38 caliber slug caught Cartwright in the gut and knocked him back six drunken steps before he collapsed in a heap, his face contorted with surprise as his own gun fired into the air.

84

Agent Burley was dead, but Tyler hadn't found Virginia anywhere inside or behind the house. When he came back to the front, Cartwright was gone. Gunfire echoed from the depot.

Tyler ran for the bridge, crippling pain radiating from his wounds with every step, his boots fast soaking, their flat leather soles barely reliable on the treacherous snow.

Von Hofmann whirled, astonished to find another FBI agent behind him. *No one misses from that close.*

Lascomb and DeGrey came onto the platform from the other end. DeGrey shouted, "Associate Director?"

Parnell stared at von Hofmann. His prize. "It's okay, men. Keep him covered." He carefully climbed onto the platform. The hunter who'd run the wolf to ground.

Von Hofmann retreated a few steps, maneuvering his human shield back and forth in front of him.

Virginia was lightheaded. She could barely breathe. Fear threatened to overpower her. She needed focus. Her eyes found Cartwright. His eyes were filled with pain. He would be dead soon, and as frightened as she was for herself, it became in that instant more important to bolster him. He didn't deserve to die alone. To die for her. She fought to hold him in her gaze.

He fought to hold onto Virginia.

"J. Edgar Hoover thinks you're an extremely important man, Standartenführer von Hofmann," Parnell said.

"I'm sorry I don't have time this trip to meet him."

Von Hofmann studied the angles between his three adversaries. The Luger waited, firm against the small of his back.

"Oh, but I think you do. Listen carefully, von Hofmann. You surrender to me now and Hoover will make you a free man when we reach Washington. You have my guarantee."

Von Hofmann almost laughed. The conceited twit was serious. But it wasn't what he said that was important. The man just had to keep talking.

"Go on." He dangled his wounded arm along his coat-flap.

"Our fear is the Reds, Standartenführer. We all know this war is only a prelude to a much larger confrontation with the Soviet Union. In order for us to prevail, Mr. Hoover believes, and the president has agreed with him, communism in America must be absolutely wiped out. A man with your training—"

"Your J. Edgar Hoover wants me to help you people sift out this country's undesirables?" said von Hofmann.

"Correct," Parnell said.

"Please, why should I believe any of this?"

"I didn't shoot you, did I?"

Von Hofmann nodded. He addressed Lascomb. "I shall release the girl to you. And you"—he indicated DeGrey with another jerk of his head—"you may handcuff me."

He dragged Virginia around so she faced Parnell completely and hid his free hand from view. "My surrender meets with your approval?"

His fingers crept to the back of his coat.

Cartwright knew a sucker play when he saw one, but he didn't have the strength to move, let alone speak. The muscles behind his eyes were relaxing. His vision dimmed. With his right cheek pressed hard against the icy wood of the dirty platform, all he saw were feet.

Von Hofmann's boots braced—

Virginia hurled away and spinning. Her feet pedaling to recapture lost balance—

Parnell: a shoe lifting hesitantly, a reflexive step backward—

The first gunshot: Parnell lifted off his feet—

Virginia colliding with Lascomb, his shoes shuffling backward on the impact—

The second gunshot: Lascomb firing into the ground.

Von Hofmann pivoting, legs bending, body moving into a crouch—

A pair of handcuffs dropping in front of DeGrey's black Oxfords—

The third gunshot: *crack.*

DeGrey down—

Lascomb's feet bracing—

Virginia thrown to the platform into Cartwright's view—

The fourth and fifth gunshots: are simultaneous. Von Hofmann's and Lascomb's.

Cartwright watched the feet. Von Hofmann's came together, relaxed, as Lascomb's body thudded down.

Von Hofmann dragged his hostage to the engine where the old engineer and the fireman cowered. "We go. Now."

He forced Virginia into the engine compartment and was right behind her as the engineer released the red-handled brake and opened the throttle.

ACROSS THE BRIDGE, and twenty yards from the platform, Tyler heard the hiss of steam and watched smoke belch from the stack as the *Apache Flyer* lumbered forward. A crowd of passengers lurked, peering out around the corner of the freight house, like dogs waiting to steal a bone.

Tyler threw a leather-clad messenger boy out of his way as he charged onto the platform. The last boxcar pulled ahead of the platform and Tyler staggered to a helpless stop.

He scanned the bodies, fearing the worst.

The three FBI agents had died fast and bled little, but the pool of red spreading from Cartwright more than compensated for their lack of gore. It was as if Cartwright's heart was a broken faucet. Tyler kneeled in the blood. Cartwright didn't look at him, but he blinked and Tyler took one of his bloody hands in both of his.

"Why did you leave me?"

Cartwright didn't react.

"God damn it. I could've helped."

TOM CARTWRIGHT WATCHES Tyler Keyes as if from inside the moment itself. There is nothing he wants so much as to apologize, but he cannot remember why; life and the passion of men losing its meaning as the world becomes an image reflected on a glassy surface: colorful in detail, yet transparent, untouchable, without depth. For the first time in as long as he can recall, he has no desire for a cigarette. Then the glass is gone and time and change, success and failure, imperfection: these things do not exist.

From this place beyond himself, Cartwright does not look back.

TYLER DROPPED CARTWRIGHT'S HAND. He rose and looked after the train, then turned and faced the morbidly curious passengers slinking forward. Tyler strode into their midst and they moved to let him pass. He left the platform and located what he was looking for.

The messenger boy's Harley-Davidson motorcycle leaned against the freight house wall. Its snow tires were studded with spikes, its flathead 45 engine still warm. It wasn't a horse, but it was the next best thing for catching trains.

85

"HEY, YOU!" the messenger boy hollered as the cowboy in the bloodstained range coat straddled his bike and roared away from the freight house.

Tyler headed for the tracks. He braked in a skidding turn and almost lost it there, but the studded tires did their job, biting through ice and snow, and he regained his balance. He kicked up a gear, opened the throttle, and sped after the train.

VON HOFMANN PUSHED Virginia against the wall beside the cast-iron door to the coal hopper. "Don't move. Don't speak."

Virginia did as told. She didn't return the sympathetic look she got from the fireman who worked his shovel between the coal and engine furnace, eyes furtive, waiting for his chance.

Don't you get it? Going against von Hofmann is going up against the Devil.

She'd known that from the moment von Hofmann came out killing from her father's study. To go up against the devil and die trying was to fulfill something sacred. It meant everything, and it quashed her fear. All she hoped now was that she could somehow take von Hofmann with her and that Tyler would be allowed a last look at her remains before they buried her.

Virginia shivered and buried her hands in her pockets. Her fingers found the lumped fabric of her mourning rosette. She sealed it in her fist.

Von Hofmann stepped to the engineer's side. Keeping his eye on the fireman, von Hofmann pulled out the red flannel rag that poked from the engineer's back pocket. He tied off his wounded arm. When he finished, he addressed the engineer. "About sixteen kilometers ahead, there are a series of three tunnels, correct?"

"Yes, sir," said the engineer.

"And we have enough fuel in the fire to get us that far?"

The engineer glanced into the furnace. He didn't consider where the conversation might be headed. "Yep."

"Also good."

Von Hofmann shot the fireman first, followed by the engineer. As he kicked their bodies out the door, Virginia withdrew the black rosette concealing the Victorian hatpin along her wrist.

BEYOND OTOWI, the tracks of the Denver and Rio Grande Western Railroad entered the mountainous wilds of the Santa Fe National Forest. Tyler paralleled the railbed as it twined through the snowcapped mesas beyond Otowi, racing the Harley after Virginia and von Hofmann, every inch of the way a battle against powder, ice, and the rough terrain hidden beneath, brutally paid out in a ceaseless hammering of machine against earth that ripped to the center of his wounds. Tyler raced past two bodies, one after another. They weren't Virginia. The tracks curved, heading into a steeper grade. Tyler saw the *Apache Flyer*, the last of its freight cars bouncing along the tracks less than a mile ahead. Tyler increased his speed.

AT SIX THOUSAND FEET, Nestor Cooney quit trying to rise above the storm. Fighting the turbulence that had dogged him since take-off, he began his descent.

VON HOFMANN STARED at the black silk flower in Virginia's hand. The sight of it and its meaning caught him off guard.

"Who's that for?" he said.

His voice was calm. He met her gaze with unexpected honesty.

"Go to hell," said Virginia.

"We're all going to hell. Every one of us, all over the world, for what we're doing. All that counts now is who gets there last," said von Hofmann. "Who are you mourning? A brother? Cousin? Uncle?"

Virginia didn't answer.

Von Hofmann scratched his chin with the front sight of his pistol. "You were better than all the rest of them." He primed the pistol. "Too bad so much spirit was wasted in an American."

He pointed the gun at her. It was over. It was time.

"My husband."

To Tyler's right, the earth fell forty feet to the icy Rio Grande. He surged to the rear of the last freight car. The steel rungs of a ladder on the back of the car were a tantalizing foot from his grip. Tyler angled the front wheel as close to the crossties as he dared. He let go of the handlebars and reached out with his left hand. A foot of space turned into mere inches . . . Almost there—

Whack, whack—! Whack! The front wheel hit the tracks. The Harley lurched out of control, swerving toward the precipice before Tyler grabbed the handlebars, working down the gears, slowing the bike as he fought to bring it under control.

The precipice narrowed. Ten feet of room became five. Tyler continued to slow.

The *Apache Flyer* barreled on.

Tyler accelerated again. This time he angled for the tracks, jumping the motorcycle to the other side, his left now protected by the stone wall of a mesa.

"The war took him?" said von Hofmann.

"It did," said Virginia.

Von Hofmann studied Virginia and allowed himself the truth. She did resemble his wife twenty years younger, but only as a sister might, had there been one.

But Virginia wasn't Agna.

The odd attraction, the lust—they were gone. Put simply, von Hofmann's feelings for Virginia had nothing to do with her and everything to do with his wife. At the ranch, in darkness, in mortal, close-quarter combat, the flash of lightning that illuminated Virginia's face had sparked his loneliness for Agna to life. What he shared with Virginia was only their personal and separate losses. He would be merciful in killing her, but the lightning had burned out. His fascination with her was over.

He said, "We have something in common."

She said, "Agna."

He said, "Yes. My wife. You reminded me of her."

A preamble to her murder. Virginia understood Von Hofmann was telling her this to calm her. Absolve himself. She had to keep it going. She stood close to the engine controls. She'd seen the engineer squeeze the brake handle, pushing the metal rod forward to free the train to movement. One hard tug back.

"You let me live because you feel guilty," she said.

"I have no guilt. No one is guilty."

She could see in his eyes that he was lying. That he knew the opposite.

"It was the last night of August," he confessed. "The British bombers fly under cover of night for protection against our fighters and anti-aircraft. Due to that, they kill many civilians. Do I blame the pilot for Agna's death? For my son's? I blame only the war."

Virginia relaxed with the sway of the train, her back against the engineer's console.

"My husband was British." She let the words hang.

She could see his need to hear, a fire in his eyes. She met them with intimacy. "He died the last night of August, dropping his bombs on your Nazi bitch wife."

The foulness of her words gave Virginia the extra seconds she needed. She cranked the brake before his bullet tore into her and both she and von Hofmann fell.

He swung his gun to finish her, but Virginia lunged past it, her fist aimed for his face.

Von Hofmann missed his second shot, the bullet ricocheting off the floor. Virginia drove the rosette's four-inch hatpin through his cheek. He reeled backward in pain and momentary shock, mouth filling with blood, the steel point impaling his tongue.

Virginia pushed away from the Standartenführer and staggered for the hatch. He clipped off a third shot in her wake. Virginia heard the bullet sing past her as she wrenched her body onto the catwalk that ran back along the coal tender.

TYLER CAUGHT UP WITH the train once more. The ladder was now on the wrong side and hopelessly out of reach. Tyler's only chance lay ahead. He increased his throttle, speeding past one boxcar, another, and another. He set his sights on the rear landing of the second passenger car.

The track curved as Tyler came parallel to the iron railing. The engine was nearing a tunnel, trapping him in an eight-foot space between the speeding train and a granite wall that narrowed into almost nothing as the train approached the tunnel's black mouth.

Tyler's left handlebar scraped the wall. His eyes flashed to the wheels and the track, ready to suck him in and grind him.

He braked. Downshifted. Let the train overtake him before launching the Harley back over the tracks. Balancing along the rim of the river-gorge, Tyler watched the *Apache Flyer* thunder into the darkness.

Von Hofmann's veins coursed with rage. He wrenched the pin out of his face. He spit a mouthful of blood. He slapped his final magazine into the butt of his Luger. He went out after Virginia into the pitch black of the tunnel.

Unstable air buffeted Nestor Cooney's Twin Beech. At three thousand feet, he brushed the dark underbelly of the storm, flying up the Rio Grande Valley, navigating by the stitches of the Denver and Rio Grande tracks. He caught sight of the *Apache Flyer* two miles away as it headed into the first tunnel. Nestor Cooney grinned at the perfection of the operation.

He dropped his starboard wing and banked toward the field where he would land. That's when he saw the motorcycle.

Tyler waited for the last car to enter the tunnel before kicking the motorcycle into high and charging for the angled side of the tunnel abutment. He toiled upward in a spray of snow, gravel, and rich red mud.

Amplified by the tunnel, the scream of the *Apache Flyer* assailed Virginia's eardrums. It voiced the pain in her side where the bullet punched through. Smoke and sparks choked and buffeted. They burned her hair and eyes. The physics of a steam-fired steel mass hurtling through freezing air trapped inside the stone shaft increased the velocity of the brutal slipstream that fought to suck Virginia from the back of the coal tender. She couldn't see her hand in front of her face, but she visualized von Hofmann close behind. As soon as they were out of the tunnel, he would shoot her. Risking the turbulence and the death it promised, she crawled forward.

THE TUNNEL CUT through the steep shoulder of La Capilla Mesa. Gravity pulled at Tyler as he struggled between boulders, lashed by the snow-heavy branches of sprawling Douglas firs and the thick, shorter spruce. He used his arms and legs, his every ounce of strength, to beat the train through the mountain. The air was freezing, his face and hands numb with the burn that precedes frostbite, but the fire inside him fueled his fight. He would fight until it killed him, because no pain, hell, or death would be worse than what he'd suffer if he lived but in this had failed.

LIGHT BLED INTO THE DARKNESS as the engine neared the tunnel's end. Von Hofmann saw Virginia's form appear gray out of the black, no more than five meters away, lowering over the edge of the coal tender. He fired the Luger at her head.

VIRGINIA HEARD THE GUN's thunderous report the same instant the sting of hot lead creased her skull, and then she was down the ladder and out of sight behind the tender. Light grew complete. The airflow velocity decreased. Snow returned in buckets of whitewash. She could see the tracks, a blur of speed beneath the coupling. The next car was a baggage car converted from an old-fashioned caboose. With its narrow platform and door, it offered Virginia the hope of escape.

Keep moving. Keep moving.

But the gap between her and the baggage car was too far to reach in one step. To jump would be suicidal.

That left only one alternative.

Virginia extended her foot to the swaying steel coupling below.

TYLER DUG HIS FOOT into the snow, braking hard, the motorcycle slewing around at the lip of a thirty-foot drop as the engine of the *Apache Flyer* rocketed out of the tunnel below. Tyler whipped the Harley around. He sweated every inch back up the slope, then spinning around, opening the throttle, engine howling at full power, he rode straight for the edge.

VIRGINIA RAISED HER ARMS out from her body for balance and took two careful steps out onto the coupling.

No different than walking along a fence.

Virginia took another step.

But a fence isn't hurtling over track at forty-five miles per hour. Do it!

The train lurched. The coupling bucked. She tilted one way, then another. Her arms desperately tipped in counterpoint to keep her center of gravity. She steadied and looked to the steps ahead. Just like showing off at the county fair.

THE APACHE FLYER clattered past the rendezvous point, heading for the second tunnel. In his rage, von Hofmann had let this woman get the better of him. He couldn't jump. The train was moving too fast for that. However grotesquely humiliating giving up on Virginia might be, it was his fault. He'd opened up to her. Wanted to show mercy in her death. Mercy he'd denied Agna in life.

Von Hofmann was headed back to the engineer's compartment when the motorcycle roared from the sky.

For the first time in his life, von Hofmann was astonished. He knew without seeing him, the rider of the motorcycle was Virginia's cowboy, and by this did he have his one true glimpse of the raw power of a force he'd once been given and failed to protect. A force that existed beyond good and evil. Beyond the terrible, unadmitted guilt that drove him. He'd killed Agna. He'd killed his son. Incinerated them; by forcing them to remain in Berlin it was as if he'd dropped the bombs himself.

His precious Nietzsche was powerless in the multitude faces of love.

For the briefest instant, man and machine were united, flying through the air, then gravity played its tricks and the motorcycle smashed onto the back of the second freight car. Tyler flipped over the bars, skidding across the roof, the bike tumbling onto him, dragging him for the edge.

Von Hofmann fired the Luger at the careening mass of steel and chrome. The *Apache Flyer* entered the next tunnel. For a second time, darkness swallowed the train.

TWO MORE STEPS to go. Virginia heard the crash atop the train, von Hofmann's subsequent gunfire, but she couldn't concern herself. One false step and she would die. Yet was there any sense in remaining where she was? So far she'd been lucky, but she couldn't keep her balance much longer. Virginia put her trust in God and stepped forward.

The train swung ever so slightly, but it was enough. Virginia pitched forward. She blindly reached out with groping hands as she fell. She cried out in blinding pain that threatened to plunge her into unconsciousness, but the constant blast of arctic wind wouldn't allow for the comfort of conscious surrender. Catching the baggage car railing, she hung on with a fierce determination to survive as her legs dangled over the tracks.

BULLETS PINGED and ricocheted. Pinned beneath the motorcycle, Tyler slid headfirst for the end of the car to strike a ventilation dome at the edge. He seized it with raw, frozen fingers. His body skated around, dropping over the side, and the bike flew from the speeding train. It shattered against the tunnel's stone wall in a blast of fire.

AT THE SIGHT OF THE EXPLOSION, von Hofmann's ego reasserted control over his weaker emotions. The cowboy was a fool to try such a stunt, and Virginia—if she wasn't dead already—he'd relish as his last bit of destruction before he flew away from this pathetic land. The Standartenführer spat blood from his mutilated mouth and turned back to the engine compartment to stop the train.

THE MOTORCYCLE BOTHERED NESTOR COONEY. He hadn't seen it jump and had no idea where it had gotten to, but it was obvious it didn't belong out here trailing the D & RGW, and that meant trouble. He forced it from his mind. To be of any help to the Standartenführer, the first thing he needed to do was land.

Three miles out, at an altitude of five hundred feet, Nestor Cooney lined up the empty field. He reduced his throttle to 70 percent, but as his claw-like fingers grasped the landing-gear lever, he recognized his dilemma. The *Apache Flyer* was all the way into the second tunnel. If the Standartenführer stopped the train directly, he'd have over a mile of open ground to retrace before he'd reach the aircraft. If the Standartenführer was in trouble, a mile could make the difference between success and failure.

Nestor Cooney increased his throttle and climbed. The second tunnel was three quarters of a mile long. There were four miles of track between it and the third tunnel. There the railbed paralleled

Horseshoe Lake, surface frozen like every other body of water at this altitude since early November. If the Standartenführer stopped before the third tunnel, Nestor Cooney decided he could risk a landing on the ice. Hell, the Soviets had managed it more than once with planes larger and heavier on Lake Ladoga in the winter resupply of Leningrad. First, he had to see what the Standartenführer would do.

The Twin Beech made a circling pass over the frozen lake.

TYLER'S LEFT ARM was just short of useless, his bullet wounds open and hemorrhaging as he torturously clambered back onto the freight car's roof. The one good thing about the incredible pain in his arm was it distracted his attention from the frostbite attacking his nose and hands, and the blood running down his brow and cheeks from where the stitches had all ripped from their skin seams.

VON HOFMANN STOOD at the controls, waiting until the engine burst into the light. He jammed the throttle control forward, cutting power to the engine. At the same time, he yanked the brake lever to a full stop. The drivers locked. Sparks poured in fountains from the wheels. The *Apache Flyer* reacted as if it had rammed into a wall.

VIRGINIA'S HANDS ripped from the railing. The last thing her mind would register was her body hitting the corner of the coal tender as it flew from the train and hit the shrouded earth in a bloom of white powder.

TYLER WATCHED Virginia glance off the coal tender and roll like a bundle of rags down a snowy embankment to the frozen surface of a wide lake that lay to the left of the *Apache Flyer*. She didn't move. Tyler refused to believe she was dead.

STANDARTENFÜHRER VON HOFMANN climbed from the engine compartment. He took one look at Virginia, then raised his eyes to the Twin Beech aircraft circling for a landing. The ice was solid. Von Hofmann checked his pocket to make sure he still had the three notebooks he'd come for. One, two, three. Safe. He pressed his free hand to his wound and, keeping his Luger aimed at Virginia, walked along the track in her direction.

TYLER DREW HIS PISTOL. He opened the cylinder and checked the cartridges. Six shots. One way or another, they'd be enough to end it. The last one to end everything if Virginia was dead. Tyler jumped to the next freight car. Keeping to a crouch, he lurched along the top until he was above von Hofmann. At the same time the Nazi killer assumed an executioner's stance above Virginia.

Von Hofmann raised his Luger as Virginia stirred. Had he not been the man he was, he'd have put a round into her brain without further hesitation, but von Hofmann was a sadist. He wanted to look into her eyes at the moment of death.

Virginia raised her head, blinking away unconsciousness.

Their eyes met. "What was it you said to me, *Fraulein,* one of your clever little phrases?" he said.

Tyler took aim with the pistol.

Virginia saw Tyler. Her eyes widened with a surprise von Hofmann interpreted as submission.

Tyler took the slack from the trigger only to realize Virginia's body would backstop his bullet were it to pass through von Hofmann.

"Ah, yes, 'pushin' up roses.'"

"'Daisies,' you son of a bitch," Tyler cried, launching onto von Hofmann's back.

Virginia watched the two men flip over the embankment. They hit the ice hard. Their bodies, thrown apart, skated in separate directions. Von Hofmann was the first to stop. He'd lost his gun. He scanned the ice for the weapon, but it was gone somewhere in the drifted snow.

Tyler rolled to his stomach. Fire raged through his broken ribs. He was helpless with pain. Fifty feet away from him, von Hofmann struggled crazily to his feet. Tyler clutched his pistol. He tried to will his body up one last time, but he'd already asked too much of it. The abuse he'd pounded into it over the past seventy-two hours had caught up with him.

The roar of engines echoed across the lake as Nestor Cooney came in for his landing.

Von Hofmann and Tyler's eyes met through the blowing snow. The Standartenführer recognized his opponent's defeat and smiled as Tyler shakingly pointed the pistol in his direction, fired, and missed. Von Hofmann turned his back in contempt and headed toward the middle of the lake.

Virginia pushed to her hands and knees. Her right leg broken and useless. She dragged her body toward Tyler.

Von Hofmann's figure grew smaller behind the curtain of snow. Tyler rallied. He wrapped his other hand around the pistol and fired again. This shot was wider.

Von Hofmann had won.

Nestor Cooney touched down and guided the plane toward von Hofmann. The Standartenführer stopped. He pulled the notebooks from his pocket. He raised them in the air not only as a sign of defiance toward the cowboy and Virginia who he could now hardly see, but as a symbol of Nazi superiority—his superiority—over this entire arrogant land.

Operation Steppenfeuer: successfully completed. America would bow before Hitler.

The gun drooped in Tyler's shaking hands. The cowboy fired a third time. The bullet furrowed the ice three feet in front of him. He didn't bother firing again. He had gone against von Hofmann man to man and von Hofmann had beaten him.

The Twin Beech taxied past von Hofmann. It executed a perfect turn around him. The hatch dropped open.

Virginia collapsed at Tyler's side. Von Hofmann boarded the plane and pulled the hatch closed behind him.

"Ready, Standartenführer?" Nestor Cooney shouted over the roar of the engines.

Von Hofmann strapped into a seat in the rear.

"Better weather in Mexico, I hope."

Nestor Cooney released the wheel brakes and increased the throttle.

VIRGINIA WRAPPED HER HANDS around Tyler's. Fifty yards away and running across their sightline, the plane commenced its take-off run. Virginia steadied the gun in both their hands. They aimed for the starboard mainwheel. The first bullet struck the tire, the second and third tore into the hydraulics and the landing-gear assembly. The plane was almost past and gathering speed.

"Shoot it again, Tyler!"

Tyler clicked the hammer uselessly onto empty brass.

"GET READY for a lift-off, Standartenführer."

The wheel wobbled. When it blew, it caused the weakened mainwheel oleo to shear. Nestor Cooney lost his starboard mainwheel, and the aircraft jerked powerfully to the right. He increased the throttles to maximum to get some lift, but it was too late for that, and the Twin Beech swung around out of control.

This wasn't the lift-off he'd been told to expect. Von Hofmann tore out of his seat harness, only to be hurled against the port bulkhead.

Tyler and Virginia hugged each other as the aircraft whipped in a violent circle before them. The broken landing gear threw a diamond-sparkling fan of frozen water as it dug into the lake. Fissures zigzagged lightning paths across the lake's surface as the starboard wing hit the ice and buckled, and with a sound of thunder, the ice gave way.

Von Hofmann pulled himself to the hatch. He had to get out before—

The propellers of the starboard engine ate into the ice. Metal shrieked as the airplane dug itself a grave.

The plane bucked. In the cockpit, Nestor Cooney crowed as water and chunks of ice filled his vision. The air inside the aircraft went frigid from the ice water embracing the fuselage. Von Hofmann fought for balance as the plane descended below the surface.

Escape!

He twisted the hatch handle. With every bit of his considerable strength, he forced open the hatch. Freezing water flooded inside. It broke von Hofmann's grip on the doorframe, slamming him backward into the fuselage as the plane rolled onto its side in water and ice. Von Hofmann's bloody face slammed against a window.

Four . . . six . . . ten snowflakes danced on the glass as water pressed mercilessly from behind.

Snow fell on the day I was born.

Von Hofmann summoned every atom of his being. He tried to push from the bulkhead, but the pressure behind him was too great. The freezing water stole his strength. His core temperature plummeted.

Light, life, and freedom glowed beyond the window through the hole in the ice above. Right there and utterly out of reach. The hole and the world beyond diminished as the plane sank. Von Hofmann held his breath.

I can't drown—Anything but that!

The plane fell deeper and deeper into the black water.

. . . and I am drowning, as helpless as my mother . . .

Von Hofmann could hold his breath no longer. He opened his mouth to scream his horror. Water filled his lungs. In his last moment, Standartenführer Jürgen von Hofmann saw the fire consume his wife and son. A firebomb delivered across continents and time from a girl lit in a lightning flash.

TYLER AND VIRGINIA watched until all that was left was the tip of the port wing, then that too slipped below.

86

THURSDAY, DECEMBER 31, 1943

N O FRESH SNOW HAD FALLEN since Christmas Eve and patches of grass stared at the sky, wet eyes of snow-burned yellow stalks. A bitter wind blowing out of the Sangre de Cristos had tormented Santa Fe since before dawn. As it gusted through the headstones of the National Cemetery, Virginia Hendricks clutched the front of her jacket together and transferred her weight from her cane and leg cast to Tyler Keyes beside her. He put his good arm around her shoulder. She nestled in closer.

The Army chaplain finished the graveside service. There was no twenty-one gun salute, no flag folded and presented to a widow. Indeed, when the chaplain walked away, only Tyler and Virginia were there to say goodbye to a man they'd hardly known.

The coffin sat at the bottom of its grave. Inside the coffin lay the remains of Tom Cartwright.

Two Mexican gravediggers waited with their shovels by the iron fence a short distance away. They shared a hand-rolled cigarette and watched the skirts dance around the slender brown legs of the girls who boarded at St. Catherine's Indian School across the street walking to chapel in two straight lines.

"I wonder who he was," Virginia said.

"What do you mean, 'who he was'?" said Tyler.

"The things he believed in. Not chasing criminals. I don't mean that. I mean his point of view. How he got it. His life. You know . . . Who he was."

"He was a man. Maybe worse than some, but better than a lot I've known from hereabouts."

From the way Virginia stirred beneath his arm, Tyler could tell she found his answer unsatisfactory. "Just get on with it. You've been aching to read it all this time anyway," said Tyler.

"I told you I was going to send it back with a note."

"You'd have done that already."

Virginia looked away, back to the coffin. "You told me it was private."

"It is private. I'd return it. But if you want to read it, I don't reckon he'll care too much."

Tyler had convictions about the world, strong convictions, and things either balanced with him or they did not. There was black and white, right and wrong, love and hate. There was alive and dead, and all it meant was what it was. He never questioned his side of it. But that only took you to the grave, and then what? Where was the final reckoning? Not with God, but with man. If one didn't leave behind memories, what did one leave behind at all?

Virginia had never told Tyler how Tom Cartwright had fought to hold on to her, looking at her with eyes that in dying had communicated more to her about life than anything she'd ever be able to express. She needed to know this man. Keep alive in the world a memory beyond violence. Tyler didn't understand.

An Oldsmobile sedan drove onto the grounds past their waiting taxicab and approached along the narrow road that split the middle of the cemetery.

"That time already?" said Virginia.

"The government's usually on time when they're coming to take you away," said Tyler.

"I wish I was going with you."

"You've things to settle at home . . . They say I'll be busy for a while and unable to see anyone but the tough sons-a-you-know-whats whipping me into shape, so . . ."

The driver got out of the car. He stepped around the front and waited on the curb.

"C'mon," Tyler said. "I'm sure he'll give you a ride back to the hotel if you want. We can send the cab on back."

Virginia shook her head. Tears welled in her eyes, but goodbye would be worse if she prolonged it. She folded into his embrace. Tyler kissed her hair. She raised her chin. Their lips met and held until Tyler tasted her tears and she believed—as she'd always believed her mother since the day she'd died—that he'd never be without her.

He gently eased away. "You sure you'll be okay?"

"I'm as capable as you," she joked, feinting at him with her cane.

Tyler clicked his tongue. "See you soon, Gingersnap." He touched his hat, then headed for the car.

TYLER AND VIRGINIA HELD EACH OTHER, watching until all that was left was the tip of the port wing, then that too slipped below the ice. They couldn't believe it was truly over, but the snow continued to fall and the silence of the world remained unbroken.

Virginia shivered. Tyler was colder than he'd ever been. If they lay there much longer, hypothermia would kill them faster than any of their wounds.

"C'mon, we got to get back to the train."

They staggered to their feet and stumbled across the ice, each carrying the other.

The Army, led by a contingent of military police from Los Alamos, was the first to arrive four hours later. They found Tyler and Virginia huddled by the coal stove inside one of the passenger cars both of them suffering from exposure and shock and a collection of other more physical wounds. Still, for all of that, Tyler was clearheaded enough to insist upon speaking to Colonel Donovan of the OSS before speaking to anyone else.

"Colonel Donovan?" the provost marshal from Los Alamos asked. "What do you know of Colonel Donovan?"

"Just tell him I was party to his conversation this morning, and that I'll tell him everything that happened—and I mean everything."

When Tyler awoke in a hospital recovery room late Christmas day, a major introduced himself as a representative of Colonel Donovan and was ready to take his statement. "I already have Miss Hendricks's. As soon as I have yours, they will be couriered to Washington."

Now Donovan had a file of his own. In the interest of National Security, the events of December 20–24 were withheld from public and federal scrutiny. The deaths at Los Alamos would go down in history as a laboratory accident. Mr. J. Edgar Hoover and his Federal Bureau of Investigation retreated from the entire von Hofmann affair like cockroaches from a sudden burst of light.

And that was that. Or almost. J. Edgar Hoover was a vindictive man. He wanted revenge against those who'd denied him von Hofmann, and he wanted the Red agent inside Project Y to rub in everyone else's noses.

Hoover went to work. Security measures, already extreme, he doubled at Los Alamos. Six "engineers," including Klaus Fuchs, were investigated, interrogated, and put under permanent twenty-four-hour FBI surveillance. No evidence of spying was uncovered against them.

Fuchs, realizing what he had almost inadvertently given to his enemies, laid low for over a year before contacting his Soviet friends. He prepared new notebooks more complete than those he'd given to von

Hofmann. On Saturday, June 2, 1945, with the Trinity Site test of the first atomic detonation a little over a month away, Klaus slipped away from the surveillance team that had followed him for the past seventeen months and met his contact at the Castillo Street Bridge in Santa Fe. He turned over the notebooks and the Soviets entered the nuclear arms race.

Klaus Fuchs continued as a spy for the Soviet Union until his arrest in London on February 2, 1950, by agents of the British government. J. Edgar Hoover quickly claimed personal credit for his capture.

As for vengeance, Hoover took that much quicker, and he took it against Tyler Keyes. Of all the charges he'd been ready to bring against Tyler, one had been legitimate. Kidnapping of Federal Agent Thomas Cartwright. Hoover pressed it for all its worth.

HENRY W. LARKIN III entered Colonel "Wild Bill" Donovan's office and addressed his superior. "Sir, I just got off the telephone with our people at Justice. With Cartwright dead and no witnesses, Keyes's plea bargain has been accepted. After his release from the hospital tomorrow morning, he'll be inducted into the Army and transferred to a frontline rifle company overseas."

Donovan laughed. "Score another one for us."

"I don't follow, Colonel."

"What's there to follow? I can have anyone I want from the armed services and want him, Larkin. Get him."

"Are you serious, sir? He's not a college graduate. He's just some yahoo cowpoke."

"He's got what it takes."

"For our work?"

There was no way to get Larkin to understand, but for the record, he gave it a try. "Larkin, you got what it takes to sit at your desk and analyze complex matters of intelligence. I got what it takes to run this service. But Tyler Keyes, he's got what it takes to go after a group of ruthless Nazis and take them down one by one. Larkin, Tyler Keyes did what over 300 hundred professionals found impossible. He's the man who got Standartenführer von Hofmann."

"Sir, Miss Hendricks had a great deal to do with that."

"And you can bet your ass I'll take her too, when she's ready. Get it straight, Larkin, I'd take Joe Stalin into this service if I thought it would help me finish Hitler. Get him."

"How DO YOU DO, Mr. Keyes? I'm Henry Larkin the third. It's good to make your acquaintance."

Tyler shook his hand.

"Would your girlfriend like a ride?"

"No. She's okay."

Larkin nodded. Fine by him. He opened the passenger door for Tyler.

Tyler hesitated. "You promised I'd have some time with her after I finish training."

"You'll get a three-day pass."

"Can a fella get married in Washington in three days?"

"I'm told these days it can be done in less than ten minutes."

VIRGINIA'S EYES followed the Oldsmobile until it turned out the gate and disappeared among the bare cottonwoods bordering that section of Griffin Street. She pulled the letter from her pocket. She knew she'd find nothing new from the bloodstained envelope, but it had told her much and begged so many questions she considered it again. Handwritten, not typed, it was addressed to: *Mr. Thomas Cartwright, c/o The Federal Bureau of Investigation, Santa Fe.* The return address: the naval station at San Pedro, California. That it was handwritten and not typed indicated a personal rather than official correspondence. The handwriting itself was feminine, so the letter was from a woman. The return address told Virginia the woman's husband served in either the Navy or perhaps the Marine Corps, while the formality of the mailing address and the fact it was sent to Cartwright's office and not his home didn't indicate much of a relationship between them.

In preparing for the funeral, Virginia had already discovered Cartwright had no living relatives.

Should I open it?

Virginia's fingers tore the envelope down the side and slid out the single sheet of vellum.

December 17, 1943
Dear Mr. Cartwright,

My name is Stella MacKenzie. I am the little girl whose life you saved in Mexico. I am thirty-six years old now and I am—

The word married was crossed out.

—widowed. My husband, Frank, was a major in the Marine Corps. He was KIA at a place called Fish Hook Ridge on the Island of Attu in the Aleutian Islands. It has taken me almost two years to find you. I am writing to you now to tell you about my child. On January 5, 1943, I gave birth to an eight-pound baby boy. It was before Frank shipped out and I thank our Gracious Lord he was there to know his son the first few weeks of his life. We named our son Thomas Cartwright MacKenzie.

If you and your family ever make it out to California, I would be happy for Tommy to meet you. I hope this letter finds you and yours well and in God's care.

*Each day of my life, I remember you and what you gave
me. I always will.
Merry Christmas,
Stella MacKenzie*

Virginia dropped the letter onto the coffin. She didn't belong here anymore. She folded the envelope and returned it to her pocket. She hobbled to the taxicab. How much she hated this war and the pain it brought to so many people's lives. How frightened she was that Tyler would die in it.

The bitter wind beat its fists against the windows of the cab as Virginia rode back into town.

EPILOGUE

THEY SOUNDED NOTHING LIKE THE CRICKETS he had known at home, or, for that matter, anywhere else in Europe. Here, as each sticky day dimmed, it was as if someone threw a massive switch. With a sound like raw voltage running through electrical wires, the insects churned out their noise. A horrible sound SS-Sturmbannführer Kurt Behr—late of the *Fallschirmjäger*, paratroopers, now an agent of the SD—would never get used to, or forget, and he always would despise. Ugly, like the sound of spoken Southern American English.

No matter. After the trials of Greece, Berlin, and Italy, he was in place. America. Camp Roseboro, North Carolina. Quite a distance for a thirty-year-old doctor of bacteriology from Würzburg to have come in the service of his Führer and the Third Reich.

The camp gates opened and the battered jeep driven by Lieutenant Mallory rolled into the prisoners' compound, tossing loose seashell from the tabby concrete lane. Kurt Behr straightened his doctor's smock. He watched the jeep from where he stood inside the doorway of the prisoners' infirmary. Some of the other prisoners stopped what they were doing and pursued the jeep with wolf whistles.

Sturmbannführer Kurt Behr didn't blame them a bit. Lieutenant Margaret Mallory was a truly beautiful woman. Beauty that went beyond her cinema-style features and full-figured shape. She had a rapier wit, a dauntless optimism and, although the American military relegated her to the position of "nursing assistant" to the feeble camp doctor, Lieutenant Mallory was possessing of the talent to one day finish medical school and become a brilliant surgeon.

Lieutenant Margaret Mallory stopped the jeep in front of the prisoners' infirmary. Dust swirled.

"Good evening, Major," she said in her honey-whiskey voice. She swung muscular dancer's legs out of the jeep. "You'll be happy to know I've gotten everything you requested."

"In three days? But how?" Behr said.

"Let's say that's my secret," Maggie said.

Kurt Behr followed her with his eyes around to the back of the jeep, waiting for . . .

"A gentleman would help a lady with these boxes," she said.

"And break regulations?"

"Because I'm a woman and you're a Nazi?"

"You know I am certainly not. But that is an unguarded vehicle." Kurt grinned.

"I should be afraid, I suppose. But *I'm* not." And she grinned right back.

Kurt Behr chuckled. He moved toward her. Close. Lieutenant Mallory's perfume smelled of wildflowers. She wore more of it lately. Her hand brushed his as he took the largest of three boxes. Up until Christmas Eve, they'd pretended not to notice their smoldering attraction—shocking to Maggie, studied for Kurt—but the heat of sex, too real between them both, had ignited into something illicit at the New Year's dawn. Now they pretended she wasn't falling for him in a way beyond what they could manage in the world they occupied. At least *she* pretended. Kurt, through sexual seduction, something he was trained at, slowly enslaved her will to his charms. She languidly brushed against him, carrying the boxes to his infirmary. And that—considering yesterday he'd achieved success with the *Bacillus anthracis* spores, awakening them from their dormant state to where they were now, secretly, silently, lethally, reproducing Vollum strain anthrax at an accelerated rate—*that* was exactly the way he needed her if, one week from now, Sturmbannführer Kurt Behr was to keep his appointment in Washington.